*KYLA knew instinctively that Desmond was the one man in her life who would have preferred that she give voice to original thoughts, rather than those she had been taught. She was at once more drawn to him than ever and it was suddenly important to her that he know her feelings of awakening love for him.*

*"Desmond . . . I hope I please you. I want to please you," she said shyly.*

*"And what about pleasing yourself?" he asked.*

Fawcett Gold Medal Books
by Joan Dial:

**LOVERS AND WARRIORS**

**SUSANNA**

# LOVERS AND WARRIORS

## Joan Dial

FAWCETT GOLD MEDAL • NEW YORK

*LOVERS AND WARRIORS*

© 1978 Joan Dial

Published by Fawcett Gold Medal Books, a unit of CBS Publications, the Consumer Publishing Division of CBS Inc.

ISBN 0-449-14072-5

Printed in the United States of America

10  9  8  7  6  5  4  3  2  1

# BOOK ONE

# 1

*A mist hung over cold sand as the October dawn found* two figures making their way down the shifting trail; the girl winced as rocks penetrated her thin slippers.

She was wrapped in a long cloak, and the hood had slipped back to reveal strands of hair, pale as cornsilk, plastered damply to her forehead. Even in the fretful light of the new day, her eyes were an arresting shade of blue.

The girl's companion was as dark as the girl was fair, a slim youth with a sensitive mouth which was at odds with a stubborn chin, with expressive black eyes that searched the foggy sea anxiously. Miguel Marques carried himself proudly, and his square-set shoulders promised that when his body developed a man's muscles, he would be a tall and imposing figure.

"Miguel, perhaps we should wait another day," Kyla whispered. "The fog is still so thick."

"No. Today. We must go today. The boat is ready, and Golden Feather will be waiting for us on the far side of the bay. He will guide us along a trail only he knows, so they cannot follow."

"Golden Feather will understand if we are not there. The fog—" Kyla said, shivering as tendrils of icy mist penetrated her cloak. A fog horn wailed, a crab squirmed beneath her foot, and she wanted to be back in bed, and warm.

"It will be all right. The fog is lifting," Miguel said.

Kyla cried out as a ghostly shape loomed before them.

"It's all right. Just a part of a ship that washed up on last night's high tide," Miguel said. "Our boat is safe above the high-water line."

Kyla clutched at Miguel's arm. "Look!"

A man's body lay on the wet sand near what had once been the bow of the ship.

Miguel silently gestured for her to remain still while he cautiously approached the inert form. The man was large. He had yellow hair and and ragged beard.

"Is he dead?" Kyla asked through chattering teeth.

"No. But there's blood in his hair." Miguel straightened up and returned to where she stood. "Come on, we must be on our way before they awaken in the *hacienda*."

"But we can't just leave him there," Kyla said.

"We must. He is a *gringo* who probably fell overboard from his ship and clung to this wreckage. He was lucky it washed ashore. Someone will find him when the sun comes up."

"Miguel, no. He might die." Kyla moved uncertainly toward the man and stood looking down at him.

"He's a dead man anyway." Miguel shrugged. "A *gringo* this far south—someone will kill him even if the sea doesn't get him. Come, Kyla, or you will awaken to find it is your birthday and you are married by proxy to a stranger."

"But *I* am a *gringa*. This man is of my blood. Perhaps he came here to find me. Look, his hair is the same color as mine."

"If he came to find you, then *he* could be the proxy sent by Lord Talmage, and it is even more imperative that we leave. Kyla, I can't let you marry him. I love you."

Kyla dropped to her knees beside the unconscious man and, not looking up at Miguel, said, "And I love you. You are my brother."

"No! Not your brother," Miguel said savagely. "We are not even distantly related by blood. I don't want you to think of me as your brother."

The man on the sand groaned and stirred. Kyla studied

the man, not wanting to look into Miguel's eyes. Already she regretted her promise to run away with him. Surely it was better to try to solve a problem by facing it. Besides, her birthday was months away, and she could not understand Miguel's haste to leave the *hacienda*. "He looks like a Viking," she whispered. "I saw a picture in a book once."

"He will be a dead Viking if my father finds him," Miguel said grimly. "And as for you and me—"

A tremor passed through Kyla's body, as the fear of her guardian was added to the chill seeping into her bones.

The yellow-haired man opened his eyes and looked at Kyla. "Help me," he whispered. "I'm being followed." His pale eyes were filled with pain and fear. "Must hide from them. They'll kill me if they catch me." The words were spoken in English and seemed to echo hollowly in some remote chamber of Kyla's mind. Her heart began to thump, and on the far reaches of her memory, vague shapes stirred.

"We could take him to the cave beyond the *Bufadora*. Then Golden Feather could come later to guide him back to his own people. Miguel, we must."

"No. It's too dangerous. It's difficult enough to get across the rocks of the *Bufadora* on a clear day. In the fog it would be impossible to carry an injured man of his size. Besides, we can only get across the rocks at low tide. What if the tide turns before we can get back? We would be trapped in the cave for most of the day."

"I won't leave him here," Kyla said, with unexpected determination. "Uncle Eduardo hates *norteamericanos*. You know how many of his friends were killed when they took Texas away from us."

"The *gringos* will never hold Texas—" Miguel began.

"I—can—walk," the man interrupted. "Fell down the cliff and struck my head on a rock, that's all. If you will help me—"

Miguel's instinct told him this man was a threat to more than the keeping of their rendezvous with Golden Feather across the bay. "Who are you? What are you doing on this beach?" Miguel asked suspiciously, fumbling for the English words.

"Trying to reach—other side of bay. Saw the hulk from the top of the cliff . . . thought maybe it was seaworthy."

Miguel did not believe him. The man had intended to steal their boat, he was sure.

They heard the voices then, muffled by the mist. A dog barked on the cliff top. The three figures on the beach froze as the shouts from above became audible.

"He must have gone down to the beach. Bring the dogs."

"Let him go. He did not steal the horse—"

"He is a *gringo*. Who knows what he will do?"

Miguel looked down at the yellow-haired man. "My father's peons are looking for you. From what they say you are a horse thief."

"Please, don't let them catch me," the man begged. "I was going to pay for the horse. My own died. My Spanish isn't good."

"Kyla, if they come down the cliff they will find us as well as this thief," Miguel said. "Come, we shall have to hide in the *Bufadora* cave until they give up the search."

The man was struggling to his feet, swaying drunkenly. "Let me go with you. I followed a dangerous man to the Marques *hacienda*. Didn't mean any harm to you people."

Kyla said, "The man you followed, could he be Lord Talmage's proxy?"

The man nodded, clutching at Miguel for support.

"Miguel, you see!" Kyla said. "We can't leave him. Perhaps he can tell us something to help us."

Miguel paused to glance in the direction of the craggy bluff, where at high tide the sea went rushing into the underground cave and was forced upward through a hole in the roof in a gaint waterspout. The adventurous Miguel had one day discovered that at low tide it was possible to crawl across the slippery rocks, around the sheer face of the cliff and into the next cove, where a chaparral-covered cleft opened to a small dry cave. The dangerous rocks of *la Bufadora* proved to be the only access to what had become their hideaway as children when the Padrone's bellowing rages sent them scurrying for safety.

From the top of the cliff came the unmistakable sound of shifting rocks, and the voices of the pursuers were closer.

"Give me your arm then," Miguel said. "Don't touch the señorita, you will crush her with your weight. Come, we must hurry."

They crawled into the chilly darkness of the cave as the tide began to send the first plumes of white spray through the blowhole, cutting off their return route to the beach.

"Do you think they saw us?" Kyla asked breathlessly.

"I don't know," Miguel replied shortly. "Thanks to you, señor, we shall have to stay here until the tide turns. You appear to know of the Marques family, may I ask again who you are?"

"Garett Ramsey. I was following a swine named Delleroc."

"He is Lord Talmage's proxy?"

The steel-colored eyes roamed calculatingly around the cave. "Lord Talmage. Yes. He's coming here from Mexico City. Meeting Delleroc—" His eyes glazed and he slumped forward.

Miguel and Kyla exchanged startled glances as Miguel turned the inert body over. "Concussion—" Miguel began, but Kyla had already torn a strip from her petticoat and was sliding down the rocks to dip it in to the cold sea. Scrambling back up to the cave, she pressed the wet cloth against the man's head, wiping away the dried blood.

"I don't trust this man," Miguel said, watching her resentfully. "He has cold eyes that do not rest long in one place. And if Lord Talmage is in Mexico, it is even more urgent that we run away, for then your marriage to him will be the real thing and not a proxy."

As the fog dissipated, the sea began rushing noisily into the *Bufadora* and rose in a triumphant column of water and stinging spray. The rocks they had come over were fast disappearing under the incoming tide.

Ramsey mumbled incoherently, repeating the name Delleroc, which was unknown to Miguel and Kyla. Then Ramsey muttered, "Kill him, kill him. China girl." He started to make whimpering sounds, which could have been caused by his pain or by some memory he was fighting to suppress in his delirium.

*Gringos,* Miguel thought. They brought only trouble. He did not think of Kyla as one of them. She had been born in Upper California, despite her foreign blood.

Kyla had been like a little golden princess and his constant and devoted shadow when they were children. How she had admired him and how he had strutted and performed dare-devil feats to impress her—until the day he had looked into those eyes filled with all the mystery of a moonlit sky, and at lips so tender he thought of the sweetness of the roses that climbed about the *casa grande,* and had felt a churning of the blood he had never felt before.

He knew that Kyla was promised to a man chosen by her stepfather and that one day she would be mistress of a *rancho* in the north. Miguel's older brother, Cervantes, had been sent to the de Rivero *rancho* some seven years earlier as *mayordomo.* It would, their father said, be good training for the day when Cervantes would become Padrone of their *hacienda* here in Lower California.

At least twice a year Cervantes returned for a reunion with his family. But Miguel knew his brother was putting down roots on Kyla's *rancho.* Cervantes was not anxious to turn over all he had worked to build to a man only half-Spanish—a man who had never cared enough about his inheritance to travel to the New World.

When Miguel and Kyla decided to run away, they planned to leave by way of boat across the bay and then on horses, which Golden Feather would provide. There would be no tracks from the *hacienda* that way. They hoped Cervantes would continue to manage Kyla's *rancho* and secretly help them until they established their own home. They had not, however, taken Cervantes into their confidence. Miguel believed it better to act boldly and worry about difficulties later. Kyla, who still looked upon Miguel as a brother, wanted only to run away from a proxy marriage to a stranger. But that was another problem Miguel had chosen to ignore.

Looking down at Garett Ramsey, Miguel silently cursed

the fates that had brought him into their lives. Not only had the man brought searchers to the normally deserted beach, but there was something else; a vague warning, deep in his senses, which told Miguel that this man was an enemy.

Miguel suspected Ramsey was merely feigning unconsciousness in order to avoid their questions and, later, as the tide receded, Miguel shook him roughly. "Listen to me. We must leave. As soon as we are safely on our way I will send my friend Golden Feather back to help you escape. Do not be afraid of him. He is an *Indio* outcast."

"Surely Golden Feather will not have waited for us," Kyla said.

"He will wait." Miguel seized her hand and she barely had time to wish Ramsey a speedy recovery before they were on their way.

It was already late in the afternoon and the short fall day was fading into a fitful twilight. To the east, clouds were gathering over the Sea of Cortez, and small animals scurried for shelter under boulders and cactus.

Kyla and Miguel scrambled over the slippery seaweed-slimed rocks, eyes fixed on the precarious footholds. They were almost around the point, approaching the sandy beach where their boat waited, when they saw the silently waiting circle of peons.

Miguel stopped, looking around wildly for a way to escape.

"Come, Señor Miguel," one of the peons shouted. "It is useless to run. Come and face your father like a man."

Kyla whispered, "They have been searching for us. They may not have seen the stranger. Don't tell them about him."

Dejectedly, Miguel helped her from the rocks to the beach, avoiding the eyes of the grim-faced peons.

The last rays of autumn sunlight were swept from the adobe walls of the *casa grande* by the storm shadows as Miguel and Kyla, wet and hungry, were ushered up the verandah steps. Their progress through the house was observed by fearful eyes from a crack in the kitchen door, but Nana did not dare go to her charge to protect her from the Padrone's wrath.

He was waiting in the *sala,* his back turned to them, hands resting on the stone ledge above the fireplace. On the ledge also was the note Miguel had left. Sitting on the sanctuary bench nearby was Miguel's sister, Maria, her lovely features a study of malicious anticipation as Kyla came through the archway from the outer hall.

Slowly, Eduardo Marques turned, heavy brows arching up, the threat in his black eyes as ominous as the storm clouds that now erupted with rumbling thunder and lightning bolts. A heavy rain began to fall outside, and Kyla thought of the semiconscious Viking hiding in the small cave.

"Father—" Miguel began.

"Silence," Eduardo thundered. "You have been gone all day. Alone. The two of you. You were forbidden to be alone together years ago. You gave me your word, Miguel, and I hold you responsible for this dishonor. You will be punished appropriately. I will ignore the foolishness of the note you left."

"Uncle Eduardo, nothing happened," Kyla said, her voice shaking as badly as her knees.

"You are no longer a child," the Padrone snapped. "You are a woman. You spent the day without a chaperone."

"But Miguel is my brother."

"No!" Miguel said, the anguish twisting his handsome features. "Father, I love Kyla. I want to marry her. I beg of you, allow us to go away together."

Eduardo sprang at his son with a roar of rage, his hand slicing through the air and clapping against Miguel's cheek. The sound of the slap echoed about the room and Maria jumped to her feet, with her hand raised as though she would strike Kyla. "Father, no. It is not Miguel's fault, it is hers," Maria shrieked. "She is a *gringa,* she is evil. She bewitched him."

Eduardo turned to his daughter. "This is not your affair. Do not speak again until spoken to," he said curtly.

Miguel's lips were white and his eyes blazed, but he

stood silently as his father paced back and forth glaring at the two of them.

Miguel's cheek was slowly darkening from the blow and Kyla raised her hand to touch him gently on the arm, tears coursing down her face. She was as appalled at Miguel's declaration as at the impact of the blow. Miguel was her brother. He had always been her dearest and closest companion, and how could he imagine any other kind of relationship between them? True, she did not want to marry Lord Talmage, a man she had never seen. But she did not want to marry her brother, either. All at once she was grateful to the man in the cave who had prevented her running away with Miguel.

"Kyla," the Padrone said in a voice heavy with doom, "I gave my sacred word to Raul de Rivero, your stepfather, that I would raise you as my own daughter and on your eighteenth birthday see that the proxy marriage he arranged would take place. You know this. You have always known it, from the time you were a little girl. I told you the story of how we rode to the *rancho* in the north after the messenger from your stepfather came to ask our help. We rode day and night, but when we arrived it was too late. Those who had not been killed, when the *Indios* attacked, had fled, all except my old friend Raul, and he lay dying from the pox in a peon's hut. The *Indios* had spared him because they feared the disease."

Eduardo Marques turned back to look into the leaping flames in the grate, remembering the burned *casa grande* of the *rancho* where Kyla's mother had died. After all these years it was still painful to remember the death of Raul, who had saved Eduardo's life during the Revolution. If only they could have reached the *rancho* in time.

They had ridden through burned fields littered with bodies of *vaqueros* to discover that their women had been caught in the *casa grande,* and the house had been reduced to a charred shell. Eerily, the chapel bell still tolled its frantic warning as they approached.

As Eduardo began organizing burial parties one of his *vaqueros* came to tell him they had found one hut left standing. From within the hut, a man called out to warn that he was dying of the pox and they should not enter if they had not had the disease.

When Eduardo entered the hut he thought his old friend, Raul de Rivero, was already dead, but then the encrusted eyes blinked open and looked at him in alarm.

"No, Eduardo. Do not come so close," Raul begged.

"Old friend, old friend," Eduardo said sadly, shaking his head as he drew a chair close to the bed and sat down.

"Eduardo—the child Kyla—she escaped, I know she did. Nana took her—" Raul gratefully accepted the cup of water Eduardo pressed to his lips.

"Raul, I cannot lie to you. We have seen no sign of life in the *hacienda*," Eduardo said. "If any of your peons survived, they have taken to the hills."

"Nana took her away before the massacre—told. her to bring Kyla to you. Eduardo, promise me, promise me—"

"Raul, save your strength. I have sent for a physician."

"No—no time. Listen to me, Eduardo. This *rancho*—I cannot leave it to Kyla. You know that—the deed—"

"I know, old friend. The king was very specific about his land grants," Eduardo answered. "The child has no Spanish blood. Ah, Raul, why did you not marry in your youth and produce heirs like my fine sons Cervantes and Miguel? Or even a daughter like my baby Maria?" Eduardo had never understood why his friend had married a *gringa* widow with a small daughter.

"Please—" Raul begged, feeling the precious minutes ebb away.

But Eduardo continued, thinking aloud. "Your sister, who returned to Spain, she will now inherit your land. If the *gringa* child lives, I will see she is given to your sister. Rest now, Raul."

"My sister—died—a year ago. She, too, married not of our blood—an Englishman, the Viscount Talmage. But Eduardo, they had a son. He is the last of our line, Desmond Gaspar de Rivero Talmage. Nana has documents I prepared—a will—instructions."

Eduardo leaned closer to hear the words as his friend's eyes burned with fever and his voice died to a whisper.

"Take Kyla. Raise her with your own daughter. Promise me, Eduardo—to pay your old debt to me. Give me your word."

"I promise. I will take the child."

"When she is a woman—she is to marry my sister's son. I have already made the arrangements. The Englishman has only a title and a military career—no personal holdings—" Raul groaned softly and squeezed his eyes shut for a second. The exertion of speaking had caused his body to shake.

His eyes blinked open again. "A marriage—by proxy—on Kyla's eighteenth birthday—so that the *rancho* will be hers, whether Talmage comes to the New World or not. Promise me, Eduardo. Swear to God—"

"I swear it by all that is holy and sacred to me," Eduardo said, making the sign of the cross.

The ravaged face looked almost peaceful when death claimed Raul de Rivero a moment later.

Days later, the *mestizo* woman, Nana, had brought the four-year-old Kyla to Eduardo. Fourteen years ago. Nothing must go wrong now, at the last minute.

"Kyla, go to your room," the Padrone said. "Do not speak to anyone, not even Nana, about this episode. We will devise some suitable story for the servants' ears. Today I received word that Lord Desmond Gaspar de Rivero Talmage is at this moment on his way here. He will arrive in time for your birthday, and you will be married to him."

"Father—no!" Miguel pleaded.

"And you who have disgraced the family," the Padrone said coldly. "You will immediately present yourself to our friend Colonel Apolo Ramírez, who will arrange a commission for you in the army. Perhaps you can redeem yourself, and forget this foolish infatuation."

Kyla dragged her leaden feet along the corridor to her room, the sound of Maria's hysterical sobbing following her. Maria had resented her presence before. Now she would have even more reason to dislike her adopted sister.

From her bedroom window an hour later, Kyla saw the lonely figure move slowly across the patio. Miguel carried saddlebags, but had scorned wearing a *serape* against the rain that now filled the night in a solid sheet. A moment later Kyla heard the plodding steps of the horse, and Miguel was lost in the blackness of the night.

# 2

*The great wooden wheels of the chandeliers were ablaze* with candlelight above the banquet table, which groaned under the weight of silver and gold dishes filled with abalone, roast pigeon and an *olla* of well-spiced beef with red beans. Tall-stemmed goblets sparkled with rich wine and ripe mangos in crystal dishes added their subtly appealing scent to the aromas of all of the other delicacies.

The families from neighboring *haciendas* had been invited, as well as a dozen officers from the nearby garrison, resplendent in their gold-braided uniforms. In the adjacent *sala* the mariachis waited, their guitars, fiddles and flutes ready for the fandangos they would play when the guests moved into the great hall for the dancing.

Every eye was fixed on the man who sat on the Padrone's right, and who returned the glances of the women too boldly for propriety. Lord Desmond Gaspar de Rivero Talmage had a tall and lean Anglo-Saxon body and bright copper-colored hair that contrasted oddly with hawklike features. In those handsome features was the indelible stamp of Castilian blood. Most startling of all, however, were the man's eyes. Not quite green, nor gold, yet somehow both, and with feline pupils. Those eyes were able to send primitive messages that made the señoritas hide behind their fans or suddenly become opaque if Lord Talmage felt one of the men's questions was too leading.

At her father's side, Maria Consuela Augustine Marques was having a great deal of difficulty concentrating on the tiny portion of shellfish on her plate. As she picked daintily at the abalone, her dark eyes moved restlessly beneath fluttering lashes. She wanted to devour this interesting stranger with her gaze, examine him from his bright hair to his thickly muscled legs. She had never seen so exciting a man. His glance had the power to make her tremble, and the fact that he was betrothed to her adopted sister made him even more appealing.

The assembled guests were clearly impressed when they learned that Lord Talmage, who had spent some time in Mexico City, was well acquainted with El Presidente, Antonio Lopez de Santa Anna, although some wondered why Talmage had tarried there instead of rushing to meet his beautiful golden-haired bride. They were even more confounded when he mentioned he had been living in Monterey, which was far to the north. Evidently, Lord Talmage had been more interested in exploring the New World than in satisfying his curiosity about his bride-to-be.

Eduardo Marques was most interested in Lord Talmage's acquaintance with El Presidente and pressed for details of the current mood in the capital city. Would there be war with the *norteamericanos*? Was it true that Santa Anna had vowed to wipe the last vestiges of Spanish rule from Mexican soil? Eduardo was Spanish, and not a *criollo* born in the New World. Since the advent of Mexican independence, the Padrone had grown increasingly apprehensive about retaining the land granted him upon his retirement from the army of occupation. He had never dared look into the *expedientes* to see if the title was honored by the Mexican government.

"Perhaps those are topics for later discussion, when the ladies have retired?" Desmond Talmage answered in his lisping Castilian Spanish, which was disguised somewhat by his deeply resonant voice.

"Yes, of course. But tell me, why did you not stop to

see your inheritance when you journeyed from Monterey?" Eduardo asked.

Talmage's eyes turned opaque. "I was unaware that your son, Cervantes, was in residence. But I saw the land. It seemed little better than a desert after the beauty of northern California. I have a friend in Monterey, you see, and I spent some time with him." His eyes were gold now and glinting slightly, as though he were secretly amused. "I find the climate and terrain there as close to paradise as is anywhere on earth. Frankly, I was disappointed to learn the inheritance is so far south."

Cervantes bridled at this disdain of the land he had nurtured so lovingly for seven years, and he indulged himself in a burst of resentment. "And no doubt the señor feels protected in Monterey by the proximity of the British presence in Oregon," he said. Cervantes was a young Eduardo in looks, word and temperament.

His father frowned slightly in his son's direction but Desmond Talmage's lips curled into a faint smile. "I can assure you that I have no allegiance to any foreign power," he said. "I make this explanation as a courtesy to my future brother-in-law and feel compelled to urge him to exercise caution when aiming such remarks in my direction in the future. I'm sure the color of my hair has not gone unnoticed. In my former country it is believed to be the banner of sudden and violent temper. Let me warn you there is some basis for the belief."

Eduardo cut in quickly to cover the awkward moment. "We were surprised when we learned you were coming in person for the wedding. We had understood from your letter you were sending a proxy."

Green eyes traveled the length of the table and found the light golden head of Kyla. "It's true," he said, "that I would have received a handsome income from the *rancho* without ever setting foot in this country. However, since I would also be deprived of the right to a wife who would be more than a name on a legal document—" He paused, eyes flickering over Kyla. "I was curious about the woman who was willing to forgo being a real wife for the sake of a piece of land."

At the far end of the table, Kyla, who could not hear the exchange, surreptitiously removed two of the sharpest hairpins from the bun at the nape of her neck and hoped that she had not been observed by Maria. As she did so, she noticed that Cervantes and Lord Talmage were exchanging dagger glances at one another and that a slow flush was spreading over Cervantes' brooding features. How like his father he is, Kyla thought. Anger can spring to those faces more quickly than the desert hawk can scoop up his prey.

She moved her neck uncomfortably, sorry she had allowed Maria to dress her hair. "Your hair is too straight to hang well under the mantilla," Maria had said ingratiatingly. "It is not prettily waved like mine. Let me fasten it into a coil for you."

The unaccustomed bun made her feel matronly, an effect not helped by the fawn-colored satin dress that Maria had presented her as a trousseau gift. The color of the dress blended with Kyla's hair to produce a rather drab look. Maria herself was devastatingly lovely in brilliant red silk, her black hair soft and wavy beneath a lace mantilla.

Kyla wished miserably that Miguel were here, seated in his customary chair across the snowy damask tablecloth. There had been no word from him. Yet he was not in the army. One of the guests, Colonel Apolo Ramírez, the cavalry officer to whom Miguel should have reported, had told the Padrone, with some embarrassment, that Miguel had not arrived. Apolo and his younger brother, Carlos, were both vainly trying to attract the attention of Maria, who had fixed her large black eyes on Kyla's red-haired suitor and was ignoring all of the other *caballeros*.

Kyla was worried about Miguel. Something terrible had happened to him, she was sure. Kyla had always been able to read Miguel's thoughts and he hers. It was the mystical bond between them that shut out others and infuriated Maria. Her eighteenth birthday was but a few days away, and Kyla knew that only some disaster would have kept Miguel from returning, or at least sending her a message.

She squirmed suddenly and, raising her eyes, saw that Desmond Talmage was studying her intently. The fork in her hand slipped from her fingers under that relentless gaze. She had spent only brief moments in Lord Talmage's company since his arrival the previous day, and even then she had been always chaperoned, but those moments were enough to convince her that this man was dangerous in a way she could not imagine.

The Viking in the cave, Garett Ramsey, had said Talmage's name, as well as the name he spat out like an oath: Delleroc. There had been hatred and vengeance and undertones of evil in the delirious mutterings they had overheard that day. Perhaps, Kyla thought, she only imagined this because that day had brought such misery to the *hacienda*: Miguel banished to the army, she herself locked in her room for a week. When she was at last released she had slipped away to the *Bufadora,* but found the cave empty. Like Miguel, the Viking had disappeared.

The dancing began, and Maria was quickly surrounded by a hopeful crowd of *caballeros,* whom she regarded speculatively, dark eyes flashing mischievously above her fan as she decided which was the most handsome and accomplished in the fandango. Desmond Talmage was still deep in conversation with her father, and Maria wanted to be the center of attraction when the guest of honor entered the *sala*.

Kyla sat on a straight-backed chair on the edge of the dance floor, her eyelids beginning to droop from the long and wearying day. It was not proper for the bride-to-be to dance with anyone except her future husband or the Padrone. She hoped Desmond Talmage and the Padrone would remain talking at the dining table all evening. Kyla felt that Desmond's expression had been somewhat dismayed when he greeted her and now, unreasonably, she wished she looked as pretty as Maria. Not that she cared about this flame-haired foreigner with his peculiar lion's eyes. She was sure Miguel would return shortly and deal with him.

Eduardo Marques came into the *sala,* Desmond Talmage at his side, and the music died abruptly as the Padrone raised his hand to command attention.

"My friends, ladies and gentlemen," Eduardo said, "one announcement only. You are all most cordially invited to stay in my *hacienda* until the wedding of my adopted daughter, Kyla de Rivero, and Lord Talmage, which will take place within a week."

The murmuring faded away and an expectant stillness hung in the room. Kyla was aware only of a pair of opaque green eyes and of fiery hair glowing in the candlelight like a warning beacon on some distant shore. Then the tall foreigner bowed before her and offered her his hand to lead her out onto the dance floor as the musicians struck up a sprightly refrain.

"You will forgive my awkwardness," Desmond Talmage said to her in English, "but I am more accomplished with the waltz and minuet than in your Spanish dances." He paused for a moment, observed the other dancers, then proceeded as though he had been bred to the dance. He added with a mocking glint in his eye, "Of course I quickly become proficient in everything I attempt."

Kyla looked up at him, astonished at his conceit and wondering if he were teasing, but she looked away hastily as the green eyes slipped from her face to briefly caress her body. All at once the memory of Miguel, forlornly going out into the stormy night, crossed her mind and she resented this sleek stranger with his fancy clothes and conceited conversation. She wanted to comment icily on Desmond's dancing prowess, but good manners prevailed.

After only a few steps of the dance she grew uncomfortable under the assault of those strange green-gold eyes and, feeling compelled to say something, blurted out, "Do you intend to spend the rest of your life on the de Rivero *rancho,* or will you return shortly to Europe?"

The smile hovering about the impertinent mouth broadened. "Tell me," he said softly, "is there a handsome Latin lover waiting in the wings for the husband to depart?"

Kyla flushed. "Of course not. In our society, sir, unmarried girls are closely chaperoned."

"Yes, I know," he replied, bowing to her as the music ended, but the bow was spoiled by the insolent way he raised one eyebrow. For one horrified instant, Kyla was sure he knew that she and Miguel had been alone all that day, and it was several minutes before she remembered that they had in fact been caring for the wounded Garett Ramsey. Lord Talmage managed to make her feel guilty even though she had not done anything.

It was, she decided, those strange eyes; so restlessly seeking, then focusing suddenly and becoming unnaturally calm, as though to lull unsuspecting prey into a false sense of security. She had never met a man like Desmond Talmage before. His true self was ill-concealed beneath the finely tailored clothes and old-world manners. He exuded restless vitality and an air of secret amusement.

She was breathing rapidly when she returned to her seat, although she had not really exerted herself dancing. There was something about Desmond Talmage that seemed to awaken every nerve in her body. He was a physically attractive man and well aware of the fact. It showed in every movement, every gesture and lift of the eyebrow.

"Have you ever seen our mutual inheritance?" he asked.

"No. Uncle Eduardo always felt that it would be better to wait until the house was completely restored and I was—married. He thought the burned *casa grande* might be distressing. My mother died there in the Indian attack. Cervantes has only recently been able to obtain all of the materials to finish rebuilding the house. Also, it is a long and arduous journey."

"Your adopted brother, Cervantes, has been undisputed *hacendado* there then, and you've had no say in *rancho* affairs?"

"It was the Padrone's decision. I do not question Uncle Eduardo's actions," Kyla said.

"He is like all of the others in his position, I suppose," Desmond said. "Lives a life of ease and luxury while his peons work themselves to death for him."

"You will shortly embrace that way of life yourself,"

Kyla pointed out, amazed at her own temerity. Since Miguel's departure a sense of bravado had overcome her. Beneath it was a feeling that no matter what she did or said, somehow she would be saved from the consequences. Wellbred young señoritas did not question or criticize their men, nor listen to derogatory remarks about them.

The pupils of the green eyes had narrowed to tight black lines, but the mouth continued to smile. "I saw what appeared to be hundreds of peons' huts within the *hacienda,* and large herds of cattle and horses. Did you know that our estate in the North is at least twice the size of this one? It covers almost seventy square miles."

Maria danced by, fluttering her black eyelashes provocatively, her red skirts swishing bewitchingly.

"The Padrone should find a husband for her quickly," Desmond said dryly. "I never saw a woman who needed one more."

Kyla was appalled at the ill-bred remark, despite the fact that she secretly agreed. Maria, who was two years younger than Kyla, had turned down every suitor who had begged for her hand, and seemed inclined toward a lifetime of light-hearted flirtation.

Cervantes made his way across the *sala* and bowed stiffly to Desmond Talmage. "My father would like to speak with you. He begs your forgiveness, but wants me to point out that wedding festivities usually last at least a week, and since you have expressed the wish to leave for your *rancho* in the North as soon as possible, he felt you should use this time before the marriage to acquaint yourself with *rancho* business."

Desmond rose unhurriedly, and picked up Kyla's hand to press to his lips before moving away from her. Even when he had disappeared through the archway of the *sala,* she could still feel the hot imprint of his lips on her flesh.

A feeling of panic swept through her body the moment Kyla awakened on the morning of her eighteenth birthday. A thin beam of spring sunlight slashed across the room and touched the ivory lace wedding dress hang-

ing from the bed canopy. The dress swayed slowly back
and forth in a slight breeze, like the lifeless form of a
hanged man—or perhaps, Kyla thought as she came fully
awake—a sacrificed woman.

Miguel, she thought sadly. Surely if you were alive you
would have come back to see me married. She still felt
as though she were clinging to the edge of a cliff, below
which some unseen savior waited to catch her when she
fell. During one of the prenuptial parties, as she had
watched her bridegroom-to-be flirt audaciously with Maria,
Kyla had told herself that if Miguel did not return in time,
she would simply run away before the wedding. But there
was nowhere for a woman to run in this wild country. To
the west lay the ocean and to the east the harsh desert.
Along the coastal plains a woman alone would be set upon
by *bandidos,* or—worse—*Indios*. To leave the hacienda
meant certain death and Kyla had much living to do.

She had endured a childhood of Maria's constant taunts
and secret pinching and pummeling. For many years
Kyla had been convinced she was as ugly as Maria
claimed, with her washed-out hair and blue eyes that
Maria said were cold and watery. She thought that even
Miguel had only tolerated her in those early years because they discovered they could read each other's
thoughts. *Gringa!* How many times she had heard that
scathing word flung at her in anger. How passionately
she had wished she looked like them, with their beautiful
dark hair and eyes and smooth olive skins.

It was only fitting, Maria had said so many times, that
Kyla should be betrothed to a man who was only half-
Spanish. It was more than a *gringa* deserved. Yet Maria
was now acting like a coquette, simpering and giggling in
Desmond Talmage's presence. Clearly Maria found him
fascinating. She cast envious glances in Kyla's direction
whenever Desmond engaged Kyla in private conversation.

Kyla rose from her bed and went to the window. The
breeze whipped the bougainvillea vines and sent a shower
of bright purple blossoms dancing across the red tile roof
toward the chapel, where this day she would become the

wife of Desmond Gaspar de Rivero Talmage. The shiver that passed through her body was one of excitement rather than fear, but she did not have time to analyze it as Nana knocked on her door at that moment and entered, carrying a pitcher of steaming water for her bath.

Nana's wrinkled old face was happy this morning. "Today my child becomes her own woman," she said, splashing the hot water into the tub she dragged from the closet. "And Nana goes home at last."

"Why, Nana," Kyla said, "you never once in all these years said that you considered your home to be in the North."

Nana shrugged. "What purpose would it have served? We had to live on Marques charity until today."

Kyla tested the bathwater with her toe. She was indeed about to become mistress of a very large estate. No longer dependent upon the Marques family, free of Maria's bad temper, it had to be the prospect of freedom that was making her blood race so.

Surreptitiously, so Nana would not notice, Kyla looked down at her body as the warm, scented water dripped from the sponge in her hand. Would Talmage find her desirable? She was not as voluptuously curved as Maria, but she did have a tiny waist. She scrubbed her legs furiously, feeling her cheeks grow pink at her thoughts. The revelation that she was physically attracted to Desmond was new and startling to her. The sheer presence of the man would have been difficult for even a sophisticated woman to ignore. He exuded masculine power the way a caged tiger soundlessly conveys his desire to be free.

As much as she told herself that she wanted a husband whose thoughts and moods were known to her—someone like Miguel whom she knew and trusted—some wild part of her nature was impatient to learn what it would be like to be alone with her fiery-haired bridegroom.

Nana handed her a towel and her robe. "The stars shine in your eyes. That is good. Remember what I told you. A moment of pain, that is all. I am an old woman now, ah, but I remember how it was."

Impulsively Kyla leaned closer and kissed the wrinkled cheek. "You have been more than a mother to me, Nana. All these years I always knew it was more important to have you than to have all that Maria has."

Kyla wondered, as Nana helped her don her wedding dress, if her feelings would have been more of terror and less of excited curiosity had she not had Nana to tell her of the joys of the marriage bed.

It was a pity Nana could not also explain the complex personality of the man Kyla was marrying. His quicksilver changes of mood had soon become evident. One moment stern and forbidding, the next cynically mocking, yet always capable of spontaneous and unexpected humor. To be able to present such chamelionlike facets of conflicting character traits surely indicated that he was at times acting a part. But at which times?

As Nana adjusted her veil, Kyla felt her excitement surge again. She was a fine one to think of conflicting personalities. One moment she was in a panic and thinking of running away, and the next she could hardly wait to see her bridegroom again.

During the long wedding ceremony Kyla stood stiffly, knelt awkwardly and gave her responses in a stilted and hollow voice, until the moment a large bluebottle fly buzzed lazily through her mantilla and then came to rest in a whirring confusion of wings on the Bible in the padre's hands.

At that moment Kyla turned her head slightly and her gaze met twinkling green eyes that were full of mirth. Kyla hurriedly coughed to cover her desire to giggle.

The sunlight was bright with the promise of approaching summer, and she noticed for the first time that Desmond's hair was sun-bleached about his face and temples, giving the coppery hair the look of a lion's mane. His eyebrows came together in a frown of mock disapproval at her sputtering, and she looked away again. She felt lightheaded, almost as though she were floating somewhere above the whole scene, so great was the sense of unreality. Somewhere at the back of her mind hovered the thought that it would be exciting to try to turn a lion's roar into the purr of a domesticated feline.

Later, when the wedding feasting began, Kyla quickly drained several glasses of wine and retreated behind a pink haze. Wedding celebrations customarily lasted many days, and it was unthinkable for the bride and groom to leave the festivities until they were ready to drop from exhaustion. Tonight there would be dancing and entertainment. Tomorrow the whole party would move outdoors for the rodeo and bullfighting. The *vaqueros* would race their swift horses, show off their abilities with the lariats. They would partially bury a rooster in the sand, then come galloping along to swoop down and try to retrieve the squawking bird.

During the next few days there would be only brief *siestas,* and it would be considered ill-bred for the newlyweds to begin their honeymoon until the guests departed.

She wished now that she could cancel the outdoor celebrations for her wedding, and she wondered if her bridegroom's Spanish ancestry dominated his English blood. Her eyes searched the guests for his red hair.

Desmond was moving among the guests with practiced ease, and Kyla was aware that his eyes examined every female with the same insolent scrutiny. Strange behavior for a man just married. Kyla felt a stab of an emotion she had never experienced before, and she could not bring herself to believe it was jealousy. She picked up her wineglass again.

The next moment Desmond was taking her hand to lead her out onto the floor for the beginning of the dancing. When she resisted for a second, still angry that he had flirted so outrageously, his fingers gripped hers like an eagle's talons. She stumbled over her gown and would have tripped, had he not wrapped his arm about her waist and lifted her effortlessly to her feet. He frowned slightly.

"If you drink too much wine, my sweet," he murmured through unmoving lips, "you will soon be senseless and miss all of the pleasures I have in store for you." He smiled suddenly in a way that was more terrifying than his frown.

His closeness, the hard muscles of his arm enclosing

her body, the peculiarly masculine scent that clung to his jacket, all at once sent warning ripples through her body, and the enormity of what was happening to her brought back the panic she had felt upon awakening that morning. She wanted to say something that would punish him for making her feel so frightened. "I want you to know," she said, her voice shaking, "that I considered killing myself to avoid marriage with you and now I wish I had not been so cowardly."

*Death before dishonor*—Miguel's words—the creed of Spanish men who protected the chastity of their women unto the death, and who expected their women to kill themselves rather than submit to a man who forced himself upon them. Though this creed was not applicable to the two of them, it seemed relevant at that moment since Desmond was not behaving in a manner proper for a new husband.

"You are monstrously bad-mannered and insufferably conceited and I wish you had remained on the other side of the earth," she added.

His mouth opened slightly in surprise, which he quickly disguised as a tolerant smile. "It's not cowardly to choose to live, Kyla, my fair bride. And I couldn't agree more with your assessment of my character. In fact, I must admire a woman who would give voice to such an opinion. My wake is littered with empty-headed women who either bored me to tears or were so afraid of me that they invited mistreatment. You've just grown in stature, my dear. I'm weary of women who cower before me."

Kyla was not sure why she told herself at that moment that she would never cower before her husband. After all, if he tired of her, she would simply be left to run his household while he pursued a mistress, and was that not the state of affairs she would prefer? Yet his utter contempt for all women made her angry, and it was a new emotion for her. He seemed able to arouse as many contrary emotions in her as he himself displayed, and the total effect was bewildering. She had always accepted her lot questioningly, because there had always been Miguel to run to. But now there was no Miguel. She felt like a colt taking its first precarious steps alone.

To her horror, Desmond was dancing toward the archway leading from the *sala,* and when they were in the shadows of the hall he suddenly slipped his hands about her waist and under her knees and swung her up into his arms. She was so surprised she did not speak or struggle as he sped away with her toward the rooms that had been prepared for them. He was carrying her over the threshold before she was able to gasp "No. We must go back—"

He lost no time with preliminaries. His fingers deftly dealt with buttons and hooks in a manner that said plainly the intricacies of female clothing were well-known to him. Her wedding gown, train and mantilla were soon joined by underclothing and stockings, all tossed carelessly in the direction of the long bench at the foot of the bed. Then his fingers encircled her arm, and she was dragged closer to the candles casting their fragile light from pewter candlesticks on the credenza.

"Now," he said softly, "we shall see what we have traveled so far and paid so dearly to possess. You must forgive my impetuousness, but time is fleeting."

Her cheeks flaming, lower lip stinging under the pressure of her teeth as she closed her eyes against his appraising stare, she nevertheless was aware of his examination of every part of her body as his fingers lightly touched and probed and he commented casually on her attributes.

"They were afraid I would find you a trifle too slender, but to my eyes you are just right. Your breasts are full without being pendulous and your waist is tiny enough to compensate for your boy's hips. After you have borne a child or two your body will be more feminine in the Spanish way. But I'm not sure I will prefer it that way. There are times when I might crave boyish hips."

He reached suddenly to pull the combs from her hair and the golden mass slipped about her shoulders.

"Open your eyes," he commanded.

Feeling him relinquish his hold on her arm, she

obeyed. She saw with dismay that he was slowly removing his own clothes.

"I take it you have never seen a naked male?" he
asked in a conversational tone as he discarded his ruffled shirt. The hair on his chest was a lighter red than
that of his scalp and curled over well-developed pectoral
muscles, but Kyla saw only his eyes, and they burned
into hers with fiendish anticipation.

She met his gaze unwaveringly, her body rigid. He
bent to remove his breeches, and in the candlelight the
fiery mane of hair falling over his face transformed him
into an apparition, a cougar about to pounce. She swayed
on her feet as he straightened up and caught her to him.

The shock of the hard warmth of his body against
her sent a ripple of fear through her, and she tried to
pull away from him and that part of him that pressed
insistently against her thigh. The hooded cat's eyes were
close now, and his breath was hot against her lips.

"I've been everywhere and done everything. Taken
more virgins than any man alive," he said. "There were
those who fought and those who begged me to take them.
There is nothing new under the sun, Kyla, always remember that. You are merely a new face, a new body.
A diversion for an hour or two. You are unimportant in
my life. But your marriage—ah, that is significant. And it
must be properly consummated while there is still time.
You are too beautiful to be imprisoned in the Talmage
chastity belt."

None of what he was saying made sense to her. Between the wine and his insistent seeking fingers, she
scarcely knew where she was or what was happening to
her.

"It can be easy for you, or it can be hard, depending
upon your state of mind," he continued. "Would you
prefer that I take you brutally? I've found some women
do."

"I would prefer, sir—" she said, her voice coming in
painful gasps as her breasts were crushed against his
chest and she strained to keep her head away from that
mouth that seemed about to devour her, "to be on the

far side of the earth. Whatever you do to me, it will be rape, because I do not love you or want you."

"Ah, Kyla, never throw down a challenge like that. For now I must make you love me and want me." His mouth closed over hers and his hands slid around her waist and upward over her breast. She felt his tongue between her lips and she was struck by the pulsating life that passed from his mouth to hers and seemed to strike some exquisite chord in the core of her being. It was like that split second after the ringing of a giant bell when all of the senses are lost in its echo. Then his tongue was in her mouth, and she remembered that when that other part of him likewise penetrated her body she would lose her girlhood forever.

She raised her hands to push him away, felt a tear slide down her cheek. His mouth released her instantly and he held her in a less fierce embrace. He looked down at her and he said softly, "Don't be afraid, Kyla. I won't hurt you. It's been so long since I was with an innocent woman that I've forgotten how to act. Come, my dear, let us merely lie down together and talk."

Kyla was acutely aware of his naked body next to hers under the sheet, despite the innocuous conversation. She was scarcely aware of his remarks about the difference between Spanish customs and those of other countries or his comments about the beauty of the Californias. He whispered that he had brought her a gift—a complete riding outfit such as English ladies wore.

Her body tingled from head to toe and her blood surged as though waiting for some explosion of emotion she could not even imagine. As he spoke he caressed her, his fingertips skimming lightly over the softly rounded shoulders, tracing the long lines of her back, hesitating for a second on her smooth thigh.

She mumbled an incoherent response, hoping he could not sense the tumult that was raging within her. She lay trapped in his arms, dizzying sensations making her feel weak.

She was unaware how much time had passed, but her body seemed to be melting against his. The hypnotic voice was lost in the silken folds of her hair as his hands found her breasts, teased her nipples, slid downward to the tightening between her legs. She heard her own swiftly indrawn breath, felt herself arch toward him, her arms going about his neck, her lips seeking his mouth. His kiss sent heightened longing racing through her body and the rapture that waited, hidden in that dark recess of her body, was now a palpable force, uniting them in its aura.

His mouth had found her nipples, tongue lightly flicking, and he murmured ancient words of seduction against the trembling warmth of her skin. He took her hand and guided it to the hard swelling of his manhood. His tongue was causing a strange blending of pain and pleasure in her nipples and she felt an unbearable tension between her thighs.

When his tongue found that secret place she could not stop the moan that rose to her lips, nor the wild movement of her body as she sought deeper sensations. She parted her thighs willingly as he swung himself over her and the hard warmth of his body awakened the last of the senses that had been sleeping until this moment.

His thrust was swift and sure and the pain erupted like a volcano, yet within the pain was the promise of fulfillment.

# 3

*In the cramped cell a rat scurried over the foot of* the man who lay on the rancid straw, staring fixedly at the wall with dark eyes that in unguarded moments mirrored anguish too great to be borne. Scratched into the adobe of the *calabozo* wall was a series of grouped notches, seven to a cluster, marking the weeks Miguel had languished there.

This day was Kyla's birthday, her wedding day, and very probably the day of her death, for she would surely kill herself rather than submit to the marriage. There was nothing he could do. He might as well be dead himself for all that life had to offer now.

Faintly he heard the tapping on the other side of the wall separating his cell from the next one. He had ignored the signals all that morning, too dispirited to continue the game of plotting escape with the unseen *gringo*.

Miguel had been thrust harshly into manhood in the brief weeks before he and Garett Ramsey were arrested. If only he had not gone back to the cave and allowed the *gringo* to persuade him to steal a horse so they might travel together! In those crowded hours and in the soul-destroying weeks of his incarceration, Miguel's eyes had begun to reflect the questioning glance of one who has learned never to take others on trust. There was evidence

35

too of a haunted desperation born of the knowledge that
man's destiny is seldom within his power to determine.

The boyish handsomeness of his features was now
marred by a newly acquired, cynical set to his mouth.
And the weeks he and Ramsey had lived with the *Indios*
had given him a stealth of movement and sixth sense of
impending danger that had failed him only once. On that
occasion he had lingered too long at the *cantiña*, where
men met to plot the overthrow of the dictator-president
Santa Anna. Don *Demonio*: Sir Devil, to many of his
own people and "the Naploeon of the West" to the North
Americans.

The abject poverty and harsh injustice that prevailed
outside the ordered existence of the *hacienda* had shocked
and enlightened Miguel. Independence from Spain had
evidently done little to improve the lot of the peon.

"The whip has merely passed from Spanish hands to
Mexican," one man told him bitterly, "and it hurts just as
much."

Garett Ramsey proved to be man alternately driven
by thoughts of revenge and a maudlin self-pity for the
raw deal he believed the world had inflicted upon him.
Miguel did not know why Ramsey cursed the name of the
mysterious Delleroc. Apparently Ramsey's only connection with Lord Talmage was through Delleroc. And
Delleroc, Miguel conjectured, was either to meet Lord
Talmage, or was on some mission for the man. Ramsey's
contempt for the Indians and the dark-skinned Mexicans
was obvious. Rather than accept graciously the help
offered by the peons, Ramsey behaved as though it were
his due. Barely disguised by a filthy serape and large sombrero, Ramsey's enormous size invited suspicion among
the slightly built Mexicans. Were Ramsey to push the
peons too far in the name of hospitality they might,
Miguel concluded, take him for a Texas marauder, and
treat him accordingly.

There was also the possibility that some of the peons
from the Marques *hacienda* would recognize Ramsey as
the horse thief they had chased down to the beach.
Yet Miguel and Ramsey each had reason to linger near

the Marques *hacienda*. Ramsey awaited Delleroc and
Miguel desperately tried to form a plan to rescue Kyla.
But Miguel's money was rapidly running out. He had
been given enough to sustain him only until he reached
army headquarters.

"We'll have to steal, that's all," Ramsey said when
Miguel brought the matter up. "You're an outcast and
I'm a *gringo*. There's no other choice."

Miguel glanced about the pathetic one-room hovel in
which they had spent the night. The owner was already
at work in the tiny patch of dusty earth, which was all
the family of eight had to sustain life. The elderly grand-
parents were quietly starving to death in a corner, while
two of the children tottered on legs deformed by rickets.
Miguel had always felt guilty that the peons who worked
his father's *hacienda* appeared to have so little compared
to the affluence in the *casa grande*, but he realized now
that his father's peons were at least spared hunger and
disease, which were rampant throughout the country.
Looking at Ramsey's well-fed frame, Miguel's anger
erupted.

"Steal," he exclaimed, "from these people? What kind
of man are you?"

Garett Ramsey's eyes paled to transparency. "One who
doesn't have much love for your people, Mexicanner, or
for anyone else with a brown or yellow skin. Oh, you
helped me and I'm grateful. But make no mistake, as
soon as I find Delleroc and settle my score with him, I
never want to see this stinking country again."

Miguel pondered briefly Ramsey's reference to yellow
as well as brown skins, remembering his babbling about
a "China girl" while he was delirious from the blow on
the head. Then he caught Ramsey stealing from the poor
farmers, and after an ugly scene, Miguel insisted they
travel north immediately. As soon as Ramsey was safely
delivered to a *yanqui* settlement somewhere, Miguel would
wash his hands of the man.

That very night they were rounded up with the plotters
in the *cantiña*. Ramsey had pleaded eloquently in surprisingly good Spanish with the *carcelero* of the prison.

Ramsey shouted that he was a personal friend of Lord Talmage, who in turn was a friend of El Presidente and the *carcelero* had better check on the story. Miguel he said was the son of a *padrone* and the two of them were on secret government business. Ramsey explained that they themselves had been on the point of exposing the plotters. In all, it made an impressive story.

The *carcelero* noted the aristocratic bearing of the slim youth, and the proud thrust to his jaw. The young one was neither a wild-eyed fanatic nor a groveling peon. And it was known that El Presidente had a friend with an English title. It seemed prudent to delay sending the pair to the firing squad with the other plotters.

Miguel did not like or trust Ramsey and was glad when they were flung into seperate cells. Some of the *norteamericanos* who settled the territory to the north were honest and hard-working men. They tamed the wild land and put down roots, became Mexican citizens, embraced the true faith, and lived law-abiding lives. But there were *yanquis* who arrived in California via the coastal trade and even some who came over the mountains to settle the fertile land, and among their number were those who would plunge the country into war for their own profit. Ramsey was such a man.

Four years earlier, a United States sea captain named Thomas ap Catesby Jones had actually stormed into the California port of Monterey and hoisted the Stars and Stripes on Mexican territory, a flagrant act of provocation. The withdrawal of the U.S. Navy and later apology by the U.S. Government did little to enhance relations between the two nations.

When Miguel tried to speak of these matters, pointing out that great care and patience would be required to insure harmony between the new settlers and their Mexican neighbors, Ramsey had given him a surly response.

"You mean like the care and patience your Santa Anna showed at the Alamo and to the Goliad prisoners in '36?" he asked sarcastically.

"That was ten years ago," Miguel said, "and in Texas

they have used it as a whip to punish the innocent Mexican as well as the guilty. Reasonable men must work for peace."

Miguel stirred in the straw of his cell, trying to find a more comfortable position. His father had ordered him to join the army, to go to the Rio Grande to help put down the constant fighting across that bloody river. Perhaps he should have done so. It would have been better than slowly dying in jail.

During the first week of their imprisonment, Ramsey had managed to relay a code for communication between the cells by the simple means of a note written on a scrap of material torn from his shirt. This he had slipped into the covered canteen of beans he knew the guard would deliver to the next cell.

The pattern of the taps on the wall intruded upon his thoughts and, in spite of himself, Miguel found one word registering on his brain. F-R-E-E. Again Ramsey tapped out the word. Their code was simple. The English vowels were allotted from one to five taps, the consonants six to twenty-six. It was a slow process and, since Miguel sometimes forgot the exact order and was a poor speller in English, the messages often made little sense.

Y-O-U F-R-E-E T-O-D-A-Y. Miguel sat up and reached for the small piece of adobe he had carefully chipped from a corner of the cell and kept concealed inside his tattered shirt. He tapped back: H-O-W?

The answer came back, a single word: *L-E-P-E-R-O*.

*Lepero;* convict. Then, D-O-N-T L-E-A-V-E M-E.

The sound of heavy footsteps and the clanging of a cell door not far away prevented further communication. A moment later Miguel's door burst open and two guards entered. Miguel felt the boot of one in his side before he had a chance to scramble to his feet.

"Come on, haughty one," the guard growled. "There's someone to see you."

The man sitting in the commandant's small office wore the uniform of a colonel in the Mexican cavalry. Miguel's eyes were unaccustomed to bright light, but he recognized the light amber eyes and the dueling scar that crossed the colonel's cheek.

"So I find you at last, Miguel Marques," Apolo Ramírez said. "Instead of coming to me to begin an honorable career, you fall in with thieves and revolutionaries and end up in the *calabozo.* A fine state of affairs for the Padrone's son."

"No charges have been brought against me yet," Miguel said.

"You were found consorting with known revolutionaries, a serious offense. However, there is a way I can get you out of here today. I am here to form a special shock battalion of *leperos.* Prisoners who distinguish themselves on the field of battle will be given full pardons. Anyone attempting to escape or shirk their duty will be immediately shot. I have great need for an officer I can trust to ride with my *leperos.*"

Miguel glanced toward the window, at the golden sunlight dappling the outer walls of the prison compound where the guards stood, watching, muskets pointing.

"Miguel, without money for *mordido,* you could rot here forever, and your father will not help you. In the coming months there will be great opportunities for a young officer. We shall soon fight the *yanquis.* El Presidente has sworn to drive them from Mexican soil forever. The Republic of Texas seeks annexation with the United States. We must hold on to our lands now, or we shall lose Upper California too."

"Apolo, today is my sister's wedding day. Do you know whether the marriage is taking place?"

"I escorted the red-haired one to the *hacienda* myself. Orders were issued for his protection by El Presidente himself. All the preparations for the wedding appeared to be made. I could not stay because I have a rendezvous with a ship bringing supplies for my *leperos.* Ride with us, Miguel. I have not the time to go through all of the channels necessary to have you released. I must be on my way within the hour. You will soon distinguish yourself well enough to earn a full pardon."

"I will go with you," Miguel said. "But first, would you lend me some money?"

Apolo hesitated, then reached into his pocket.

"And I would like a minute to see the gringo, the one who was arrested with me."

Apolo glanced toward the *carcelero,* who nodded. Dealings with the military were always risky and he wanted the cavalry officer to be on his way with all speed. In Mexico, whoever controlled the army controlled the country.

The guard waited as Miguel went to Ramsey's cell.

"Ramsey, are you awake?" Miguel called.

A hand emerged from the bars and the faint light caught the thatch of dirty blond hair and the gray eyes that were as cold as steel.

Miguel placed the money in Ramsey's hand and stepped backward. "That should buy you some help when you go to trial," Miguel said. "I can no longer be responsible for you. As it is I have the uneasy feeling I shall live to regret helping you at all. Still, *vaya con Dios, gringo.*"

"*Hasta mañana,* Mexicanner," Ramsey responded with a sly smile.

Two years earlier, Garett Ramsey had squirmed under a justifiable dressing-down in front of his fellow-students at Harvard. His crusty old professor would not tolerate cheating. Ramsey had stormed out of that institution of higher learning and, afraid to face his father, had signed on for an education of a very different kind aboard the brig *Constantia.* The ship was bound for California by way of the Horn.

By the time Ramsey arrived in Monterey Bay, he had had more than enough of the brutality of life in the forecastle. He had witnessed three floggings, the victim of one dead a raving lunatic several days later. The body was casually thrown to the sharks without benefit of a canvas covering or any words of common prayer.

Men died from minor injuries as gangrene and infection occurred within hours in the tropics. Others were lost in falls from the yards and the skipper refused to put about to attempt to pick up a luckless deckhand who fell from the shrouds.

Ramsey's size and strength kept him healthy. But it was a tolerance for the first mate's personal perversions that brought Ramsey through the voyage without suffering the harsh punishment meted out for even minor infractions.

At last the ship lay at anchor in the pleasant bay. Ramsey looked over the red tile roofs of Monterey, to white adobe walls and lush green foliage. He heard the singing of the birds in the woods and felt terra firma beneath his feet again. That the flag of Mexico was flying from the little square *presidio* mattered little to him. As soon as the cargo was sold and he received his pay for the voyage, he vowed to find a place for himself in California. According to Mexican law, the entire cargo had to be unloaded and examined in the customs house, and then returned to the ship before it could be sold.

His interest was immediately caught by a man who came to bid for the cargo of spirits, tea, coffee, sugar and various items of clothing and hardware. The man was taller than most of the *Californios,* with bright red hair and sideburns. However, he had swarthy Spanish features. An old hand at California trading told Ramsey that Spanish blood in California—no matter how little— usually meant a person of upper caste, probably a landowner. Ramsey wondered idly why the man came to the ship like a common merchant. But then that red hair wasn't Spanish. A señorita must have been captivated by a visiting Irishman. Ramsey saw to it that when the man made his purchases, it was Ramsey who carried the casks and crates up from the hold to the trading room in the steerage.

Piercing green eyes went over Ramsey appraisingly as he lowered the crate of Chinese fireworks from his shoulder. Normally two men were required to haul a case of that size from below decks.

"I am Quintero Delleroc," the man said, his voice so soft that only the meticulously pronounced syllables carried his words to Ramsey's ears over the hum of trading activity surrounding them. "And I could use a man of muscle. I'd pay you well. Unless, of course, you are dedicated to a life in the forecastle." The thin lips twitched in amusement. Delleroc was well aware of the harshness of life at sea for the common sailor.

"Where can I find you when I get ashore?" Ramsey asked.

"I own an emporium. Anyone can direct you."

Two days later Ramsey stepped into the tiny store that was a hodge-podge of goods of every type, from bolts of silk and cotton to crockery, tinware, cutlery, furniture, jewelry and boots.

An exquisitely lovely young Oriental girl stepped forward to greet him. She wore a close-fitting silk dress of brilliant green, and her ebony hair was drawn upward into a circlet of flowers then flowed down her back well past her waist. He was instantly conscious of his size and bulk in the cluttered and confined surroundings.

"Morning, ma'am," he stammered, removing his hat and accidentally brushing against a small chest with his boot. Almost without appearing to move, her tiny hand steadied the vase that rocked atop the chest.

"May I help you, sir?" Her voice was as soothing as a shallow brook flowing over smooth pebbles. When the full red lips smiled, the almond eyes glowed like dark jewels. Ramsey's blood surged in his veins, and for a moment he forgot why he had come to the emporium. The need to erase the memory of moments spent in the first mate's cabin aboard the *Constantia* swept over him as he feasted his eyes on soft female flesh and delicate bones.

"I—my name is Garett Ramsey—I—"

"Oh, yes, Mr. Ramsey, sir. Mr. Delleroc told me you might come. If you will excuse me for a moment, I will summon someone to take my place here, and then I will conduct you to Mr. Delleroc's house."

She bowed and disappeared through a beaded hanging at the back of the shop, her movements so graceful that Ramsey was reminded of a tropical bird he had once glimpsed in the Sandwich Isles.

A moment later the girl reappeared with a wizened old

woman, Oriental like herself, who gave him a toothless grin and seated herself behind the counter. She placed in front of her a card which stated: "I am mute. If the item you wish to buy is not priced, please return later."

"I am Shansi, manager of Mr. Delleroc's emporium," she explained, holding the door for him to pass through into the street.

"I'm delighted to meet you, Miss Shansi," he said, tripping over the threshold. "I take it Mr. Delleroc does not run the emporium himself?"

"Mr. Delleroc has many interests, sir," she answered enigmatically. "At this time of morning, however, he is usually at home."

Home proved to be a handsome single-story house on the edge of town, surrounded by flowering shrubs and vines and built around an inner courtyard so that all rooms faced a tiny garden containing a waterfall, and a profusion of flowers shaded by a pair of olive trees.

Quintero Delleroc lounged upon a satin-upholstered couch, smoking a cigar and sipping from a large glass of brandy. He expressed neither surprise nor greeting as Ramsey followed Shansi into the room. The furniture was exotic—Oriental, Ramsey guessed, although he was not sure.

"Join me for a spot of breakfast?" Delleroc asked, inclining his head toward the decanter standing on an ebony chow table near his elbow.

Ramsey murmured a refusal. He was not invited to sit.

"I came here the same way as you," Delleroc said. "I suspect my career at sea was as brief as yours. I was previously a soldier, but that's a long story. I take hides in trade for my goods which in turn I barter for more goods from the merchants' ships. There are no banks or any kind of credit system here. Our only circulating medium is silver or hides. No doubt you've heard the sailors refer to California banknotes. Hides and silver are what they mean. Shansi runs the emporium, but I must buy the merchandise and barter for the hides. Neither the ships' captains nor the ranchers will deal with a woman, especially not one they consider to be a coolie.

I need a man to buy the merchandise and barter for the hides."

"I'm interested," Ramsey said. "When can I begin?"

"You already have," Delleroc said softly, his eyes opaque.

Before the month was out, Delleroc's instruction was no longer needed by Ramsey. Any gratitude he felt at his new position in life and escape from the forecastle was soon eclipsed by his envy and resentment of Delleroc's affluent life, and by lust for Shansi, who was Delleroc's mistress.

There had been one puzzling incident, soon forgotten. As Ramsey awaited Delleroc at his house one day to report on the latest purchases of cargo, Ramsey's attention had been caught by a leatherbound writing case lying on the chow table beside Delleroc's satin couch. The case bore an impressive coat of arms and below it, elaborately lettered in gold leaf, was the name DESMOND GASPAR DE RIVERO TALMAGE.

# 4

*Kyla was awakened by Nana in the early dawn. Blinking,* she sat up. She was alone in the bed.

"Come, you must hurry and dress," Nana said. "No one is about, and he is already outside choosing horses and mules."

"But we can't leave so soon. Why, the wedding celebrations have hardly begun! What will the Padrone say?" Kyla gasped.

Nana shrugged. "*He* is your *padrone* now. You must obey him. He says we must leave for the north today."

The exhausted wedding guests were snatching an hour's sleep before the outdoor activities began. The Padrone, much the worse for an excess of wines and spirits, opened one eye long enough to bid them goodbye and to order two *vaqueros* to accompany them. Foreigners, Eduardo thought disgustedly. *Gringos,* they had the manners of pigs. He was well rid of both of them.

Before the sun came over the hills, Kyla was riding along beside her new husband while Nana plodded along to the rear in the company of the *vaquero* leading the mules. The other *vaquero* scouted ahead.

Kyla wore Desmond's gift of a beautifully tailored deep blue riding habit with matching plumed hat, silk shirt and cravat. She was sure that the outfit would have been ideal for riding through cool English woods, but it was obviously unsuitable for the searing heat of the terrain through which they must ride.

The road was rough and the horses lurched precariously close to the edge of the bleak headlands high above the sea. They caught glimpses of sandy beaches in hidden coves far below, and to the east lay an unbroken chain of gray hills looking peculiarly like a collapsed elephant train. Beyond those hills lay the searing desert valleys. There would be no shade there and even the tall saguaros seemed to implore the blazing sky for mercy as they raised spiny arms.

They rode in silence, Nana's eyes fixed on the hills and Desmond's sending outrageous messages to Kyla. Her husband continued to surprise her with his abrupt changes of mood. He could be terrifyingly stern and domineering one moment and the next boyishly playful. There were moments when she believed he was deliberately trying to frighten her and she wondered if this was some test of her fortitude. She was careful to respond coolly. The trouble was, she was mesmerized by him and wanted to know all there was to know of his life and thoughts and hopes.

*"Madre de Dios!"* Nana cried suddenly. At the same moment their scout shouted *"Indios!"* and came galloping back toward them. Kyla reined her horse and came to a halt amid sliding hooves and the startled snorting of her mount. Almost before she realized he had moved, Desmond was in front of her and his rifle was in his hand. "No need to get alarmed," he said over his shoulder. "There's only one Indian as far as I can see, and he is approaching with his arms in the air."

Riding slowly toward them was a familiar figure, the sunlight gilding the single feather he wore in the rawhide headband, his buckskin-clad legs seeming to barely touch his pony.

"It's Golden Feather, Miguel's friend. Don't shoot him!" Kyla screamed, slipping from her saddle in her agitation, and landing in an undignified heap in a cloud of dust. Desmond rode back and scooped her up in the same manner the *vaqueros* retrieved the buried rooster in their games. He grinned at her. "Calm down, my dear. No one is going to shoot anyone. You've lived too long away from your own kind, I can see. You are as excitable as any Spaniard."

Despite the upraised arms, everyone tensed as Golden Feather drew near. He presented a fierce and forbidding figure. His bearing was regal and his movements swift, belying the gray that now touched his hair. Silently he slipped from his pony. He had ridden from the desert valleys for as long as Kyla could remember. He had saved Miguel from a cougar when Miguel was small, and a friendship had grown between the Padrone's son and the Indian who lived alone. Kyla had always felt a bond of sympathy with Golden Feather, since she too had been separated from her people.

Golden Feather had never spoken aloud in her presence. She did not know if this was because he did not speak Spanish, or whether he simply chose not to speak.

"Peace be with you, Golden Feather," she said. "Have you seen Miguel?"

The Indian reached below the blanket on his pony's back and pulled out a piece of cloth, which he handed to Kyla. She unrolled it slowly. It was a flag, dominated by an eagle standing boldly on one claw, the other claw upraised. In the eagle's beak was a writhing serpent.

"So you have a Latin lover, after all," Desmond said softly. "And he sends you his battle flag."

They reached the mission San Luis Rey just after dark and spent the night there. Kyla lay on a hard bed and waited for her husband to join her. He had not come to her on the previous nights, but had remained with the *vaqueros,* drinking and laughing noisily. Kyla avoided Nana's questioning eyes when the old woman helped her undress.

About midnight the wind began to howl down the canyons, bringing dust and the pungent aroma of sagebrush on its fiery breath. Kyla struggled from the deep sleep of exhaustion to get out of bed and close the shutters. She was still alone in the room.

Here there were no tall trees to slow the fury of the

desert wind and she felt her hair crackle and her lips parch in the hot dry air.

Tossing fitfully, she hovered between sleep and wakefulness as the wind lashed the mission and giant tumbleweeds careened across the plaza below. The horses whinnied and thrashed about in fright.

At length she rose and opened her overnight valise and took out the flag Golden Feather had given her. Kyla fondled the cloth with its proud Aztec symbol.

Why did her husband avoid her at night? Surely, even if he was fatigued from traveling, he could at least come to bed. What had she done? She was too proud to ask.

During the first night of their trip she had looked at him shyly and asked if he were ready to retire, and for a moment his eyes had been unguarded. Kyla thought she saw dismay written there. Yet she knew that her own emotions must be apparent. At that moment she wanted him to caress her and make love to her. She was about to tell him that she had not meant what she said about not wanting to marry him, but before she could speak he had told her harshly to go to bed. He was not ready to retire.

When they were again on their way the following morning he had asked a very strange question, suddenly, without leading up to it. "Are you shocked by physical deformity?" he asked.

"I—don't know what you mean. A cripple? No, I don't think so. There is an old man—"

"The bullfights," he said. "There must be men who are gored."

"Yes. But, of course, Maria and I did not care for them."

He was silent and stared moodily ahead.

In her room at the mission San Luis Rey she clutched Miguel's flag to her breast in fright as the bedroom door burst open and her husband lurched into the room. He held a candle in one hand and peered at her drunkenly, his hawklike features thrown into sinister relief by the flickering light. His red hair seemed touched by the fires of hell. Indeed, he looked like the devil himself.

Kyla stifled an impulse to cross herself. *Don't cower!* she thought frantically.

"Ah. So the new bride clutches the flag of her departed lover," Desmond said, his words slurred and the reek of brandy reaching her across the space that separated them. "I must admit that not many women have tired of me as quickly as you did, fair Kyla. I must be getting old." He stumbled toward the bed, placed the candle precariously on the pillow and sprawled backward.

Kyla reached the falling candle quickly enough to prevent the pillow from igniting, and she blew out the flame.

"Miguel is my brother, nothing more," she whispered. "I told you." So that was the reason for Desmond's coldness, she thought, he did not believe me.

"*Nada más, nada más.* Nothing more," Desmond mumbled. "Pull off my boots, there's a good girl."

Kyla was glad the room was now only illuminated by the moonlight. She fumbled with her husband's boots and, tugging with all her strength, pulled them from his feet.

Desmond gave a contented sigh and reached for her, enfolding her in his arms and caressing her body with his strong, insistent hands. She felt her breath grow uneven and longing ran through her veins like liquid fire. He kissed her, his hands cupping her breasts, his darting tongue exploring her mouth. Her body was taut with tension and desire as he positioned himself over her, his hands and lips still fondling and delighting. Then he thrust inside her, long, slow driving movements that sent quivers of pleasure racing out in every direction from the source of their passion.

His voice came to her, low and sensuous, and it seemed the whole world was spinning and she was weightlessly twisting and turning in a whirlwind of exquisite delight, building toward a climax that every nerve in her body rushed to experience.

The fever that gripped them both was pressing them to some brink of exquisite madness. Here they lingered for a blissful eternity before plunging over the precipice in wild delight that brought a cry of pleasure to her lips. The moment of release came for them simultaneously, their sighs blending as they breathed deeply of each other and were lost to everything but a supreme joy and contentment.

For a long time they lay locked together until casually, playfully, he picked up her hand and guided it to the caresses he wanted from her. Then his lips sought her body again and she shivered, the memory of pleasure making her flesh tingle as though an invisible flame had passed over her skin. He pressed his mouth to her ear and whispered to her, then playfully touched her lightly with his tongue.

He kissed her lips tenderly, then his mouth went slowly downward, pressing a delicious trail over rounded breasts, downward over stomach and thighs that were suddenly tense. She wanted to cry out, beg him to stop—she could not bear it—no, never to stop. Her hands went to his head and her hips moved upward toward him.

The madness overcame her again as, laughing and teasing, he awakened all of her senses and then, sternly, demanded that she do the same for him. This time when he was poised above her he hesitated and she could feel the tip of his organ against her. With a low cry she seized his buttocks and pulled him closer, arching her back and wanting him deep inside her.

· They moved together again, slower, more deliberately, until at last the exploding moment of their zenith could no longer be delayed and they tumbled together into the breathless void.

When he withdrew from her and lay on his back she clung to him, never wanting to move from his side. She lay beside him, her mind and her body filled and satiated with him.

It seemed impossible that she had been so frightened of him only a short time earlier. How could he frighten her so one minute and the next drive her out of her mind and into some mysterious vortex of the senses that was ancient, yet new? He made her feel that she had just been born, but had spent eternity with this man who was still a stranger.

She felt a sudden tightening of the muscles of his arm enclosing her. "Did I make you forget your Latin lover

for a moment, my sweet?" he asked lazily and although his words were carefully casual, she detected a certain edge to his voice that puzzled her.

Raising herself on one elbow, she placed her hand over his heart and looked into the depths of his veiled eyes.

"My husband," she said slowly, meaning what she said more than anything that had ever passed her lips before, "in your embrace I forget everything I ever knew or dreamed of."

"Well said, my dear," he said and then lapsed into a long silence. At length he slept and, contented and warm in his encircling arms, Kyla drifted away to a deep and satisfying sleep.

As they rode the following day, Desmond asked her a bewildering array of questions. He wanted to know every detail of her life and, in particular, how she had been educated. She and Maria had shared a tutor and had been taught to read and write, basic arithmetic and a rather vague and rudimentary knowledge of world history and geography. Although Kyla spoke English when she first went to live at the Marques *hacienda,* she had not been given books written in English to read, and now she confessed she was more adept at reading in Spanish. The rest of their schooling had been directed toward the lives she and Maria would lead as mistresses of large *haciendas.*

Describing her upbringing to her husband, Kyla realized for the first time that she had been carefully molded to fit the role the men in her life expected her to play. It was a disturbing revelation. She knew instinctively that Desmond was the one man in her life who would have preferred that she give voice to original thoughts, rather than those she had been taught. She was at once more drawn to him than ever and it was suddenly important to her that he know her feelings of awakening love for him.

"Desmond, I hope I please you. I want to please you," she said shyly. She had never practiced the coquetry of señoritas and she spoke with quiet sincerity. "I didn't mean what I said about not wanting to marry you."

"And what about pleasing yourself?" he asked with unexpected harshness. "No, don't look so perplexed. Kyla, why don't you reserve judgment on your marriage and me until you really get to know your husband? First impressions can be dangerously misleading." He did not look at her now, but she could see the frown creasing his brow and his profile was stern.

She wanted to reply that her first impressions of him had been terrifying but that he had the power to fill her with a zest for living she had never known before, but the words would not come in time, and he was galloping ahead to speak to the scouting *vaquero*.

The day had been hot, and with relief they reached the mission of San Juan Capistrano late in the afternoon. Desmond did not linger with the *padres* or the *vaqueros*. He came to their room as Kyla was preparing for bed.

He stood for a moment, and watched her take down her hair. "You're very lovely, Kyla," he said and she turned to look at him, puzzled by the regret in his voice.

She rose and went to him, wrapping her arms about him and laying her face against his chest. She felt him tense and she could feel his heart pounding against her ear.

"Oh, God," he groaned. "What have I done?"

She looked up at him in surprise, and the moonlight caught the tender curve of her lips, illuminated the endless blue depths of her eyes. Before she could speak, his mouth came down on hers, hungrily, demanding and receiving the response that rose between them in a swift crescendo. He swept her into his arms and carried her to the bed.

His lovemaking was tender, reverent. She felt she would burst with joy and happiness. As her own passion grew, she clung to him and invited him with her lips, her fingers, the pressure of her body, until he was breathing rapidly. Their flesh joined, became one, soared away on wings of ecstasy that gave no hint that pleasure was fleeting.

In the comforting afterglow of their lovemaking, Kyla tried to tell him in English of the feelings he aroused in her, of the great love that was being born inside her, but he cut off her words abruptly with his lips.

He sat up, slid his feet over the edge of the bed and was reaching for his breeches.

Kyla tried to shake off the pleasant languor that robbed her body of any desire to move. "Desmond, where are you going?"

Without a word, he pulled on his shirt and boots and stumbled from the room.

When he returned, two hours later, she was still wide awake. He staggered toward the window and flung open the shutters, despite the wind.

"I'm going to tell you a story, Kyla, and in the morning probably will curse my drunken foolishness," he said.

"A story? I don't understand." She huddled beneath the sheet, afraid of what he was going to say.

"It is the story of a man. The illegitimate son of a roving sea captain and a dishonored lady. He wandered the face of the earth until he found himself by a strange set of circumstances in the army—the British Army, as an officer no less, which was really a huge joke, because his father was Irish and his mother Chilean. Anyway, since he had a certain disregard for danger and took pleasure in any kind of brawl, the army appeared to be his natural home.

"That was, until he was asked to resign his commission. He had, his superiors claimed, committed every indiscretion, sin and folly known to man and was not only unrepentant, but actually boasted of his misdeeds. He had taken up the occult practices of yoga and hypnosis while stationed in India and made a detailed study of the sexual perversions common to the various provinces of that British colony. It was this last that caused the commotion. You see, he published his findings in the mistaken belief the information would aid in the governing and understanding of the colony. The details were devoured in the officers' messes and clubs, but when the report escaped from army control there was a public howl of outrage. Officers of the old school were quick to point out his numerous other crimes, including the seduction of a commissioned officer's wife and several high-caste Hindu ladies. I might add that all of this was true. The man was pure rogue.

"After leaving the army, our ne'er-do-well managed to gain entry to the forbidden city of Mecca, then continued his travels through the Dark Continent and Asia, always ready to be initiated into whichever sect he was currently curious about. He managed to be on hand for any minor insurrection or major war and, some said, caused some of the furors himself.

"By the time he arrived in the New World, to escape a firing squad, by the way, our friend boasted of a reputation the devil himself would be proud to claim."

Desmond's voice trailed away and he was silent for so long that Kyla said, "And this man, who is he? What is his name?"

"Quintero Delleroc," Desmond said, "the last name being a corruption of his mother's maiden name. He had no right to his father's name, you see."

"He sounds like a dreadful person. Oh! I've heard that name before," she added, remembering Garett Ramsey, the Viking in the cave.

"Oh? In what regard?" Desmond's voice had lost some of the careless lilt that had crept into it during his strange narrative.

"Miguel and I helped a North American. We hid him from the Padrone. This man said he was looking for a man named Delleroc. That he was going to—" She broke off, but it was too late to avoid telling him the rest.

Desmond soon had the whole story, in response to a few pointed questions. Surprisingly, when she had finished, he laughed a hard laugh that was as chilling a sound as Kyla had ever heard.

"So he does the devil's work even when far removed from the scene. I'm sorry, Kyla, that because of Ramsey's pursuit of me you did not run away with your Miguel. It's all very ironic."

"No. Not you," Kyla protested. "The man named Delleroc."

"Kyla, my lovely. I *am* Delleroc," he said. "My friends call me Quint."

# 5

Garett Ramsey had lasted only a short time as Quint Delleroc's assistant at the emporium in Monterey. Ramsey had made the mistake of seizing Shansi one day, behind the shelves laden with bolts of cloth.

She felt like a fragile China doll in his hands, lying limply against him and offering no resistance as he pressed the soft swelling of her breasts and let his hungry hands slide downward over her thighs. The coal-black eyes regarded him with haughty indifference.

If she had struggled, or cried out, he reflected later, he would have begged her forgiveness and told her that he wanted her desperately. But she was infuriatingly unmoved by his kisses, his whispered declarations of his awe. She was neither moved nor afraid. She simply hung against him like a rag doll, her flesh cold and unyielding and her lips closed tightly against his searching tongue.

She made no sound as her waist-length hair came free and tumbled about her face. Nor did she take her eyes from his as he placed her down on the hard floor and ripped open her dress to expose the smooth flesh beneath. Her eyes were remote, uncaring, unfeeling.

He was whimpering like some animal, hands and lips trying to make her feel what he felt, but succeeding only in turning her into a corpse so cold that his own desire died as swiftly as it had arisen.

Shansi stared at him with those uninvolved eyes that chilled him to the marrow. He rose unsteadily to his feet and looked down at her. "Damn you," he said hoarsely. "Damn you—" Then he turned and stumbled past the grinning old woman who went to help Shansi to her feet. Outside in the sunshine he shivered, as though an unspoken curse had been flung at him.

There was no point in returning to the emporium the next day, he decided. Shansi would surely have told Delleroc of the incident, and Delleroc was not going to have the satisfaction of firing him.

Arrogant swine, with his fancy house and fancy Oriental mistress, a man who clearly was not as well-born as Ramsey, whose family had been established in America since the earliest Jamestown settlement. Delleroc. Who was he? A petty merchant and cashiered army officer of doubtful parentage, he had heard . . . who was he that he should possess the beautiful Shansi?

Garett Ramsey drank himself into oblivion and was easy prey for the two crimps who threw him in a longboat and collected a handsome fee for shanghaiing a brawny and experienced crewman. He awakened to find himself back at sea, opening his eyes in horror to the damply smiling lips of his former first mate on the *Constantia.*

When the nightmare voyage ended, Garett Ramsey staggered ashore filled with hatred and self-pity for all of the brutalities and indignities he had suffered. Making his way back to Monterey, he knew that the demons that haunted his dreams would not be laid to rest until Delleroc had paid for shanghaiing him.

But Quint Delleroc was no longer in Monterey, and neither was Shansi or the toothless old hag who accompanied her everywhere. The house was closed and shuttered and the emporium had been sold to a blandly smiling Mexican, whose English was experimental and who had some difficulty understanding Ramsey's broken Spanish.

Eventually, Ramsey surmised from their rambling conversation that Delleroc had departed for Mexico City. Delleroc had confided to the new storekeeper that an English viscount by the name of Desmond Gaspar de Rivero Talmage was going to become a close friend of

Antonio Lopez Santa Anna—who had been returned to
the presidency. This Englishman, Delleroc had claimed,
was going to negotiate the purchase of a large part of
the California territory from Mexico.

The new owner of the emporium added that, of course,
the man Delleroc had been drunk at the time. Still, one
never knew. It was well known that both England and
France were interested in such a purchase, and Santa
Anna could ill afford to garrison the sparsely settled land.
A powerful ally against the encroaching *yanquis* might
solve more than one problem.

And Shansi?

Ah, yes, the man remembered the lovely Oriental girl
with the long shiny hair and strangely remote black eyes.
The man's hands expressed his thoughts as his English
failed him, and he sighed deeply. He wished, he said
distinctly, that he could have afforded to buy the girl
himself, when Delleroc told him she was for sale. But
then Delleroc had laughed that devilish laugh of his and
said that the girl was for Desmond Talmage.

"You are only an hour or two ride from your *rancho*
now," Quint Delleroc told Kyla. "The *vaqueros* will take
you and Nana the rest of the way and I will remove my
loathsome presence from your life."

"But why?" she whispered, disbelieving. "Why did you
impersonate Desmond Talmage?"

"Actually, I was to be his proxy," Quint said. "It was
at his request I came to America. Can you believe it? The
farmer asking the fox to look in on his chickens! Lord
Talmage had no desire to come to this wild and remote
place. Still, the inheritance was considerable, and although he himself had no interest in it, he felt it unfair to
deprive you. I was to see you married and installed at the
de Rivero *rancho* as Doña Kyla de Rivero Talmage."

"A proxy is only supposed to stand in for the groom
at the wedding," Kyla said bitterly. "He is not supposed to
consummate the union."

It was almost dawn, and the wind had died, leaving
the air crystal clear and the chaparral baked to tinder-

dryness. When the sun rose the day would be hot, but at that moment Kyla was shivering so violently that he went to her and covered her with the warmth of his body.

"You are a very beautiful bride, Kyla. I don't have a conscience, so I can't offer any regrets for taking you under false pretenses. In fact, I rather glory in it. I am a thoroughly bad lot, as your rightful husband will no doubt tell you when he arrives." His voice was carefully impersonal.

Kyla raised a tear-stained face to look at him. "He is coming to California?"

Quint grinned. "I don't see how he can avoid it now. He's vegetated too long, it's time he rejoined the living. Old Des will be too noble to refuse a mission for queen and country."

"What do you mean?"

"I posed as Lord Talmage in Mexico City, and Santa Anna was quite taken with me—so much so that I convinced him England is ready to go to war over the Oregon dispute, and if he were to sell them a slice of northern California, he would have a powerful ally against the *yanquis*."

"Is that true?"

"Not a word of it," he answered cheerfully. "But I told El Presidente to be sure to insist that Lord Talmage handled the negotiations. That will bring Desmond out of the hills."

"But if he is sent to Mexico City on behalf of the English government, what makes you think he will come to California to see me?"

"He's your husband, isn't he?" Quint asked lightly, stroking her hair.

She wanted to scream at him: No! You are my husband! Instead, she said, "And you, Quint Delleroc, what will you do now? Where will you go?"

"Back to Monterey to pick up some pieces there. Ah, 'tis a fair city, Kyla. I was as happy there as anywhere I've seen."

"What about that man, Garett Ramsey? He said he would kill you. Oh, Quint, why does he hate you so?"

Quint shrugged. "Who knows? But Kyla, believe me, you are well rid of me. When you hear evil things about me, rest assured they are never exaggerated. Now I must be on my way. I wish you a happy life. Smile for me, Kyla. Thanks to me and old Des, you are going to be mistress of a huge *rancho*. One day, when you are a very old lady, you will look back on this little episode and chuckle quietly to yourself. And if your husband growls at you, you will smirk privately and remember that you once made love to a likeable rogue."

She watched him finish dressing and leave her with never a backward glance. Then she buried her face in her pillow and wept.

Dust swirled under the hooves of the horses of the dragoons and artillery teams and the sun glinted down on the eighteen-pound siege cannon being drawn by oxen. Rolling along behind this monster were the lighter field guns.

Across the muddy river, near the town of Matamoros, Miguel and Apolo watched the arrival of the *yanqui* army under the command of General Zachary Taylor. They could not see the infantry yet, but the number of horsemen told them all they needed to know.

Their superiors had decided to send the *lepero* battalion as far from their home villages as possible, and it appeared now that this was not merely to discourage desertion.

"It's to be war with them, then," Miguel said.

Apolo looked at him sharply. "Did you ever imagine otherwise?" They were both aware that the United States Government had promised protection to Texas if that republic agreed to the annexation terms. And this despite the fact that the Mexican Government announced that they would consider the incorporation of Texas into the United States a proclamation of war.

"Look at the aggressors, Miguel, massing their army on Mexican soil, far from the boundary of the Nueces River. And tell me you think war can still be averted?"

Miguel climbed back onto his horse. "There were provocations on our side too. The slaughter at the Alamo and killing of the Goliad prisoners, among other things."

"Watch your tongue, Miguel," Apolo growled. "Or I will think you are a traitor, despite your skillful though wrong-headed handling of the men in that unfortunate incident the·other night."

Miguel shrugged. "The men are peons. I was born to rule them. If you would forget they are *leperos* and think of them as soldiers, you would rest more easily at night, my friend. You cannot treat men as though they are mindless cattle and expect loyalty from them."

"Nevertheless, I admired your courage in preventing the mutiny with your impassioned pleas. I had no idea you could be so eloquent. For myself, I would have killed as many of them as possible before dying myself."

"Death and dying seldom solve anything," Miguel said, almost to himself, as though he were reciting a lesson to be learned.

"What did you say?"

"That we are poorly equipped, by comparison with the *yanquis* across the river. Our men are armed with discarded British muskets that are no match for their Kentucky rifles. And the *yanquis,* I understand, made a careful study of the use of field artillery in the Napoleonic wars. Their cannoneers will ride horses instead of the limbers of the gun, and they will employ their weapons much more rapidly in support of their infantry."

Apolo's amber eyes flickered briefly. For a reluctant soldier, Eduardo Marques' younger son had proved to be a keen student of military history. "Perhaps," Apolo answered. "But our lancers are superior. We can break any enemy square with our lances and·lariats. And our troops can make long marches as well as fight. The *yanquis* will sicken and die if they are forced to march any distance."

By the time they had rejoined their men, the *yanquis* across the Rio Grande were making camp. A rooster, mascot of one of the regiments, was crowing lustily and a band could not resist striking up "Hail Columbia" as the two armies eyed each other across the river.

In the dusty streets of Matamoros, the women went about their work nervously. Even the dull-eyed prostitutes cast anxious glances in the direction of the massed troops. Those who had somewhere to go and could afford to travel began to pack their belongings.

If the mood among the men was defiance and bravado, the creeping fear among the women was as old as time. They had always been part of the spoils of war.

Kyla's red-rimmed eyes uninterestedly took in the straggle of adobe houses as the party came to the top of the rise and the valley unfolded before them.

"There. See?" Nana asked, excitement in her voice. "It is called *El Pueblo de Nuestra Senora la Reina de los Angeles.*"

"A grand name for such a dismally small place," Kyla commented.

Nana ignored the remark. "We are close to the *rancho* now. Soon you will be home again."

The heat generated by the desert wind had followed them all the way and despite only her thin *rebozo* over her lightest dress, Kyla wilted in the uncomfortable saddle. Her riding habit had been discarded days earlier.

Nana appeared not to notice either the heat or her mistress' tear-filled eyes. Nana was going home, and her tired old eyes lit up as familiar landmarks loomed before her. Wait until the golden-haired one saw the vast and beautiful land that was now hers. The husband's purpose had been fulfilled. It did not matter if he never returned. The rancho now belonged to Kyla and to Nana. Neither of them would ever have to suffer the moods of the unpredictable Marques family again.

In this latter assumption, Nana was wrong, for Cervantes Marques awaited them at the de Rivero house.

Kyla barely had time to glance at the stout adobe walls of the *casa grande* and note the strong Moorish influence of the architecture, when Cervantes came striding impatiently down the steps.

"Cervantes," Kyla said in surprise. "How did you get here so fast?"

He greeted her perfunctorily, then led them into the house. "I rode day and night to be here before you. I reached the mission San Juan Capistrano while you still slept this morning, and I learned the man posing as your husband had already left. I decided to come here to organize riders to search for him. Nana, you may go. The kitchen is to your right, and there is a woman there who will tell you all you need to know."

Kyla sat down weakly in the nearest chair. "You know then—that he is not Lord Talmage."

"The real Lord Talmage arrived at the *hacienda* shortly after the impostor spirited you away," Cervantes said grimly. "Do you have any idea the direction he might have taken?" Cervantes glared at her and Kyla was uncomfortably aware of his resemblance to the Padrone.

"No," Kyla lied.

"You can imagine the state the Padrone is in. He wanted me to reach you before Lord Talmage arrives, so that you will know what to tell him. You will swear that the impostor Delleroc did not violate you, that he acted only as Lord Talmage's proxy. We told your husband that you were never alone with the man, that he and the two *vaqueros* accompanied you here to insure your safety on the journey. Nana will swear she shared your room at your lodging places. It is very fortunate for you, *gringa* sister, that your husband's Spanish is poor and in the general confusion of the wedding celebrations we were all able to think quickly enough to avert a crisis. Believe me, it is not for your sake we do this. Lord Talmage was accompanied by a military escort chosen by El Presidente himself. We cannot afford to offend Santa Anna. With his tainted *criollo* blood, he has no love for Spaniards like Father. He would jump at the chance to seize our land and we may have given him the means, if he decides we are part of a plot against him."

"A plot? But what has that to do with me and Quint . . . the impostor?"

"Delleroc posed as Lord Talmage and ingratiated himself with Santa Anna. It seems they are both womanizers. Lord Talmage has somehow straightened out the matter. He has an almost mystical power for soothing ruffled feathers. All would have been well, had it not been for the news Apolo brought about Miguel, and the man Ramsey, who was jailed with him."

"Ramsey? He was in jail? But I thought Miguel was in the army," Kyla said.

He told her briefly of their arrest. "Apolo Ramírez had been searching for Miguel because he had not reported to him. When he discovered Miguel in the *calabozo* with Ramsey, Apolo sent word to father that Ramsey claimed to be a friend of Lord Talmage."

"Miguel—he is not in danger?" Kyla asked, a cloud of fear darkening her blue eyes.

"As I said, Lord Talmage has a healing tongue. The man Ramsey was released and sent north. Miguel and Apolo are leading a *lepero* regiment. Your husband is a diplomat. He deftly put everything in order. We must keep him happy and he in turn will protect us from any sudden whim of El Presidente."

"Cervantes, what is he like?"

"Tall, handsome, dressed in a magnificent uniform and riding a magnificent charger. You have seen pictures of him," Cervantes said.

"No—not El Presidente. My husband, what is he like?"

Something that was almost pity flickered in the depths of Cervantes' dark eyes. He shrugged enigmatically. "You will soon see for yourself. He was anxious to come here and meet you as soon as possible. Remember, the man Delleroc never touched you. We shall try to find him and silence him."

"No!" Kyla cried, and a slow flush spread across her face. She looked away quickly, certain that the shame of her moments alone with Quint Delleroc must be emblazoned in her eyes. It had to be shame, she told herself desperately. It could not be fear for the life of the man who used her as carelessly as if she were a *puta*.

# 6

*Thankful that the fading light would help conceal her* dismay, Kyla rose uncertainly to greet the man who limped across the room toward her.

Shock followed upon shock as her eyes went reluctantly from the stiff right leg and empty right sleeve of his coat to his face. He held his head awkwardly, and she realized he was turning the right side of his face away from her in an effort to conceal the cruel scars that distorted that side of his face. She saw all too clearly the pulpy mass of tissue extending from just below his eye to the mouth pathetically pulled upward in a permanent grotesque mockery of a smile. The left side of his face, and high intelligent forehead, were untouched.

"I hope they prepared you adequately, Kyla," Lord Talmage said in a gentle voice, but he could see they had not.

Kyla wanted to speak, but her mouth hung open and she stood frozen, her eyes wide as she stared at the broken body of her husband.

He sighed deeply. "Would you mind if I sat down? Thank you. Please sit down yourself, Kyla, while I quickly assure you that you need have no fear that I will ever come closer to you than I am at this moment." He lowered himself carefully into the nearest chair, right leg extended stiffly in front of him and his profile thoughtfully turned to hide his scarred face.

He had once been a handsome man, Kyla thought, as she began to recover her senses and fixed her gaze on the unblemished half of his face. He had the dark good looks of his Spanish mother combined with brilliant blue eyes. Now the eyes were filled with soul-deep sadness and there was only half a face, only one arm, only one good leg. She fought rising hysteria, her hands gripping the edge of the table in front of her.

"Please, my dear, sit down," he said, and his voice was filled with infinite patience and compassion; almost, Kyla thought wildly, as if *he* were sorry for *her*.

"I would never have come to you, never put you through what you are suffering at this moment," he continued, and his gentle voice was beginning to calm her fears, "but for the urgent summons of the Mexican president. I should, of course, have realized that my old friend Delleroc would not have been able to resist stirring something up. Please don't look alarmed, Kyla. Once we are sure your inheritance is secure, I will return to where I came from."

At the mention of Quint Delleroc's name, Kyla found her voice at last. "You call him *friend?*" she asked in amazement.

The unscarred part of his mouth smiled. "My dearest friend. You do not believe I would have sent an enemy to be my proxy? You see before you a pitiful wreck of a man, Kyla, but, although it may be hard for you to believe, life is sweet even to one such as I, and had it not been for Quint Delleroc, I would be dead. He did not tell you our story?"

"He told me he was a rogue and vagabond who was forced to resign from the British army for certain indiscretions." Her voice sounded hollow, she thought. She concentrated on keeping her eyes on that handsome profile, although she wanted to turn and run.

Desmond Talmage chuckled softly. "We met in India. He saved me from the tribesmen who were very successfully torturing me. My entire company had been wiped

out, you see. Quint spirited me away to be cared for by
friends of his and it amused him to take my place when
the replacement troops arrived under a new commanding
officer. I became a recluse. I had no desire to face the
world again. The deception was incredibly easy. I en-
couraged him to continue with it and coached him in army
protocol. He learned faster than any Sandhurst cadet.
While we were in India he won several decorations for
bravery—in my name; that, no doubt, gladdened the
heart of my father back in England. After my father died,
Quint and I inherited the title. I suppose you could say
that for many years we have shared a life. I lived
vicariously through him, and he gained the advantages of
my birth and position—until he offended some influential
staff officers, mainly, alas, by dallying with their wives,
although the officers claimed his crime was the publication
of inflammatory material about the colony. He had such
a thirst for knowledge, you see, and wanted to learn
first-hand all there was to know about everything and
everyone. Deep in his soul he has a great awe for the
mystery of humanity that he strives constantly to understand. A rogue and a vagabond? Yes, but a brave and
keenly intelligent man also. He simply lives by different
rules than the rest of us do."

Kyla's breath escaped in a long sigh. "Oh, Desmond,
what will become of him? Cervantes has sent men to kill
him and there's another man, Ramsey."

"I visited Ramsey in the *calabozo* because I was told
he claimed to know me. Ramsey told me he was a close
friend of Quint," Desmond said, "and seemed to know
enough about him to verify this."

"He lied. He plans to kill Quint. Oh, I'm so afraid for
him."

"Don't be. Quint can take care of himself. I will send
men to search for Cervantes' party and bring them back.
Don't distress yourself, Kyla. Everything will be all
right."

Desmond Talmage had a way with servants and *vaqueros*. Without appearing to command, he was able to

move them to accomplishments they would have believed beyond them. Under his gentle insistence, work was begun to improve the peons' huts, which had been neglected for years. Cervantes had restored the *casa grande,* but none of the outbuildings.

When Cervantes and his men returned, unsuccessful in finding Quint, Desmond asked him to remain as estate manager. Kyla had misgivings, but Desmond pointed out mildly that since he would shortly return to Europe, she would need the protection and services of a manager. Who better than Cervantes, who had managed the *rancho* for almost eight years and was her adopted brother?

Kyla did not argue. She quickly learned that Desmond Talmage always looked for the finest motives in those around him and did not appear to be aware of the resentment in Cervantes' gaze. Desmond was a gentle, sensitive man who harbored no bitterness about the gruesome hand fate had dealt him. It seemed, in fact, that he had probably invited it, since he had allowed a domineering father to bully him into military service, despite an inborn horror of war and suffering.

In no time at all, Kyla hardly noticed the shambling walk, the empty sleeve, or even the scarred face. She was so busy the first weeks, supervising the spring cleaning of the house, directing the planting of trees and flowers, that she did not have time to think about anything else.

She rode the softly rolling hills and green valleys of the *rancho* and observed the subtle differences between the terrain and the Marques *hacienda* on the southern peninsula of California. Unlike the bare gray hills about the *hacienda,* the mountains forming a backdrop for the *rancho* were capped by snowy peaks in winter and thickly covered with pine and spruce. While the cactus did not grow as tall and impressive here as it had on the Marques land, Kyla delighted in the wildflowers that formed a vivid carpet beneath the mesquite and sagebrush of the foothills. She began to understand how Cervantes had developed such a passion for this beautiful valley.

Kyla had always loved children, and now that she was mistress of her own *rancho* she quickly organized lessons for the children of the peons and *vaqueros*. She was seldom seen without a small olive-skinned child in tow. Her soft voice and gentle ways inspired their love and trust. And more than one small boy or girl would mistakenly pray at night to the golden-haired madonna, who was more real to the children than the invisible saints.

Sometimes, when Kyla lay in her bed late at night, she would remember the short hours of her honeymoon and the dizzying passions Quint Delleroc had awakened. She hated herself for wishing he, instead of the kindly but hideously scarred man who slept chastely in the next room, was really her husband. She wondered if Desmond's high regard for Quint Delleroc would survive the knowledge that Quint had taken it upon himself to be much more than just a proxy at the wedding.

While she had become accustomed to Desmond's presence Kyla still occasionally jumped in fright when he came upon her unexpectedly. Cervantes rode in to join them for dinner two or three times a week and report on *rancho* business. At these times Desmond often asked Cervantes his opinion regarding the political situation in California. In the Marques *hacienda* the men never discussed either business or politics in front of the women, and when Kyla started to withdraw politely one evening, Desmond restrained her.

"Please stay, Kyla. You should be aware of what is happening," he said in his softly insistent way.

Cervantes' volatile nature soon led to a heated exchange with Desmond. "The *yanquis* come like a plague of locusts," he declared bitterly. "First by way of the coast, and now they are even coming over the mountains from the east, a double assault on our land. They talk of their manifest destiny and of the golden gate to the Far East. They want the whole continent to be gobbled up into their United States, and us Mexicans swept into the sea."

"But it appears to me that it is not strictly a territorial dispute between the Americans and the Mexicans," Desmond said. "From what I have observed, there is a third group, the *Californios*. What of them? They seem to gain little from Mexican rule and appear to want an independent republic, similar to the republic of Texas."

"Texas!" Cervantes spat out the word like an oath. "We allowed the *gringos* to settle there and they repay us by stealing our land. But they made a grave mistake when they allowed Santa Anna to live after they captured him. Believe me, he will not let them have Texas. The Rio Grande will run red with *yanqui* blood." He paused, catching sight of Kyla's widening eyes over the rim of his wine glass. "Forgive me," he said, with no apology in his voice. "I love this land. I have a great rage I cannot control when I think of foreigners dividing it up to plant their miserable crops, fencing it off."

"Of course," Desmond said, then added in a deadly quiet voice, "but I am the nephew of the man who was granted the land in the first place, and Kyla was born here, a true *californio*. So your rage cannot be directed at us, can it?"

Cervantes glowered for a second, a hovering whirlwind of anger, then put down his glass and excused himself from the table. After he had gone, Desmond turned to Kyla. "An impetuous young man. But he knows and loves the land. Will you be able to handle him, when I am gone?"

"Oh, Desmond." Her dismay was plainly written in her eyes, the smoky blue depths of which could never conceal her feelings. "I wish you would stay," she said impulsively.

He bent suddenly over his wine glass, and she was startled to see his eyes glittered strangely in the moment before he lowered his head. "Kyla, before our friend Quint thrust me so unceremoniously back into the world, I had been living in a monastery." He was speaking rapidly, as though he were afraid he would run out of time before he finished what he had to say. "Then I was approached by the British Government to look into the possibility that we might settle the Oregon dispute and acquire some of the California territory. I believe they were astonished that the Mexican president asked for Lord Talmage, not only because of my leaving the army under a cloud, but because of my disability—which, they thought, occurred after I resigned my commission. Before we left India Quint wanted to confess the deception and clear my name, but I persuaded him that all I wanted was to leave the army and fade quietly into obscurity."

"But the British Government still asked you to come here, even when they learned of your—injuries?" Kyla asked.

"I persuaded them I was capable of handling the matter. Knowing Quint, I felt it better to come and see for myself what he had been up to. I was unaware when I sailed from England that Quint had also instigated a military inquiry into the last months of our service in India. His letter relating the whole story was on a ship bound for England as I was sailing for Mexico. A copy of that letter reached me in Mexico. He wanted to clear my name of the charges brought against him. Since he has little interest in political intrigue and certainly no loyalties to any one government, I believe the purchase of California territory from Mexico was his idea of a way to restore the tarnished glory of the name of Talmage."

"I'm not sure I understand," Kyla said. "You are the owner of a vast *rancho*. Why would he believe you would want to see California go to the English?"

"My father was English and I lived my entire life there until I was commissioned at Sandhurst and sent to India. I regard England as my country, Kyla, and never seriously considered the inheritance here. Frankly, I felt the Spanish land grants were too tenuous, that long before you were old enough to marry me, the land would have been divided up among the neophytes of the missions. The English, you see, are a nation of empire-builders. It is never possible for an Englishman to look at virgin territory without thinking of acquiring it for the Crown. Quint knows this. But he is wrong about me. I am no longer the eager young conqueror of foreign territories, if indeed, I ever was. I don't care that the name of Talmage is a vile one throughout India. All I want is to return to the peace of the monastery, to my books and plants and butterflies and all that I find beautiful in the world, which in turn does not look upon me as ugly and pathetic."

Kyla felt a tear prick the back of her eyes. "Desmond, are we married legally?" In her heart and soul she was Quint's wife and it seemed to her inconceivable that mere words on paper could bind her legally to another. She knew too that her body would never willingly be given to another man.

"I'm not sure," Desmond replied thoughtfully. "The priest who conducted your wedding to Quint had left the *hacienda* by the time I arrived. I sent a letter to him, but am not sure if I shall receive a reply unless we send a messenger. I was not aware at the time that there is no postal service here. In all of the excitement of the wedding celebrations, I don't expect anyone looked to see exactly how Quint signed the marriage contract. If he signed as proxy, in accordance with my written consent and your father's will, then we are legally married."

"You've been waiting to hear? That's why you stayed?"

"Yes, Kyla. Once the *rancho* is yours, it would be better for both of us if I return to my monastery. In time, you could—" He broke off. "You are young, beautiful. You will one day want a real husband and children. The one thing I am confident I shall be able to give you is an early widowhood."

"Desmond! Please don't say that," Kyla cried. In her distress she jumped to her feet and ran around the table to stand beside him, her hand dropping to his shoulder. It was the first time she had ever touched him and he raised his face slowly. Too late she realized she had moved to his right side and the candles sent fingers of relentless light and cruel shadows probing the scars. She started and drew back involuntarily. Obviously despite the fact that she was comfortable in his presence, she was still affected by his appearance.

He stood up so suddenly that the chair toppled over behind him and she stood, frozen, as he dragged his withered foot from within the prison of the carved wooden chair legs. He lurched away from her before she could find her voice.

In her dreams that night she was riding over rough trails, her horse galloping furiously after the shadowy figure who raced away from her, cloak flying like a great bat. She was calling to him to come back, oh, please come back. . . .

She awakened with Nana's hand patting her cheek gently. *"Muchacha,* wake up. He's here," Nana was whispering urgently.

"What? Who?" Kyla struggled to the surface of consciousness.

"The man who pretended to be your husband. A Chinese girl brought him. He is outside in a cart."

"A cart?"

"He's been shot."

# 7

*Colonel Apolo Ramírez cursed the loss of Captain Marques, his right-hand man.* Though the country was not yet officially at war, it was certain that a confrontation with the *yanqui* army across the Rio Grande was imminent. Still, compassionate leave had been ordered for Captain Marques because of an unfortunate accident at his father's *hacienda*.

Only hours after Marques left the encampment, an American patrol had unintentionally crossed the Rio Grande and stumbled into the path of the *leperos*. The Mexicans had butchered the patrol quickly, without waiting for orders. "It was them or us," they shrugged, as though there could have been no other course of action.

Incident followed upon incident and tensions ran high. But it was General Mariano Arista's move that finally brought about open warfare. He ordered his troops across the Rio Grande to capture a detachment of American dragoons, and then successfully cut off General Zachary Taylor's supply base.

The disreputable-looking *yanqui* general—whose own men referred to him as "Old Rough and Ready," quickly pulled back to defend his rear. His twenty-three hundred men met the six-thousand-man Mexican army head-on.

The artillery of both armies roared simultaneously, the American shells bursting with deadly effect. The Mexican gunners had only round shot and poor-quality powder, and their cannonballs rolled harmlessly through the tall grass. The advancing American ranks merely moved aside to allow them to pass, and a captain's dog, barking excitedly, set off chasing one of the Mexican cannonballs.

Now the cavalry, dragoons against lancers, went into action, and the infantry moved forward behind a bristling array of bayonets. The battlefield lay under a pall of smoke that was filled with choking cries of human agony and horses' screams.

When the moon rose over the burning prairie, more than seven hundred Mexicans lay dead or wounded. The rest had quit the field, including Apolo Ramírez, carried away with a shattered thigh.

General Zachary Taylor and his elated men followed the retreating Mexicans across a land harshly beautiful, through towns built around pleasant plazas filled with lovely señoritas. The advancing soldiers, envisioning *caballeros* serenading the señoritas beneath romantic balconies, sang their own ditty, the words written by the Scottish poet, Robert Burns:

> Green grow the rushes, O!
> Red are the roses, O!
> Kiss her quick and let her go
> Before you get the mitten, O!

*Green grow, green grow*, the Mexicans repeated, enraged. We will drive the *gringos* from our land!

Kyla found Desmond was already standing beside the cart, a lantern in his hand as two servants lifted the blanket-wrapped form from the oxcart. Watching them was an exquisitely lovely young girl whose almond eyes left Quint Delleroc's unconscious form only long enough to flit appraisingly over Kyla.

"Is he badly hurt?" Kyla asked, her heart beating so loudly it seemed they must all be as aware of it as she was.

"I'm not sure. He seems to have been shot in the back, on the left side. We'll learn if any vital organs were damaged when the doctor arrives from the pueblo," Desmond replied.

"But that will take hours," Kyla said.

"He will live," the Chinese girl said. Then she added something in her own language and they were all startled to see a wizened old woman emerge from the back of the cart. Her brown face was a finely crossed network of wrinkles and her mouth opened in a vacant and toothless grin. At a nod from the young girl, she followed the servants carrying Quint into the house.

"I am Shansi," the girl said to Kyla. "Old Woman will keep Mr. Delleroc alive until your doctor arrives."

*"Mr.* Delleroc," Kyla thought, relieved. The girl was a servant.

"I am Doña Talmage, and this is my husband. Please, come into the house. Have you journeyed far?"

Shansi looked Desmond full in the face, then bowed. Kyla envied the Oriental aplomb that kept any hint of revulsion or shock from appearing on Shansi's lovely features.

"We traveled for two, three days."

"But why did you not seek a doctor's help before?" Kyla cried. "You could have killed him, bringing him so far in that condition." She could not hide the anger in her voice, and felt Desmond's eyes on her.

"He told me to bring him here," Shansi said simply. "We rested frequently and Old Woman cared for him. She could cure him without the help of your doctor."

Desmond surprised Kyla by saying firmly, "Go back to bed, Kyla. There is nothing you can do tonight. I'll sit with Quint until the doctor comes. It won't be the first time we've looked after each other's wounds. Nana can find a room for Shansi."

Kyla hesitated, wanting to order everyone to leave so that she could rush to Quint's side, but knowing she could not. "Who shot him?" she asked Shansi, to delay the moment she must go.

"A man named Garett Ramsey."

"You're sure?" Desmond asked.

"Yes."

Desmond drew in his breath. "Then it was my fault, for having the man released from prison."

"You couldn't have known then that he would do this," Kyla said quickly. "He told you he was Quint's friend."

"A former employee," Shansi said. "Ramsey wanted me, even though he knew I belonged to Mr. Delleroc." There was no emotion in her voice, as though she were discussing a trivial matter. "He knew he would have to kill Mr. Delleroc to get me."

Kyla felt all of the implications of this revelation go spinning through her mind. Looking at the breathtakingly lovely girl, it was easy to imagine two men fighting over her. Kyla turned away, a mumbled "good night" on her lips, afraid her face would reflect the jealousy that rose within her.

A little later Nana brought her some warm milk, and the old eyes were quick to note the young woman's clenched fists gathering the sheets at her side into tight knots. Kyla's blue eyes were misty in the early dawn light.

"The Chinese is a woman of the night," Nana said softly. "A woman bred for man's pleasure only. She has no other destiny. She could never be mistress of a *hacienda,* or stand at a man's side as his wife. There is no need for you to fear her."

Kyla turned her face away. "Who said I fear her? What is she to me? What is either of them to me? He is merely a friend of my husband."

She lay awake until the sun began to rise.

The wounded Quint had been taken to Desmond's room next to hers, but the thickness of the adobe walls shut out all sound. When she arose and went out into the stillness of the morning the door to the room was closed. She hesitated for a second, then tapped on the heavy oak. A moment later the door swung open and the toothless old woman grinned at her.

Desmond was sitting at the bedside and Quint's eyes were open and filled with pain, but he smiled broadly as he caught sight of Kyla. "Hello, Lady Talmage," he said, his voice weak. "Sorry to burst in uninvited."

"How do you feel?" she asked, praying her composure

would not desert her as her eyes took in the blood-stained sheets.

"Better, now that I can feast my eyes on you again," Quint said, with a sidelong glance toward Desmond.

"To think that we helped him so that he could do this to you," Kyla said.

"Who?" Quint asked.

"Why, Ramsey, of course. Shansi said it was he who shot you."

"Shansi doesn't know who shot me any more than I do. I was ambushed on a dark street. It could have been anyone. Shansi's never liked Ramsey for some reason. Probably because he took over her job at the emporium. Unlike you señoritas, Shansi came from a society where a woman's worth depended on her usefulness as much as on her looks."

Kyla bit back the retort that flighty señoritas became hardworking señoras, who ran vast households and supervised many workers. This did not seem to be the time to argue the point. Instead she said, "Is there anything I can do to make you more comfortable?"

"It's just a flesh wound. I'll be fine when the hole in my hide is stitched up."

"The doctor should be here any moment," Desmond said to Kyla. "Quint has made his own diagnosis. He rather fancies himself as a physician, having read a few medical books," he added dryly. "Why don't you go and get someone to make us some tea, my dear?"

It gave her something to do, she realized as she went reluctantly to the kitchen. Desmond knows how I feel about Quint, she thought.

The doctor arrived before the tea was made and Desmond shuffled into the kitchen to tell her. His face was gray from the long night's vigil, but his voice was cheerful. "He'll be all right. It will take more than an assassin's bullet to kill Quint Delleroc. I shouldn't wonder if either a silver bullet or a stake through the heart might be necessary. He told me some interesting news in his moments of lucidity, by the way. There has been a revolt of the American settlers in the north and they have declared a republic, the Bear Flag Republic. As usual, old Quint found himself in the thick of things. There are also rumors that Mexico and the United States are already at war in the south."

"*Madre de díos,*" Kyla whispered. "Miguel—"

"It's only a rumor, Kyla. According to Quint, the situation here is fraught with more intrigue than the French court. Secret emissaries of the United States Government have apparently been in California for some time and there are fears that England or France may soon get into the picture. Quint feels the whole affair is beginning to take on comic opera overtones. Still, the Americans apparently believe an English man-o'-war is on the way to Port St. Francis and the United States government has seen fit to send a squadron to the upper California ports. It looks as though the *yanquis* intend to occupy the territory, Kyla, and there are too few *Californios* to stop them. As for the Mexicans, I don't know their strength, or whether Santa Anna would send an army up here."

"What will that mean to us?" Kyla asked, her eyes drifting to the door to see if the doctor had yet emerged from Quint's room.

"Perhaps nothing very much, or perhaps we will be caught in the middle of a war, like a bone pulled between two dogs. The *yanquis* may stay in the north, and decide that Southern California is too close to the Mexican army and perhaps too arid for them to bother with."

"But you say the American settlers have declared a Bear Flag Republic. Couldn't the *Californios* unite with them, and then we could be independent of both the United States and Mexico?"

The brilliantly blue eyes in the ravaged face regarded her with keen interest. "The land here could be richer than any European country and certainly stand alone, given the population. But there are too few settlers now. You have no postal system, no police force, no courts. No schools, books, newspapers. Santa Anna himself told me that only a nominal garrison is maintained here to protect the settlers from Indian attacks, and the only system of justice is that of fining the Spanish for their misdeeds, and whipping the Indians. In short, you have a primitive society ripe for plunder."

The sickroom door opened at that moment, and the doctor emerged. "Your friend will live, but he has lost much blood. He will be weak and should remain in bed for as long as you can keep him there."

"Desmond," Kyla said, after the doctor left, "what about the girl, Shansi?"

"What about her?"

"I believe she is—" She looked at the floor, her color rising. "His concubine."

"I doubt he's in any condition to act improperly at the moment," Desmond said with a faint smile. "But if you're concerned, we can arrange to have the girl move into one of the peon's huts."

Kyla felt uncomfortable as her husband's knowing and infinitely wise eyes searched her face. She quickly excused herself and went to see what was keeping Nana and the other servants from serving breakfast.

She was unable to visit Quint until the following day, as the doctor had given him a stiff draught of laudanum which caused him to sleep for sixteen hours. Kyla followed the maid who took his lunch tray into his room. Old Woman still sat at his bedside, and Kyla wondered if she ever slept.

"You're a sight for sore eyes," Quint murmured. "Get rid of the women and give me a kiss." The latter was added *sotto voce* in English, but Kyla cast a nervous glance in the direction of the servant girl, who, fortunately, did not speak the language.

"I see you are feeling better," she said.

"I'd be better still for a kiss."

"Please be serious."

"All right. Take off your clothes and get into bed with me and I'll be very serious."

Kyla hastily dismissed the servant girl, but did not ask Old Woman to leave, since someone had to act as chaperone. Kyla was not sure if Old Woman understood English or not.

"Desmond tells me you are in some kind of trouble again."

He grinned, eyes glowing in the manner of the hunter, despite the bloodless pallor of his normally swarthy features. "Caught in the middle again," he admitted. "Never could resist stirring up the underdogs in any dispute. I'm afraid your California will end up in Yankee hands, no matter what." He was silent, reflective, for a moment.

He had learned that a United States Marine Corps lieutenant named Gillespie had brought instructions from Washington to the U.S. Consul in Monterey, Thomas Larkin. Gillespie, it was believed, had brought word from the Secretary of the Navy, and possibly President Polk himself, that California should be seized at the first sign of trouble with Mexico. Quint Delleroc would have understood had the giant to the east simply declared that he coveted the Mexican territory. The fact that the U.S. was resorting to underhanded political maneuverings to acquire it angered him.

"And which underdogs are you stirring up?" Kyla asked, glad to be on safer conversational ground, though she didn't want him to stop flirting with her. She felt something of the fascination the prey feels for the hunter, which prevents flight until it is too late.

The *Californios,* of course. I had an Irish father, my dear, and although I never knew him, his blood runs in my veins. I believe land should belong to those born on it."

"And yet you brought Desmond here on behalf of the English Government."

"I brought Des here because he was fading quietly away in a monastery in Wales."

"You might have warned me—what to expect."

"You would have run away, gone to your Latin lover, and ended up a camp follower. Couldn't let that happen to you."

"Why—why did you marry me? No—I mean, why did you *consummate* the marriage?" She barely whispered the word. "It seems Desmond is your friend, yet you did that to him—to me." She had forgotten the presence of Old Woman.

"You mean, apart from my appetite for virgins?" he asked mockingly. Then, in a quicksilver change of tone, he added, "If I'd left you in your virginal state, you would have settled down to living the life of a nun with Des. I know him. He is able to bind people to him in blind loyalty and devotion. And I know you. Oh, yes, I do. You wouldn't have hurt him by taking a lover. A case of what you have never had, you never miss. Des has that effect on everyone. Once anyone accepts his physical appearance, Des becomes a sort of god to him. I felt it my duty to arouse some earthly passion in you before you wasted that fine lithe body and those beautiful breasts."

"Stop! Please," Kyla said, blushing furiously. "You appear to be telling me that you are an incorrigible meddler in other people's affairs."

"That I am," he agreed cheerfully. "Most people would live dull lives if left to their own devices."

"You'd better try to take some of your soup," Kyla said, realizing the food on the tray was growing cold.

"Feed me," he demanded.

After she left his room, almost an hour later, she realized that, during the course of her spooning soup into his mouth and breaking pieces of tortilla for him to nibble, his eyes had managed to make love to her every moment until her heart was pounding and her hand trembling. She went quickly to her room to splash cold water onto her burning cheeks.

She was still flustered from the encounter at dinner that night, but if Desmond noticed, he made no comment. Silently Kyla pondered what Quint had told her. Was Desmond all that Quint seemed to think he was, and Quint what Desmond believed him to be? *Masks for faces*, she thought. Where had she read that? Shakespeare, of course. We all wear masks for faces. People are never quite what they seem to be.

Their second unexpected guest arrived just as they were rising from the table. Nana hurried to open the door in response to a vigorous pounding, and Miguel stood on the threshold, splendidly attired in his army officer's uniform, his dark eyes boldly sweeping the room until they came to rest on Kyla.

"Miguel!" Kyla gasped joyfully and rushed to fling herself into his arms, laughing and crying and pushing him away to examine the gold braid, the enormous shoulders and newly acquired muscles. "Oh, you've turned into a fearsome warrior in such a short time," she said. "Just look at your shoulders! Oh, you look so well, so fine, and I'm so happy to see you."

"And you, *chiquita*," Miguel said softly, "are more beautiful than I remembered all these lonely months. I had forgotten how your hair turns into a golden halo in the candlelight and your eyes are lagoons of warm, blue water." He was holding her hands at arm's length, to gaze at her, when Desmond rose from the table and shuffled toward them.

Miguel's fingers tightened on hers for a second and the look of horror on his face was quickly masked as Kyla introduced her husband.

"Your *brother?*" Desmond repeated, in surprise. "Ah, the brother of Cervantes. I see." It was clear from the way he looked at the two of them that he did not see at all, but Miguel's next words immediately diverted his attention.

"I'm afraid I have bad news. Where is Cervantes?"

"Out on the far boundaries of the *rancho*. We can send for him," Desmond answered, one hand reaching for Kyla in an unaccustomed gesture of possession.

"It is my father. He is dying," Miguel said. "An accident with the bulls. He was badly gored. Cervantes and I must ride back immediately. There is no need for you to come, Kyla. The war could start at any second and I don't wish to put you in danger."

"But of course I must go with you," Kyla said at once. "Uncle Eduardo has cared for me all these years. I cannot let him die without going to see him and tell him of my gratitude."

"I'll make the necessary arrangements," Desmond said. He was the only one who noticed that Quint Delleroc's bedroom door was slightly ajar.

# 8

*Quint Delleroc sat in the window the following morning,* despite Desmond's protests, and watched as Cervantes and Miguel helped Kyla into her saddle and then mounted their own horses.

"Look at her, damn it," Quint said, "that pale gold hair and blue eyes. She'll never reach the *hacienda* unmolested. I tell you, they are already at war, the Mexicans and the Americans. She's a *gringa* and the first Mexican soldier who lays eyes on her is going to do to her what any soldier does to his enemy's women."

"If you don't calm down, Quint, all those stitches holding your wound are going to come undone. As you yourself will surely be undone one day, my friend.

"She is protected by her adopted brothers, one of whom, in case you hadn't noticed, happens to be an officer in the Mexican cavalry."

"And in love with her," Quint said. "Which won't help her after some disgruntled peon kills him. You haven't been here as long as I. The officers in their army are hated by the men—most of whom are ill-fed, ill-equipped, and seldom paid."

"What makes you say Miguel is in love with her?"

"I watched their reunion last night. I was curious about all of the excitement going on beyond my bedroom door. And don't tell me you didn't see how he looked at her."

The riders outside had moved out of sight and, sighing, Quint moved stiffly back to his bed.

"There will be nothing to prevent his marrying her after I'm dead," Desmond said. "It would probably be best for both of them."

"The flame of love could well have flickered and died by the time you're shoving up daisies, old sport. You're a fool, Desmond. There are more years ahead of you than you'd guess, despite your infirmities. Pass the brandy, would you?"

"No. If you drink you won't eat, and you need the food to build up your strength. Tell me, is anyone likely to come after you here?"

"I shouldn't think so. Shansi is convinced Ramsey is after my hide, but I don't believe he was the one who shot me. Some of my business acquaintances in the North probably felt they had a reason, but Ramsey—hell, I gave him a job and treated him fairly until he moved on one day, without any notice, but I know how it is to get the urge for a change of scene."

"Suppose I were to get the urge to leave, so that Kyla and Miguel could be together?"

The green eyes were opaque. "What does it matter to me?"

"Kyla is in love with you. Not Miguel."

Quint Delleroc's lips compressed into a tight line. "She'll get over it. And damn it, don't look at me like that. It was all your idea, my coming here in the first place. So don't give me one of your saintly looks, because I have no conscience, and you know it. There's no place in my life for an innocent who closes her eyes when I kiss her. I'm used to women of more sophisticated accomplishments."

"I didn't think even you would take a virgin."

"Why not? I've taken other virgins."

"But none, I believe, as sheltered as Kyla. Or taken under such circumstances of deception. Sometimes you are like the small boy who constantly gets deeper and deeper into mischief, all the time hoping against hope that his father will call a halt to his misdeeds."

Quint gave a derisive chuckle. "The analogy being, the sinner who wants God to step in? I knew it was a mistake to let the monks have you. You've become a religious fanatic. How about sending Shansi to me, now that the mistress of the house has departed?"

"The doctor said you must rest."

Quint grinned. "Shansi knows how to bring a man to his zenith without his moving a muscle—well, maybe moving *one* muscle."

Desmond was watching the dust settle outside. He silently wished the riders godspeed.

They were both startled when Old Woman rose from her chair in the corner of the room and began to unwind fresh bandages. She had the eerie power to fade into the background more completely than a chameleon.

Desmond sighed. "We haven't talked about it—but tell me, why didn't you do as I asked—stand in for me as proxy and leave me to the peace of my monastery? I should have insisted you stay away from the New World until it was time for the wedding. I should have known, when you suggested coming a year before necessary, that you would be in some kind of trouble before the wedding."

Quint looked pained. "Is that all the thanks I get? El Presidente is not my idea of the type of companion I would choose for myself. I honestly believed if he requested Lord Talmage's presence to negotiate a land purchase on behalf of the Crown that the British government would feel the mess in India was absolved. I went directly to Mexico City, then hid out in Northern California while Santa Anna sent word to England for me to return. You know as well as I that if you had arrived before the *yanquis* crossed the Rio Grande, you might have pulled it off."

"Why didn't you simply handle the matter yourself, posing as me? You certainly never hesitated to use my name in the past."

Quint grinned. "'I was afraid it wouldn't be legal. Besides, you're more of a diplomat than I am. I'd have

lost my temper and botched it. I was growing impatient
with El Presidente's excesses."

"Then, too," Desmond said, his eyes fixed on Quint's
expression, "you wanted me to come here. Why, Quint?"

"Because I'm a meddler." There was a twinkle in
Quint's eyes, but Desmond knew Quint was being honest
with him.

The Padrone did not live long enough to see his sons or
his adopted daughter, and the Marques *hacienda* was already in deep mourning by the time they arrived. Eduardo
Marques' body lay in state as his peons filed silently by.

They were met by a tearful Maria and the priest who
had married Kyla. After the burial the following day,
Kyla drew the priest discreetly aside and inquired about
her marriage contract. She learned that Quint Delleroc
had duly signed as proxy. She was legally married to
Desmond Talmage.

Kyla was so shattered by this news that she retired to
her room. As she paced restlessly back and forth, she
realized that all the time she had been hoping that the
marriage had been to Quint. He *was* her husband, in the
eyes of God and the church and she wanted him and
loved him! She wished she were dead, too, and lying in
the ground beside the Padrone.

News that the country was officially at war with the
*norteamericanos* reached the *hacienda* late that day and
Miguel went to tell Kyla. He knocked on her door, begging her to let him in.

He was shocked to find her disheveled and red-eyed.
The Padrone had been a stern and unloving surrogate
father, and Miguel had not expected Kyla to show such
grief at his passing.

Dispiritedly, Kyla turned back into her room and, dis-
regarding propriety, Miguel followed, although he left the
door wide open.

"Kyla, I must return immediately to my regiment. I
came only to say goodbye and to promise you that I will
find a way to dissolve your marriage to that monster."

She looked at him sharply. "Desmond isn't a monster,"

she said quickly. "He is a kind and sensitive man. He can't help the way he looks. It happened while he was in the army. Oh, why must men make wars? You will go away, and perhaps something dreadful will happen to you too."

He was beside her, his hands on her waist, moving longingly across her back, his eyes dark with passion and anguish. "How can you bear to let him touch you?" he whispered.

"He has never touched me. We live as brother and sister."

Kyla and Miguel had never lied to each other, and often their spoken words were merely an echo of what passed between their minds. He knew she was telling the truth and he let out his breath in a long sigh.

"Yet," he said slowly, "you are no longer a girl. I feel it, the awakening of passion in you. Oh, Kyla, Kyla, you do love me as I love you. You've dreamed of my flesh as I've longed for yours. Tell me it's so."

She allowed him to pull her close and bury his face in her hair and she held her breath and forced her mind to block out the memory of Quint's kisses. When Miguel's lips found hers, she relaxed her body against him and held him in her arms fiercely, but tears were spilling down her cheeks and in her imagination she was running away, far from the feeling of unutterable dread, which was all she felt in Miguel's arms. It was as though he had turned into the monster he accused Desmond of being. She felt as though all of the saints in the chapel were pointing at her accusingly, as if she were committing some unspeakable sin. She felt his tongue brush lightly along her lower lip and she wrenched away from him, sobbing.

"No! Oh, please, Miguel. I don't feel that way about you. You've been my brother for as long as I can remember and I can't think of you in any other way."

She covered her face with her hands to blot out the stricken look on his handsome features, the desperate longing in his dark eyes. His voice came to her through a fog of pain. "Then who—who is it, Kyla? There is someone. I know it. Who is he? I'll kill him."

Blinded by anger and humiliation, Miguel seized her shoulders and shook her roughly. He released her suddenly, and she fell backward to her bed, staring at this frightening stranger who no longer resembled her beloved Miguel, trying to keep him from reading her thoughts.

He stiffened in sudden realization. "Cervantes told me that the proxy sent by Lord Talmage pretended actually to be your husband, but Cervantes swore you left immediately after the ceremony. Yet I felt he was concealing something. No doubt he was afraid I would ride after the man and kill him, had I known he was stealing your heart from me. But I will not become a deserter now that we are at war. I shall wait for you to come to your senses. We are meant for each other, Kyla. It has always been our destiny. Why else were you sent to me? Why can we communicate without words, if we are not two parts of the same whole?"

Kyla looked at him through her tears. He was young and brave and handsome and she loved him dearly. Oh, why can't I feel about Miguel the way I feel about Quint Delleroc, she thought miserably. How much simpler the world would be if love only came to two people simultaneously.

Before Miguel left the *hacienda,* word came that the *yanquis* had crossed the Rio Grande and there was fierce fighting. When Miguel began preparations to return to his *leperos,* even more staggering news arrived. The land no longer belonged to the Marques family; it was to be divided among new owners. The old grant had ended with Eduardo's death, according to the priest and *alcalde,* who came to try to explain to the Marques heirs that they were virtually penniless and certainly homeless.

"I don't believe them," Cervantes declared, his eyes wild with rage. "We must appeal, go to El Presidente himself, if necessary, or all the way back to Spain. The land is ours; Father would have told us if the grant was going to die with him."

"Cervantes, my brother," Miguel argued sadly, "in normal times, perhaps we would have a chance. But the country is at war and Santa Anna is more dictator than president. You know that. Feeling runs high against foreigners and the people have not forgotten the Spanish plunder of the land. Father was Spanish born. We must persuade Kyla to take Maria back to the Alta California *rancho* and you must come with me. Perhaps if we distinguish ourselves in battle, when the war is over there may be a way to recover what is rightfully ours."

Cervantes ranted and raved, but he knew Miguel was right, and he reluctantly agreed. He and two trusted *vaqueros* would escort Kyla and Maria to the de Rivero ranch. Miguel had to leave immediately to replace the wounded Apolo.

The little group that traveled cautiously back to the ranch might have been riding together, but each was an island of private emotions. Cervantes cursed the fates that had reduced him to a man without property. He had restored the Alta California *rancho,* only to have to turn it over to a foreigner, and now his own inheritance in Baja California was to be denied him. Cervantes' lust for blood grew more insatiable as he journeyed northward.

Maria, her dark eyes flashing venom in Kyla's direction, had emerged from the wild grief at her father's death to the realization that she was not only no longer the pampered and adored daughter of a wealthy *padrone,* but was actually to live on the charity of the hated *gringa.* Maria had always resented the attention Kyla received. When they were children, visitors to the hacienda always exclaimed over the unusual golden color of Kyla's hair. Maria, being dark in a land of dark-haired people, was second-best.

When Maria was seven years old, she even went so far as to creep into Kyla's room one night and slice off one of her braids. Fortunately, Nana came rushing to see what all the shouting was about, and stopped her before Maria could do any further damage.

As they rode, Maria regretted not accepting one of the proposals of marriage she had received. Now it was too late, at least during this period of mourning for her father. When that ended, she promised herself, she would marry

the richest man in Mexico and would find a way to remove her adopted sister so that Cervantes could have the
*rancho* in the north. Her dark eyes glowed as she contemplated the downfall of the *gringa*.

Kyla, too, felt dismay at the turn of events. But she had
a duty to Cervantes and to Maria, as well as an obligation. Oddly, the knowledge that Quint Delleroc was still
recuperating from his wound at the *rancho* concerned her
most. Maria was so lovely and Quint so susceptible.

Cervantes was anxious to return to the *rancho* as
quickly as possible, and on the third day of their journey
they rode until dark before he suggested looking for a
*hacienda* or a mission where they might spend the night.

Night shadows were moving rapidly through the valley
as they came to the crest of a hill. Below they could see
the distinctive quadrangle and *companario* of a mission.

Cervantes peered through the diminishing light for signs
of life. Since the secularization of church lands many of
the missions had been abandoned by both *padres* and
neophytes, but occasionally the priests remained despite
loss of their land. There did not appear to be so much as
a flickering light within the adobe walls. Cervantes
frowned as Maria began to complain that she was too
tired to travel further that day.

"It looks deserted," he said at last. "You will wait
here while I ride down to see. Remember, we are at war,
and I do not wish to encounter soldiers of either side, we
are too few to deal with them. In the event we run into
soldiers, you will both hide, do you understand?"

"Yes, yes. You have told us enough times," Maria said
impatiently. "Oh, I hope someone lives there. I would
like a hot meal."

Cervantes still hesitated. "I am uneasy. I have a premo-
nition of danger." He slipped his pistol from its holster
and handed it to Kyla. "If you are ever threatened by
soldiers, you will kill Maria and then yourself. You will
not submit to them." He spurred his horse and galloped
down the hill toward the mission.

"He gave you the pistol! How dare he?" Maria exclaimed.

"Probably because I am older and married," Kyla said tiredly. "But don't worry, if the worse comes to the worst, I shall let you do the shooting." She looked at the gun with distaste and pushed it into her saddlebags.

The mission was deserted. Cervantes rode back and the group made their way into the *convento* where a few sticks of furniture remained, despite the fact that one end of the building had collapsed. It saddened Kyla to see the ruins of what had once been a fine old building. Although from the outside the mission appeared intact, within the adobe walls there was little that had not been destroyed, either by vandals or the elements, since the departure of the *padres*. Most of the collonade had crumbled and it seemed certain the roof would not withstand a heavy rain.

Before she retired for the night, Kyla went into the cool gloom of the chapel to pray.

Kneeling before the ruined altar, she looked up at the empty alcoves that once had housed statues of the saints, saw the primitive painting of the neophytes on the interior walls and, as her eyes were lowered to the floor upon which she kneeled, she saw the imprint of two tiny bare feet in the rough tile. An Indian child had stood in that spot before the tile hardened. Her fingers drifted over the indentations, and she shivered as though a cold wind had touched her. She had always looked forward to the day she would bear a child. She did not remember her own parents, her father who had died before she was born, her mother killed by Indians, and her Spanish stepfather who had died of disease. Kyla longed to have a child to love and care for. Perhaps then she would know again the love she herself had forfeited as a little girl. But there would be no child while she was married to Desmond Talmage.

Cervantes had not allowed them to build a fire for fear of calling attention to their presence. If they met *yanqui* invaders, Maria and the men would be in danger, and Cervantes was uneasy about the possible reaction of Mexican soldiers to the golden-haired Kyla.

A little after midnight Kyla stirred, suddenly tense and chilled. A sound coming closer. Voices and horses. Laughter. Many riders galloping into the mission patio. She shook Maria, who lay at her side, and the girl opened her eyes and asked irritably what was wrong, as Cervantes came silently toward them. He crouched down and whispered urgently, "Soldiers. Mexican, but they are drunk and there is only one officer with them. You must slip out of the ruined end of the *convento*. Run for the hill and wait for us there. We will come as soon as we can."

He clapped his hand over Maria's mouth as she began to protest, while Kyla scrambled to her feet and felt around in the darkness for her riding boots.

"No! Don't waste time. Go—take only the gun," Cervantes ordered.

Kyla took Maria's hand and they went to the far end of the convento, scrambling over the fallen wall and hiding behind the remains of the colonnade as Cervantes went out to greet the soldiers.

They were tying up their horses and staggering about noisily searching for any wine that might remain.

"*Buenas noches, amigos*," Cervantes said. "My friends and I were sleeping and heard you arrive. Alas, there is no food or wine left in the mission, but we have a little *carne seca* from our own supper."

"We are not hungry, we have just come from a very hospitable casa," a voice answered out of the darkness. "But the woman there was old and ugly. You do not have a pretty señorita hidden away, do you?"

Maria gave a little gasp of alarm, and Kyla yanked the girl out of the shadows, and the two of them sped toward the nearest cluster of trees.

"What was that? Are your friends fleeing from us, *amigo?*" the drunken voice asked.

"No. It was just a deer. We disturbed several when we arrived," Cervantes said hastily.

"Then why did you not kill one for your supper?" A second voice asked suspiciously.

"Too tired. We have ridden far. We are carrying important dispatches to the commander of the garrison in the *pueblo* of Los Angeles," Cervantes improvised quickly. "We are traveling as civilians because we heard there were *yanquis* in this area."

Kyla and Maria huddled in the shelter of the oak grove, trying to regain their breath as Cervantes' voice faded in the distance. Cervantes and the soldiers had gone inside the mission. Kyla prayed the soldiers would not find the female belongings left in the *convento*.

Dawn was lighting the hilltop before Cervantes and the *vaqueros* rode to join the two women who were by now numb with cold.

"We could not leave before, it would have looked suspicious," Cervantes said. "Come, you will have to share our horses. Yours were confiscated by the army. They thought we were returning them to the *rancho* from which we had borrowed them."

Trying to tuck her bare feet under the warmth of her skirts, Kyla rode within the circle of the *vaquero's* arms, the horse slowed by the double weight. She could not stop shivering. We are at war. We are really at war, she thought. Oddly, it was the tiny imprint of the child's feet in the adobe tile of the mission that came to her mind.

# 9

*Quint was on his feet, though still bandaged and weak,* and Shansi still had a room in the *casa grande,* when they reached the de Rivero rancho. Kyla was greeted by Desmond, his poor tortured lips smiling and his bright blue eyes lighting up with joy at her safe return. Impulsively, Kyla embraced him, but her arms dropped quickly as she felt the empty right sleeve under her hand.

"Eduardo?" Desmond asked, pretending not to notice how swiftly she withdrew from the greeting.

Kyla shook her head. "He was dead when we arrived. Desmond, you have already met my sister, Maria, I believe?"

Maria's horror at Desmond's appearance was written plainly on her lovely features, and Kyla quickly gestured for Nana to show the girl to her room. They had barely disappeared when Quint entered the room. He walked stiffly, but the pain was gone from his eyes. Kyla searched in vain for the joy she herself felt at seeing him again. His greeting was casual.

"Welcome home, Lady Talmage. As you can see, I am still imposing on my old friend. Did you run into any trouble along the way? See any soldiers? What news have you of the fighting?"

"We saw only a small group of Mexican cavalrymen," Kyla said.

"Quint is champing at the bit, knowing there is a war going on and he's not part of it," Desmond said, his eyes still following Kyla fondly as she went to the table where Nana had placed a tray of cool drinks and refreshments. "Kyla, I am glad you are safely home. Had we known when you might return I would have sent men to meet you. It seems the war may come to us, without our going to search for it."

"What do you mean? Surely we are far from the fighting here," Kyla said, feeling a pair of green eyes examine her.

"The Spanish *californios,* they are organizing to fight," Desmond said. "They are serious about independence. Already they have a group of superb horsemen, and a dedication to their cause that is probably lacking in either the *yanqui* or Mexican armies. Gallant, but foolish, I'm afraid. Their cause is already lost."

"Who is their leader?" Kyla asked absently. She had caught a glimpse of the Oriental girl, Shansi, padding silently from the direction of the kitchen.

"We have heard of several." Desmond did not add they had been informed that every Mexican citizen from fifteen to sixty who did not take up arms would be declared a traitor, or that any Mexican or foreigner who aided the enemy would be put to death and his property confiscated. "We shall be losing Cervantes, I'm afraid. Tell me, Cervantes, have you decided whether you will join the *californios* or the Mexican regulars?"

Cervantes' interest had been caught by the possibility of the confiscation of property of foreigners, and he hovered for a moment on the brink of a decision between joining the rebellious *californios* in the hope of acquiring a *rancho,* and his deeply inbred love of his country. After all, as Talmage had pointed out, the *californios'* cause was already lost, there were too few of them. "My duty is clear," he said, "I will join the Mexican army now that I have delivered my sisters safely in your keeping." He bowed in their direction, ignored Quint Delleroc, and left for his own quarters.

The girl Shansi bore a tray of fresh drinks, and Kyla

frowned as she came boldly into the room. She glided, rather than walked, her head held high like some exotic princess. There was an instantaneous change in the two men who watched her entry; Kyla felt it as clearly as if a warm wind had come into the room. It was an awareness, a certain tension, as though the girl generated the electrical force of a storm.

"Shansi very kindly offered to help in the house," Desmond said, catching Kyla's glance. "Nana is getting old and so many of the women have left to follow their men in the fighting that we are very short of workers."

The almond eyes met Kyla's frosty blue stare in what seemed a challenge, and Kyla fought the impulse to order the girl to leave the room. To her horror, she heard herself saying, "Then we must find some suitable clothes for her to wear. Something more befitting a servant in the *casa grande*." Oh, why had she spoken without thinking! She did not dare look in Quint's direction.

Shansi looked down at her own close-fitting silk dress— palest pink with deep red embroidery around the hem and mandarin collar. The dress opened at the sides and gave daring glimpses of slender and shapely legs when the girl walked. "I dress in the manner of my country and position in life," she said coldly. "And I was under the impression I am a guest in your house, who chose to make herself useful—not a servant."

Kyla's mouth opened in amazement. She had spent her life waited upon by docile and subservient Indians and *mestizos* who hardly dared look her straight in the eye, much less speak back in such a manner.

In the background, Quint laughed. "You'll have to excuse her, Kyla. She's never had to kowtow to the lady of the manor before. Nor has she ever had to deal with a woman's jealousy. Shansi—" he spoke to the girl softly in Chinese while Kyla blinked back tears of mortification, which were not made easier to bear when Desmond reached across the table and patted her hand gently.

"I'm sure you must be very tired from your journey, my dear. Why don't you take a *siesta* before dinner?"

Kyla thought angrily that the mistress of the *rancho*

ought not to be sent to her room like a naughty child, but it seemed that Desmond's advice would be well-taken.

She was very tired and slept soundly, awakening to total darkness and unfamiliar surroundings after the nights spent in different places. As she stumbled from her bed, Kyla experienced a moment of disorientation. She opened the door to the silence of the hall beyond, and realized she must have slept through dinner and into the small hours of the morning. No doubt Nana had decided not to awaken her. She returned to her room and was about to close the door when the door to the room next to hers opened. A slim silhouette glided silently away— a silhouette with a long curtain of black hair that fell down her silken back.

Kyla slammed her door shut. Quint Delleroc had the audacity to allow the Oriental concubine to go to his room while he slept under Kyla's roof, taking advantage of her hospitality. Oh, how dare he do this, betray her with that woman? In her anger she forgot completely that Quint was guilty only of impropriety, not infidelity. He was not after all, her husband, or anyone's husband. But Kyla did not stop to consider this as she paced her room for most of the remainder of the night.

An armed band of Americans from the East, under the command of Lt. John Frémont of the U.S. Army, supposedly on a mission of exploration, had seized the villages of Sonoma and San Francisco. The Spanish *californios,* who had been prepared to unite with the American settlers to proclaim California a republic, quickly changed their minds when Frémont and a mountain man named Kit Carson showed their true and bloodthirsty colors. Asked why Mexicans and Spanish *californios* were shot at the slightest provocation, without a chance to speak on their own behalf, Carson replied laconically that the U.S. Army had "no room for prisoners."

When John Sloat sailed into Monterey Harbor and occupied the town, and the American flag replaced the Bear Flag and the Mexican flag in all of the northern settlements, the *californios* in the southern part of the state belatedly took up arms against the invaders.

A group of Americans stumbled into an encampment of red-mantled *californio* lancers under the command of Andres Pico, and were astonished as the much-smaller force charged on sleek horses, wielding, with deadly effect, eight-foot willow lances tipped with knives.

*"Viva* Mexico! *Viva* California!" they yelled, putting on a display of horsemanship and reckless disregard for danger.

There was fierce fighting in the desert and mountains east of San Diego and it was soon evident that Southern California would be the main battleground.

Kyla was not sure when she first realized Quint's absences from the *rancho* were growing more frequent and of longer duration, but there was no doubt he was involved in the fighting, when he came home late one night with blood soaking through his shirt in the vicinity of the old wound.

Everyone had retired for the night and Kyla was alone, unable to sleep and feeling strangely apprehensive. She sat in front of the dying embers of the fire, a book open on her lap and a mug of chocolate growing cold on the table beside her. She tensed as she heard the footsteps across the tile of the hall, uneven, furtive. Then Quint moved into the small circle of light cast by her lamp. He was swaying slightly on his feet, his red hair damp from the thin drizzle falling outside. She saw the blood on his shirt instantly and leaped to her feet.

Gratefully, he lowered his arm about her shoulder and she helped him to the nearest chair.

"It's all right," he said, with a ghost of a smile. "I fell off my horse, that's all. No lead in me this time."

"I'll get some water, to bathe the wound," she said.

He caught her wrist before she could move. "No. There isn't time. I must leave tonight. Go and wake Shansi."

Her eyes narrowed, but she tried to keep her voice level. "But why? You can't ride. You're hurt. Oh, Quint, you've been riding with the *californios,* haven't you?"

"Do you take me for a fool?" he answered, which was

no answer at all and when she opened her mouth to protest, he added, "Look. American sailors and marines landed at San Pedro. That's less than twenty miles away. And they're marching in our direction. Another detachment of Americans is headed this way from San Diego and probably more from the north. It's hopeless, they will be in Los Angeles in a matter of days. Anyway, I must return to Monterey. I've already tarried too long here."

"Oh, Quint. You stayed and fought with the *californios* because of me, and your friendship with Desmond?" The last was added quickly when he raised one eyebrow at the starry admiration in her eyes.

"Don't endow me with noble attributes I don't possess," he said shortly. "I stayed because I enjoy a good brawl, like any self-respecting Irishman. I'm only interested in one cause, the gratification of my own selfish desires. I don't give a damn about your Bear Flag Republic or Mexico or the United States or any other national boundary. I'm an expatriate, and the expatriate never breathed that was worth a damn."

"But you've been fighting for California, it doesn't matter why. Oh, Quint, stay here, please. Quint, I love you. I'll always love you." The words were out before she could stop them.

In the second before his brows came down and his eyes turned opaque, Kyla recognized a look of pity that softened the hawklike features. That look was to her more soul-destroying than anything he could have said or done. She felt herself cringe in every cell of her being. His hand dropped from her wrist.

"Then you're more of a fool than I thought." His voice was harsh. "Love! A word invented by men to get a woman to raise her skirts. And not a word I've ever used, to you or any other woman."

She drew in her breath, turning her face from him and wishing she could die. She wanted to turn and run from the humiliation of his rejection, but she stood riveted to the spot.

His expression softened somewhat as he added quietly, "You're too good to waste yourself in the shadow of a scoundrel like me, Kyla. I'm incapable of feeling anything but temporary lust for a woman. Let me give you the best piece of advice you'll ever receive: live for yourself. Don't build your hopes on anyone else. The foundation will be too fragile."

She closed her eyes briefly, her head drooping on her shoulders as she searched her mind frantically for a way to save her pride. She had been brought up to believe her only happiness would be in serving a man's needs and bearing his children, but now she wondered if that was a whole life.

"I don't understand what you mean," she said in a small voice, "but I'm sorry I threw myself at you. I'll go and fetch Shansi now."

"Good," he said. "But I wasn't finished talking to you like a Dutch uncle. Stay with Desmond. He'll be good for you. He'll help you develop your mind, show you there are more things on earth than pretty dresses and fandangoes. And he'll turn a blind eye to any handsome *caballeros* who climb the balcony at midnight. If I were a woman, I'd consider myself fortunate to have old Des, this *rancho,* and your looks and intelligence. With all of these advantages, life never need be dull. Believe me, that's the deadly sin—boredom."

Somewhere in the back of her mind a raw nerve was touched and she felt anger race through her blood. "How dare you—" she said in Spanish, the words tumbling from her lips in a raging torrent, "presume to tell me how I shall spend my life, or assume that all I want is moonlight romance? What do you know of me, of my people, or my country? You are a stranger here whose only interest is that we might amuse you for a time, relieve your boredom. Don't pity me, Quint Delleroc. I shall get over my foolish infatuation now that I know what kind of a man you are. It is you who needs pity. You calmly boast that you are incapable of deep feeling. It chills my blood that you don't realize you are a soulless monster, with less reason for being than the blind worm that crawls through the bowels of the earth."

She stopped, her knuckles going to her teeth as she

realized her voice had risen to the point they might be overheard. She turned to run from him, blinded by her tears and unaware of the changed expression in his eyes.

Despite his weakness, his hand snaked out and caught her, pulling her back to him, crushing her against his chest. He looked down at her with a raw fire burning in his eyes, and she struggled to pull away from him.

She held herself stiffly, her lips clamped together, as he bent over her, his face close to hers. He kissed her, without passion, lingeringly, like a long goodbye. For a moment her treacherous body responded to his nearness. Then she fought him, pulled free, turned and ran. Tears streamed down her face.

Her words lingered in his mind as he rode through the night. Kyla was not the first to accuse Quint Delleroc of having no soul, but on other lips he had relished the taunt.

He felt that creeping lethargy that was due, he knew, to loss of blood, and he fought to stay conscious and reach his destination. As his horse plodded through the darkness flickering images from his life came and went.

On his ninth birthday Quint had stowed away aboard an English ship. The crew found him a week later, half-starved and reeking of bilgewater.

He was put to work in the galley with a bad-tempered old cook who tried to hold his hand over a steaming pot one night when he dropped the skipper's dinner. Quint promptly elbowed the cook in the stomach and fled from the galley into the waiting arms of the first mate, who gave him a taste of the cat for his insolence. This had laid him low for the rest of the voyage. His flayed skin became infected, and the skipper had dropped him ashore among the army of orphans and beggars that swarmed the London docks.

He was found, feverish and semiconscious, by an aging whore who worked the waterfront and whose former good looks had faded under the onslaught of too many beatings. Her name was Nellie, and she took him to a medical student of her acquaintance who tended her black eyes from time to time in return for free favors. The student cleaned his back, explaining gravely that it was his personal belief that it was not so much the wound that killed a man, but the filth that was able to gain access to his body through the torn flesh. Then he threw Nellie onto his narrow bunk and Quint watched, fascinated, as the two of them went through various forms of coupling.

Quint worked odd jobs when they were available, picked an occasional pocket and between times found his way to the medical student's room and listened solemnly while the student agonized over his books and cursed the inept physician-teachers at the hospital.

Quint stayed with Nellie until the night one of her clients left her beyond the ministrations of the medical student. He stood by her pauper's grave, battered cap in hand, and said goodbye to her, then set off on foot for Liverpool, where he had heard it was possible to stow away on a boat for Ireland.

Along the way he joined a gypsy caravan. With his swarthy features and bright red hair hidden under a bandanna, he looked the part of a gypsy. He rapidly learned the Romany ways and was most interested in their clairvoyant powers and fortunetelling. All of them agreed *his* fortune lay far across the water in some distant land. When he was sent to prove his worth by stealing a horse from a local squire, he was promptly caught. The gypsies moved on without him, leaving him with his first taste of the lure of exotic nonconformity.

He escaped hanging when the jailor's wife came upon him performing a necessary bodily function and was impressed with his fourteen-year-old dimensions. After a few rapturous visits from her in the stealth of the night, he was spirited out of the cell of the condemned convicts and found himself among those to be transported to the penal colony in Australia, that dumping-ground for English incorrigibles.

It was one of the supreme ironies of fate that, when he managed to slip his gaunt wrists and ankles from his chains and jump from the deck of the ship into the murky depths of the Mersey, instead of scrambling aboard a ship for Ireland, he found himself aboard a ship bound for the west coast of Africa on a slaving expedition.

The crew of the ship consisted mostly of Hindus and, when he was able to escape the constant chores the first mate found for him, he listened to an old Hindu tell him stories of the vast and mysterious land of India and the beliefs of some of its people. He was particularly fascinated in reincarnation and the laws of karma. The Hindus believed the blacks they bought from the African tribal chiefs had not only committed some folly in this life, but were paying for crimes in earlier lives by now living in servitude.

In his desire to learn whether the blacks—who were crammed like cordwood in the holds below—believed this too, he painstakingly learned one of their languages while feeding them. He was caught speaking Swahili and, red hair notwithstanding, sold to a sugar planter in Jamaica. The plantation slaves had an interesting belief in voodoo and he began to see the pattern between their practices and the laws of karma of the Hindus of India. But several more years were to pass before he reached the northern provinces of that land and fate led him to the lone Englishman, dying by inches at the hands of the Khyber tribesmen.

He forced the Englishman to live. Perhaps it was their karma—they owed it to each other from some previous existence. Oddly, it was Delleroc who looked the part of a half-English, half-Spanish army officer. The role was easily assumed, and he played it to the hilt—until he faced the fact that playing the part of Lord Talmage had not solved the problem of Delleroc's identity. So the search had begun again.

There had been one man—the right age, the same new copper-penny hair and green-gold eyes. Skipper of a decrepit merchantman plying the China seas which had foundered during a dread *taifung* wind. Quint found him, stupid from a week-long binge, in a Singapore bar. He had been smuggling opium since the loss of his ship, and aye, he'd sailed the Caribbean and the South American ports many times. A Chilean girl? A crafty look had come into the cat's eyes. Well, now—that depends—

It's all right, Quint had said quickly, it doesn't matter. Tell me about yourself. Do you have a family somewhere? Where did you come from? What are your politics and religion? What do you believe in?

Dublin, long ago, but he hadn't seen the city for over twenty years.

Yet you feel you belong to that city, to that country?

Of course, where else? The older man had passed out into drunken oblivion without answering any further questions, and while Quint looked for a rickshaw to take him home, the skipper disappeared, and Quint could not find him again. Twenty years, Quint thought, yet he knows he's a Dubliner and Irish.

Quint did not think of himself as Chilean, and he had never seen Ireland.

# 10

*Matamoros was in American hands, and volunteers* poured into the dusty, flea-ridden town in ever-increasing numbers. It seemed every man in the United States wanted to fight Mexicans. "The Halls of Montezuma" was a phrase on everyone's lips and men couldn't wait to see for themselves the exotic señoritas, the volcanos and desert, to say nothing of the silver mines and other riches that glittered beckoningly in their imaginations.

Congress, however, had limited enlistments to fifty thousand, and state after state was turning applicants away from recruiting offices. Some of these men merely headed in the general direction of the Rio Grande, and it appeared most of them came to Matamoros.

They came to black clouds of flies, searingly hot days, desert-cool nights that were filled with mosquitos so enormous the men called them "night hawks." Sickness was rampant among the "seven-dollar targets," as the recruits called themselves, their pay being seven dollars a month. And the tent-hospitals were crowded with men wasting away from dysentery and in the throes of fever. For every man killed in battle, ten would die of disease.

The new arrivals, however, came full of bravado and high spirits, and the town boomed. Hotels, lunchrooms, bars, brothels, even a couple of bowling alleys and a theater sprang up. There was a fountain selling "soda with syrups," along with a daguerreotypist and a dentist's office.

Among those too late to be accepted into the army was Ramsey. He had lingered too long in Monterey, trying to find out what had happened to Shansi and Old Woman, who had both disappeared into thin air after the shooting of Delleroc. The local mortician, improbably named Merciful Smith, refused to disclose the funeral arrangements and Ramsey had been unable to find out what other interests Delleroc had in Monterey. Eventually, for want of something better to do he drifted south. The lure of marching into Mexico and possibly looting some of the rich *haciendas* sent him to the recruitment office, only to be told no more volunteers were needed.

Ramsey prowled the town restlessly, noting that he was not the only would-be volunteer to be turned away. Men brawled and drank and loafed about the town, in the hope that more volunteers would be needed to replace the men dying in the fly-filled tents.

There was one regiment that Ramsey noticed more than all of the others. These men were feared and despised by the Mexicans and even their fellow Americans gave them a wide berth. *Los Diablos Tejanos,* the Mexicans called them, and with good reason.

As fighters and scouts, the Texas Rangers were unexcelled. No one could fire a six-shooter with more accuracy, or wield a bowie knife with more deadly effect in close combat. They were utterly fearless and dedicated. Remembering the Alamo and the slaughter of the Goliad prisoners was a religion to them. They were also, as General Zachary Taylor himself said, "licentious vandals," who raided and pillaged Mexican villages and farms. They were wild and uncontrollable, and on one occasion Zach Taylor lost his temper and threatened to jail the lot of them. They swaggered about the streets of Matamoros, spurs jingling on their boots, Colt revolvers on their hips and pistols and bowie knives tucked into their belts. They frightened the citizens and picked fights with the regulars in the United States army.

Ramsey promptly offered himself as a volunteer to ride

with them. He was told, curtly, that the Texans didn't want any "outsiders."

One towheaded youth from Kansas, who watched Ramsey's unceremonious dismissal, unwittingly gave him the solution to his frustration.

"Hell, I reckon there's enough men in this stinkin' town to make up our own regiment. Any fool can ride into a Mex village and shoot down men without guns and take what he needs. Who needs their lousy seven bucks a month?"

Ramsey looked at the boy for a moment, then let his gaze drift down the street to where a group of loiterers were idly shooting at a tin can.

And Ramsey's Raiders came into being.

Maria resented being plunged into what she called a life of gloom and misery. There was no social life at the *rancho* and all of the young men were off fighting each other. Kyla pointed out that they *were* in mourning, and even if there had not been a war, they certainly could not have entertained or been part of any social activities. Maria had stormed away. She took her meals in her room and adamantly refused to spend a moment longer than necessary in the company of Desmond. His appearance so offended her that if she chanced upon him in the halls she would cross herself and murmur, "*Madre de Dios!*" Evidently she had not minded Desmond's presence while Quint was still in the house. Then she had come to dinner with a becoming sparkle in her eyes.

But Kyla herself was too miserable about losing Quint to concern herself with Maria's tantrums and constant sulking.

Kyla battled her emotions, telling herself that if Quint Delleroc had taught her to love, then from his rejection she must also learn to hate and mistrust. But just as she could never willingly hurt another living creature, neither could she understand what drove someone else to deceive and deliberately cause pain. She taught the children and did all she could to relieve Desmond's burden. With so few *vaqueros* to help take care of the vast *rancho,* he had all but exhausted his limited strength. He no longer spoke of returning to the peace of his monastery, and for this, at least, Kyla was grateful.

As Quint predicted, the revolt of the *Californios* appeared to be crushed. Americans marched into the pueblo of Los Angeles and promptly declared martial law. Lieutenant Gillespie, who had been left in charge of Southern California, did not understand the *Californios*. The restrictions he imposed on them could not be tolerated by proud and hot-blooded men. In the pueblo of Los Angeles, two or more persons must not walk together on the streets, and galloping through town on horseback was forbidden—a humiliating rule to *Californios,* who practically lived in the saddle. There were to be no gatherings held in the homes, an even more unthinkable edict to the party-loving *Californios*—especially with the annual *matanza* approaching.

When the small American garrison began to swagger about the streets, showing off the cockiness typical of the conqueror, they quickly earned the hatred of *Angelino* youths and rekindled a surge of patriotism. Small groups of *Californios* armed with old flintlock muskets, began to harass the garrison.

Gillespie promptly arrested the most prominent men in town and conducted a humiliating interrogation in his office.

Desmond was summoned by several of their wives to see if he could intercede and he immediately rode into the pueblo, alone. Kyla waited anxiously for his return and was sitting on the verandah watching the sun set as he climbed wearily from his horse.

"Are you all right? What happened?" Kyla asked, running down the steps and standing on tiptoe to kiss his cheek.

His arm went about her shoulders in an encouraging hug. "Excellent, excellent. They have been released. But the mood is one of anger. I believe the *Californios* are actually considering digging up *El Conico*." They walked into the house together as a vaquero ran to take the horse.

"El Conico? What do you mean?" Kyla asked.

"I forget you did not know. There was an ancient bronze cannon—it used to be mounted in the plaza for ceremonial salutes in local fiestas. It was a culverin, a long gun with a flare-shaped muzzle that gave it the nickname of El Conico. The townsmen decided it would not fall into *yanqui* hands, so they hauled it away and buried it in Doña Reyes' peach orchard."

Kyla laughed delightedly. Doña Reyes was a sweet but fiercely patriotic old lady.

Later, when they heard the ladies of Los Angeles had sent Gillespie a gift of plump California peaches as a peace offering, Kyla thought about the buried cannon—especially when it turned out that the peaches had been rolled in the tiny prickles of cactus apple and it took the American commander a week to get them all out of his mouth.

Except for the shortage of men, life on the de Rivero *rancho* continued untouched by war. They were not close enough to the pueblo of Los Angeles to suffer from the indignities of martial law. The summer slipped by, and there was no word from either Quint or the Marques brothers.

The time for the annual *matanza*, the roundup and slaughter of the cattle, was approaching. Kyla did not look forward to this, as the animals were killed for their hides and tallow and much of the flesh was left to rot, its stench permeating the hot air and attracting coyotes and wolves. Some of the meat was dried into *carne seca,* and, normally, great parties, barbecues and bullfights and much socializing would have taken place. But not while the family was in mourning and while young men died in battle, to say nothing of the American law forbidding such gatherings. Maria was indignant when Kyla refused to invite a group of officers from the Los Angeles garrison to dine on some of the surplus meat. Maria felt any party was better than none, and their martial law surely did not apply to themselves.

"But they are *norteamericanos!*" Kyla protested incredulously, "and Cervantes and Miguel are at this very moment fighting them."

Maria shrugged. "You are also a *norteamericana* and your grotesque husband is an Englishman. You could have some of your own people over to eat the meat without making such a fuss."

"Absolutely not," Kyla said. "We are *Californios* and do not fraternize with invaders. And if you ever call my husband grotesque again, I shall—slap you."

They confronted each other, blue eyes clashing like sabers with dark ones, until Desmond quietly separated them.

When he had time, Desmond talked to Kyla of his travels and of life outside the confined world of the *hacienda*. A large crate of books arrived aboard a clipper from England, and Desmond greeted them like long-lost friends, running his hand over smooth leather covers and exclaiming softly as his brilliantly alive eyes found a well-remembered title. In his quietly insistent way, he urged Kyla to begin reading books written in English and learn something of her heritage and origins. He suggested for entertainment she begin by reading a book by a young Englishwoman named Jane Austen. As Desmond predicted, Kyla was enraptured by *Pride and Prejudice*.

Late in September, fighting flared again in the pueblo of Los Angeles as a group of *Californios* attacked the small American garrison there. They were repulsed, but the next day Captain José Flores of the Mexican regular army, rallying five hundred men, proclaimed the independence of California. The garrison in Los Angeles was under heavy seige.

Desmond immediately began to disappear every evening after dinner and sometimes for most of the night, and Kyla watched and worried. He had told her he personally did not believe that soldiers slaughtering one another was a civilized way to settle territorial disputes. Neither did he know of a way to get men to sit around a conference table and talk—although, for all the *yanquis'* talk of "Fifty-Four-Forty or Fight," the Oregon dispute with the British had been peaceably settled on the forty-eighth parallel.

He couldn't be involved in the fighting, Kyla thought.

Apart from his beliefs, he has only one arm and an almost-paralyzed leg. He is merely busy with *rancho* business in preparation for the *matanza*.

Sometimes, when he returned late at night and she had waited up for him, he would look at her in a quizzical way and there were times she felt he was about to tell her something important, but the words never came. It was the fighting, she thought, he wanted to spare her details of the bloodshed.

It was not the fighting. Desmond was looking at her though Quint Delleroc's eyes, the memory of Quint's conversation about her still fresh in his mind. Quint was still in Los Angeles and Desmond met with him and the other men who planned to resurrect the cannon, *El Conico.*

Quint had felt it better that he remove himself from the rancho the night he was almost caught leading a raiding party against the garrison in Los Angeles. He and Shansi and Old Woman were now installed in an adobe hut in an area populated mainly by poor Indians on the outskirts of the pueblo. Quint always asked about Kyla. Was she happy? How was their relationship progressing? Had she heard from Miguel?

"For a rake and a roué," Desmond said mildly, "you show an inordinate interest in my wife. She is busy; therefore she is happy. Our relationship is one of mutual trust. She has not heard from her adopted brothers. Does that satisfy you?"

Quint's eyes twinkled, he laughed, and slapped Desmond lightly on the back. "Are you sure you had a Spanish mother?" he asked mockingly. "I believe your English father contrived to produce you alone and unaided. You are all English ice, Des, old friend. Doesn't your wife's beauty resurrect any latent feeling in you? Surely you are still a man under all that godlike goodness. I for one don't believe saints walk the earth among us mortals, so you can stop masquerading for me. Have you slept with her yet?"

Desmond looked away to hide the pain in his eyes but he spoke lightly. "I gave up such antics years ago.

You know that, Quint, so don't mock me. I came to tell you we've found an English carpenter who says he can make wheels for *El Conico*. And Flores has the sulphur and saltpeter, so we'll have powder."

Quint leaned back, his long legs extended in front of him and his hands clasped behind his tousled bronze hair. A grin still puckered the corners of his mouth. "You lead a celibate life because you won't give a woman a chance to love you like a man, not because Master Johnny Inigo can't act like an instrumentalist any more. Your mind can't get an erection—not your body."

"If you are going to quote Rabelais to me—Johnny Indigo, indeed! I shall go home and leave you to resurrect the cannon yourself. Or perhaps for spite I shall quote *Lysistrata* to you. Perhaps that would solve all of the problems. We shall simply ask all the women hereabouts to behave like the Trojan women and withhold all sex until the men promise to stop making wars."

Quint laughed, jumped to his feet, and thumped Desmond again affectionately. "Why don't you stay overnight and let Shansi work her magic on you?"

"So that you can ride to my house and seduce my bride? Oh, no, my dear Quint."

"Remind me to tell you the story of the dog in the manger again sometime, old sport," Quint murmured. "But not now. Here come Flores and the others, and it's time to make war."

The cannon was hauled across the Los Angeles river and up a hill overlooking the pueblo. Behind the gun was Don Ignacio Aguilar, who had served as an artilleryman in the Mexican army. With the muzzle of *El Conico* staring at Gillespie's small garrison, the *Californios* sent a formal request for surrender, punctuating it with a shot from *El Conico*.

Five days later an excited *vaquero* rode into the *rancho* with the news that the Americans in Los Angeles had surrendered. All of Southern California was in revolt, and the Mexican army was marching northward.

Desmond Talmage looked thoughtfully at his wife's

light blond hair and remembered what Quint Delleroc had said about the women of an army's enemies.

"Kyla, we've been lucky so far. We've had to donate a few head of cattle to the Americans and lost most of our peons to the army, but the Americans have not bothered us. If the three factions are going to be fighting near here, I wonder if it wouldn't be prudent to send you and Maria to a safer place."

"But I'm a Mexican citizen," she protested. "If I was safe here when the Americans were in control, why should I fear the Mexican army? My brothers are serving in the cavalry."

"You may be a Mexican citizen, Kyla, but you look like a *norteamericana*. Please. The war can't last forever and I would sleep easier at night knowing you are somewhere safe. Perhaps you would like to visit Europe. Spain, perhaps, to visit some of the friends of my mother's family. Or England, where I have many relatives."

Unobserved, Maria entered the room and, apparently forgetting her revulsion at Desmond's physical appearance, burst out, "Oh, yes! Kyla, say we'll go. Please! I'm afraid to stay here with all the fighting going on."

"We shall have to find out which port it will be safe for you to travel to first," Desmond said as Kyla looked from one to the other uncertainly.

"What about you? Will you come with us?" Kyla asked Desmond.

"No, I shall stay and take care of things until Cervantes returns. When peace is restored, then I'll think about returning to my monastery."

"Then I shall stay too," Kyla said firmly, and ignored Maria's wail of protest. Nor did Kyla allow herself to consider the possibility that they could have sailed from Monterey. After all, if Quint Delleroc was still in Monterey, what good would it do to see him? He had made his feelings abundantly clear. She was a fool to hope that he would ever love her as she loved him. In time, she promised herself, I shall be able to forget him, but I can't hate him no matter how much I try.

The following morning they awoke to the sound of distant artillery fire and Maria ran screaming through the *casa grande* that they would all be killed, because Kyla could not make up her mind to leave while there was still time. A strange stillness had fallen upon the house and, as Kyla went to the kitchens and then from room to room, she realized why. The last of the servants had run off in the night.

Desmond came in from the patio, dragging his withered leg. The half-smile that puckered at the mutilated side of his mouth made the worried look in his eyes more ominously significant.

"The sound of the fighting seems to have brought about the defection of the last of our people," he said, "and I see dust from a group of riders coming our way. Kyla, I want you and Maria to hide somewhere. Don't come out until you are sure the riders have departed, do you understand?"

Kyla nodded, frightened by his concern for their safety. Maria sobbed hysterically, but did not resist as Kyla took her firmly by the arm and dragged her from the house.

"We shall go to one of the peons' huts. Come, we must run as fast as we can," she said. There was one hut, on the furthest boundary of the *hacienda,* which had been empty since their arrival and which superstitious Indians and *mestizos* refused to enter, saying it was a "plague hut." From its decay and uninhabited look, Kyla thought it would probably escape being searched.

# 11

*Ramsey and his men had found killing and robbing* Mexicans almost too easy. The war had given them license to plunder and murder at will. When tales of *Los Diablos Tejanos* reached them, Ramsey's men wanted not only to emulate, but to outdo the dreaded Texas Rangers. And the name *Los Diablos Ramsey* brought pleasure to their conscienceless leader.

The Raiders usually kept a respectable distance between themselves and old Rough and Ready's regulars, but they had heard there was fighting in California and the riches to be gained there were greater than those in the poor Mexican farms along the Rio Grande.

Not knowing the territory, he and his men had become lost in the vast Mojave Desert. They would have perished had they not found an encampment of friendly Indians. Ramsey realized then he would have to plan more carefully. He chose to head for the pueblo of Los Angeles, which, he had heard, was in American hands. When he learned there had been a revolt and one hundred and fifty *Californios* with one ancient cannon had routed four hundred Americans to recapture Los Angeles, Ramsey detoured quickly.

He had learned much about ruling by fear while he was at sea. He found, too, that brute strength and the kind of intelligence and education he alone among the men possessed, were valuable assets in keeping the men obedient.

The towheaded boy from Kansas who had given him the idea of forming his own band of raiders still followed blindly and was good with a gun. When it was necessary for Ramsey to beat a man into submission for questioning an order, "Kansas" would stand by with a six-shooter in each hand and make sure no one went to the aid of the unfortunate victim.

Most of the time, however, the rewards of plunder and rape were all that it took to keep the group following him. But Ramsey had made a bad mistake, getting them lost in the desert. He could not afford to make another one.

His men found an old Mexican sitting beside the trail, his mule dead at his feet and his pathetic belongings scattered in the dust.

"A greaser, Ramsey," Kansas called to him. "Shall I waste a bullet on him, or do you want him tied to your horse for one of Ramsey's famous rides?" The Raiders found that dragging a man through the cactus was almost as entertaining as stringing a naked señorita up by her heels and devising new ways to violate her.

"Find out from him what's up ahead," Ramsey said.

Ramsey was intrigued to learn that they were approaching de Rivero *rancho*. He remembered that Talmage, the crippled Englishman who had sprung him from the *calabozo,* now owned the de Rivero *rancho*: a good place to stop for supplies and water. Delleroc was dead and, therefore, there was no way for Talmage to know Ramsey had lied about their relationship. Nor was there anyone to connect Ramsey to the ambush shooting on the dark street in Monterey.

"Slit that Mex's throat quietly," Ramsey said. "Then the rest of you wait here while Kansas and I ride ahead to pay our respects to my old friend Lord Talmage."

Desmond came looking for Kyla and Maria at dusk, softly calling their names as he limped among the silent and deserted huts. Fearfully, they emerged from their hiding place. "Have they gone?" Kyla whispered.

"No, but the two who came to the house are asleep. It was Ramsey and his lieutenant."

"Ramsey! But—"

"Kyla, I asked him point-blank if it was he who shot Quint, and he denies he was even in Monterey at the time. Quint himself does not suspect Ramsey. There is only the accusation of the girl Shansi."

"Yes, but—" Kyla stopped. She was hungry, and tired of being confined with Maria, who had spent the day complaining and blaming Kyla for her discomfort.

"Ramsey's men are camped nearby, and he and the boy Kansas are extremely polite and most grateful for my hospitality. There is something else. He tells me that you and Miguel saved his life and that he will always be indebted to the Marques family, that he is a close friend of Miguel. Is this not true?"

Kyla nodded and relayed briefly what had happened, without telling Desmond that she and Miguel had been running away that day.

"Then I'm sure we have nothing to fear. Come, let's go back to the house so you can have some food," Desmond said.

Since there were no servants, the next morning Kyla and Maria had to prepare breakfast. They had just finished setting the table and had prepared the *champurrado,* a thick chocolate enriched by beaten eggs, when Ramsey and another light-haired man came into the dining room.

"Morning, ma'am," Ramsey said, and although he spoke to Kyla, his eyes went immediately to Maria, who was putting the remains of yesterday's ground-corn porridge into a pot to be heated.

"Good morning, Señor Ramsey. I'm happy to see you again," Kyla said. "I trust your injuries healed without complications?"

"Never did get a chance to thank you personally for saving me from the Padrone's men that day on the beach."

"We were only too happy to help. Maria, this is Señor Garett Ramsey. May I present my sister, Maria Marques?"

"Most happy to meet you, ma'am. Kansas, go and tell the men my friend Lord Talmage has given permission for them to slaughter as many steer and replace as many horses as necessary. I'll be along after a while."

The light-haired lieutenant glanced longingly at the two women and at the elegantly set table, but obeyed instantly.

"It is my deep regret that I now find myself on the opposite side from my good friend Miguel," Ramsey said. "But you little ladies need have no fear. Garett Ramsey doesn't forget a kindness, nor a stab in the back, for that matter."

Ramsey's eyes never left Maria, and her eyes flashed invitingly in return. She had not had a man admire her so openly since she left her father's *hacienda*. She had not worn her customary black mourning dress but had come to breakfast wearing a colored skirt topped by a low-cut blouse, and the thin *rebozo* she wore seemed to slip frequently to reveal a rounded shoulder and plump breasts straining against the taut cloth. The unspoken messages passing between the two were quickly discontinued when Desmond arrived, looking tired after a sleepless night.

Ramsey presented a very different appearance from the one on the beach that October morning, Kyla thought, as she brought the porridge to the table. She apologized for the meager breakfast and explained that neither she nor Maria had ever learned to cook. Ramsey disagreed politely as he tasted the rich *champurrado*. Although his clothing was obviously trail-worn, he wore an impressive uniform of his own design, patterned after the uniform of Old Fuss and Feathers himself, General Winfield Scott. And he no longer wore the untidy beard which Kyla remembered. Ramsey was a somewhat florid man, and his enormous size made him appear clumsy, but his manners were good for a *norteamericano*. His pale gray eyes were disconcerting, as they sometimes appeared to totally lack color and give the impression of cold-blooded malevolence, but Kyla told herself this was merely a trick of the light, for he was acting anything but cold-blooded toward Maria. And he did sound genuinely grateful to herself and Miguel. Still, she felt a twinge of dismay when Maria began to tell Ramsey they hoped to visit Europe until the fighting ended and would certainly have to leave the rancho now, since all of their servants and *vaqueros* had abandoned them.

"Why, ma'am, two women and a—one man alone—certainly can't travel in times like these," Ramsey said. "In return for your hospitality, I insist that my men accompany you to whichever port you intend to sail from."

"But surely you are under military orders?" Desmond asked, with an uneasy edge to his voice.

Ramsey grinned slyly. "Oh, I make my own orders. I can take a few days to escort you. When would you like to leave?"

"I'm afraid I can't leave," Desmond said. "Someone must stay to protect the property. I'm sure our *vaqueros* will return when things quiet down. Perhaps some will return today." He turned to look at Kyla, exposing the scarred side of his face to the cruel early morning light.

Kyla forced herself to look at her husband without blinking. She felt more pity than revulsion, but was annoyed with herself for reacting to his appearance. Sometimes she was able to disregard it. "We appreciate your offer, Señor Ramsey," she said, "but we can't leave now."

"Then I shall go alone," Maria declared, her eyes flashing fire. "I need the protection of a man. Who will protect me if I stay here? A man with only one arm?"

"Maria!" Kyla gasped, horrified beyond words at Maria's insensitivity.

"Kyla," Desmond said quickly, "I must insist that you go also. Mr. Ramsey is a gentleman, and he himself says he owes you a debt of honor."

Kyla had grown to love her land. She wanted to stay and face whatever ordeal the war brought. She did not think of herself as being brave, but she knew she would find the strength to cope. "Please, Desmond. I can't leave," she said.

"You must, my dear. Maria can't go alone. She is unmarried. She must have a *duenna.*"

They were all startled when the door opened and Nana appeared, breathing heavily, her *rebozo* still covering her hair.

"Nana, where were you?" Kyla cried.

"Trying to bring back some of our people, but they are all afraid of the *norteamericanos,*" Nana replied, watching Ramsey warily. "Soldiers are coming this way. A large number of soldiers."

"Americans?" Ramsey asked.

"Mexican regulars," Nana said, a gleam in her old eyes. "More than five times the men you have camped in the *hacienda,* señor. They are only an hour away."

Ramsey was on his feet instantly. "Discretion, as they say, is the better part of valor. If you ladies want to be escorted to the Coast, you've got ten minutes to make up your minds and pack your belongings."

Desmond looked at his wife's pale blond hair. "You must go, Kyla. Nana, go and pack for the ladies and yourself."

"No," Kyla said. "I will go, but Nana will stay here and take care of you, Desmond."

"I'll give you the name of my bank in England. Letters of introduction—" Desmond was already dragging himself toward his study but paused to give Ramsey a long hard look. "I am entrusting you with what is more precious to me than my own life. I believe that you owe both the Marques family and myself a debt and will guard my wife and her sister with your life."

Kyla went with her husband while Nana and Maria ran to pack and Ramsey went to muster his men. As Desmond feverishly wrote instructions for their journey, Kyla again voiced her doubts. "I can't stop thinking that he once said he hated Quint."

The brilliant blue eyes looked at her carefully. "Kyla, my dear, you know Quint is my dearest friend. But I have no illusions about him. To Quint, truth is relative, and he sees varying degrees of it, according to circumstances. I am not sure what he might have told you, for Quint revels in the role of villain. Sometimes he strives to earn hatred as other men try to deserve love. He is too complex a paradox for me to explain to you. You would have to know him as I do to understand. What we do know is that you and Miguel saved the life of Ramsey, and I had him released from a Mexican jail. He is obviously educated and seems to come from a good family. I believe you will be safe in his care."

Maria came into the room, dressed in a pretty, dark red traveling dress and matching *rebozo*. "Come, we must hurry."

Kyla glanced down at her own black mourning dress, and a brief vision flashed into her mind: the Padrone cursing the fates which had put a *gringa* child into his care.

She said goodbye to Desmond with a heavy heart, surprised at how much she hated to leave him. If it had not been for Maria, she would have defied convention and openly refused to obey her husband's order to leave. But she could not humiliate Desmond by doing so in front of witnesses. She had, after all, promised to love, honor and obey. Sometimes, she thought, as she tried to overcome her misgivings about running away, the role society forced on wives was a difficult one.

# 12

Shansi had not questioned Delleroc, when he left the *rancho* in the middle of the night without saying goodbye to his old friend Lord Talmage. Nor was she surprised when he announced they were leaving the pueblo of Los Angeles after the successful recapturing of the town. Shansi was accustomed to such sudden departures. Delleroc had simply decided it was time to go, as he had so many times before. Nor did she ask him why they journeyed southward, after she had distinctly heard him tell the pale-haired woman they were returning to Monterey when they left Southern California. She and Old Woman obediently climbed into their saddles and followed. South. Toward Mexico.

Long ago in China, Shansi's father had been a powerful *yamen*, symbol of state power. He had been the first to be killed, his house sacked and burned, when, in the year of the withered harvest, the peasants revolted. Her mother and brothers had also been trapped in the house, but Shansi and her nurse had been walking near the great river that day.

Old Woman had quickly divested the little girl of her rich clothes and removed the binding from Shansi's feet, which had not yet taken on the shape and configuration of the high-born. She stole peasant's clothing when women laundering the garments on the river bank were not looking. The two of them remained in hiding until at last, driven by hunger, they returned to the *yamen*'s house.

Afterward, Shansi was never able to recall exactly what she saw in the charred remains of her home that blotted from her mind forever all memories of what had gone before. Had Old Woman been able to speak before they went sifting through those terrible ashes?

Sometimes, Shansi awoke late at night to the echo of a blood-chilling scream. She did not know if it had come from her lips or whether it was part of the nightmare.

In the dream, she was slowly pushing aside the ashes and blackened wood, knowing she would soon find the hand. Yet she was unable to stop. The hand was not burned, nor was the arm she so carefully dusted clean, for the body had been carelessly thrown into the burned house after the fire died and had been buried when the roof collapsed. When she reached the shoulder, she would awaken to the sound of the scream. She must awaken, for if she were to look upon the horror beyond the arm and shoulder, she would go insane.

Old Woman went to the leader of Ke-Lao-Hui—the "Elder Brother" society, and told him the child was hers, born out of wedlock while she served in the house of the *yamen*.

The secret society acted as a mutual-aid group and welcomed women to their ranks, knowing a woman's lot was particularly hard among the peasants in the Chinese countryside. Besides, to assert equality of the sexes was in sharp contrast to Confucian principles and custom. In the Ke-Lao-Hui, women were allowed to rise to high rank and were not excluded from the esoteric cults, initiation rites, trial by ordeal, or knowledge of the mediums and charms.

During a peasant uprising, the secret societies, supported by the masses, freely took the lives and goods of the rich and powerful, but in quiet times it was necessary to survive at the expense of the peasants. This shifting between rebellion and banditry and the resulting loss and recruitment of members made Shansi and Old Woman part of a large cross-section of the population, ranging from well-born dissidents—black sheep of powerful families—to itinerant musicians and beggars.

Awakening from her nightmare one night, Shansi had been comforted by a man with eyes strangely at peace; he had showed her how the "magic cloud" could quiet her slumber. She and Old Woman never retired after that without first immersing themselves in the soothing vapors.

As she approached womanhood, the Western powers were beginning to penetrate China. The age-old contradictions between peasants and feudal holders of power were ready to erupt, and the country hovered on the brink of the first Opium War. Into this social and political crisis came a startling Westerner, a red-haired vagabond with peculiar eyes—even for a Westerner—who wanted to probe the mysteries of the Ke-Lao-Hui society.

"I seek the *vox populi,*" he said, the first words in halting Chinese. The last, he said, were Latin and meant "the voice of the people." He would work for them, even kill and plunder for them, if he were allowed to learn all of their secrets. No one thought he would endure the trial by ordeal, but he did.

At the time Shansi was the woman of the new leader of the society, Li Tzu-chung, whom she had found lying upon her one night when she drifted to the edge of wakefulness. Lost in the magic cloud, she had felt nothing at first in the man's embrace, but he seemed well pleased after plunging up and down like a horseless rider for a few minutes. Shansi returned to her dreamless sleep.

As the nights passed, she began to look forward to the coupling of her body with Li Tzu-chung, and she forgot there had ever been a time that making love was not a part of the pre-sleep ritual. First the magic cloud, to soothe the mind, then the hands that ran slowly over breasts and thighs, the seeking lips and tongue, the ultimate caresses—the shared intimacies that became more exotically refined as time went by.

The red-haired Westerner was interested in her. It appeared that, in the West, women did not enjoy as free a way of life as hers, and he was particularly intrigued by the difference in Shansi's status within the Ke-Lao-

Hui and that of the women of the wealthy class, with their bound feet and arranged marriages or enforced concubinage. It was Delleroc who gave her the name of Shansi.

"Westerners will find it easier on their less-nimble tongues," he said. "My own last name is a corruption of my mother's name."

"I know no other Westerner but you, Mr. Delleroc," she had replied.

"Perhaps one day you will travel in the West," he suggested.

"Perhaps," she said, not really believing she would ever travel beyond the province in which she lived. But then the First Opium War had erupted.

Li Tzu-chung was killed almost immediately, and Shansi found herself at the mercy of his henchmen, who fought over her like a pack of wolves. All the professed emancipation of women in the society did not save her from being the object of sexual pursuit.

When Delleroc returned from a skirmish several days later, he found a bruised and terrified Shansi, shivering and sweating, her body wracked with demon pains. She was begging Old Woman to kill her, but Old Woman was enduring her own private hell.

Delleroc cared for them, hiding them and bringing food, holding Shansi in his arms when her limbs writhed like serpents and she shrieked her agony and need for her magic cloud.

In time her body recovered, but her nightmare had returned. She dutifully followed the Westerner when he told her he was returning to his own people.

Shansi did not like England. The weather was cold and damp and the women stared at her when she went out to the shops to buy food. Delleroc did not like the fashions worn by Englishwomen and insisted she wear the clothes which they had bought in China and India on their way back to the chilly little island of England.

Delleroc told her, "Hold your head high, like a princess, and always remember, they are merely in awe of your beauty. Look at them scornfully and never, ever, lower your eyes and cower before a white woman or a white man. Do you understand? If you do, I shall beat you."

He never did beat her, but then, she never gave him cause.

At length Delleroc went to visit a holy man who lived in a monastery in the Welsh mountains, and when Delleroc returned he told her he was going to the New World—America. Did she and Old Woman wish to return to China or accompany him?

She and Old Woman were passengers, but Delleroc worked his passage, first to Boston and then on an American clipper around the Horn. The money given by Lord Talmage for Delleroc's fare had been used for theirs.

They settled in Monterey and Delleroc rented the emporium and began trading. "Next year," he told her, "I shall have to travel south and see to Lord Talmage's business, and you cannot accompany me. But by then I'll have enough money for you to be comfortable while I'm gone."

"You won't go back to England?" Shansi asked fearfully, remembering the incessant rain.

He laughed. "I can never go back to England—not after I send a confession to the army that it was I and not Lord Talmage who was the culprit in the scandals in India. I expect if they ever get their hands on me, I shall be shot for impersonating an officer."

After Delleroc left for Baja California, Old Woman learned about the Chinese seaman who had come to Monterey aboard a whaling ship and found a job ashore as a cook. The man was able to obtain their magic cloud from other seamen who came to the port. Soon the money Delleroc had left for their care during his absence was used. He had sold the emporium before he left, and now Shansi moved out of Delleroc's house and in with the Chinese cook. She was living there, lost in a constant magic cloud, while Ramsey searched Monterey for Delleroc and his China girl.

Delleroc returned and found them. He was angry, but he did not beat her. This time he did not make her suffer the agonies she had suffered before. She and Old Woman were allowed to have their magic cloud, but in ever-decreasing quantities. He believed her when she told him she no longer needed it. More Chinese were arriving in California every day and while most deplored the use of the magic cloud, there were always those who understood and provided.

Shansi had taken care to bring enough of the magic powder for an extended journey, but nevertheless she grew apprehensive as they rode into unfamiliar territory after leaving the pueblo of Los Angeles. They rode hard and it was several days before he announced, "We are going to Monterrey."

"Then we are traveling in the wrong direction," Shansi said.

He laughed. "This Monterrey has two *R's* and is far to the South, in Mexico, not California. The Americans are invading Mexico, and I've studied all of the possible areas where invaders might be stopped. I believe Monterrey might be impregnable. It is rimmed by mountains, and the only large open area is to the east, guarded by three forts. There is a narrow road to the west, which passes through a gorge where heavy artillery could be employed."

"You will go and fight now for the Mexicans?"

"No, Shansi. I fight because there is a splendid order and purpose to the clashing of two armies. I fight for myself, but it's more of a challenge to be on the side of the underdog. You and Old Woman will wait for me at a mission still occupied by *padres,* not far from San Diego."

"A seaport? Ships stop there?"

"Yes. It's in American hands. You'll be safe there until I return."

She understood his craving for excitement. It was similar to the one she felt for her magic cloud.

Quint Delleroc was not traveling deep into Mexico merely to be part of a fight. As always, it was partly the lure of studying first-hand a group of men that interested him.

Just before the war started, an Irish sergeant in the U.S. Third Infantry, John Riley, had been hounded by an officer, to the point of desertion. Several of his countrymen went with him and all were eagerly accepted by the Mexican army. The word was sent back that conditions for foreigners in the Mexican army were excellent, far better than with the "Protestant Yankees." The pay was higher, discipline less harsh and, best of all, generous land grants were promised for their services. They were also assured they could practice their religion without fear of persecution.

When the war started, the *San Patricios* swore a blood oath to fight to the death, well aware that capture meant execution. Since the Mexicans lacked artillerymen, they became crack cannoneers and Quint Delleroc had no difficulty being accepted into their ranks. The prospect of a fight to the finish was interesting, and his ever-curious mind could not rest until he had learned all there was to know about the motives of the *San Patricios*.

"I won my stripes the hard way," John Riley told him bitterly, "but there was this young officer who hounded me. Mocked me and all Irishmen, reviled the Mother Church. I couldn't take it any more. Especially when it looked like we'd soon be fighting true believers. But you, Delleroc, are you sure you want to join up with the *San Patricios?* We're all deserters and we'll either get shot in battle, or shot by the Yankees if they capture us. Either way—"

"The odds are pretty hopeless," Quint agreed, "but there's just a chance we can hold Monterrey."

He had fought on many sides by the time he joined the *San Patricios* in Mexico, but had always emerged from the conflicts unsatisfied, still without a country or any reason to be anchored to one place. Perhaps it would have been easier if he knew for what he searched.

The *San Patricios* had accepted him readily at first sight, because of his bright red hair and claim to an Irish father. But some of them were growing uneasy about his constant questions and the fact that his speech reflected a strong English influence. Was he a spy?

John Riley himself came up with the answer to their

dilemma. "We have a special mission for you, Delleroc," he said. "You are to pass yourself off as a European."

Quint blinked at this piece of Irish superfluity, but Riley continued unabashed. "The Yankees are camped at Bosque de San Domingo, and we want you to go down there and see what they're planning, which way the main thrust of their attack will come."

Quint looked at him steadily. "They'll make a two-pronged attack," he said, "from the northeast and along the Saltillo Road to the northwest."

"Well, now, that's possible. But to tell you the truth, we're all cannoneers and I don't know how we can use you if you won't go and spy for us," Riley said. "I'd like to know for certain where to deploy the guns."

"Very well," Quint said. "I'll try to get back before they storm the city, but I hope you realize it's going to be very soon."

There was no road from Matamoros to Camargo, which was to be the jumping-off place for Monterrey. The American force had to travel the winding river in steamboats, unreliably fueled by green mesquite. And when they reached their destination they found that they had journeyed into hell.

Camargo, too far from the Gulf to be reached by sea breezes, was held in the relentless grip of desert heat. The air was thick with flies and fleas and blowing sand choked their lungs. The San Juan river, a tributary of the Rio Grande, was their only source of drinking water and also served as their sewer. Cholera and dysentery struck swiftly, and men lay dying in the blistering heat. Those still on their feet swore the mockingbirds had learned to trill the death march.

They ate beans, pickled pork and weevil-infested biscuits, and they moved listlessly. Their drinking water was two-thirds yellow mud and the rest sand. As many as eight men were placed in the suffocating closeness of one nine-by-nine-foot tent.

In desperation, General Taylor sent word back to

Washington, begging for medical officers to care for his men.

No one was exactly sure when the red-haired civilian, who spoke English in a combined British and indefinably European accent, appeared. No one questioned his medical training either, for he moved quickly in an attempt to stop the rampant disintegration of the bowels of the gray-faced troops. Forcibly he stopped thirsty men from drinking the brackish water.

"You have to boil their drinking water," he told the sergeant who came upon him dragging a limp youth to the shelter of one of the tents. "And make them travel further from the river for their ablutions."

He lifted the sodden bandage from a man's putrefying leg and said briskly, "Gangrene. It's got to come off today or he'll die."

The open-mouth sergeant was not surprised when the fiery-haired stranger asked for a knife and saw as he learned there were no doctors available.

A few days later the Texas Rangers, despite Taylor's orders, began their attack. Letting out their ear-splitting yell and, riding singly, the Rangers swept around the fort between them and the city of Monterrey.

"They're like boys at play," one regular said, shaking his head in disbelief.

There was occasional fire from the Mexicans, but the riders were too swift. The Rangers vied with one another in attempts to see who could come closest to the walls of the fort. Each flirted more perilously than the next with death.

General Taylor could do little but order them back to camp. The entire army, 6,230 strong, now prepared for the battle precipitated by the Rangers. No one noticed that the red-haired man, with the fierce hawklike features and gentle healing hands, had disappeared.

The main American column struck the northeastern section of the city and General Worth's division, led by the Texans, flanked Monterrey and approached along the Saltillo Road. Federation Hill and Fort Salado fell, then

Independence Hill and the Bishop's Palace—which the Texas Rangers, shrieking like banshees, captured almost single-handedly.

On the third day of the battle, thunder rolled through the canyons and lightning flashed across the top of the buildings. A heavy rain began to fall. The Rangers and light infantry were in the city proper now and fighting house to house, tunneling through adobe walls with picks, dashing through narrow rain-drenched streets filled with debris and corpses. They were ordered to withdraw, so that General Taylor's artillery could shell the city before the main attack. The Texans scornfully sent back word that they had taken the lower part of the city by themselves and they would not budge. Miraculously, none of them were hurt in the ensuing bombardment.

The Mexicans were not giving an inch. Outworks, forts, every street and house had to be forced at the point of a bayonet.

Taylor succeeded in bringing his big guns to bear against the cathedral, and the Mexican General Ampudia, knowing there was enough gunpowder stored there to blow up the entire city, sent out a white flag.

At first Taylor refused to consider anything but unconditional surrender, but then he looked around at his men: drenched with rain, many of them barely able to stay on their feet, much less fight. And the Mexicans were still well entrenched and would have to be prised out one by one. He was running short of supplies. Five hundred dead would have to be buried soon, or he risked a cholera epidemic. There were the wounded to be cared for.

He granted an eight-week armistice, providing the Mexicans withdrew from the whole Rinconada Valley, which would leave the road to Saltillo open. They could keep their muskets, but all cannon and munitions, as well as the city itself, would become the property of the invaders.

They ran up the Stars and Stripes and the band played "Yankee Doodle" to the weak cheers of the men. Angry shouts and raised fists greeted the appearance of the *San Patricios*, marching out of the city with their Mexican compatriates, and many Americans screamed for the blood of the deserters, but they were allowed to pass. Quint Delleroc was not one of them.

# 13

The mood among Ramsey's Raiders had shifted from loyalty, based on fear of Garett Ramsey's physical strength and mental cunning, to one of suspicion and distrust. It was one thing to raid the helpless villages and farms along the Rio Grande, especially after the Regulars had gone ahead clearing out any remnants of the Mexican army, and quite another to deliberately ride into territory where they not only had the Mexican army to contend with, but also armed men who were prepared to fight fiercely for their homes. The announcement that they were to escort two señoritas to the coast came as the spark to ignite open rebellion.

Kansas approached Ramsey warily to try to convey the risks. "They want to ride south, Garett," he said. "They've heard these *Californios* fight like madmen. There may not be many of 'em, but there's not many of us either. And there's a rumor that five hundred Mexican regulars are headed our way. If we stumble into them between here and the coast, hell, killing greasers is one thing, but we can't risk coming up against artillery and trained dragoons."

Ramsey had spent the day riding at the side of the lovely Maria, through pleasant country with no sign of the army which the *mestizo* woman Nana had warned about. They made camp in an abandoned farmhouse

135

when the sun set, a wooden house, probably built by American settlers who did not appreciate the cool durability of adobe. He was looking forward to an evening of light-hearted conversation with the women and perhaps—who knew where Maria's obvious admiration might lead them?

The role of knight rescuing damsels in distress was new and exhilarating. Ramsey had concealed a secret from his men that was becoming increasingly burdensome. He was unable to satisfy himself with a woman taken by force. The frozen terror of the señoritas whom his men had captured quenched his amorous thoughts faster than a dose of saltpeter and, although he always ordered his men to leave him alone with one of the women captives, only he and the woman knew that he did not rape her.

Whenever possible, he slipped away to one of the brothels that marked the path of the advancing army, but he lived in constant dread of his men finding out that he paid for what they took so freely.

"Watch your tongue," he snapped at Kansas, glancing over his shoulder to the other room of the farm house where the women were washing away the grime of the day's ride. "Miss Maria is a Mexican. And I told you—I owe them this. Their brother saved my life and the lady's husband got me out of the calaboose."

Kansas shifted his feet uncomfortably. Ramsey was a man given to spiteful vengeance toward those who questioned his orders. "Well, sure, Garett. I understand. But the men are still jumpy since we got lost in the desert— and there's been no loot or women since we rode into California. They're getting restless."

"Who is the ringleader?" Ramsey asked, his eyes cold as flint. "Has he forgotten what I did to the last man who questioned my orders?"

Kansas looked away. "No ringleader, I reckon. Just a muttering among them. I just thought you should know."

"Go and tell them this is a natural stronghold. The hills are behind us and there's only a narrow approach to the mesa the house is built on. Tell them to relax for tonight and tomorrow we'll deliver the ladies and head south again."

"I'll post a couple of lookouts," Kansas said. There was no use arguing, he knew. Ramsey could never admit he had made a mistake, and riding into California was a mistake. They had been plagued by bad luck since leaving Matamoros. First the harshness of the unknown desert terrain and then Ramsey going soft when they came upon the unguarded *rancho*. They'd taken all the meat and horses they needed, but Ramsey had not allowed them to loot the *casa grande*, which was surely full of treasures. Ramsey was headed for a fall, and Kansas had no desire to go down with him.

Maria brushed her wavy dark hair until it gleamed and there was a sparkle in her dark eyes as she came to stand beside the fire Ramsey had built. She smiled up at him, feeling tiny and fragile, close to this huge man who exuded brute strength. Yet Ramsey was almost boyish in his open admiration and fumbling compliments.

The presence of his band of ruffians outside also produced an excitement Maria relished. Those men had looked at her boldly, in a way no *caballero* would have dared regard the Padrone's daughter. In all of her sheltered life, she had never experienced such raw, masculine lust. And Maria enjoyed it, protected as she was by this great bear of a man who obviously inspired terror in his followers.

There was no chaperone other than Kyla, and Maria could always handle her adopted sister, who had ice water for blood. Since Kyla had rarely attempted to defend herself against Maria's rages, Maria had long ago decided that *gringa* women were incapable of any kind of violent emotion. This did not appear to be true of *gringo* men, however. When Garett Ramsey looked at her, his pale eyes were bright as polished crystal. And she could feel the electricity pass from his body to hers as he handed her a flask.

"Sorry. No glasses. And it isn't wine, it's whiskey," he said. "There'll be some stew soon, and I've cleared off the table so we can eat in here. The seating accommodations are—"

Maria giggled as he gestured to the only other piece of furniture in the room, a sagging bedspring hung precariously from a tarnished brass bed devoid of mattress. Ramsey had placed a couple of saddle blankets over the spring and Maria sat down, sipping the whiskey daintily and looking up at him from beneath fluttering eyelashes.

"You should not drink undiluted whiskey, Maria," Kyla said from the doorway. "You are not used to it."

Maria was already coughing and gasping as the fiery liquid burned her throat and she was not able to reply. Ramsey thumped her awkwardly on her back, sitting beside her on the bed. Kyla approached them uneasily, wishing, for the hundredth time that day, they had not left the *rancho*.

"Oh, Kyla, you are such a killjoy," Maria said, her face flushed. "Just because you are afraid to try anything new, you certainly don't have the right to tell me what to do or not to do." She turned to Ramsey and added, "She lived her entire life on my father's charity, and thinks now she is married she can give herself all sorts of airs and graces."

Ramsey grinned at the display of female cattiness, comfortable with a woman who wanted nothing more from life than a man to call husband. Pity she was a Mexicanner. She was beautiful enough for any man to be proud to call wife, and a virgin, he was sure of it. Those high-born señoritas were well guarded against amorous advances. "I should have offered you water to go with it, I'm sorry," he said. The thought of a sheltered virgin offering herself to him willingly was making him grow inside his britches, and he wondered if she would give herself to him with Kyla Talmage sleeping in the other room.

They were halfway through their dinner of barely cooked stew when the lookout came riding furiously up to the house, his face pale in the moonlight.

"Mexican regulars, and they've got a cannon, cavalry and infantry."

A moment later Kansas appeared at the door, rifle in hand.

"Send six men to guard the gorge leading up here," Ramsey ordered. "Tell them to shoot anything that moves. They're not likely to attack until morning, but they may try to send scouts in."

Maria was on her feet, her eyes wide. "Attack, but what about the señora and me? If the army is going to attack, we must be conducted safely from here immediately."

Ramsey looked speculatively from one woman to the other. "Just settle down, Miss Maria. No one is going to hurt you, I've given you my word, haven't I? But there's no way to get out of here except through that gorge—the horses couldn't climb those hills behind us. We're safe here. The Mexican army isn't going to waste time trying to blast us out. We'll hole up for a couple of days until they leave."

Maria relaxed visibly and did not argue when Ramsey suggested she and Kyla share the bed and try to get some sleep while he went outside to talk with his men.

Outside the men had doused their campfires and waited in an angry group for their leader. Once again he had led them into danger. Ramsey carried a shotgun and lost no time in relaying his plan.

"Kansas, you ride down and meet them. With a white flag." As there was a growl of disbelief, he added quickly, "Give them a message. Tell them we're holding two highborn Mexican women as hostages. One is the daughter of a padrone and and the other the wife of a Californio don. Get something from the women's saddlebags to help convince them. Tell them we want safe passage out of here at dawn, or they'll find the women's bodies on their way in here."

Kansas nodded amd made his way to the tethered horses, unfastening the leather pouches that contained the women's belongings. In their haste to leave the *rancho*, Desmond had urged they take only what was necessary for the journey and buy clothes upon their arrival in Europe. Kansas quickly withdrew a black lace mantilla and tortoiseshell comb and then, fumbling in Kyla's bag, he produced a rolled-up piece of cloth.

"Well, looky here," he said softly, unrolling the flag to display the eagle and the serpent. In the corner of the faded material a name had recently been embroidered. Miguel.

Miguel stood stiffly at attention, his eyes fixed on the articles dangling from the colonel's hand. "It is the flag I sent to Kyla, my adopted sister. There is no doubt of it, she has even embroidered my name in the corner. And the mantilla and comb belong to Maria, my natural sister. Sir, I beg of you, agree to their terms. When the women are safe, we can pursue Ramsey." Kansas had thoughtlessly identified his leader and the group when he stated his terms, and Miguel knew too well the kind of men he was dealing with.

"For the moment, Captain, you will return to your men. Those bloodthirsty *leperos* of yours make me nervous. I am never sure whether or not they will turn and bite the hand that feeds them as readily as that of the enemy. I understand your brother has taken the place of the wounded Apolo Ramírez?"

"Yes, sir. He is out with the party scouting the Raiders' stronghold. It appears there is only one way in, through a gorge so narrow it will be necessary to approach in single file."

"Have your men dismount and make camp. I'll let you know what I decide."

Miguel paced the perimeter of the camp restlessly, his eyes fixed on the small knot of officers who conferred thoughtfully for the next hour. The towheaded American, who had brought the message from Ramsey, waited nervously, two soldiers guarding him. Miguel wanted to fasten his hands about the scrawny throat with its bobbing Adam's apple and choke from the man the assurance that the women had not been molested.

Cervantes returned and spent several minutes in agitated discussion with the commanding officer and then strode toward Miguel. Anger was written in every line of his face, every movement of his body. "They cannot get out and we cannot get in," he said grimly. "But with enough men there may be a chance, if we wait until the moon goes behind a cloud. Some might get through. I have volunteered to lead the assault."

"No!" Miguel said, "we must not rush them—we must agree to their terms. We cannot risk them harming Maria and Kyla."

The moonlight illuminated Cervantes' profile, and fear caught Miguel's breath as he saw the expression on his brother's face.

"They are better dead than dishonored," Cervantes said. "We cannot give in to them. Those men are Ramsey's Raiders. You've seen their handiwork all along the Rio Grande. *Dios*! We thought *Los Diablos Tejanos* were evil, bloodthirsty fiends, but even they do not torture and rape as sadistically as Ramsey's men. No. The sooner we attack, the less time they will have to torture Maria."

His words were echoed a moment later by the colonel, who came to tell them that there was no guarantee the Raiders would release the women even if they were guaranteed safe passage. Such men could not be trusted, their word was meaningless. Their representative would be sent back with the message that if they did not harm the women they would be taken prisoners of war and treated accordingly. They would be given until dawn to surrender.

"Dawn!" Cervantes repeated angrily. "You would give them all night to mistreat our sister?"

"Calm down," the colonel said. "As soon as the American has returned with our terms we will light campfires and give the appearance of settling down for the night. Your *leperos* will then be given the opportunity to try to storm the stronghold. We believe when the moon disappears behind a cloud you might have a chance, especially as we shall be diverting their attention with our campfires. I have chosen your *leperos* not only because your sisters are captive, but because your men are felons with more stealth and cunning, to say nothing of ability with a knife. My soldiers have been trained only to march and point a musket in the general direction of the enemy."

As Miguel and Cervantes saluted and withdrew, the colonel added quietly, "If they do not succeed, we will withdraw, make the Raiders believe we have moved on, then return and try to catch them by surprise."

Miguel was telling Cervantes, "I'll take three men and approach on the mesa side. We'll remove anything from our uniforms that might catch the light, and we'll smear our faces with dirt."

Ramsey watched the flickering campfires in the arroyo. Silhouetted figures moved about leisurely, preparing for an evening meal. "Keep your mouth shut about the Mex not accepting our terms," he told Kansas. "Tell the men we'll get safe passage out of here in the morning."

"But in the morning they'll pound us with cannons," Kansas said fearfully.

"I've got a plan. Don't worry. Now go and calm down the men, and leave at least a dozen lookouts on either side of that wash."

Ramsey's plan was simple. He would save himself. The Mexicans would show them no mercy, and one man was easier to hide than many. Ramsey glanced regretfully toward the farmhouse and thought of Maria's dark and inviting eyes, but he sauntered as casually as possible toward the well. As he brought the dipper of cool water to his lips, he reflected that the months he had spent at sea would at last prove useful. He had climbed the rigging of a ship, clinging to a swaying yardarm using his legs and feet as his hands reefed or let out sail. The hill beyond the farmhouse was almost as sheer. He also remembered what the desert Indians had taught him when they became lost in the Mojave: there is always a foothold—an animal trail. Walk the ridges, do not try to climb straight up. Once over that hill, he could hide out in the desert beyond until the Mexicans moved on.

The moon slipped behind a cloud.

# 14

*Maria clung to Kyla in terror as the sound of rifle fire*
cracked through the night. They heard the shouts of the
men outside, more shots, then silence. Minutes passed,
then the sound of voices, coming closer.

Kyla looked about the empty room. Their unfinished
dinner was still on the table. Ramsey had not returned,
and neither had anyone else, since the Mexican troops
had arrived and camped in the valley beyond the narrow
gorge. There were no weapons of any kind in the room
except for the blunt dinner knife lying on the table. Kyla
snatched up the knife and buried it in her skirts as the
door was kicked open. She did not have time to regret
leaving the pistol Cervantes had given her outside in her
saddlebags.

Three of Ramsey's men burst into the room and more
were milling about outside.

"He ain't here," one of them growled. "Less'n he's
under the bed. I told you, he's vamoosed. Where the hell
is Kansas? Get him in here."

They ripped the blankets from the bed, cautiously
kicked open the door to the adjoining room, poking into
the dark corners as though expecting to find the large-
framed Ramsey cowering in the shadows. It was several
minutes before they turned their attention to the women.

"Where's Ramsey?" a black-bearded man shouted into

Kyla's face as she and Maria were pushed apart. Maria screamed hysterically and tried to claw the man who held her, and he began to smile as her body squirmed softly against his sweat-stained shirt.

A white-faced and disarmed Kansas was pushed into the room.

"We don't know where Ramsey is," Kyla whispered, fighting to control her trembling, her face ashen.

"Hold on there now," Kansas said, his voice a croak, "he's here someplace. Give him a minute, he's probably out back. No need to panic. We got all of the greasers that tried to sneak up on us. I'm sure of it."

"You lied to us," the black-bearded man yelled. "Told us the Mex colonel had given us safe passage out. Was you going to sneak off too?" The man's bowie knife was in his hand and the point close to Kansas' throat.

"No! I swear. Ramsey said he had a plan. That's why I lied."

The word ended in a gurgle of blood as the knife sliced into his throat, and at the same instant there was a shout from outside. One of the Raiders casually jumped over Kansas' body to bring the news. "They're leaving. Reckon that patrol was just to test our strength."

"What are you talking about?" Blackbeard demanded.

"They're dousing their fires and breaking camp. I was on lookout and right after we killed their patrol I saw a rider come in on a lathered horse. They must be needed elsewhere."

Kyla held her breath as several of the men rushed outside, uncomfortably aware of her captor's grip, the stale tobacco smell of him. What would happen if the Mexican troops had indeed left? And there was no Ramsey to keep the men in check.

The black-bearded man was jubilant when he returned a few minutes later. "They're leaving all right. The cannon's rolling away and the horsemen have already left. The infantrymen are forming up ranks." The excitement that had taken hold of the men now died away. They were safe, and two women stood before them.

The man holding Maria flung her backwards onto the broken iron springs of the bed. Two other men moved toward her to hold her down. Kyla sprang at them, dinner knife upraised.

Dimly she heard their laughter and that peculiar yell they had copied from *Los Diablos Tejanos,* the yell that had frozen the blood of Mexicans all along the Rio Grande.

Kyla felt the knife wrenched from her fingers and their hands on her body. She was pushed backwards and the bedsprings jabbed at her back. Maria was lying alongside of her thrashing and twisting, trying to evade the pawing hands.

Kyla's dress was ripped from neck to hem and hot, sticky fingers fumbled with her pantelettes. Her ankles were held fast in a merciless grip, while her arms were stretched upward over her head. She felt as though her arms would break and pain shot from her ankles to her hips as someone jerked her legs apart. Her body arched in rebellion as the first man came down heavily upon her, crushing her with his weight.

As she felt him try to enter her a surge of terror-induced strength freed her arms and she clawed at the bearded face. Vaguely the scene beyond focused for one awful second. The room was filled with men, pushing and jostling to get near the bed. At her side four men were holding Maria down, while a fifth was bouncing up and down over the slender body. Maria's screams subsided to whispered pleas that the Holy Mother end this suffering.

Above Kyla, the black-bearded man cursed as she twisted away from his searching organ, and her hands were again viciously dragged over her head. Her hair was in her eyes, in her mouth, and she was biting her lips and trying to close her thighs.

"Hell, she's worse than a wildcat," Blackbeard said disgustedly. "Ever try to slip your knife into a sheath on the saddle of a bucking bronc?" He roared with laughter at his wit, and then his breath was in Kyla's face and he said, "I changed my mind. That ain't where I want to put it anyway. You'll get the idea pretty damn quick, you little she-cat, I promise you."

Kyla had time to give only one scream in the instant before she realized what he was going to do. It was a scream that continued to echo in the shocked and disbelieving recesses of her mind long after the sound had been cut off.

The scream dragged him back to consciousness. Miguel struggled to sit up and realized he was enmeshed in a spiny clump of *cholla,* suspended head downward. Pain throbbed fiercely in his shoulder and warm wetness trickled down his neck. There was a dull pounding in his head, and the inch-long cactus spines imprisoned his leg like a cluster of knives.

What had happened? They had reached the lookouts and killed the first of them before they were seen. Miguel was not sure what happened after that. He was on his feet, racing toward the farmhouse, when something crashed into his shoulder and he fell into the black pit.

The moon shone briefly and flooded the arroyo with pale light. There was no sign of the rest of the men— horses, men, cannon, everything was gone. In the instant before the moon sailed behind a cloud, something glinted within a shadowed cluster of trees. The cannon. They had not withdrawn, they had moved out of sight.

Miguel's numbed mind grasped the situation slowly. The *lepero* assault team must all have been killed. The rest had withdrawn to gain the advantage of surprise for the next attempt on the mesa. He stifled a groan. The Raiders believed they were safe from further attack. They had left lookouts and the rest of the men . . . *Madre de Dios!* Miguel writhed, trying to seize some solid object in order to pull himself free of his cactus snare.

He heard the scuffling along the dry wash then, and knew more men were about to move in.

"Look out," a voice over his head yelled in English. "Here come some more greasers."

Rifle fire cracked through the night. When the burst of sound died there was an eerie stillness. Straining his ears,

Miguel could hear nothing to indicate any of the men had succeeded in gaining the mesa.

He moved his uninjured arm over cold rock, felt the smashed bone of his shoulder, touched his head and felt the ragged skin where the second bullet had creased his forehead. He braced his other leg against the rock and grasped the *cholla,* unable to stifle the groan as the cactus bit into his fingers. Afraid he would black out again, he rested for a moment before flinging himself into the center of the *cholla,* feeling for the sturdy roots that pushed through the rocky face of the cliff. He was covered with tormenting cactus spines, but his senses were returning.

A moment later the silence was shattered by the roar of the cannon. He heard the sound of bugles below and realized gratefully that the colonel had ordered the storming of the stronghold. Then Miguel remembered Kyla's scream and fought to free himself from the clutching *cholla,* forgetful of the agony of his shoulder.

A cannonball went crashing over his head and there was a burst of rifle fire. It was too dark for the cannoneers to fire with any accuracy, but they would cause some confusion among Ramsey's Raiders and raise the spirits of the men who had to charge through that narrow gorge into the murderous hail of rifle fire.

Miguel had lost his weapons and had no plan in his mind. Only the driving urgency to reach Kyla and Maria kept him going. He inched over the edge of the mesa as Ramsey's men came bursting from the farmhouse, stumbling into positions overlooking the dry wash.

Miguel rolled over onto his stomach and raised his head cautiously. In the canyon below, the Mexican troops were running up the dry wash while Ramsey's men fired feverishly from the cover of the boulders.

Miguel began to crawl along the ground, intending to come in behind the Raiders. He moved from rock to sheltering scrub, making a wide circle toward the farmhouse. His progress was agonizingly slow, and he wondered how he would clear the final obstacle. Between Miguel and the house was a corral with the rearing and

careening horses of the Raiders. The gunfire had un-
settled the animals. But Miguel dragged himself forward,
the memory of Kyla's scream a maddening spur to reluctant flesh.

Reaching the corral, he raised his hand and grasped
the wooden fence and pulled himself to his feet. Then he
plunged through the writhing horses, using them as cover.
An agonizing pain gripped him as a large mare crashed
into his injured shoulder. But he clutched the sweat-
streaked backs of the horses, hanging on to tails, being
flung dangerously near to kicking hooves. Panting, he
found himself on the far side of the corral, only feet away
from the ominously silent farmhouse.

All of the Raiders were defending the narrow approach
to the mesa. Miguel stumbled toward the single window
of the wood frame house, from which emitted a faint glow
of firelight. His blood dripped on the splintered window
ledge as he peered into the room.

He thought at first the room was deserted. The fire was
almost out, a few embers glowed feebly. He could see
the vague outline of a table and a bed. Then the moon
slid out from behind the cloud and flooded the room,
silvering the hair that trailed over the edge of the bed.
The pale light touched the naked girl, softening the
bruises that covered her body, but Miguel's breath escaped
in a sob as he looked at her face. He could not tell
whether she was alive or dead, she lay absolutely still.
Had it not been for that cloud of golden hair he would
not have recognized Kyla, for her face was blackened
and swollen.

Maria was on the floor beside the bed and, mercifully,
he could not see her face which was turned from him.
She, too, was naked and covered in bruises, but she was
moving, he could see her shoulders shaking as her body
wracked with silent sobs.

In his anger Miguel forgot about the Raiders, the
horses, his own wounds. He ran toward the door of the
house. Inside the house he stumbled over the body of a
man lying in a pool of blood.

"Miguel! Oh, Miguel," Maria sobbed when their eyes

met. She came up on her knees, arms protectively across her breasts. Her face was not as badly battered as Kyla's, but her lips were swollen and bleeding and one eye was blackened.

Miguel dropped to his knees beside Kyla. He reached out to touch the dangling arm and she stiffened, a hoarse moan escaping her lips.

"Maria, can you stand up?" Miguel whispered urgently. "We must leave here. Can you help me with Kyla?"

Maria was sobbing again, her hands over her face. "They would have killed us. They said they were going to kill us." The words were torn from her constricted throat in a series of choking sobs and she made no attempt to rise to her feet. "They heard the cannon and ran outside. They will come back and kill us."

Miguel seized Maria's hands, pulling her toward him to gently kiss her fingers. "Maria, little Maria, it's all right, I won't let them hurt you again. Look at me, Maria. It's me, Miguel. Listen to me. We are going to rake all of those embers from the fire, scatter them about, under the table, around the walls."

Maria's dark eyes blinked uncomprehendingly.

"Set fire to the house, Maria," Miguel said. He went to the fire and began to stir the embers with an iron poker lying in the hearth. "Find your dress and get Kyla's clothes. Hurry, we must get out of here. The blaze will give the cannon something to shoot at and perhaps divert the Raiders' attention. Then our men can break through the gorge." The room kept receding into a misty haze. There was a peculiar squeezing sensation about Miguel's temples, and he prayed he would not lose consciousness. "Maria! Help me!"

Out of the corner of his eye he saw Kyla slide from the bed, steady herself for a second against the wall, then pick up the torn remnants of clothing lying on the dirt floor beside Maria. Kyla's hands then went to Maria's shoulders and she shook the girl slightly. When Maria still did not respond, Kyla raised her hand and slapped her cheek, and Maria scrambled to her feet and slapped Kyla's pathetically beaten face in return.

Miguel wanted to weep at the sight of the two of them, but the aged wood of the dining table burst instantly into flames and they started toward the door, Miguel still grasping the iron poker.

They scrambled up the rocky hill behind the leaping flames as the cannon roared again. The chilly night air revived the women and they pulled their tattered dresses over their shivering bodies. Miguel lay weakly back against the unyielding rock, blood seeping from his shoulder. His mind tried to shut out the memory of the blood smeared over bruised thighs. He wondered whether he would have the fortitude to kill both women with the poker if the Raiders came back.

The cannon roared again and the sight of the flames from the house flickering against the sky diverted the defenders' attention so that the first men were able to reach the end of the canyon. Moments later they were engaged in hand-to-hand fighting as the Mexican troops stormed up the wash.

Miguel was unconscious when the colonel came upon the three of them clinging to the hillside, their faces black with smoke.

Garett Ramsey was safely over the hill and crossing the desert valley on foot. Most of his Raiders were dead. The rest would be, soon.

# 15

All of the leperos who led the first assault against the stronghold were dead, including Cervantes Marques, shot through the heart. Only Miguel survived, although he lay near death from loss of blood and, eventually, still in a coma, was left behind when the troops moved on. American reinforcements were arriving in strength, and as the sympathetic Mexican colonel prepared to withdraw to the south, he detailed a party of men to accompany the two women and the unconscious Miguel back to their *rancho*.

Maria continued to sob hysterically, until they reached the *rancho*. Approaching the protective walls of the *casa grande* she became quiet. Except for her black eye and cut lip, her scars did not show. Kyla had not cried, nor shown any sign of emotion, even when they were told of Cervantes' death. She did not utter a sound, but moved woodenly, her eyes blank.

The Mexican escort was relieved when their charges were put into Desmond's hands. They were particularly glad to be rid of the stone-faced woman with the blond hair. She seemed to be the symbol of the outrage one country was committing against another. The trouble was, she was a *gringa*—and the emotions she aroused among them were anathema.

"When can we continue our journey to Europe?" Maria demanded the instant they were inside the *casa grande*.

Desmond led Kyla to a chair and, when she was seated, he turned to Maria and said quietly, "You won't be leaving now, Maria. Kyla cannot travel, and I will need your help to care for her and for Miguel."

"Care for her!" Maria said indignantly. "What about me? Everything that was done to her was also done to me. But I am stronger, I do not hide inside my head and refuse to come out. I shall survive."

"Of course you will, my dear. Be patient. Better times are coming. There will be no more fighting in California, I'm sure of it."

Nana stood weeping silently in the background, and Desmond gestured for her to leave and take Maria with her. He then sat down and looked into his wife's unseeing eyes and began to talk to her. The *vaqueros* were returning. They were lucky there had been no damage and no great loss of either cattle or horses. He had sent for some new books from England and had found several species of butterfly he had never seen before. It did not matter to him that she gave no sign she had heard, much less understood, what he said. There was nothing to do but wait for the passage of time.

Miguel regained consciousness and Maria devoted herself to his care. He did not mention that harrowing night again and saw no purpose in telling anyone that Ramsey had tried to barter his life for the safety of the two women. Sometimes, however, when Miguel was alone, he would pace his room and slap his fist into his open palm until he could feel nothing but the pain in his wounded shoulder.

The bruises on Kyla's flesh began to fade, but she seemed lost in some secret world of her own. Desmond and Nana were beginning to despair of ever bringing her out of it when they had unexpected visitors.

Desmond was sitting with Kyla on the verandah, watching the setting sun weave a litany of vivid hues against the endless sky, when the two figures, on foot, approached the house.

Kyla rose to her feet, her body tense, the dark blue eyes coming to life as she recognized the women who were coming hesitantly toward them. Desmond reached out his hand to steady her, but Kyla stepped forward, her movements purposeful.

"What are you doing here?" she asked coldly. "And where is your lover?"

Desmond stared at Kyla and gave a long sigh of relief. She had come back to life.

Kyla turned and looked at him, her lips parted slightly, as though surprised to see him. Then she looked around wildly—at the house, at Shansi and Old Woman and, with a great shudder, at her own body. Then Kyla ran from them, tears streaming down her cheeks.

"Please—come inside," Desmond said hastily, "and forgive my wife. She has just awakened from a nightmare. I must go to her." He limped after Kyla as Shansi, unperturbed, made her way into the house.

Christmas came and Miguel's strength was rapidly returning. His dark eyes followed Kyla constantly, and he was polite but curt with her husband.

Shansi had slipped inobtrusively into the role of housekeeper, as Nana was bent with arthritis and unable to cope with more than her own simple needs.

Delleroc had not returned from Mexico, and Shansi and Old Woman had come to the de Rivero Rancho, they said, upon his instructions.

John Frémont's band cut a bloody swath southward from Northern California and when they reached the San Fernando Valley a few miles north of the pueblo of Los Angeles, representatives of the *californios* met with them to negotiate a settlement. Meaawhile, in Mexico it was rumored that Antonio Lopez de Santa Anna had mustered twenty-five thousand men and was marching for Monterrey.

"I must go south," Miguel told Kyla. "I am well enough to fight again." He had come upon her curled up in a chair in the *sala,* reading one of Desmond's books.

The blue eyes darkened slightly. "Yes. I've been expecting you to leave. I shall miss you, Miguel."

He looked at her, biting his lip, and started to speak several times but his words trailed away in embarrassment. At last he dropped to his knees beside her, clutching her skirts with his hands. "Ah, Kyla, Kyla," he said brokenly. She had not told him, not in so many words, but he had seen her depart hurriedly from the breakfast table, handkerchief pressed to her lips. She had swayed dizzily several times and he or Desmond had caught her before she fell. Miguel read her mind and confirmed his worst fears.

She stroked his black hair gently. "I'll be all right, Miguel. Desmond will take care of me."

"He knows?"

She nodded. "I'm sure he does. He hasn't mentioned it—but the way he looks at me—" There was a terrible calmness about her he could not understand. If she had been hysterical it would have been easier to bear. She was ruined, and the evidence of her ruin would soon be there for all the world to see. He sighed and stood up awkwardly, not knowing what to say. Guiltily, he wished that it had happened to Maria instead.

"Desmond will accept the child as his own," she said. "He does not speak of returning to England any more."

"I shall return to you. When the war is over," Miguel said. But his eyes did not meet hers, and after a moment her gaze returned to the book on her lap.

Miguel left the following day and a week later Maria found Kyla vomiting in the early morning and she, too, surmised Kyla's condition.

"You must have one of the old women get rid of it," Maria said. "If Nana won't do it, we must ask the Chinese woman. Your husband will kill you if he finds out."

"No, he won't kill me," Kyla said weakly, pressing her handkerchief to her lips. "I think he already knows."

"*Madre de Dios!* You don't even know which one of them was the father," Maria said, shuddering.

"What difference would it make if I did?" Kyla asked shortly.

That afternoon, while she was taking her *siesta,* there was a soft tapping on her bedroom door and when she called out to her visitor to enter, Shansi and Old Woman padded silently into the room.

"Maria told me of your problem," Shansi said, her black eyes staring off into the distance. "Old Woman can end the problem for you."

Old Woman stepped forward, grinning, and for a second Kyla did not see the long bamboo sliver in the wrinkled brown hands. Then the old woman held it up and nodded knowingly, and Kyla screamed and could not stop screaming.

By the time Nana had summoned Desmond from outside and the two of them rushed to Kyla's room, both Shansi and Old Woman had discreetly withdrawn.

Desmond dragged himself to her side. "It's all right, Nana, I'll take care of her. Come now, Kyla, don't distress yourself. It is bad for your child. The time for tears is past and you must resolve to be strong and face the future without fear. Put what is past behind you and go forward in the knowledge that you will overcome and perhaps even benefit in some mysterious way from what happened to you. I know that seems impossible to you now, but our character is shaped more by our adversities than our triumphs. Believe me, my dear, I know that better than most men." He stroked her hair tenderly and spoke soothingly until at last, lulled by his voice and gentle hand, she slept.

Kyla moved listlessly about the house, the terrible fatigue etched in dark circles under her eyes. Her cheeks were sunken and her body shriveled. Desmond spent most of the time caring for her, neglecting the *rancho*. Often, when she slept, he would pace up and down restlessly outside her room, dragging his withered leg and sometimes stopping to pound his fist futilely against thick adobe walls.

In the shadows Shansi watched and remembered what Quint Delleroc had told her about his friend Lord Talmage.

One night Desmond awakened from a restless sleep to find he was not alone in bed. Soft female flesh was pressed against his side and tiny hands moved expertly over his body, while a cloud of black hair softly brushed the scarred side of his face.

"Des-mond," she whispered. "Ah, my lord, do not send me away. I have lost my protector. You have cared for me and I want to care for you. No, do not resist me. See— see how I am able to arouse you, in spite of yourself. Here in the darkness together, we can be whole, you will see. You can forget all of your fears and burdens. My lord, don't deprive me of your manhood. I want you, Des-mond—I want you so much."

He tried to speak, but her lips were on his and in the warm sweetness of her mouth the specter of the knives and fires of the Khyber tribesmen faded for the first time.

He pondered the irony of fate when Quint Delleroc's letter was brought to them by a messenger from the mission the following day.

"I am a prisoner of the Americans," Quint wrote briefly. "Go to Lord Talmage and see what he can do."

Desmond wondered briefly if Shansi had really been instructed to come to him in the event anything happened to Quint. The letter seemed to indicate that Quint had expected her to remain at the mission.

The Americans were moving quickly to entrench themselves and had begun construction of a fort on the hill overlooking the pueblo. This time they were in Los Angeles to stay. They had marched in to take possession, while native hotheads sat on the hill above the plaza, catcalling and waving pistols. All buildings and homes were locked and bolted against them, but the war for California was over.

Amnesty was offered and an emissary even sent among those in hiding to assure them of their safety, but the doors remained barred. It was, therefore, with an astonished expression on his face that an aide to General Stockton announced that one of the California *rancheros* was asking for an audience.

"Show him in," the general said quickly. Then, noting the aide's hesitancy, he asked, "What is it?"

"He's a cripple and badly scarred, sir. I thought you

should be warned in advance. But he is apparently the owner of a large *rancho* a day's ride south of the town."

"I've seen more than my share of scarred men. Show him in."

The man who entered the room dragged a stiff leg and one sleeve was empty, but he stood erect and saluted the general in a military fashion. He wore the *calzoneras*—the fitted trousers that could be unbuttoned to flare out over the boot—of a *vaquero,* but when he spoke his accent was English. The general could not bring himself to look into the hideously scarred face.

"Desmond Gaspar de Rivero Talmage, at your service, sir." He spoke the name proudly. In spite of himself, the general found his gaze drawn to magnetic blue eyes.

"Please sit down, sir."

Before the interview ended, the general had promised to look into the matter of the friend who was a prisoner of war and the soft-spoken *ranchero* had made an excellent suggestion for a way to restore peace to the troubled pueblo of Los Angeles.

That evening at sunset, the American military band set up their instruments in the plaza, and surprised dark eyes peeped around corners and through windows as the warm air was filled with music, Spanish as well as Yankee. Before the concert ended, the plaza was filled with *Californios,* clapping their hands and shouting their *vivas.*

"He was right," General Stockton mused, watching the scene. "He said music would soothe ruffled *angelino* feathers faster than bayonets."

They had found him, long after the other Mexicans left Monterrey, tending wounded men in the ruins of a church. A bloody bandage was wrapped around his head, completely covering his hair, and he wore the uniform of a Mexican artilleryman.

"Are you a doctor, señor?" an American officer asked him, puzzled as he noted the uniform. "I see you have some of our wounded here, as well as Mexicans—"

"Neither a doctor, nor a señor," Quint answered absently. "I'm on holiday here."

"Your troops have evacuated the city, hadn't you heard? There has been an armistice. You were all supposed to leave."

Green eyes flickered upward over the officer. "Sorry, old bean. Nowhere to go at the moment." He was carefully cleaning a shattered kneecap.

"Wait a minute." A sergeant stepped forward. "This man came to our camp at Camargo, before the attack. I remember that accent and those eyes. I bet the hair under that bandage is nearly as red as the blood."

"A spy?" the officer said. "He wasn't wearing a uniform when you saw him last?"

"No, sir. But sure as hell a lot of our boys are alive because he helped them, just like he's helping these poor devils," the sergeant said vehemently.

One of the junior officers, who was passing by and who overheard the latter part of the conversation, paused, frowning. "Did someone mention red hair? During the worst of the house-to-house fighting, some of my men reported seeing a red-haired man fighting like a maniac, and one dying Mexican called out to him, '*el tigre colorado*' which someone translated to me as meaning 'red tiger.' Is it possible this is the same man? We believed him to be one of the San Patricios, and if that is the case—"

"What exactly are you, sir?" the first officer asked Quint.

"Now there's a question to tempt a facetious answer," Quint said with a tired grin. "I am, sir, Satan incarnate. You see me in the act of mending bodies so that I may possess souls."

"I think we'd better put you under arrest," the officer said. "But you can continue what you're doing until we decide what to do with you."

"On your way out, would you see if your men have left any of the señoras and señoritas alive? If so, I could use some bandages. And tell your general if he doesn't start burying the dead, we shall have cholera to add to our woes. Oh, yes, one other thing. I'll be glad to help with the wounded in return for a favor. Would you send a message to a mission near San Diego for me?"

"I'll take care of it for you, Red Tiger," the sergeant whispered as he bent to close the eyes of a dead soldier.

General Taylor took Saltillo, still deeper inside Mexican territory, and moved in the direction of Victoria. There had been little opposition.

An embarrassed sergeant duly reported to his commanding officer that the Red Tiger had escaped just before Saltillo and was later found helping the Mexican wounded. It was suspected the man had again fought on the Mexican side.

One of the newly arrived replacements jerked to attention. "Delleroc! You have him?" the big yellow-haired man asked in amazement. "Do you know who he is? He is a personal friend of old el Presidente himself: Santa Anna."

The officer blanched visibly. The man Ramsey had arrived in their midst with a heroic tale of being the only man to escape a Mexican massacre in California. He had, he said, been taken prisoner, but managed to escape before the greasers slaughtered all of the other prisoners in cold blood.

"You're harboring a spy," Ramsey said grimly. "He's an Englishman who came to negotiate a land purchase from Santa Anna before the war started. After that he fought with the Spanish *californios*. He's been killing Americans from the very beginning."

The officer said, "We've got to double back to Monterrey. I've had a report that Santa Anna has twenty-five thousand men marching in that direction. I haven't time to verify your story. And the man Delleroc has served us as a medical officer, despite his escape. I hesitate to shoot him as a spy."

"Then let me take care of him," Ramsay said, his pale eyes transparent. "I'm not one of your regulars and bound by army regulations. And I've an old grudge to settle with the swine."

"You won't kill him in cold blood," the officer said curtly. "But I will detail you to take him back to our base camp on the Rio Grande and order an investigation into his activities. If he is a spy from Santa Anna, perhaps we can learn something from him." Two problems solved at once, the officer thought, relieved. He did not need another volunteer of Ramsey's type. The regulars would win this war. "I'll send one of my noncommissioned officers to accompany you," he added. "Sergeant Morgan, you and Mr. Ramsey will leave at once."

Sergeant Morgan was a young volunteer from Ohio, who had the gray pallor of sickness about his face and was silently battling stomach cramps. He watched, paralyzed with disbelief as well as his own internal misery, when Ramsey dragged Delleroc from his horse the following day and proceeded to attach a rope to the handcuffs the prisoner wore.

They were in a desolate valley, strewn with boulders and cactus. Sunlight struck them like a sword thrust, despite the black clouds that clung to the distant mountains.

"You're going to have one of Ramsey's famous rides on your belly through the cactus," Ramsey said, giving the rope a vicious jerk.

"Whatever amuses you," Delleroc said indifferently. "I am curious, however, as to what inspired your hatred? Not that I mind, I've always preferred to be hated than ignored. But in your case I fondly imagined that all I did was give you a job. Perhaps the wages were inadequate?"

Ramsey's fist smashed into his mouth. "Goddamn you, don't pretend you didn't have me shanghaied."

Quint licked the blood from his lip. "Shanghaied? What for? As I recall, you were doing an excellent job in the emporium. I had been hoping to leave you in complete charge when I went to fulfill my promise to Lord Talmage. That was really the reason I hired you in the first place. Instead you simply disappeared one day and I had no alternative but to sell the emporium."

"Oh, sure. And the girl never said anything about—"

"Shansi? Ah. I see," Quint said, and his eyes were opaque.

"Shut your goddamned mouth," Ramsey yelled. "You'd tell me anything now to save your neck." He climbed up on his horse.

"Sir, wait," Sergeant Morgan said, finding his voice at last. "What are you doing?" The sergeant doubled over with the pain in his stomach, and when he tried to straighten up the bleak landscape spun dizzily.

"Bring his horse," Ramsey said. "I owe him this."

Quint stayed on his feet longer than most men, but then the horse was whipped to a fast gallop and he was flung on to his face. Surprisingly, it was the pain in his arms that was greatest. Like being stretched on the rack, he thought distantly, as he was aware of but not impressed by the jarring of his body over the rocks and through the spiny cactus clumps. Long before the sergeant had summoned the strength and will to gallop after them and to cut the rope with his knife, Quint had removed his mind from the agony of his body. It was something he had learned years ago, from the yogi in India.

The black clouds over the mountains had begun to move toward them.

# 16

*Kyla stood at her bedroom window, watching the riders* climb into their saddles. It was one of those February days of crystal-clear air and golden sunlight, and her garden was thriving. Beyond the patio, the newly planted peach and plum trees reached spindly branches eagerly toward the sun, and a pair of fat puppies were frolicking boisterously in the grape arbor.

They would have to leave. All of their work, all of Raul de Rivero's hopes for them, Desmond's long journey—they had all been for nothing.

She had been too shocked to remain in the room while those men had explained to Desmond about the new American Land Commission and its findings in the case of the de Rivero *rancho*. She had heard little beyond the news that Cervantes Marques had petitioned the Alcalde of Los Angeles to be granted a portion of the land, and the Commission's attention had been drawn to some ir-regularities in the *expedientes*. And then there was the fact that debts and taxes were outstanding against the *rancho*.

The bile had risen in her throat then, and, mindful of the constant nausea that plagued her, she had fled from the room.

The Americans had been polite and concerned. Des-mond was known to be one of the few rancheros who had extended the olive branch to the conquerors, and the Americans regretted he was going to be one of the first to be evicted from his land. But it would have happened anyway. Whether or not California had become part of the Union, the wheels were put in motion months before by the embittered Cervantes Marques. When the annexation of California was official, there would be few of the old Spanish land grants honored, so perhaps the crippled *ranchero* was fortunate in being spared the suspense.

Desmond knocked on Kyla's door, then entered the room and stood, waiting for her to turn from the window. She was numb with an overpowering sense of loss, and the intruder in her womb was sending waves of dizziness and nausea through her body. She did not look around, but said to Desmond over her shoulder, "Now you can return to your monastery with a clear conscience. There is nothing for you here, and you won't have to stay and be a witness to my final humiliation."

He dragged himself across the room and stood at her side, his hand reaching for hers, refusing to be deterred. She had noticed on other occasions that he seemed to have the strength of two hands concentrated into his one.

"Kyla, I won't leave you now," he said softly. "There's no need for anyone to know the child is not mine."

She turned to look at him and her eyes were haunted by memories too terrible to bear. "There is no need for you to stay because of my shame."

"The shame is not yours, Kyla," he said. "And the child is innocent of any crime. Let me take care of you, and after the child is born, you can decide then what you want to do. But there is something you must know. Come, sit down, you should not tire yourself by standing for long periods."

She allowed him to lead her to a chair, but sat stiffly, her lips pressed together, her eyes glistening slightly. How she had longed for a child. What a cruel answer to her prayers was this parasite that grew inside her, sapping her strength, destroying her life.

Desmond said, "I didn't want to tell you this before, because there seemed no point in your being concerned

with the matter. But I cannot return to England, at least,
not to England and freedom. Unfortunately, after I had
been sent to Mexico by the British Government, when
Quint confessed to our little deception in India he believed
he was acting in my best interests. But I am sure the army
will bring charges against both Quint and myself. Desertion, party to a conspiracy, and so on."

"But you said he fought so bravely in India. He was
decorated."

"He did and was. But, alas, there is no one quite as
angry as a man who has been made to look a fool. And
Quint and I made the army look like fools. So you see, I
cannot take you back to England and make a home for
us."

"I don't want to live in a foreign country," Kyla said.
"This is my country and my home. Surely there's something we can do to keep it?"

"I was shown a copy of the original grant," Desmond
said. "I can quote it word for word, I read it so many
times. 'The Viceroy, on behalf of the King of Spain,
makes the grant to Raul de Rivero, soldier of the Royal
Presidio of San Diego, and to his progeny being of pure
Spanish blood. The petitioner is granted the permission
of having bovine stock and horses at the place south-
east of the Pueblo of the Queen of the Angels known as
the de Rivero *rancho* and its environs; provided no harm
is done to the Pagan Indians or the mission lands and
providing also that the petitioner have someone watch
over the lands at all times.'

"You see, it was specifically stated that Raul's progeny
to whom the lands could be left must be of pure Spanish
blood. Neither of us qualifies on that account. Then, too,
Raul precipitated an Indian attack, willfully, from what
I have learned, by luring young men and women from
both the missions and the nomadic Indian tribes to work
on the *rancho*. Unfortunately, he took a young woman,
who was betrothed to the chief of a much more warlike
tribe from the east. The deed was probably invalid after
the massacre and during the time the *rancho* was left
unattended. Even though Eduardo Marques later sent an

estate manager and eventually his own son, Cervantes, to take care of things, that does not change the stipulations of the grant. It was, by the way, Cervantes who unearthed the original land grant. Since he was serving in the Mexican Army at the time, he petitioned to be given the land by virtue of his residence there and service in the Mexican Army. Of course, as it turns out Cervantes is dead and the land is now in American territory."

"Then where can we go?"

"I thought perhaps we would journey along the El Camino Real until we found an abandoned mission. I understand there are many, and some of them are for sale. Although the taxes and other debts are going to take a large bite out of the money we will realize from the sale of the stock and furniture and so on, there should be enough for our needs. There are so many old and sick Indians who would welcome a chance to move back to the safety of a mission. I know that secularization has removed control of the mission lands from the *padres,* but we could plant small gardens for our own needs and help the Indians sell their handicrafts. It would be a spartan existence, Kyla, but we would be doing God's work and be useful. There would be no one to point a finger of scorn at us."

Kyla sighed. Once what she had yearned for more than anything else was to have a child of her own to love and care for. She had pictured the child even before she imagined the man who would father him. Suddenly she wished savagely that the child she carried could be exchanged for the land she had grown to love.

Desmond was watching her, and she quickly stifled the useless, resentful thoughts. "How long do we have?"

"We should begin the sale of the stock and make arrangements for the journey immediately, before you —before your condition—"

"What about your friend Delleroc?"

"General Stockton promised to send word to General Taylor that Quint is a British subject, and have him released."

"Is Quint a British subject?" she asked in surprise.

"No. But I didn't know what else to tell him. Quint is a citizen of the world. I'm not sure where he came from originally. Every time he told me the story of his life, he claimed a different ancestry. To my knowledge, he speaks at least five languages."

"He told me his father was Irish and his mother Chilean."

"It's possible. He once told me that too. But oddly, Ireland is the one country he has never visited. He also told me once when he was very drunk that he was the bastard of the King of Spain and a Scottish governess. The only story I really believe is that he ran away from home as a nine-year-old boy and stowed away to England. If you are worried about him, Kyla, don't be. I don't know anyone on earth more capable of taking care of himself."

Kyla turned away from the searching eyes uncomfortably. She never wanted to see Quint Delleroc again. How could she face him in her shame? "There's the question of Maria, and Shansi and Old Woman, and Nana."

Desmond smiled ruefully. "I seem to have acquired quite a harem for myself, but, of course, they will all come with us."

She felt the sudden tension in his hand and glanced at him in time to see his expression turn to one of abject misery, well-laced with guilt. It was an expression she had seen on the faces of men and women about to enter the confessional. But that was ridiculous. No man had fewer sins to confess than Desmond Talmage.

When the women were called together to be told of the plans, Kyla noticed that Desmond looked at all of them except Shansi. Not once did his eyes glance in the direction of the coolly composed Oriental, even when she immediately protested that such a course of action was unnecessary.

"We can go to Mr. Delleroc's house in Monterey," she said. "It is not as grand as this, but it is far better than living at a mission."

"Shansi," Desmond said uncomfortably, still not looking in her direction, "you don't understand. We shall have a purpose in life on a mission, besides, there will not be a great deal of money. We shall have to work for our daily bread."

"Mr. Delleroc's business maintains his house," Shansi said.

"But he told me he had sold the emporium." Desmond was staring at the handsome, beaten-silver plaque which hung on the wall.

"Mr. Delleroc did not sell his *other* business," Shansi said. "The one run by Mr. Smith and the woman Felice. It makes much money. There is a mortuary and a gambling house."

Everyone, including Desmond, was staring at her with great interest now.

The wind shrieked toward them, filled with blinding, swirling dust and the heavens exploded with thunder. Quint Delleroc lay in a narrow wash, the rope still attached to his handcuffs. Inches from his face, a small gray lizard slithered down a smooth boulder and paused to regard him curiously before proceeding to shelter from the oncoming storm. Rain pelted the dry sand but did not clear the air of the driving dust.

His arms felt as though they had been torn from their sockets, and his body was being devoured by unseen demons. He heard the horses whinny faintly, as though far away, but could see nothing. He buried his face in his arms and slipped gratefully into oblivion.

Dust clung to his eyelids, and when he tried to blink it away he was tormented by sand scratching his eyes. There was water under him, flowing down the wash, and he dragged himself to his knees to crawl to higher ground. Fifty-foot dust devils were dancing across the valley and the wind slammed the breath from his lungs. He rolled under the meager shelter of wind-bent mesquite, choking and gasping. There was no sign of either Ramsey or Sergeant Morgan.

While the storm raged, Quint alternated between periods of consciousness and oblivion and he was not sure how much time had passed when he opened his eyes to a blaze of sunlight and still air. Sitting up slowly, he saw first the dried blood on his shredded trousers and shirt, and then the maddening thirst struck him and he staggered to his feet to search for the canteens. The gravelly sand was bone-dry, as though it had never rained.

He saw Ramsey then, sitting with his back to a large boulder, looking dazed. There was no sign of the horses.

Ramsey hauled himself up on his feet and approached Quint cautiously. "They said you knew a bit about doctoring," he said, the dust cracking on his face as he spoke.

"So?"

"Better come and look at the sergeant."

"How about a little water?" He didn't expect to get any, but Ramsey tossed him a canteen and then trudged off in the direction of the boulder.

The sergeant was lying on the other side of the rock, and they could smell him before they saw him. His skin was a pallid green, and his nose had been bleeding so that his face was smeared with clotted blood. He moaned and twitched convulsively.

"Unlock the handcuffs," Quint said quietly.

Ramsey hesitated, then withdrew the key with his left hand and his Colt with his right hand. He held the gun on Quint as he bent over the sergeant and raised his eyelids. The whites of the eyes were yellow and, when he pulled back the lips, the gums were bleeding.

"He's been vomiting?" Quint asked.

"Yes, he did yesterday. Black stuff. Is it dysentery?"

"*El vomito negro,*" Quint said. "The medical term for what the sergeant has is *Leptospira icteroides*. I believe you will recognize it by the name of yellow fever."

Ramsey leaped backwards in alarm. "Yellow jack!"

"He'll have an insatiable thirst. How much water do you have?"

"Two canteens. The horses ran off in the storm, and I haven't seen them since. I'd better start off on foot and see if I can catch up with the troops, get help for the sergeant. Look, I haven't touched him. You have. Besides, you're in no condition to walk."

Green eyes regarded Ramsey levelly. "You'll at least leave me a gun and one of the canteens?"

"Like hell I will. The sergeant's a dead man and you soon will be too. I hear it's not too pleasant a death, yellow jack. Think about what you did to me when you start getting the stomach pains. That was how the sergeant started."

"Ramsey, thinking about you would bore me to death. I wouldn't need the fever to kill me. For all your size, you sniveling, self-pitying coward, you are a very small man. You imagine others are bent on your downfall when, in actual fact, most men would not go out of their way to step on a cockroach like you. You are simply not worth the effort."

Ramsey took a step toward him, but the sergeant moaned again and Ramsey stopped. "You stand there and tell me you wouldn't like to kill me for dragging you behind my horse?" he asked incredulously.

Quint's eyes flickered contemptuously over Ramsey's large body. "You stupid bastard, the mere fact that you crave my enmity is reason enough for me to deny it to you."

Ramsey glared at him speechlessly for a second, then the man on the ground whimpered piteously. Ramsey stepped backward, then turned and headed in the direction of the distant hills. Quint watched him go and then started looking for a place to shelter the sick man from the noon sun.

The sergeant opened his eyes briefly and thanked Quint for remaining with him. He begged for water. Quint had already knocked the top from a barrel cactus with his boot, and the moist, bitter-tasting pulp was the best he could offer, but the dying man accepted it gratefully.

"Will you do something for me? Let my brother know what happened to me?" he whispered. "Only the two of us left. His name is Nathaniel Morgan. He went to Northern California, a place called Sutter's Fort."

The sergeant died the following day, which was the sixth day of his illness. Quint piled rocks over the body and began the trek toward the hills. There were deep cuts all over his legs and lower body, and as time passed and he did not develop the symptoms of yellow fever, he remembered what he had been told in China: that the wounded warrior rarely succumbs to sickness. It was believed that the body's defenses, once harnessed to heal the wounds, were able to withstand the invading illness.

In the chilling drizzle that soaked the battlefield, the sentries patrolled nervous perimeters, shooting instantly if a challenge were not properly answered. The password of the Americans that night was "Honor to Washington," and flashes of red flame stabbed the wet darkness frequently during the tense night. Far away in the American capital, President Polk was attending a banquet honoring the birthday of the country's first President, unaware that a decisive battle was about to be fought.

The Americans occupying Monterrey had noticed that the townspeople were turning more sullen, that the town seemed to be preparing for a siege. Shops and *cantiñas* were closed and barred; houses stood empty, and every day more residents left for the mountains. The rumor that Santa Anna's vengeful army, numbering over twenty thousand men, was close by made the volunteers under Taylor's command increasingly jumpy. For the most part they were recruits who had not yet tasted combat. Their battle-tried comrades had gone to Tampico with Scott.

Reports of Mexican cavalry movement, and the glow of Mexican campfires in the hills around Monterrey, spread alarm through American ranks. The dragoons and Texas Rangers were sent out on patrol missions and came back with gloomy news. Half a dozen American outposts had been overrun, and Santa Anna's infantry and cavalry were wheeling around to take Taylor's army from the rear.

The advance positions would have to be given up. They would pull back to a sheep ranch called Buena Vista, where a wide mesa offered a regrouping point. The Americans retreated to the new positions through the choking smoke of blazing supply dumps.

"Who goes there?" the sentry barked as the shadowy figure materialized in the gloomy drizzle.

"Friend. I'm a friend." The hoarse whisper came back, but the sentry's rifle spat fire, and the shadow fell heavily to the ground, rolling away into the brush. The sentry did not go to investigate who he had shot. Time enough for that in the morning.

When the gray dawn broke the plain was filled with the awesome sight of Santa Anna's army, row upon row of troops, each regiment wearing its own colors, flags and banners fluttering in the breeze. The plain was a blaze of color—red, blue, yellow, scarlet, green and white. The bands were playing, the men were cheering. On their flanks were the lancers, while gunners stood at fieldpieces and the *San Patricio* battalion's flag flew over the batteries of eighteen and twenty-four pounders.

Apolo Ramirez, his wound healed, sat upon his horse at Miguel's side. Their veteran *leperos* would be among the first to charge.

"Now we shall show the *gringos*," Apolo breathed.

"Apolo," Miguel said, "if I die—"

"*Madre de Dios!* It is unlucky to think of it. Cross yourself and vow to live, Miguel."

"Maria and Kyla, I worry about them. If anything happens to me, will you go and see that they are all right? They have only the crippled Englishman to protect them."

"Listen to me, Miguel. I made some inquiries and found that you and your brother left your *hacienda* somewhat prematurely. While it is true that most of your lands have been reclaimed by the State, your house still belongs to you, with enough land, so that you will have a modest beginning when the war is over. El Presidente will be grateful to his loyal officers. I am sure that we shall be able to do something about getting more of your land deeded back to you. Fight well today, Miguel, and no more talk of dying. You have much to live for."

Miguel was silent as the bands began to play a stirring call to battle. Kyla, he thought, she would be heavy with the unknown *gringo's* child now and forever lost to him. No man of honor could accept a woman so shamed. The husband could have been sent back to where he came from, and Delleroc, the man who had bewitched her, he could be dispatched in a duel. But a bastard? There was no solution to that horror.

The signal gun sounded, the bugles blared, and the men swept forward. "*Viva* Mexico! Death to the *gringos!*" burst from their throats, as they attacked with such fury that the Americans reeled back under the assault.

They fought at bayonet point, peons and farm boys dying in muddy streambeds and cactus gardens under a thick pall of gunsmoke. Horsemen clashed, saber against lance, and the blood of the horses and men ran in ravines and trenches, their screams mingling in a hellish cacophony. The batteries of the *San Patricios* were red-hot, so rapidly were they firing. In their midst was a man whose hair was as red as some of the other Irishmen, but whose features were more Castilian than County Cork. He had crawled to their lines under cover of darkness, red hair matted with blood where the sentry's bullet had creased his skull.

John Riley looked at him in amazement and said, "Delleroc, we thought you'd gone over to the other side. How bad are you hurt?"

Delleroc grinned fiendishly. "They can't hurt me when they shoot at my horns. Can you use another cannoneer? My services are for sale for a canteen of water and a meal. And as for going over to the other side, as you can see, they didn't want me."

Now the *San Patricios* paused as the cavalry charged and the *leperos* thundered after a fleeing American regiment.

Miguel was unaware of his horse streaking forward, and the sound of bugles and cannonade was only a distant accompaniment to the rushing of the blood in his ears and the terrible hatred that drove him toward the men who had torn the fabric of his life to shreds. He fought like a man possessed, slashing, mutilating and maiming in a great orgy of vengeance—for Kyla, for Maria and for the dead Cervantes—for the loss of his home and the humiliation of his people. His horse reared as a riderless horse crashed into them, and at that second a bullet grazed his leg and buried itself in his horse's side. They both went down in a flurry of hooves and rolling bodies.

The horse shuddered and died, and Miguel's leg was pinned beneath the carcass. He struggled, but could not move, looking up to see the *yanqui* bearing down on him, pale blue eyes flashing as silver as the upraised weapon.

Two of the *leperos* swung low on their mounts to help him, while a third beat back the *yanqui*. The next moment Apolo was pulling him to his feet.

"Look—they ran from us!" Apolo shouted, and Miguel watched through a red haze as the enemy retreated in confusion. He tried to take a step, but his leg twisted uselessly beneath him and he fell again, his face in the mud.

Early in the afternoon a thunderstorm added its roar to the sound of battle, but slashing rain did not slow the bloody pace of the fighting. As the afternoon waned, the Mexicans made another all-out attack and overran a battery of cannon.

Flying artillery was set up near Taylor's observation post, and he ordered double-shot rained down on a ravine crowded with Mexican infantry. The murderous fire tore into the ranks and the Mexican attack melted away as the dusk began to fall.

The first daylight the following day illuminated a ghastly scene. The dead lay piled body upon body, and the dazed Americans realized the Mexicans were in full retreat.

Dejectedly, Miguel and Apolo shared a horse as they led the remnants of their *lepero* brigade back into the mountains. The taste of defeat was not a fitting reward for men who had fought so bravely.

# 17

Nana awakened Desmond before dawn, and he dragged his weary body back from the sleep of exhaustion. "It's time?" he asked.

She nodded in the darkness of the chill morning. "It will be hard for her. She does not want the child and she will not labor willingly to bring it into the world. You must talk to her, tell her she must help the child in its great struggle to be born. She cries for her own dead mother and slips into oblivion. I am afraid for her." Nana did not tell him of the other name Kyla had cried out in her agony.

"You sent for Dr. Clement?"

"An hour ago. But the labor will be long. We shall not see the child this day."

Desmond did not leave his wife's side all that long and harrowing day, as she writhed in agony and cried out her wish to die. Nana was sent from the room, crying softly. The doctor, turning his head to conceal the liquor on his breath, suggested that Desmond send for a priest to administer last rites.

"There is little I can do to help her," Dr. Clement whispered. "She fights her contractions and holds her breath. Do you want me to perform Caesarean surgery to save the child?" He regarded Desmond with bloodshot eyes, and his hands shook.

174

"No," Desmond said immediately. "If worse comes to worst, you must sacrifice the child. Is there a way you can put Kyla to sleep and bring the baby?"

"Not yet. The birth canal is not sufficiently dilated. Later, perhaps, I could give her laudanum. Who is the person Quint that she keeps calling for? A relative? Can we bring Quint here? It might help."

"I'm afraid not."

Kyla moaned and opened her eyes. She stared unseeing at the two men. Then pain gripped her body again and she gasped and went limp, her eyes rolling upward. The doctor pressed a cold compress to her forehead and looked at Desmond helplessly.

"Perhaps it's better for her to faint like this. It's the body's way of avoiding pain too great to be borne, although I feel in your wife's case there is more than the pain of the contractions. Has she had some terrible sorrow perhaps, or was she frightened by something? Old wives' tales, I know, but I have seen anguish of the mind cause physical distress. You say her brother is fighting in the war? What news have you heard?"

Dr. Clement's nervous fingers plucked at his ginger moustache. He was uneasy dealing with childbirth. His patients usually were sailors with boils and broken bones, or travelers with gunshot wounds. There were few women in his territory, and midwives usually brought their children into the world. But Lord Talmage had sought the doctor out during Kyla's difficult pregnancy.

"The Americans are still advancing," Desmond answered, taking Kyla's limp hand in his. "The Mexicans will defend their land gallantly all the way to Mexico City, I've no doubt, but they cannot win. I hear the English minister has been asked to intervene and bring about a settlement. But I believe it will be impossible for anyone to negotiate a settlement. The Mexican Congress passed a law earlier this year designating a traitor anyone who even dared to listen to terms offered by the United States. Doctor, perhaps you'd better go and ask Nana to see if she can find a priest."

Dr. Clement looked down at Kyla's waxen face and

nodded. He was gone only five minutes, but when he returned, Kyla's eyes were open and she was holding on to Desmond's hand as though she were dangling over a precipice, straining in the grip of a contraction. The doctor did not know that in those few minutes Desmond had whispered to her that she must fight for her life and for the life of her child. "Quint's child, Kyla. Quint will not forgive you if you let his child die." In her semi-conscious state she believed for a little while what she wanted to believe.

Nana had not returned with a priest when the scrawny boy was delivered at the stroke of midnight. By then Kyla was so weak, she closed her eyes and slipped into exhausted sleep before her child gave his first cry.

The doctor's eyes met Desmond's moist gaze over the puny body lying at the foot of the bed, its small fists flailing angrily.

"I'm sorry," the doctor said. "You mustn't blame yourself. It has nothing to do with your own—ah—unfortunate accident. I have seen such children born to perfectly normal parents."

Desmond looked down sadly at the child's clubfeet. "Both feet. Can anything be done?"

"I don't know. Perhaps. But I don't have the knowledge or the skill and I don't know anyone who does. It would be better not to hope."

"Doctor, come, bring the child. I must speak with you outside." Desmond glanced at his sleeping wife and led the way from the room, the doctor following with the tiny bundle in his arms.

Dr. Clement was surprised when Desmond paused for a moment in the chapel, retrieved something hidden in a saint's niche, murmured a quick prayer and then led the doctor outside to where his horse was tied to the weathered olive press in the garden.

"My wife was brutally raped. The child is the result. I believed we would be strong enough to accept him, but doctor, my wife has been through so much. Every day she must look upon her husband's vile shell of a body; I cannot let her suffer the sight of a crippled child also.

Will you help us? Take the child away with you, tonight, and find a foster home for him."

Desmond held a leather bag toward the doctor. "All the money I have in the world is in this pouch. It should be enough to pay for his care for a long time. I will tell my wife the baby was stillborn."

Dr. Clement looked down at the squirming child in his arms and wished he could reach into his saddlebags for the bottle of whiskey. "What do you want me to do with him? I don't know of any orphanges in this territory."

"Couldn't you find a family who would take care of him? And a doctor who could do something for his feet? There is enough money here so he would not be a financial burden in regard to either his care or medical treatment."

The doctor's eyes gleamed as he hefted the pouch and he licked his dry lips. "Don't you wish to have him baptized first? A child taken from his mother at birth might not survive. Not that I'm judging your actions. The child would be a constant reminder of your wife's ordeal."

"You must leave now, before Nana returns with the priest. I shall make a burial mound and tell them the child was stillborn. I ask only one other thing of you. On your way through Monterey, would you send a message to my wife's sister, asking her to come and stay with us to help Kyla over the next few weeks?"

Shansi had refused point-blank to accompany them to the tiny mission built on the craggy headlands overlooking the sea. She would return to Monterey to Mr. Delleroc's house. Maria, too, had balked at life in the ruins of a mission and had asked if she might stay in Mr. Delleroc's house while she found some position suitable for an impoverished gentlewoman.

Shansi's black eyes had been indifferent. She supposed it would be all right. Desmond had not argued with them. He said a silent prayer of thanks that his own weak will had been recognized and temptation removed from his path.

They had reopened Delleroc's house and found an

Indian couple to work for them, and Shansi had visited the woman Felice and returned with supplies.

"Perhaps Felice has an opening for me," Maria asked.

Shansi's gaze was remote. "Perhaps. I will arrange for you to meet her."

Maria went to early-afternoon tea with the infamous Felice, more out of curiosity than any desire to go to work. One of these days, Miguel would return from the wars and take care of Maria. It was merely a question of survival in the meantime.

She was surprised to find the gambling den situated in the back rooms of a very respectable-looking funeral parlor. The sallow-skinned reed of a man named Merciful Smith, who ran the establishment regarded them somberly through a cloud of cigar smoke.

"Mornin', Miss Shansi. Felice is having her *siesta*. She expecting you?" His voice was a hoarse whisper, and his throat was wrapped with a dingy yellow cravat as though to ward off a quinsy.

Maria held her skirts away from him as she passed, in case he was suffering from some contagious disease.

"This is Miss Maria. We are expected," Shansi said, waving the smoke out of her face. "Maria, this is Mr. Merciful Smith, the mortician."

He kept the cigar clamped between his teeth as he nodded in Maria's direction.

Beyond the display of coffins was a room evidently used for the preparation of the deceased, and Maria averted her eyes from the long table, which was fortunately vacant. A second door led to a large room crowded with gaming tables, upon which lay decks of cards, and there was a backgammon board on one green-covered table. Cane-bottomed chairs sat in plush red carpeting, and scarlet and gold striped wallpaper covered the walls. There was a handsome oak bar at one end of the room, above which a gilt-framed mirror reflected the garish grandeur of the room.

A heavy velvet curtain at one end of the bar was raised, and a woman came out to greet them. She was a full six feet tall, with a generously endowed figure and an intricately arranged coiffeur of red curls that put Delleroc's fiery mane to shame. Her face was handsome rather than pretty, with sculptured cheekbones and a high-bridged nose. Slanted golden eyes crinkled with good humor. She wore a white satin wrapper and was unconcerned that it did not meet over her breasts. She scratched herself absently as she dropped into the nearest chair.

"Run along, Shansi, and let me talk to Maria. Pull up a chair, girl, and stop wrinkling your nose as though you smell something bad."

Maria sat down, her mouth slightly open.

Felice looked at her visitor appraisingly. "Let's understand one another. I know you're not a *puta,* that you're from a good family. But I also know that a pack of soldiers got hold of you and you're not a virgin any more and probably won't find a rich *caballero* for a husband. *Sí?*"

Maria's chin went up and her eyes flashed. "Watch your tongue, woman. I've had *mestizos* like you whipped for less."

Surprisingly, Felice threw back her head and roared with laughter, a rich, full-bodied laugh that made the crystal jingle in the chandelier over her head.

"A little spitfire. Good. The men like spirit. It's what they expect of señoritas. Listen, I've got two other girls here, high-class like yourself. They deal cards, monte mostly, some blackjack. And if they want to make their private arrangements with their customers, well, that's all right by me, so long as they conduct their personal business in their own homes on their own time. Delleroc's business is strictly gambling and whiskey. The girls are not allowed to drink while they work."

"Cards! I know nothing of cards," Maria said haughtily.

"I can teach you," Felice said easily. "You've got the hands for it, long slender fingers, and the looks for it. The customers are going to be so busy trying to look down your bosom, they won't notice if you're slow at first. And before you go all high and mighty on me, I'd like to point out that some of the richest men in town come here to play cards and drink. It's the one place their wives never find out about, because if they get too drunk, Merciful Smith takes them home discreetly in the hearse. A girl with your looks could set herself up very nicely, if she had a mind to."

"As soon as my brother returns from the war, I shall not need to work," Maria said coldly.

"And what will you do until then? Shansi won't support you. She wants you out of Delleroc's house before he returns. Anyway, it's up to you. I'm going back to bed. Come back tonight when we're open. Won't do any harm just to watch, will it?"

Maria went back and watched. She had no choice, when Shansi made it clear there would not be a permanent home for Maria in Delleroc's house.

Felice and her ladies were richly gowned and dazzlingly bejeweled. The clients were gentlemen, not ruffians, and the atmosphere as gay as the parties and fandangos of the *hacienda*. Moreover, Maria was instantly the center of attraction. The men complimented her extravagantly, begging her to take a glass of wine and sit at their elbow "for luck" during their games. Maria graciously accepted one such invitation and the handsome cardplayer presented her with several pieces of silver when he won. In the background, Felice tossed her red curls back over her ample shoulders and winked at her.

Maria moved in to a small hotel near the funeral parlor and learned to deal blackjack and play monte. She did not take any of her clients home with her for many weeks. Then one of them made her an offer that was so staggering she accepted. So much money—why, if she were so inclined, in no time at all she could open her own place and then she would not have to deal the cards. She could just mingle with the guests as Felice did. It was not, as Felice had so callously pointed out, as though she were a virgin. If there could be no rich marriage, then there might as well be rich male protectors.

The man was young and handsome. He removed his own clothes as well as hers, amused her with risqué stories, and was exceedingly eloquent about her charms.

She lay back on her satin pillow, spreading her dark hair becomingly about her creamy shoulders, and watched languidly as he proceeded to kiss and caress every inch of her body. By the time he had reached her thighs, she found her hips were involved in some wild contortions over which she had no control.

She moaned as she reached for him, to guide him into the moist warmth between her legs, then gasped as he hesitated, teasing her with the tip of his organ, burying his face in her breasts. Her fingernails went into his back and he laughed and plunged into her joyously and they swayed and rose and fell in a symphony of the senses that lingered in her mind and on exquisite nerve-points long after he had departed. When she later found the money on her dresser it took her a moment to remember the financial part of their bargain.

Maria was irritated when the crippled Englishman sent word that Kyla's child was stillborn, and would she please come to the mission. She suffered a few days of the discomfort of the hovel which Desmond and Kyla shared with Nana, who was now bedridden.

Desmond's never-robust frame was now gaunt, but his eyes were sapphire-bright in his shrunken face. He toiled long hours at the side of the Indians who grew meager crops; he nursed their sick, taught their children, and cared for Kyla as well as Nana. Maria had no intention of giving up her own luxurious way of life, and departed hurriedly, promising to send word to Miguel that Kyla was deathly ill following the birth of her child.

"Yes," Desmond agreed, looking worriedly at his wife's pallor and thin body. The doctor had warned him to expect a period of acute depression, but Kyla grew weaker with each passing day. "Perhaps Miguel—they were very close, weren't they? But how will you send word? I hear the situation in Mexico is one of chaos."

"I have friends," Maria said vaguely. "There are many ships that call at Mexican ports after stopping here."

Maria would have promised to send a man to the moon, if necessary, in order to escape the grim life at the mission. She returned to Monterey and promised herself she would speak to one of the sea captains who patronized the gambling parlor when the opportunity presented itself. Perhaps someone would know a way to learn where Miguel and his *leperos* were fighting.

When she casually mentioned her desire to get in touch with her brother in Mexico one evening several weeks later, one of her clients told her he would be glad to take a message south and, in fact, knew of a recent arrival in town who had fought in Mexico. Perhaps the man might have some idea how she could get a message to her brother. He would bring the man to the card parlor the following evening. He hoped, however, that the beautiful Maria would not be too impressed by the man's brutish good looks and considerable fortune.

"Fortune?" Maria asked, her eyes lighting up.

"He was the only survivor of a band of raiders that did a whole lot of looting during the early days of the war," the man answered. "He's big and mean, and no man dares question him too closely, but he came into town and immediately started building a fancy American-style house, although it's more ornamental than substantial. They say he's having a fancy carriage shipped from the East and a shipload of furniture. His name is Garett Ramsey, and he was the leader of the Raiders."

Maria considered the situation carefully. Ramsey had not been present when the men forced their way into the farmhouse and raped Kyla and herself. He had apparently escaped before the soldiers charged through the canyon. Maria could not blame him for saving his own skin, although it was inconceivable that he had not attempted to take her with him. He had so obviously been attracted to her. He must have been wounded, she decided, and unable to get back to her in time. It was a rationalization made easy by the knowledge of her own allure. Men had always been willing to fight for her.

When the sea captain brought Garett Ramsey into the gambling rooms the following evening, Maria saw she had been right to give him the benefit of the doubt. Ramsey was expensively dressed, his light blond hair fashionably cut, his boots gleaming. He was tanned, clean-shaven, and his pale gray eyes met hers unhesitatingly in pleased recognition.

"Miss Maria! I couldn't believe it would be the one and only Miss Maria Marques," he said, taking her hand and bending to press his lips to her wrist. "I'm not a gambler by nature and just came tonight to see if it was really you."

"You left me under rather hurried circumstances the last time we were together," Maria said, with an icy edge to her voice despite the smile on her lips. Her large dark eyes gazed accusingly into his.

"I was knocked out and fortunately fell into some brush and was hidden from view. When I came to, everyone had left," he said smoothly, his story well-rehearsed. "But I knew you'd be all right with your own people." He smiled disarmingly.

"Of course. Please, come and sit down and let me order a drink for you," Maria murmured. "Perhaps you would like to take me out to supper later? There is a favor I would like to ask of you." He did not know what his men had done, she thought, and was relieved.

"Anything at all, Miss Maria. It grieves me to see you working in a place like this. I had no idea there was such a den of iniquity in this staid little town." He had heard she could be bought, for the right price. A high-priced whore was exactly what Garett Ramsey was looking for. He was tired of streetwalkers but still found it necessary to pay for a woman's favors.

By the time they had finished their late supper and lingered over liqueurs, they each had the measure of the other.

"The war will end soon. I don't know how you can find out where Miguel is, much less get a message to him, the way things are in Mexico. But I'll get word to him if I can. Still, I hear there may be another battle for Mexico City, so it could take a while."

"Then I shall have to go on working in that hateful place," Maria said tearfully, "and my dear sister will go on starving at the mission." She told him of the loss of the *rancho* and Kyla's stillborn son, allowing him to believe Desmond was the father.

A large hand slid across the table and closed over her slim fingers. "You need a protector," he said, his pale eyes like shards of glass. "Someone strong, and rich."

The fingers squirmed irresistibly under his hand and the dark eyes promised that he would be met more than half-way when the time came to shed the pretense that she was a sheltered virgin and he a bashful suitor.

# 18

"*I am surrounded by cowards and traitors,*" lamented
Antonio Lopez de Santa Anna. "Veracruz should have
been held to the last man, the last bullet, the last drop of
blood."

Instead, the Stars and Stripes fluttered over the city,
and the Americans under Scott were marching northward.
Santa Anna issued a proclamation. "Mexicans! You must
choose between death and slavery. It is better to die a
free man on your feet than to live on your knees as a
slave."

He was organizing a fresh field force to meet Scott.
Thousands of men joined him, inflamed by rumors that the
blaspheming *yanquis* had burned all of the churches in
Veracruz.

"I wish I were going with you, but my flesh festers,"
Miguel said, as the tent flap dropped behind Apolo.

"Miguel, there may be someone who can help you. A
man with the *San Patricios.* I have not met him, but I've
heard that when he is not loading cannon he is treating
their wounded with much success. I will send one of the
*leperos* to find the *San Patricios* and bring the man here."

"Where will the stand against the *gringos* be made?"
Miguel asked, easing himself over on to his side to look
up into Apolo's amber eyes. The dueling scar down his
friend's cheek reminded him disturbingly of the mutilated

185

face of Kyla's husband, and he wished passionately he could be riding out to fight *yanquis* instead of thinking of a lost love.

"The Cerro Gordo Pass. It is a fine defensive position. We will occupy the peaks above the winding highway and make it a *gringo* tomb. I must go. I will try to find the medical officer of the *San Patricios* before I leave. *Vaya con Dios*, Miguel."

Cerro Gordo did not become a *gringo* tomb. A young American officer named Robert E. Lee found a way around the Mexican ambush and almost lost his life doing so. When the red-haired representative of the *San Patricios* stepped into the hospital tent, the Mexican army was in full retreat to Mexico City, although neither of them was aware of it at the time.

"I must apologize for taking you away from the fighting," Miguel began, then he recognized his visitor. "You—"

"Miguel Marques, the Latin lover," Delleroc said softly. "Your Colonel Ramírez ordered me here, and frankly I'd rather be here than taken prisoner with the *San Patricios*. I've an uneasy feeling the end is near and I've no desire to be hanged by the *yanquis*. Now let's forget who we are and what's between us and let me look at that leg."

"The leg and I will rot in hell before you'll touch it. You—defiler—*degenerar*." Miguel's eyes blazed and he clenched his fists as he looked at the man who had awakened passion in Kyla. Had he possessed her? He, and the crippled Englishman, and how many others? And never once had Miguel ever touched her, in all those years when his blood cried out for her. He swung wildly at Delleroc as he bent over Miguel's wounded leg, but Delleroc caught his arm and held it in a viselike grip.

"Why don't you save that until you're able to finish what you start? I take it you have been nurturing this anger since my little masquerade at your sister's wedding." He released Miguel's arm and ripped the filthy bandage from his leg to reveal the infected wound.

"Don't speak her name, you filthy pig," Miguel said

weakly, the exertion of his rage and the throbbing wound causing him to breathe rapidly.

"I'm going to clean the wound. It will hurt like hell, but then it will heal. How is our good friend, Lord Talmage, and his wife? Have you heard?" He was rolling up his sleeves.

Miguel regarded him for a moment and realized that Delleroc did not know what had become of Kyla and Maria. Miguel felt an overwhelming sense of power.

"I expect the child will have been born by now," Miguel said slowly, in English, not flinching as the last of the bandage was torn from his leg.

"A child?" Delleroc was surprised. Miguel saw it in the instant before the veil fell over his eyes.

"It is a pity she does not at least know who the father is," Miguel continued. "But she was raped by many men."

Delleroc froze, the knife held over Miguel's leg. "Mexicans?" he asked in a small tight voice.

"*Gringos! Norteamericanos!*" Miguel shouted triumphantly. He could not stop the cry that rose to his lips as the knife plunged into his festering wound.

Men died. Horribly, bravely, foolishly, gallantly. They died at Contreras and Molino del Rey and Chapultepec where the boy cadets gave their lives for Mexico. They were thirteen, fourteen and fifteen years old; those over sixteen were serving in the regular army.

At Churubusco, seventy-five survivors of the *San Patricio* battalion were captured. Those who had deserted before the outbreak of war, including John Riley, were flogged and branded with the letter "D," for deserter, on the right cheek. Fifty were courtmartialed and ordered hanged. Riley and his comrades were ordered to dig graves for the first twenty men who were executed. The last group of thirty died on the gallows just as the Americans stormed Chapultepec Palace, the last stronghold guarding Mexico City. The legendary Halls of Montezuma were theirs.

All along the roads to Mexico City the villagers bolted their doors, and within the city itself the citizens shivered in fear when, early in December, *Los Diablos Tejanos,* well ahead of the main column of advancing *yanquis,* arrived. The citizens crowded the streets to look at the "Texas Devils," those huge bearded men with their dreaded weapons, riding by on their enormous horses. It was rumored that their "revolvers" could fire a bullet that traveled in circles, following its victim around corners and in all directions.

They rode to the Grand Plaza to await their camp assignments, and the people followed, in fascinated awe, poised for instant flight should *Los Diablos Tejanos'* dreaded yell explode on the air.

An old Mexican carrying a basket of candy, suddenly shrieked that a ranger had taken a handful of his wares and refused to pay. The old man picked up a rock and flung it at the ranger, and the next second there was a roar from the Texan's revolver. The old man was dead before he hit the ground, and the stampede was on. Men trampled each other, some fell into the sewers, everyone fled in panic from *Los Tejanos Sangrientes.*

The hatred grew as the bearded men brawled with the men of the town and made violent love to the women. Then one night a lone Texan was stabbed in the heart. In retaliation, twenty-five Texans swept through the neighborhood and killed fifty Mexicans.

In desperation, General Scott ordered the Rangers out of the city to hunt down the *guerrilleros* who hid in the villages and ravaged American trains bringing men and supplies from Veracruz.

The *guerrilleros* were indomitable fighters whom the pauper youths of the villages worshipped and the señoritas loved. They swaggered through the villages and danced at the fiestas in their handsome velvet jackets, skin-tight trousers slit open at the sides and fastened with gold buttons. Silver bells and spurs jingled as they walked, lassos over their shoulders. Every man, woman and child sheltered them and kept their secrets.

Miguel stayed with them briefly, learning their methods of warfare. Thanks to Delleroc, his leg had healed sufficiently to allow him to ride. But the war was over and

Santa Anna was again going into exile. Delleroc had disappeared in the confusion of the ending of the war and Miguel left the *guerrilleros* of Monterrey to travel back to his home in Baja California. There were other men, peons and soldiers, who would be seeking a leader and there was much to avenge. The Treaty of Guadalupe Hidalgo had ended the war, but not the hatred that burned in his countrymen's hearts.

As he rode northward, Miguel thought of the man who had saved his leg and, possibly, his life. During his visits, ostensibly to clean Miguel's wound, Delleroc had pried more information from Miguel than any priest could have. Miguel had not been aware of this at the time, for he had been interested to hear of the exploits of the *guerrilleros*.

"There is no government left in Mexico," Delleroc told him. "Only the law of the bullet. Your *guerrilleros* are bandits more interested in loot than military reprisal. Still, you'll probably work out of your system a lot of the hatred that is burning in your vitals if you ride with them for a time. Make believe the war still continues. You can be a modern Genghis Kahn. You have all the attributes of a leader."

"Genghis Kahn?" Miguel asked. No matter how he vowed to ignore Delleroc, the man always aroused his interest.

"A leader of barbarian hordes, who once said that war was the one occupation in which a man could rid himself of all diplomacy and compassion and fight with the uninhibited fury of his violent nature. You, my young friend, should consider directing your fury toward the rebuilding of your country."

"From what I've heard, you fought well yourself. But you are flawed, Delleroc. You feel you must do penance for killing by trying to undo what you have done. That is why you tend broken bodies."

"Possibly. But you forget, I did not have a country threatened by invaders to use as justification for my bloodletting."

"Will you come with me and join the *guerrilleros*?" Miguel was astonished that he asked the question. The words sprang to his lips as though placed there by someone else.

Delleroc's green eyes looked away to some distant place above Miguel's head and he replied, "No. This time even I have had enough of war and bloodshed. My fury is spent."

Quint Delleroc looked at the handsome young Mexican, with his fine, aristocratic features and proud carriage, and wondered silently what would happen to Miguel in the aftermath of war. Quint had been present at the ending of other wars and it had been his experience that the uneasy peace that came to the vanquished often brought hardships less easy to bear than battle.

Did he feel pity for the young Mexican? Quint asked himself in surprise. Something had been slowly happening to Quint Delleroc, some metamorphosis. When it had begun he was not sure, but it became evident sometime after his arrival in the New World. He was troubled by vague stirrings deep in his consciousness that were new and disturbing. Often of late he had dreamed of Kyla, and then of a small ragged boy crawling through the dusty debris of a ravaged city. He was not sure whether the image was that of Kyla's child, born out of savagery, or of his own bleak boyhood.

In his waking hours he sometimes remembered Kyla to the exclusion of all other women in his life, thinking of the smooth flesh which yielded so softly beneath his hand, the hair that smelled as sweet as summer rain upon a meadow—the pure and shy love she had offered him. It took all of his powers of concentration to obliterate the memories that came to haunt him.

Miguel rode northward, his anger growing at the plight of his people. They had been poor before, now the invaders had destroyed towns and villages, ravaged crops, filled the countryside with homeless widows and orphans. A band of *guerrerillos* could be organized in the vicinty of the Marques *hacienda*, to strike into California, which was now part of the United States.

Miraculously, his own lower California, the peninsula

of Baja California, was still Mexican. Damn their treaty of Guadalupe Hidalgo! The war was far from over for Miguel Marques.

*In the same month that the treaty of Guadalupe Hidalgo was signed, forty miles up the American River from Sutter's Fort, James Marshall stopped near the millwheel of the newly-built sawmill, his eye caught by the gleam of sunlight on yellow metal.*

*The night before he had turned the water from the mill-pond into the tailrace, so that the channel would be washed free of debris and loose dirt. Now he bent to pick up the yellow nugget and saw there other flashes of yellow metal scattered about in the clear water.*

*Holding it in his hand, heart thumping, he automatically told himself, "Fool's gold," but nevertheless he reached for a rock to pound the yellow metal. Fool's gold would shatter as it was brittle; real gold, being soft, flattens easily.*

*Four days later his employer, John Sutter, looked up as James Marshall burst into his office, wildly excited and soaking wet.*

*"There is more gold in the country drained by the Sacramento and San Joaquin Rivers than would pay the cost of the late war with Mexico a hundred times over."*

*So announced the War Department after receiving a letter from Gov. Richard Barnes Mason confirming the discovery of gold at Sutter's Fort in the newly acquired California territory.*

*It was official.*

*Along the eastern seaboard, Americans were held in the grip of a financial depression. Business had fallen away alarmingly, farms and houses were heavily mortgaged, and there were no jobs or opportunities for young men, not even the victorious veterans of the recently ended Mexican war.*

*The westward rush was on!*

# BOOK TWO

# 19

*The Indian children, who had been gathering berries, ran* to hide behind Kyla's skirts as the rider came over the crest of the hill. She raised her hand to shield her eyes from the sun, but could not see the man's face. From his lean build, she was glad to see it was not Garett Ramsey, coming to dispense his largess at the mission to ease Maria's conscience.

Kyla pushed her cornsilk hair back from her forehead and squinted at the silhouetted rider. She had long ago stopped protecting her complexion from the sun, and she was almost as tanned as the children who clung to her skirts.

If it was not Garett Ramsey, Kyla did not particularly care who was riding toward the mission. Ramsey always filled her with revulsion as did the large black beetles that sometimes invaded the mission. Ever since Ramsey had become Maria's protector, he had been trying to act as a respectable citizen of Monterey, apparently unaware that gifts to local churches and missions did not alter the fact that everyone else considered he was living in sin with Maria.

Desmond accepted Ramsey's gifts gratefully and, as usual, would hear ill spoken of no one, not even the man who had left his wife to her brutal fate. Like Maria,

194

Desmond accepted Ramsey's story of having been unconscious while his men assaulted the two women.

Kyla's scars were buried deeper now, and she could laugh with the children and brush a tear from her eye as she read Desmond's books. She could even bristle with indignation when the travelers who stopped at the mission brought stories of vigilante justice and harsh prejudice meted out to the burgeoning numbers of new Californians.

They came in droves, all seeking gold. The sleepy village on the bay of St. Francis was growing by leaps and bounds, while the harbor was jammed with abandoned vessels as crews followed passengers to the gold fields. Every day more citizens departed from Monterey to travel north to seek their fortunes. It appeared that the once thriving capital city of the California territory might soon be a ghost town. Ramsey remained in the gingerbread-fancy wooden house he had built, passing off his Mexican mistress as a housekeeper.

At the small mission two days' ride south of Monterey, there had been few changes. Nana had died and was buried beside the tiny grave of Kyla's child. Sometimes as she knelt beside the two graves she felt a gnawing sense of loss as her hands touched the empty place where she had carried her baby. During the early days of her pregnancy, when nausea and fatigue had held her in their grip, there had been times she had prayed to be released from the burden of motherhood. Yet as the new life had quickened within her a great peace had descended. The child was, after all, as much hers as the unknown father's creation.

When Kyla went into labor, the intensity of the pain had brought back the memory of the night the child was conceived and, coupled with her weakened state of health, had caused her to shrink from delivering the child. Paradoxically, after Desmond had shown her the pathetically small mound and tiny cross in the graveyard, she had flung herself down upon the sweet-smelling earth and wept with a grief more poignant than any she had ever known. She had wished the child dead and now she was paying for that wickedness. Kyla did not confide these thoughts to Desmond.

Since the secularization of the missions, most were left without the Franciscan *padres*, some passing into private hands and others crumbling to ruin. The Indians had welcomed Desmond in place of the *padre* they had lost years before.

Kyla cared for their children and the sick, submerged her own needs and desires and felt vaguely it was a form of penance. Occasionally she did rebel against the harshness of her life; but her rebellion was short-lived and quickly overwhelmed by her feelings of guilt.

The rider was dismounting, leading his horse toward her, and he pulled his hat from his head. Instantly the sun blazed down on the red hair and caught the fierce features in sharp shadows.

Kyla stood still, aware of the pulse that throbbed in her throat, feeling the warmth of the sun, the cool softness of the grass beneath her feet. Small hands clutched her skirts tightly, and a jackrabbit suddenly bounded across the trail in front of them.

"*Buenas dias*, Doña Talmage," Quint Delleroc said, making a sweeping bow. When he raised his head he was smiling. He tied his horse to the nearest tree and came forward to take her hands in his, green eyes absorbing every detail of her face and faded calico dress.

She wanted to pull her work-roughened hands from his grip, acutely aware of calluses and broken fingernails, but she held her head high and managed a composed smile. Her heart had begun to pound in slow, painful beats.

"I'm glad you are alive and well, Quint. Children, this is Señor Delleroc. Please greet him."

"*Buenas dias, señor*," the children chorused dutifully and six pairs of dark eyes were fixed on the bright copper hair.

Quint glanced from one child to the other, noting that the youngest was at least five years old. "Your own child is not with you?" he asked.

Kyla caught her breath. "Children, take the berries to the kitchen. Run along, we shall be there in a moment."

When their bare feet danced away and the sound of their laughter faded she looked up at Quint and said quietly, "My son was stillborn. I assume you have not been to Monterey, or you would have known that."

"I'm sorry about your child." His fingers squeezed hers. "No. I haven't been to Monterey. I went first to the de Rivero *rancho* and found new owners, *yanquis,* I was surprised to discover. They told me some of your belongings and Desmond's books had been sent to this mission. Knowing old Des's propensity for the spartan life of the monastery, I assumed he would still be here."

"We thought you were dead." Kyla disengaged her hands and began to walk toward the mission. "Desmond will be glad to see you. You can leave your horse there if you wish and we'll send a boy back for it."

"Ah, Kyla. Must you hurry us to your husband? I would have thought after all of this time you could spare me a moment without a chaperone, after all we were to each other." His eyes were filled with teasing golden glints.

Kyla's smile froze. He was still the old Delleroc. She quickened her pace as his long strides caught up with her. He would find, she told herself silently, that the impressionable young bride was now a woman, a woman who knew how to conceal her emotions and who would fight to suppress the longing that swept through her at his nearness. "As you can plainly see," she said shortly, "my days of being a chaperoned señorita are long behind me."

She was aware of the masculine power of his movements beside her. The Indians who came to the mission were usually old or sick. Able-bodied men stayed only briefly, on their way to the gold fields.

Walking beside her, Quint was experiencing new and bewildering emotions. He wanted to sweep her into his arms, tell her he would make everything right again. His heart bled for her loss, for her poverty. He fought the urge to hold her and comfort her and did not know why he fought it. The old Quint would have seized her and kissed her with never a second thought.

He had thought of this moment so many times and had imagined what would happen. He had even postponed it for the maximum pleasure of anticipating it. And he had never deluded himself that it was Desmond he wanted to see. He had even looked forward to meeting her child—a shy little boy, perhaps? Or a delicate little girl with big blue eyes and soft golden hair?

Now he walked beside her like a tongue-tied boy and, worse, he was in turmoil because of a feeling of panic. Why? It wasn't the obstacles—Desmond, Miguel, even Kyla herself perhaps, with her new air of reserve and guarded glances. No, obstacles were there only to be overcome; to make the final victory more worthwhile.

I'm not ready, he thought. My old ways are too much a part of me. I would be vulnerable. I'm incapable of reforming, of ever settling down. What the hell am I doing here? She's lovelier than ever, standing there in the sunlight when I first saw her, she was a madonna surrounded by little bronze-skinned cherubs. Is this tenderness, this longing that transcends lust. . . ? This unbearable urge to protect and cherish. . . ? No! A misconception, that's all.

They were at the top of the rise and remains of the mission were in sight. A chapel without a bell tower and a patched and propped addition that served as living quarters. She saw the crumbling adobe through his eyes and was ashamed of their poverty. The old Indian, whom Desmond had nicknamed Tut because of his regal bearing, was hoeing the furrowed rows of vegetables.

"You can't see them from here, but we planted fruit trees and grape vines on the other side of the patio," Kyla said defensively.

"You should get a good price for fruit in the gold towns and ports."

"Oh, we don't sell it. Look, there's Desmond. Put on your hat quickly so he won't recognize you. He'll be so surprised."

Desmond was shuffling toward Tut, calling for the old

man to leave the hoeing and cut the last of the summer's crop of maize. He looked up and saw his wife coming down the hillside with a man at her side, and Desmond sighed. Another wayfarer to feed, and there was barely enough for their own people.

Kyla had never asked him what became of the money from the sale of their *rancho* stock and possessions. There had been moments when he regretted the hasty arrangements he made with the doctor who delivered her child, but at the time a speedy solution had seemed imperative. Desmond had traveled to Monterey to seek out Dr. Clement several months after the birth, only to find the doctor no longer practiced there. Some thought he had gone to the village of Yerba Buena. Desmond had returned to the mission. It was too far to travel to the village on the bay on his limited resources.

He picked up the hoe left by Tut and leaned against it. His withered leg kept him in constant pain, and there were disturbing signs that his mutilated flesh was undergoing further deterioration. He looked again at the approaching traveler and recognized the alert bearing of the head and the feline movement.

Oh, God, must you send him to me again? Desmond asked silently. I haven't the strength to resist when Delleroc pulls the strings. He dropped the hoe and began to limp toward his friend.

Maria had no illusions about the reason Garett Ramsey offered to make her an honest woman, nor did she imagine he had changed his opinion as to the inferiority of skins that were not Northern-European white. She had made love to him with the fiery abandon she had quickly learned reaped the highest rewards among her gambling clients. And he had soon suggested she leave Felice's employ. Maria was shrewd enough to insist upon an adequate settlement in advance, just in case he tired of her. Then she moved into his flimsy wooden house.

For a time, the small population of Monterey had dwindled even further, as men dropped everything to rush to the gold fields. California reeled under

the onslaught of the Gold Rush. Then the merchants and
saloonkeepers, hotelmen and gamblers began to arrive.
Crude trails were beaten into stagecoach paths, and
financiers, bankers, lawyers and entertainers arrived from
the East. Garett Ramsey invested in mining shares, in
saloons and hotels throughout the burgeoning territory
and grew richer day by day.

The old system of an *alcalde* under Mexican rule was
replaced by the town justice of the peace, and Ramsey
knew that statehood for the rich land of California was
inevitable. He saw himself traveling back East to his
estranged family, as a representative of the richest state
in the Union.

Maria had begun to hint that as respectable families
returned to Monterey, she and Ramsey would surely be
ostracized because of their living arrangement. Increasingly, she returned to her former haunts at Felice's gambling parlor to chat with the girls and the melancholy
Merciful Smith, telling Ramsey that she was preparing for
the day when she must return to work there.

Had there been any other suitable women to court,
Ramsey would have done so. But men poured in from all
parts of the world, without women. There was nothing
else for it. He would have to make Maria his wife, in the
interest of keeping her as much for respectability sake
for his future political plans.

He put his foot down, refusing to invite Felice and the
girls to the wedding, and Maria would not hear of inviting
the crippled Lord Talmage, fearing his appearance would
horrify the other guests. Ramsey rode to the mission and
made a handsome donation and explained they had been
quietly married the previous month. He knew he might as
well get in the habit of making friends and securing future
votes.

The wedding was a disaster. None of the few respectable women or their husbands appeared, and Maria
stormed out of the house, leaving behind the musicians
and entertainers, a table groaning under the weight of
food and drink and an array of baffled servants. But the
marriage was conducted quietly, and later Ramsey's pale

eyes darted about at the wasted food and drooping bunting festooning the dining room. After the justice of the peace departed, Ramsey made an announcement.

"We're going to live in San Francisco. The hell with Monterey. It's a ghost town anyway. San Francisco is growing faster. More opportunity for a man to amount to something there."

Maria shrugged. It was immaterial to her. As far as she was concerned, their relationship had not really changed. How could they be married when there had been no priest?

"I'll go on ahead and find a place to live. I'll send for you later," Ramsey said. "You can stay here and supervise the packing. I don't suppose any of these old-fashioned citizens will want to buy an American-style house, so we'll just close it. Maybe we'll want to come back some day, when more settlers arrive."

He had been gone for two weeks, and Maria was packed and bored when she decided to visit Felice. Dressing in her newest satin dress, she had her maid lace her corset tightly. Maria saturated a handkerchief in lavender water imported from England at five dollars a bottle, and thrust the sweet-smelling lace between her breasts. Her wavy dark hair was brushed until it gleamed, and was fastened with a tortoise-shell comb.

She enjoyed the stir she created when Merciful Smith held the door open for her to sweep into the smoke-filled redness of the gambling rooms. She had always enjoyed the sense of competition with the other girls, as well as the admiration of the men and excitement of the cards. Felice's booming laugh rang out and that amazon was moving toward her with arms outstretched.

"My little Maria! How come you didn't invite us to your wedding?" she bellowed indignantly, but nevertheless enfolded Maria in a bear-hug to her expansive bosom.

But Maria's eyes had already found the most exciting man in the room. He sat near the bar, long thickly muscled legs stretched out in front of him and a large glass of brandy in his hand. He wore an embroidered velvet waistcoat over a fine linen shirt and surveyed the crowded tables with satisfaction.

"Delleroc!" Maria breathed, struggling to free herself from Felice's smothering embrace.

"Yes, he's back. Here, wait a minute. What did you wear for your wedding?" Felice boomed, but Maria was already moving swiftly and gracefully through the tables toward the bar.

Delleroc arose and greeted her like a gentleman, but the primitive appraisal of his glance angered her. How dare he believe she was just one of the card-dealing hostesses? The desire to bring this arrogant devil to his knees was almost overpowering. Maria gave him her most dazzling smile and extended her hand for his kiss.

"Señor Delleroc, how nice to see you again. I made the acquaintance of Felice through your servant, Shansi," she began.

"Shansi is my mistress, just as you were Garett Ramsey's, and I already know of your brief but profitable career here. Will you join me for a drink?"

Maria's smile froze but she accepted the chair he held for her.

"And I understand congratulations are in order? That you became Mrs. Ramsey recently?"

"One congratulates the husband, señor. Not the wife," Maria said frostily. "If you are going to speak in the ill-bred manner of the *gringo*, I shall leave. I merely stopped at your table to give you news of your friend Lord Talmage."

"Most kind of you. However, I stopped at the mission on my way here. Tell me, where is the bridegroom?"

"We are shortly moving to San Francisco. Garett is finding a house there. He is away at present." She emphasized the last words with a provocative smile and before he could speak added quickly, "Perhaps we could dine together and you can tell me all about the health of my dear sister and her husband?"

"Excellent idea. How about tomorrow night, at my house?" He was smiling conspiratorially.

"Oh, no. I think it would be better for you to come to my house. After dark."

"Naturally." His face was a study of dark discretion, but there were disturbing golden glints in the depths of his eyes.

She cast about for something to add and then, uncertainly, stood up and excused herself. Felice was laughing heartily in a corner with a fellow merchant, and everyone else was involved with cards or backgammon. Maria went reluctantly through the door and was startled to find Merciful Smith busy with a cadaver on the table in the anteroom.

"Leaving so soon, Miss Maria?" he croaked mournfully, waving his long black cigar to brush a fluttering moth from the deceased's nose.

*"Madre de Dios!"* Maria muttered. She hurried to the door and flounced through it so quickly she almost collided with a shadowy figure outside.

"Why, Maria," a young male voice said, "if I'd known you were back at Felice's I'd have been around to see you."

She looked up at the first client of her career. Garett had been gone for many nights, and she was tired of her lonely bed. Besides, Garett had been a disappointment when it came to lovemaking. It had always been hurried and furtive, and she had to coax him. There was no reason to suppose a wedding ring would change things. Not only that, but seeing Delleroc again had aroused her blood.

"Why, señor, how very pleasant to see you again. Just when I need a protector to escort me home."

They traveled by way of the darkest streets and entered Ramsey's house through the back door.

The young man glanced about at the opulence of the furnishings only briefly, then, with an exultant whoop, swept Maria up into his arms and ran up the stairs with her. She was laughing, a low and husky sound that was muffled against the linen of his shirt. Before they reached the upper floor, her fingers had unbuttoned his shirt and freed her own breasts from her bodice so that the soft flesh pressed against him.

"Which room?" he asked breathlessly at the top of the stairs.

She raised her arm and pointed, completing the airy sweep of her hand by pulling the comb from her luxurious mass of hair.

Inside her room they collapsed on the bed, laughing and panting, their clothes awry and Maria's hair a smothering cloud. She reached for him eagerly and he protested that she was too impetuous; they were not in a hurry, were they? Didn't they have all night?

But Maria *was* in a hurry. She wanted a man inside her to quench the throbbing fire that Garett Ramsey was never quite able to extinguish. She tore at the stubborn trouser buttons and by the time she had succeeded in her objective, the young man was as ready as she for quick release. She wrapped her legs around his back as he moved slowly into her, gripping him in the double embrace of legs and arms and her fingernails cut into his flesh as they moved together.

Maria rotated her hips wildly and chided him for not thrusting harder and he laughed and throbbed inside her, pressing deeply, faster and faster until she moaned and gasped and tried to swallow all of him into the sweet hot abyss that suddenly exploded in a torrent of molten fulfillment.

They lay still for a moment, still locked together, until Maria pushed him away impatiently. He rolled over on the bed and grinned at her.

"Now," Maria said, standing up to kick aside the remnant of her petticoat that clung damply to one leg. "Now, we make love." She looked down at him and smiled, running her little pink tongue over her lip and bending over him flirtatiously so that her hair brushed his chest and hard little nipples touched his thighs.

Several hours passed before she pushed him unceremoniously through her back door.

It was to that same back door that Maria went excitedly in response to a gentle tapping just after dark the following evening. She pinched her cheeks and moistened her lips with her tongue before flinging open the door to admit Delleroc.

"Good evening, Maria," he said with a deep bow, and stepped aside to allow Kyla and Lord Talmage to precede him into the house.

Maria heard herself mumbling a greeting as Quint Delleroc said, "Your dear sister and her husband were delighted to accept your kind invitation to dinner, as you can see."

"Maria, I was going to call on you today," Kyla was saying. "We only arrived yesterday afternoon. But Quint said to wait until tonight."

"Yes, of course," Maria said faintly, thinking of the table set for two, with its single candle, and of the lavender water sprinkled liberally over her bedsheets.

"As you probably learned from Quint," Desmond was saying, "we are on our way to San Francisco."

"I left that news for you to give to Mrs. Ramsey," Quint said smoothly. "I knew how excited you would all be to learn you are going to be neighbors."

"San Francisco. Neighbors," Maria repeated stupidly. She led them to the drawing room, hoping the table setting in the adjacent dining room was not visible through the half-open door. She rang the bell for the Indian maid, and the girl was given instructions to bring wine, an order punctuated by her mistress's frantic glances in the direction of the dining room.

"I've been having a bit of trouble with my leg," Desmond said apologetically, "and Quint says there may be a doctor there who can help me. I had no idea how much San Francisco has grown in the last two years." He wondered privately at his need to justify their journey to Maria, or anyone else, and closed his mind to the memory of the revelation that had really brought about the decision to accompany Quint to San Francisco.

Maria's maid returned with the wine, and Maria let out an almost audible breath of relief as she saw the cook slip unobtrusively into the dining room with additional dishes and silverware. Then she caught Quint's dangerously playful look, a look closely akin to the cat eyeing the mouse.

Maria dug her long fingernails into the arms of her chair, and wished it were Delleroc's flesh.

The meal stretched as it was by the addition of rice and beans, was poor but illuminating. Delleroc was moving his funeral parlor and gambling operations to the booming town of San Francisco. There were just not enough people left in Monterey to justify remaining. Like the Ramseys, Delleroc would have to simply close his house due to the lack of purchasers.

Delleroc had made a trip back to the East Coast, filled a clipper ship with cargo and sailed back, disembarking in San Pedro in order to call on Desmond at the *rancho*.

The ship had arrived in San Francisco and was promptly abandoned by the crew. There were no men to unload his cargo and the last he heard, the ship was still lying in the congested waters of the bay. But no matter. He would simply wait until the outward spreading shoreline covered the tidal flats and the ship was beached. It would then join the jerrybuilt banks and brokerage houses interspersed with other hulks that now comprised Montgomery Street. In a town busy dumping sand, dirt and unsalable goods into the bay—to create the more valuable commodity real estate—this would not take long.

The ship would then be his store. Meantime, Felice and Merciful Smith could keep the wolf from the door.

"I'm surprised you haven't considered going to the gold fields yourself, Quint," Kyla remarked. "I thought every man on earth except Desmond had gold fever."

"And my Garett," Maria put in quickly. "He is so rich he has no need. Other men will pan his gold. Did I tell you he has bought into several mining companies?"

"I avoid hard labor like the plague," Quint said. "Especially when there's no guarantee of riches. Unfortunately most of the erstwhile argonauts will go home empty-handed, or stay to become farmers. Even those who find gold in sufficient quantity to make them rich will fall prey to the hordes of rogues who are arriving with the express purpose of parting the miner from his precious dust."

"Like yourself," Maria put in triumphantly.

"Exactly."

They were so engrossed that no one noticed the front door open and the owner of the house step inside. He stamped the mud from his boots and strode in the direction of the sound of voices and laughter, stopping in his tracks as he saw Delleroc.

"Garett!" Maria cried, startled. She leaped to her feet to run to her husband and as she stood on tiptoe to kiss his cheek, she felt a chilling horror at the thought that he might have come home and found her in bed with Delleroc. "I didn't think you would be coming back. You said you would send for me."

"Welcome to my house, Lord and Lady Talmage," Ramsey said. "I see you managed to avoid being hanged with the *San Patricios* deserters, Delleroc."

Ramsey stood staring at Delleroc, the muscles of his jaw twitching slightly. It was incredible, but the man had somehow survived both yellow jack and the Mexican desert. A slight shiver passed up Ramsey's spine, as though he were dealing with the supernatural.

"Since I was never in the U.S. Army, I could hardly desert from it," Delleroc said, carelessly spearing a peach with his knife. His eyes looked over Ramsey as though Ramsey were an insect crawling out of a rotten log; the glance implied distaste, but of insufficient depth to warrant any action.

Ramsey flushed, wanting to smash that hated face with his fists, yet held back by a nameless fear.

"I understand you were something of a free-lance yourself during the war, despite the circumstances of our last meeting," Delleroc added. "At that time I didn't know of all of the exploits of your fearless and intrepid raiders." He was peeling the peach slowly, deliberately. Ramsey stared, fascinated, as the knife encircled the soft flesh, almost feeling his own skin fall away from his body.

"I was not with them at the end, you know," Ramsey said, running his tongue nervously over his lower lip.

Desmond glanced at Kyla, who had grown pale since Ramsey's arrival, her eyes wide and frightened. "Gentlemen," Desmond said quickly, "the war is over. Can we not forget past differences? What purpose will be served to upset the ladies?"

"Of course," Ramsey said, slipping his arm about Maria's waist to lead her back to the dining table. "I owe you a debt of gratitude, Desmond, and accepting your friend Delleroc into my house is certainly the least I can do to repay you."

"How very civilized of you," Quint murmured. "But never fear, I'm on my way. I've suddenly lost my appetite."

"If you will forgive us, Maria," Desmond said, "Kyla is not feeling very well." He looked beseechingly into Quint's cold green stare and sent the silent message that Kyla and Maria had been raised as sisters, and Maria *was* married to Ramsey.

Quint read the imploring glance and understood. Ramsey was not important enough to widen the existing rift between Desmond and himself, Quint thought. He remembered with some remorse what he had put Desmond through in order to pry him from his adobe hovel and starving Indians.

They withdrew graciously, to Ramsey's obvious relief. During the short journey back to his house, Quint wondered moodily if he would have been quite so accommodating if he and Desmond had not recently quarreled bitterly over Kyla.

# 20

*Quint Delleroc's anger had been terrible to see. On the* day he had arrived at the mission he had maintained the mask of polite greeting until Kyla retired for the night. And then he dragged Desmond outside and forced him to march into the darkness, putting distance between the sound of their voices and the sleeping mission.

Desmond stood silently, his sad eyes fixed unblinkingly upon the place in the darkness where Quint thrashed about in the autumn-dry chaparral, kicking at rocks, slapping his fist against his palm and growling like an angry tiger.

"You meekly walked away from it all. You stupid, cowardly, weak bastard, you let them come and tell you it isn't yours because you're not a Spanish blueblood and simply walked away and left it. I can't believe it. Good God, man, possession is nine-tenths of the law! You were there, you were in possession. To hell with their land grants. You should have armed your peons, recruited Apaches, told the Americans to go to hell."

"I abhor violence, Quint, you know that, and possessions are meaningless to me," Desmond said quietly. "I simply did not care enough to try to retain the *rancho.* If I had, I would have used peaceful and legal means to fight for it."

"And what about Kyla? She was born to it, even if you

were not. Did you ever really find out whether she wanted to give up her inheritance?"

"I felt, under the tragic circumstances, she also would be happier hidden away from the world, sharing the peace and solitude of the mission."

There was a long pause, and then a slowly drawn breath of realization and Quint's hands were on Desmond's shoulders, heedless of the pathetic stump of bone and the sleeve that flapped loose from the belt of the monk's robes he had taken to wearing.

"Goddamn you to hell. You hid her away from the world because she was raped and pregnant from it. You hid *her*! As though she were the perpetrator instead of the victim. Don't you see, don't you understand? She isn't a fallen woman, she's a tortured victim in exactly the same way you were a tortured victim of the Khyber tribesmen. You believe that those filthy swine who raped her had, as the Bible so charmingly puts it, 'carnal knowledge' of her? That it was sex? Hell, it wasn't sex, it was an act of violence, brutal torture as bad as any you suffered. Only her scars don't show like yours. You bloody hypocrite, you punish her by hiding her away from the world. Why didn't you just have her stoned to death in the marketplace? Isn't that the prescribed treatment for fallen women in your gentle religion?"

He released his hold on the frail shoulders and Desmond staggered backward in stunned silence.

"All right. Let's have a few facts," Quint said, breathing heavily. "There were furnishings, silver and gold dishes and ornaments in the *casa grande*. There must have been a thousand head of cattle and horses. What happened to all of the stock?"

"Most of it was sold to neighboring *ranchos*," Desmond answered dully, trying to ignore the pain in his leg. Ridiculously, he wanted to point out that Quint had confused the Old and New Testaments of the Bible.

"That should have realized a considerable amount of money. Surely enough to provide a better home and way of life than a miserable hovel in the middle of nowhere."

"I gave most of it to the doctor who delivered the

child." Too late, Desmond realized he should not have begun what he would now have to finish. Within minutes Quint had the whole story.

"He promised to pay someone to take the child East and try to get medical attention for the clubfeet. I knew it would take a great deal of money. Quint, don't you see, I had to give him all we had to be sure the child was cared for."

"You never heard from this Dr. Clement again?"

"No. He had only been in Monterey a short time. He was a ship's surgeon before settling there. I couldn't get anyone else to make the long ride out to the mission, and I didn't want to leave Kyla to an Indian midwife. When I went to Monterey later to ask what arrangements the doctor had made, he was gone."

"We'll find him. But first you're going to do what should have been done before. You're going to take Kyla back to the world of the living. We'll take her to San Francisco. I've some goods on a ship there and was going there myself anyway. That town is exploding with life, and I fancy the idea of making a fortune there. We'll get you a house, new clothes for Kyla, entertain, with parties and fandangos. She needs to feel worthy again, beautiful, loved. Confound it, Des, I didn't think I'd need to tell you this with your insight."

"I'm filled with shame that you do," Desmond said heavily. "I didn't see what you have seen, perhaps because Maria put the experience behind her."

"Maria will never be able to put the experience behind her," Quint said quietly. "She has been scarred even more deeply than Kyla."

The patrol returning to the fort had been much larger than Miguel expected and now he and his men rode for their lives, the guns of the pursuing soldiers stabbing the night. Hooves crashed through the underbrush as the riders raced across the plain toward the sanctuary of the hills, outlined against the last glow of the sunset.

One of the men riding beside Miguel threw up his arms, then slipped to the ground, as his frightened horse plunged on. Miguel turned his mount, leaned precariously close to the ground and picked up the dismounted rider. The wounded man swung up beside him and the horse labored to climb the rise and catch up with the others.

"Señor! This way!" A voice called in Spanish from the shadow of a thicket of smoke trees.

Miguel snapped the reins and the horse leaped in the direction of the voice. The man was on foot, and as they drew near, he said, "Dismount, let the horse go."

The stranger slapped the rump of the horse to send it on its way as Miguel and his passenger leaped to the ground. Then the three stumbled into the center of a boulder formation.

"We can get into a small canyon this way. Horses cannot follow," the man said and led them to what appeared to be a solid rock but which revealed a narrow crawlspace near its base. He went first and pulled the wounded man through as Miguel pushed from the other side. A moment later they were in a narrow canyon and were approaching a silent circle of men waiting about the smothered remains of a campfire.

"*Caramba!* Let us hope your men lead the *gringos* high into the hills and do not double back this way," the man said. "We barely had time to douse the fire. Who are you, *amigo?*"

"Miguel Marques. I am most grateful to you, señor."

The moon slid out from behind the hill and Miguel looked at the man who stood, proud as a king, a red sash wound turbanlike around his long black hair, his pale fair skin setting off flashing black eyes.

"I am Joaquin." The man said the name with fierce pride. "You have the honor to meet the man who will personally avenge many of the wrongs committed against our people by the *gringo*. Come, sit down and we will talk. It sounds as though your men have led the patrol in the other direction. My men will care for this one with the *yanqui* bullet in him."

"*Gracias,* Joaquin. If you have something to ward off the night chill?"

They settled down near the dampened campfire and

huddled under serapes as one of Joaquin's men handed him a bottle.

"No tequila. Only *yanqui* whiskey. I regret it is the best I can offer. Tell me, *amigo,* why do you attack the patrols from the fort? You are a foolish man. The war is over, what can you accomplish by fighting their soldiers, who are so many and you are so few? You ride like a *Californio.* Why waste your skills in picking off a few *gringo* soldiers? Their wagon trains of immigrants pour into California and they have taken much land, built rich *ranchos.* In the north they build gold towns. Miguel Marques, you should strike the *gringo* where it hurts him most, in his pocketbook. Steal from them and help our poor. This way you will be assured our own people will always be on your side and there will be many places for your men to hide. Why not ride with me, Miguel Marques? I can use a man who rides with the skill of the *Californio.*"

"Joaquin, are you Murrieta? The same Joaquin Murrieta that I heard about in the pueblo?"

"From the note of disapproval I hear in your voice, *amigo,* I would say the stories you have heard came from the *gringos.* Let me tell you something, once I admired the *norteamericanos* greatly. I met many of them in my own country and truly believed they hated all forms of tyranny as much as I. I came to California to be free of the constant insurrections of Mexico and wanted to end my days as an American citizen. I lived near Stockton. But I and my family were constantly insulted and harassed by our neighbors. They even drove me from my mining claim. When I went into business I was cheated by everyone I trusted. But the real horror was yet to be. My brother was hanged because some men believed he had stolen a horse. He had not. And then—" Joaquin paused, his voice heavy with grief.

"Five miners came to my cabin to drive me away. I was beaten insensible. When I came to, my beautiful Rosita, my wife, ah, *díos!* She was dying. She had been beaten and violated. That was how it began. Those five bodies were left for the coyotes and buzzards. I carved my initial in their foreheads. The *gringo* will pay, *amigo,* and go on paying as long as Joaquin Murrieta has breath in his body. What do you say, will you ride with me?"

"We are *guerrilleros,* not *bandidos,*" Miguel said. "I sympathize with you as I, too, had someone close who was brutalized by *gringos.* But our goals and methods are different."

"And your *guerrilleros,* do they not leave behind starving families? You take only enough to feed your men, is it not true? They will ride for you until they can no longer bear to think of those they left to starve. Have a purpose for your anger. Take from the wealthy *gringo* to feed our poor."

"Perhaps it will come to that. But I cannot follow. I must lead," Miguel said cautiously.

"Then it will be necessary for us to divide the territory. I cannot risk your men blundering into our encampments and leading soldiers to us. We will remain here in Southern California and you will ride north."

"Agreed. As soon as I find my horse and my friends. I have an *Indio* friend who will guide the men back to me as soon as it is daylight."

"I saw your *Indio,* and your fine white stallion and the silver trappings on your saddle. You make a mistake with all of them. Learn to disguise yourself. Never ride the same horse or wear the same clothes, or even travel with the same companions. These are the snares they will use to trap you."

There was much to be learned from the man who called himself Joaquin Murrieta. Fortunately for Miguel's impression of the encounter with the man who would become the Mexican Robin Hood, his sinister henchman, Three-Fingered Jack, was not present that night. Miguel did not, therefore, have to hear in blood-curdling detail the ways some of the *gringos* died at the hands of a man whose only pleasure in life was shedding blood. Even Murrieta himself was sickened by Jack's exploits.

# 21

*Where once had been the potato patch of Yerba Buena* now stood Portsmouth Square—the hub of a lusty whirl of life in a brawling infant of a city growing at a dizzying rate. Around the square, on Washington, Kearny, Dupont and Clay Streets, stood hotels, restaurants, plush saloons and gambling halls. Well-dressed citizens moved about town impervious to muddy streets and the occasional presence of an itinerant mule or donkey strolling the thoroughfare.

They had stayed at a hotel on Quintero Street, which Delleroc modestly claimed had been named for him.

"Did they really name the street for you?" Kyla asked, feeling a surge of excitement as she was surrounded by the promise of vitality.

"Of course. They were impressed by the fact that I am the son of the last of the Conquistadors and an Aztec princess."

"Don't you know by now, Kyla, that Quint will say anything for effect? To him truth is relative. He is teasing," Desmond said.

"No, I'm not," Quint said indignantly. "I never tease beautiful women who are wearing lovely gold and blue ballgowns." His bantering air and constant teasing were to reassure *her,* he told himself, despite the fact that he had to repeat to himself frequently that Quint Delleroc had never let a woman get under his skin. There were moments, usually in the stillness just before dawn, when he felt an unsettling sense of osmosis and when the bewildering longings came to plague him. He had to rationalize it because somewhere in the bloodbath of the Mexican war he had at last felt his first twinge of feeling for his fellow humans. Resuming his teasing of Kyla, he said, "Tell me, how do you make the skirts stand out like that? Did you know that when you move there is a tantalizing glimpse of lace around your ankles?" He thought, keep it light, superficial. The old ways are less taxing.

Kyla bit her lip to stop herself from giggling. The dress did feel almost sinfully luxurious against her skin, and she was looking forward to another fine dinner and a visit to the theater later. She knew that Desmond did not like to be seen in public, but he insisted that this was not so and they must taste all of San Francisco's dazzling night life. When Kyla protested that they could not afford this extravagant manner, Desmond told her that he had gone into business with Quint and not to worry about money. In the heady excitement of her new life it was easy to forget everything. There was simply no time for memories, good or bad.

They had brought nothing but Desmond's books with them from the mission. Desmond had left Tut in charge when Quint pointed out that the Indians would survive, probably better without the burden of the white man's religion to inhibit them.

Quint would not let them speak of the past. Life is now, he said, today, this minute. Only vague dreams of the future are permitted and no regrets for the past. He told outrageous stories, made terrible jokes and argued incessantly with Desmond. When their arguments turned into a battle of wits as to who could remember obscure quotations from stories and lyric poems Kyla had never read, she would ask Desmond in private for the books in order to read for herself what it was the men were twisting out of context in order to trap one another.

Desmond had been educated in English public schools,

which she learned were actually quite the opposite of American public schools, and at Cambridge, yet Quint was more than his match. The secret lay in Quint's quick grasp of both written and oral information.

Kyla found herself relaxing in Quint's presence. She told herself that if she had just met him for the first time, as a friend of her husband, she would have found him witty and charming. Never by word or deed did he remind her of what had happened between them and, because the past was so painful to recall, Kyla chose to pretend she had never believed this man to be her husband or lover.

There had been an ugly moment when they first arrived in San Francisco, when the desk clerk refused to provide rooms for Shansi and Old Woman. Quint appeared ready to pull the frightened clerk over the desk, but then a porter whispered to Desmond, who in turn spoke quietly to Quint. Kyla and Felice were escorted to their rooms and, later, learned Shansi and Old Woman had accommodations at another hotel.

A few days later, both Felice and Merciful Smith also moved from their hotel and Kyla and Desmond were able to use Felice's accommodation, which adjoined theirs. When Felice's booming laugh, Merciful's hoarse croak and cloud of cigar smoke had faded from the air, Desmond asked Quint if they were moving into a business location.

Quint, who had arrived to accompany them to dinner, was noncommittal. "Not yet. But I believe it would be better to have them live somewhere else. We are going to build a fine house on the highest hill in town for Lord and Lady Talmage. And they will live there untainted by the more unorthodox aspects of our business, or my somewhat colorful companions in the enterprise."

"My contribution to your business is embarrassingly minimal," Desmond commented as they were seated at their restaurant table. He was glad of the dim light and tried to ignore the waiter's horrified stare.

"Nonsense. Your contribution is invaluable. You know I never mastered higher mathematics, and our present dealings are beyond Shansi's abacus. We need you to keep the figures straight."

"Quint brought in a cargo of, among other things, nails. We salvaged them from the ship and he is selling them at an obscene profit in a town desperate to build," Desmond explained. "Did you know that at last count there were over a hundred beached ships being used as buildings?"

"Which are sounder in construction than most of the buildings they are throwing up," Quint commented. "And there is nothing obscene about my profits. As a matter of fact, I believe I shall take some of our nails out to the Sierra boomtowns and sell them at an even higher profit."

"Tell me, Quint," Desmond said, "what is the difference between you and the bandits who cover their faces and point their guns at innocent travelers?"

"Very little difference," Quint agreed gravely, "but where would the world be without us rogues? How could there be virtue if there were no sin to define it? Waiter, bring champagne to launch my journey."

"You are really leaving—so soon?" Kyla asked, ignoring the pang that warned she was letting down her guard. The days sped so quickly while Quint was near and there was always an air of expectancy, as though something wonderful was going to happen.

"Just for a short time. While I'm gone I would ask you to be cautious about leaving your rooms after dark. The lawless element in this town is rapidly outnumbering the honest citizens I'm afraid. Another boatload of ex-convicts from the Australian penal colony arrived the other day, and none of them rushed out to buy shovels. Those 'Sydney Ducks,' as everyone calls them, are going to be a real problem to this town. I hear our friend Ramsey is spearheading a drive to form a vigilance committee. By the way, Maria is already queen of the Nob Hill matrons. There surely is nothing quite so sanctimonious on the face of the earth as a would-be politician or a reformed whore."

"Quint!" Desmond protested. "Are you forgetting my wife is present?"

"No," Quint said, an odd half-smile hovering about his

lips, "I am never able to forget the presence of your wife. But to get back to the danger abroad on the streets of our boisterous town, I am going to send Merciful Smith over to accompany you wherever you need to go."

"Merciful Smith!" Kyla said. "But he is so slightly built, a puff of wind could blow him away. He is so sickly-looking. Surely we would have to protect him, rather than the other way around?"

"He is an expert both with a knife and with the derringer he carries at all times," Quint said. "He was a valuable bouncer, in addition to being a talented mortician. And if he appears a trifle frail, perhaps it's a natural consequence of half a life in Dartmoor."

"Dartmoor?" Kyla asked.

"A prison in England," Desmond explained.

"Merciful killed a fellow inmate and was hanged for the crime. But the hangman botched the job somehow, and Merciful came to his senses in a pine box on the way to the cemetery."

"Merciful heaven!" Kyla gasped.

"Exactly," agreed Quint. "And while on the subject of bodyguards, Kyla, Felice will accompany you on any shopping expeditions. Women are the scarcest of all luxuries in San Francisco, and not many men will tangle with Felice."

"May I ask what Merciful Smith's original crime was?" Desmond asked. "There seems to be a slight brogue lurking under that rasping whisper of his."

"In Merciful's case I never inquired. But I would suspect he was an Irish insurrectionist. Ah, here is the champagne."

Later, when the evening ended, Desmond walked down to the lobby with Quint and they stepped outside on to the planks of the rough sidewalk. Although it was well after midnight, the street thronged with people. Quint good-naturedly shoved a reeling miner on his way and remarked, "They say living for a week in San Francisco is the equivalent of a year of life anywhere else."

"How long will you be gone?" Desmond asked, standing well back in the shadows.

"I'm not sure. Later we'll find a man to travel to the mining camps for us, but I want to see them for myself first."

Desmond detected in Quint's reply an undercurrent that hinted there was more to the proposed journey than Quint cared to divulge. But Desmond knew better than to pry.

A pair of miners, hanging about one another's necks and singing loudly lurched into Desmond and drew back in alarm. "Holy Christ!" one of them gasped as he caught sight of Desmond's scarred face. Desmond turned away quickly to retreat back into the hotel.

Quint's boot went squarely into the rear of the nearest man, sending both him and his companion staggering forward to be swallowed by the crowd. "Wait a minute, Des. I wanted a word alone with you before I leave."

"If it's about Kyla, I've already told you I will keep her busy. With you out of the way we can visit Maria, since she appears to be the most sought-after hostess in town. I can perhaps find a dark corner, sit low in my seat, and pretend to myself that I am merely a one-armed gentleman with a slight dueling scar."

"Why not? That's the way your friends see you, and so would others, but you'd have to give them a chance to get to know you first. No, that isn't what I wanted to ask. It's much more indelicate. Have you slept with her?"

The blue eyes squeezed shut for a second, and there was a peculiarly poignant droop to the unscarred side of Desmond's mouth. He took a moment to collect himself before answering, "You go too far, Quint. Must I remind you again that we are not Siamese twins, nor two bodies occupying one soul? Stop living my life. It's time you found your own identity."

Quint turned away and Desmond could not see his face, but the parting words that came softly through the night were revealingly rueful. "I was not thinking of us, but of Kyla and her needs. Goodbye, my lord."

Maria had everything she ever dreamed of, a fine house, servants, clothes, a rich and handsome husband who was becoming an important man in a fascinating city that teemed with life and excitement. The only blot on her sense of well-being was the lack of news about Miguel.

In San Francisco they had quickly been surrounded by a nucleus of other *nouveau riche* families, and Maria was in her element. Word spread that she was the daughter of a Spanish don and possibly related to the king of Spain. This, aided by Ramsey's wealth, made her a natural leader among women unsure of their own pedigrees.

She did not particularly care to include Kyla and her husband in her circle of friends, but Garett admired Desmond's mind, his diplomacy and uncanny knack for finding workmen in a city where unskilled laborers could demand thirty dollars a day and still jobs went begging. Desmond also spoke the language of the bankers and brokers and was able to borrow money at three percent interest per month instead of the usual fourteen percent per month. Working with borrowed capital, Desmond had turned Quint Delleroc's original stake from his cargo of nails and hardware into real estate: gambling and billiard halls, buildings rented to restaurateurs, and even a hotel.

When Desmond graciously assisted Garett Ramsey in unraveling a complicated mining investment, Ramsey urged Maria to include the Talmages at her dinners and parties.

"But he is so ugly," Maria protested. "He frightens all the ladies. And when I invited them to our housewarming, they brought Delleroc, and he was impossible." Delleroc had baited Ramsey continuously, and Maria had been ashamed of her husband's stammering response, especially when Delleroc had ridiculed the Vigilance Committee and added, "One of these days, Ramsey, you are going to frighten yourself to death."

Maria looked at her husband with distaste, remembering the remark, which had sounded oddly prophetic. He *was* afraid of Delleroc, always speculating on the man's whereabouts and activities; obsessed with making more money than Delleroc.

"And Kyla is so dull," Maria added as another reason

for excluding the Talmages from her parties. "One would have thought she wanted the child. Instead of being glad the wretched creature was stillborn, she mopes about with her head in a book. I like to have people around me who are gay."

"You haven't seen much of her since they moved to the city. You might be surprised at the change in her. I saw them coming out of their hotel lobby on Quintero Street one night, and she was laughing and looking quite pretty in a new dress."

"What were you doing down on Quintero Street at night?" Maria asked suspiciously.

"Oh, I had some business to see to." Ramsey's eyes shifted uncomfortably as he silently cursed the slip of the tongue. There was a young Cantonese woman named Ah Toy whose place of business was off Quintero Street, and Garett Ramsey had become one of her regular customers, so much so that he was discreetly trying to have a deportation order against her dismissed. "Anyway, remember what I said about inviting the Talmages over. Desmond is liked and trusted and can be useful to me. Besides, I hear Delleroc went out to visit the mining towns and I'd like to know what he's up to."

"Delleroc, Delleroc," Maria muttered. "A nobody. What do we care what he is doing?" But she was distracted, as always, by the mention of the man's name. What was it about him that, when one had met him, it was impossible to put him out of one's mind?

When Kyla and Desmond attended her next party, Maria saw that Garett had been right about the change in Kyla. Her deep blue eyes sparkled, her dress was new and fashionable, and she walked with an eager step. When Desmond hid himself in a corner with a glass of brandy, Maria was chagrined to note that Kyla was quickly surrounded by a circle of the most important men in town. Men outnumbered women in San Francisco that it was impossible for a woman *not* to be surrounded by men but this fact did not occur to Maria. She had been undisputed queen of society and far and away the most beautiful woman in town, and the limelight was not going to be shared. The echo of sighs of delight over Kyla's golden hair, when they had been children, lingered in Maria's memory.

At the party, they had rolled up the carpet and were about to begin dancing to the three-piece orchestra hired for the evening when the Chinese servant Garett had hired to act as butler slipped quietly to his employer's side and whispered something to him. Garett glanced toward his wife and then bent to reply to the servant, who padded swiftly back to the double doors leading to the outer hall.

There was a gasp and an excited ripple of voices as the two men stepped into the brightly lit room. The first man was black-haired and handsome in the aristocratic Spanish way, tall, broad-shouldered and dressed in a magnificent embroidered velvet bolero and tightly-fitted *calzoneras* set off with gold buttons. Flashing black eyes swept the room and found Kyla instantly, but it was Maria who was running toward him.

"Miguel!" she screamed, flinging herself at her brother. Even as she hugged him fiercely, she said against his chest, "Send the *indio* to the kitchen, Miguel. He can't come in here."

But Miguel had disengaged her and was walking slowly toward Kyla, who stood waiting, conflicting emotions racing across her face and her eyes wide.

In the doorway, Golden Feather folded his arms and watched, heedless of the way the guests stared at his buckskins and feather-decorated headband.

# 22

"*I want you to come away with me,*" Miguel said. "*I cannot stay long. Someone might recognize me as the bandido who has been raiding the gold camps and stagecoaches.*"

Kyla could see the guests dancing in the background, felt Maria's eyes on her as Miguel whirled her around the makeshift dance floor. The *norteamericanos'* dance, the waltz, was ideally suited for the exchange of private conversation, since the partners danced holding each other. They were doubly secure in that few of the assembled guests spoke Spanish. Still, Kyla's eyes went apprehensively to the corner where Desmond sat when Miguel made this announcement.

"Miguel, you—a *bandido!* Oh, I don't believe you," she said, playing for time.

"I didn't intend to be. I was a *guerrillero*, but my men had to eat and have horses and they had families to support. And as the *yanquis* arrive in their never-ending hordes their treatment of our people becomes more like the whipping of an unwanted cur. *Chilenos* and greasers, they call us, and hang and flog us without giving us a chance to speak in our own defense. *Yanqui* justice! *Dios*, I thought Spanish justice was harsh, but the *yanquis* know only the law of the rope and the whip. They have no *calabozos* in their new towns, so they hang or beat a man to death for even minor crimes."

"The boomtowns—where the men go for the gold," Kyla said, "I hear they are growing even faster than San Francisco. Perhaps in time there will be law and order for all people. Why, Miguel, here in San Francisco there are men from all over the world, even convicts from the Australian penal colony. Miguel, you must stay here. Garett Ramsey will help you, for Maria's sake."

The music ended and Miguel took Kyla's hand to lead her back to her chair, his dark eyes resting briefly on his host, who was drinking with several of his friends, all of whom were Anglo-Americans. Miguel wondered cynically how long it would be before Ramsey decided that having Mexican relatives was not in his best interests.

"It's too late for me to retrace my footsteps, Kyla," he said softly. "I am already a hunted man in the South and it will only be a matter of time before the wanted posters with my name are seen in the North. Kyla, come away with me. Let us have a little while together before a *yanqui* bullet finishes me or I dance on the end of a rope."

"Miguel, please don't talk like that. I can't. I have a husband." She spoke with more conviction than she felt. Since moving to San Francisco, she had caught something of the fever of the new immigrants, but not for gold. She was increasingly aware that there were no real ties holding her to Desmond. She was restless but had been unable to define what it was she really wanted.

Later, she thought, I'll know what I want out of life. For now it's enough to spend a little time playing instead of working.

Guiltily, she realized her mind had wandered while Miguel continued to plead with her.

He pulled a chair close and spoke quietly in Spanish. "Maria told me your child did not live. You lost your *rancho* to the *yanquis*. You submitted to a proxy marriage to a hideous cripple to keep a promise to a dead man who was not even your real father. Kyla, don't you understand? You have no obligation now to anyone. Everything we had is gone, our land, our honor. How can you live with them, after what they did to you and Maria? Kyla, if I had not found Ramsey married to my sister, I would have killed him. I came here to kill him and take you and Maria away with me."

Kyla stared at him, trying to remember the sensitive boy who had been her childhood companion. This stranger with the hard and reckless eyes lived by rules she could not imagine.

"Kyla, I cannot tell Maria this, but Ramsey tried to barter your lives for safe passage for his men."

"But he is Maria's husband now. You can't destroy that. Why can't you begin a new life, Miguel? Forget the past."

"While our people are beaten and starving? While *yanqui* murderers walk free? Maria is lost to us, living in their world. But you and I—come away with me. There is a small *rancho* we can reach before morning. It is called *Los Amigos*. We will be safe there."

Kyla felt Miguel stiffen suddenly, and she knew without turning her head that Garett Ramsey was approaching. He addressed Miguel in his halting Spanish. "We are glad you come to visit us, Miguel. Perhaps it would be a good idea for you and me to have a private talk. There are some things it would be better for you to understand right away."

Miguel rose to his feet. Beside Ramsey's bulk, he appeared slim, despite his broad shoulders. His dark eyes met Ramsey's pale stare contemptuously. "You would explain to me that in your new society there is no place for Mexicans unless, like my sister, they choose to forget their proud heritage. There is no need for you to tell me this in private, nor for you to fear I came to abuse your hospitality. I shall leave shortly."

Garett Ramsey's eyes darted about to see if anyone was listening, as Miguel had spoken in English. Kyla rose to her feet also.

"Please excuse me," she said. "I must go to my husband. I will see you before you leave, Miguel."

*And I can't go with you.* Her eyes met his steadily, and

he read her thoughts very well, but sent her the silent message that the matter was far from settled.

In the shadowed corner of the room Desmond Talmage watched and wondered what had become of Quint Delleroc. Desmond closed his eyes and allowed the peaceful vision of the monastery, nestled in the soft green hills of Wales, to flit soothingly across his mind. Besides blotting out thoughts of Delleroc, the image helped stifle the longings he was unable to reveal even in the confessional.

Quint Delleroc seized the man who sprawled across the bar and jerked him to his feet. The man opened a bleary eye and mumbled something into his ginger moustache, then gasped as cold liquid was dashed into his face. The other patrons of the small *cantiña* fell back as Quint dragged the man outside. Fights, after all, were common, and a man would be a fool to take on that red-haired demon whose eyes belonged to the devil himself.

The night air revived the man somewhat, but alcohol had long ago saturated his brain.

"Are you Clement? *Dr.* Clement?"

The man nodded, his teeth rattling as Quint shook his shoulders. "Wha—what do you want? My hands—not steady enough any more if it's a bullet."

"Come on," Quint said. "You're going to drink a gallon of coffee and then you're going to tell me what you did with Kyla Talmage's son."

It took some time to piece the various conflicting stories Clement told into a coherent whole, and even then Quint was unsure how much was truth and how much the alcoholic had concocted to justify his spending all the money Desmond had given him. Clement claimed that several doctors had looked at the child and agreed there was little hope for the clubfeet. Clement had found a family of poor Mexicans who agreed to take care of the baby, but he had not seen them for some time.

"Nor paid them, I expect," Quint said grimly. "All right, come on. I've got horses waiting and we're going to ride until you lead me to the Mexicans who have the child.

So better choose the fastest route, because you aren't going to get another drink until we find him."

A week later Quint Delleroc stood at the door of a hovel in a poor Mexican pueblo far from the coast, and his eyes were moist with pity as he watched the small blond child drag himself across the dirt floor by his elbows. The boy looked about two and a half years old and, despite his blond curls, his fierce eyes were black as coals. Both feet were clubbed.

"What do you call him?" Quint asked the woman who stirred the bean pot over the fire outside the hut. Half a dozen dark-haired children played nearby.

*"Huérfano,"* she said. "He will not answer to any name. He is filled with rage, that one, and would never let me hold him without wriggling away from me. He tries to walk, and because he cannot, he screams and bites the other children. If we could have found the doctor, we would have returned the child. We are poor, and there is not enough to feed our own children."

"You will be paid for taking care of him," Quint promised, "and he will no longer be called 'orphan.' I shall call him Victor. Now, if you will fetch me some water, I am going to wash him and take him away with me. Clement—Dr. Clement, if you please—get down from your horse and get in here to help me."

The child sank surprisingly sharp teeth into Quint's hand when Quint tried to pick him up, and the boy howled furiously when the woman produced a tin washbowl.

"Now that you've found him, you won't be needing me any more, I trust?" Clement asked nervously when, half an hour later, the boy was washed, dressed in clean clothes and glaring malevolently at the two strangers who had burst into his life.

"There were surgeons in England who were operating on clubfeet while I was there. There must be some in this country. You, Dr. Clement, are going to find them for me. I don't care where they are. Meantime, we are going to take the boy to a lady of my acquaintance, who will care for him without allowing him to bully her."

Quint Delleroc looked down at the fighting scrap of

humanity in his arms, and he met the black stare of hatred with compassion. Down the corridor of memories of his own life ran a small ragged boy whose existence had been clawed from the mean streets of a forgotten seaport, living on what he could forage or steal, staying alive only because he was too angry to starve to death.

"I know, little one," he said softly. "I know how it is."

Quint Delleroc was back in San Francisco, and Kyla had no time to wonder and worry about where Miguel had gone and what he was doing. Every hour was filled with promise, plans and so much to do that the days slipped away faster than autumn leaves before the wind.

The new Californians brought a vigor and zest for both work and play that was in sharp contrast to the more leisurely pace of the Spanish society to which Kyla had been accustomed. She marveled at the energy and enthusiasm of the new citizens, who cheerfully worked all day and played most of the night.

Quint slipped easily into this pattern, plunging into business ventures, sampling all of the entertainment the city offered and sweeping Kyla and Desmond along with him on a breathless wave of activity.

There had been a disastrous fire during Quint's absence, and many of the makeshift buildings had burned. Upon his return, he quickly decided that the crowded hotel area was unsafe, and their first goal would be to build a house.

A small house was constructed atop a hill in such a way that additions could be made later. Kyla began to furnish it, while Quint and Desmond opened an office closer to their business interests in town. Kyla asked once at which hotel Quint resided and had been told he usually slept in a coffin filled with earth. Desmond had not joined in the ensuing laughter.

Kyla was surprised one day when Merciful Smith came in response to her request for someone to accompany her to the dressmaker.

"Oh, Mr. Smith, come in. I'm sorry, but Desmond must have misunderstood. I told him I wanted to go to the dressmaker and thought he would send Felice to accompany me."

Merciful adjusted the dingy yellow cravat he always wore about his neck and croaked, "I'll take you. Felice can't get away no more." He bit down hard on the unlit cigar in his mouth.

"I suppose she is busy in one of the card parlors?" Kyla asked, reaching for her bonnet. "I haven't seen her since Quint returned from the gold fields."

Merciful's eyes shifted uncomfortably, searching the room for a place to rest in a way that said he was also seeking an answer, other than the simple truth, to her question.

Kyla had grown accustomed to Merciful's somber presence and knew that he was a man constantly surprised that he was still living. Few things upset him or moved him. No emotion greater than the wonderment he felt at being alive and free ever registered on those sallow features. Usually he was terse but honest in his answers to questions, and this unexpected glimpse of him evading a question intrigued her.

"Is she still working for Mr. Delleroc?" Kyla persisted, straightening her bonnet in the hallstand mirror.

"Oh yes. Yes, she still works for him." He was studying his cigar as though it had turned into a viper.

"In one of the card parlors?"

"No. Ah—no."

"A restaurant?"

"No." His brows had come together ferociously now and Kyla decided to let the matter rest. Perhaps Desmond knew what had become of the ebullient Felice.

Merciful waited outside in the carriage while Kyla had her dress fitting. A young French dressmaker, who had created several dresses for Maria, was making Kyla's gown for the spring ball, which was to be the social event of the year. Many hoped the ball would prove that there were decent citizens in the brawling young city, who could get together and act like ladies and gentlemen. The stories of those refugees from the Australian penal colony—the "Sydney Ducks"—and about sundry other bands of roving thugs, were beginning to reach the outside world.

"Theez one, madame," the dressmaker said, shuffling through her bolts of cloth. "See 'ow ze light shimmers on it, changing ze color from white to green to blue? I will stitch into ze bodice tiny brilliants and seed pearls and some of zat blue stone ze Indians sell. Turquoise. All of the blues will bring out ze lights in madame's eyes."

"Oh, it's beautiful!" Kyla exclaimed. "Do you think— would it be all right for me to wear the dropped sleeves?"

"But of course. Bare shoulders. I insist. Madame has fine white shoulders and décolletage. Ah, *oui*, we cut ze bodice very low." The dressmaker sighed. "Madame Ramsey insists on wearing red. Always ze red. And every hotel and restaurant in California is furnished in red! She will disappear into ze walls, but I can tell 'er nothing."

Kyla was looking forward to the ball and wearing her new dress with its décolletage and flounced skirt. Quint was always most interested in her clothes. She frowned at the thought. She had been trying to ignore the spell he was again casting. But he had been such a model of decorum toward her since he found them at the mission, that it was difficult to remember the villainous Delleroc who had boldly claimed another man's bride so long ago. The passage of time had wrought great changes in all of them, but surely there was no one more fascinating than a reformed sinner.

Perhaps, she told herself, what she felt was envy of Delleroc's freedom from the bonds of conventionality. There were secret moments when she felt trapped by her marriage to Desmond. She worried about the amount of brandy Desmond drank before he retired each night. He was not happy in his new role of businessman and financier in this throbbing metropolis. But if Desmond were to return to the mission, Kyla would have to go with him, and that was unthinkable. She was too full of the turbulence of change. Half-formed ideas and goals lurked in her mind. She could not bury herself on some remote mission.

Unlike Quint, who became noisy and quarrelsome if he

drank too much, or absurdly silly, Desmond became more silent and withdrawn, and Kyla flinched from the misery expressed in the brilliant blue eyes. Desmond was often morose, while Quint was always exuberant. It was impossible for Kyla not to feel downcast in Desmond's presence, elated when Quint was near.

She would not hear any word of warning or criticism about Quint, even from Desmond. Once he had caught her by the wrist as she was about to run from the dining room to the front door to greet Quint. "Let the maid go, Kyla," Desmond has said quietly. "Don't welcome Quint as though he were some kind of messiah. He isn't. He is the same man he always was and he will drop from our lives as swiftly as he has returned, the moment he becomes bored with the game of making a fortune. It worries me that you are beginning to treat him—as—as a friend. Please don't let his present good behavior blind you to his true colors. It is just the calm before the storm, Kyla. Quint Delleroc is a walking volcano who will erupt without warning. And I regret to say an eruption is long past due."

Flushing, Kyla snatched her wrist from his grip. "How can you speak of him so? I thought he was your dearest friend. After all he has done for us, this house, your business, why, we'd still be living on corn and beans at the mission if Quint had not come along. How ungrateful of you, Desmond."

Quint's voice was calling to them, and she walked stiffly from the room, telling herself she admired Quint's attitude toward life, that was all. She had long ago conquered those other feelings for him. If she found him physically attractive—well, Quint himself had told her those feelings had nothing to do with love.

"And how are my friends Lord and Lady Talmage spending this fine Sunday afternoon?" Quint inquired as she entered the living room. He was standing near the bay window and behind him the spring sunlight cast a halo on his fiery hair. Kyla thought how appropriate it was of Desmond to compare him to a volcano. But because Quint was a man of quicksilver changes of mood and fleeting interests did not make him dangerous as a friend.

"Hello, Quint. We just returned from church and were discussing the furniture for the dining room. We've been getting along with an old table Merciful found for us, but we hope the next shipment of furniture from the East Coast will be here soon."

His eyes glazed slightly. "Lord, but that sounds boring. Why don't I take you for a spin in my new buggy? Quaint word. I learned it from a *yanqui*."

"Oh, that would be lovely. I'll run and put on my bonnet."

"And I'll get my cane," Desmond said, from behind her. Because of his leg a walking stick had become necessary. The doctors he had seen had all agreed he was lucky the leg had not been amputated along with his arm. Beyond prescribing laudanum for the pain, they offered no other relief.

When Kyla disappeared and they heard her footsteps run lightly up the stairs, Desmond dragged himself closer to Quint and stood leaning against the mantelpiece, looking at him.

"You're going to hurt her," Desmond said. "And I won't be able to stand it. I believe I would have to kill you."

"And commit suicide?" Quint asked mockingly. "How could you live if I were dead? The only way you can think your saintly thoughts and do your good deeds is by vicariously enjoying all of my sins."

"Quint, I'm not joking. I care very deeply about Kyla."

"Then why don't you claim her for yourself, instead of leaving her in some state of suspended animation?"

"Your tongue has a cruel edge, Quint. Even if I were a whole man I could not compete with you in her eyes. You are the dashing cavalier, fearless, intrepid, full of wit and lusty life, who can protect her and provide for her. And I? Any drunken miner who passes by could incapacitate me. How do you think I feel, having Merciful Smith accompany us everywhere because I am incapable of protecting my wife from the rabble of the city? We won't even go into the fact that I live on your charity."

"Oh, sit down and shut up," Quint said amiably. "I'm in no mood for a verbal battle today. Spring is in the air, and for the first time in my life I wonder about putting down roots. I haven't had gypsy feet since I came back to California."

"If I were to give her an annulment," Desmond said slowly, "would you marry her?"

Quint smiled, his eyes sending out sparks. "I love women, but hate matrimony. You know my creed. I am as much in favor of indulging in all excesses as you are drawn to lost souls. And you worry too much about your wife. She has recovered from her ordeal now, mostly thanks to my efforts. Therefore, having put the pieces back together to form a woman, may I remind you of Rabelais? 'They say it is virtually impossible for man to find in women beauty unallied . . . with arrogance or cruelty or pride.' Des, old sport, Kyla is a very beautiful woman." Incredibly, Desmond did not seem to realize how hollow the words rang, Quint thought. Damn it, I can't develop a conscience now. I'm not old enough yet, he told himself sternly.

Kyla's arrival, in a new and becoming bonnet, prevented further conversation. Desmond doggedly endured a wild ride up and down the steep hills of San Francisco, despite the fact there was a new book awaiting him at home and his leg was in a frenzy of pain. Even Kyla was beginning to notice that Desmond never left her alone with Quint.

# 23

*There was a crescent moon the night of the spring ball* and reckless *joi de vivre* in the balmy air. The spring of 1850 saw a city growing by thirty new houses a day, infused by a steady stream of gold from the Sierra mines, blighted by at least two murders and one fire daily. San Francisco had grown from a village of a few hundred people to a city of twenty-five thousand, and twice that number had disembarked at the port en route to the gold fields.

Desmond climbed from the carriage first, his cane sinking into the mud of the street as he missed the wooden plank sidewalk outside the hotel. Quickly Quint leaped down to offer a hand, but Desmond dragged himself up on to the sidewalk unaided. Quint turned immediately and clasped Kyla about her waist to lift her over the muddy chasm between carriage and sidewalk, and she felt her nerves tingle at the touch of his hands. His demeanor was frankly admiring tonight and she knew Quint Delleroc was impressed by her glorious new gown, her carefully dressed hair and the jewels that sparkled as brightly as her eyes.

"You should have brought a partner, Quint," Desmond had said with shocking pettiness when Quint arrived to accompany them to the ball. "There are those in town who are already whispering of a *ménage*. One day

our business will stand or fall on our reputations—
respectability will be essential. Perhaps we could avoid a
repetition of what happened in India."

Kyla realized with some dismay that Desmond had been
drinking. He did not want to go to the ball, to be exposed
to the bright lights and the painful scrutiny of strangers.

"Perhaps Quint should go without us," she said in a
small tight voice.

Desmond was immediately contrite. "Kyla, I'm sorry. I
know how much you've been looking forward to this. And,
of course, we must go together. I shall need Quint to
protect you from the amorous throngs seeking the favor
of a dance. I spoke without thinking. I apologize to you
both."

"No need, old sport," Quint said, watching his friend
closely. "It's a pleasure to hear you sound a little testy
occasionally. There's hope for you yet. Your husband is
jealous, Kyla. A very human emotion, especially when one
has a wife as lovely as you. Old Des is reminding you
that I am a cad and not to be trusted."

"Please—" Kyla said, uneasy at the antagonism that
seemed to have flared so unexpectedly between the two.
"The carriage is waiting. Shall we go?"

She insisted that her partners return her to Desmond
the moment a dance ended. Uncharacteristically, he sat
at a table on the edge of the floor, enduring the glare of
the lights and the obvious stares of the guests.

The ballroom was crammed with leading members of
the new society along with those of lesser repute. One lady
remarked that a year earlier the ball had encompassed the
whole of San Francisco society of which the ladies were
sixteen in number.

Eating and drinking progressed on a lavish scale in the
adjacent banquet rooms. There gin and champagne cock-
tails were much in demand, as well as the current favorite,
the Queen Charlotte, a mixture of claret and raspberry
syrup. The men tended to consume their whiskey and
brandy straight, then helped themselves to the choice cuts
of wild game, sweetbreads and cockscombs.

Kyla had not missed a dance. But Desmond, she knew,

had not stopped drinking. We should leave, she thought, but Quint had not yet asked her to dance. Surely he would come for the next waltz? He circulated among the men, asked several ladies to dance and stopped to chat with Desmond from time to time. He had even danced with the flirtatious Maria, despite Garett Ramsey's glowering gaze.

She sat, fanning herself, during the intermission. Desmond's eyes had lost their luster and his head drooped wearily.

"Desmond, are you feeling all right?" Kyla asked.

He raised his head and tried valiantly to smile, but only the distorted pucker of the right side of his lips lingered in a travesty of good humor. "I'm fine, my dear. Are you having a good time?"

"She is the belle of the ball, isn't she?" Quint said from behind her. "Des, old sport, I came to ask if I have now fulfilled my obligations to propriety and may claim a dance with the most beautiful woman here tonight?"

"By all means dance with Kyla. Perhaps you could restrain yourself long enough to await the return of the musicians?" Desmond said acidly.

Quint laughed and pulled out a chair, motioning to one of the scurrying waiters, despite Kyla's warning glance.

"Brandy for my friend, Lord Talmage. And the same for me. Kyla, is that claret? And bring us some food. You look as though you could use some solid sustenance, old sport."

"I've had no more to drink than you. I detect, in fact, more of a slurring of your speech than mine."

"I'm quite sure you never slurred in your life. As for me, well, I don't need speech to gain my ends. I'll use the language of eyebrows and fingers—with annotations in wine."

Desmond turned to Kyla. "He quotes from *Amores*, Kyla. It pleases him to exhibit his literary knowledge. Such a display is usually the sign of an insecure intellect."

Quint leaned across the table, his eyes hooded. "If we are peeling away the layers, Des, old friend, shall we dissect the reason for your animosity? Our old idol, Rabelais, was once a monk, if you will recall, just like you. And if this insecure intellect may quote him: 'Here is Master Johnny Inigo, a master instrumentalist who begs to fiddle and thrum, sweep the *viola d'amore,* play the manichord, beat the drum, wind the horn and grind the organ until you feel his music throbbing in the marrow of your bones.' "

Desmond had half-risen from his chair, his eyes blazing and his face white. "Go to hell—" he began through gritted teeth. At that moment the orchestra returned and struck up a waltz and Quint rose and extended his hand to Kyla.

"I was promised a dance. After that, I'll gladly go to hell."

They whirled about the floor in dizzying turns and flamboyant circles and she was too breathless to speak. Then all at once they had moved through the open doors and were in the deserted hall outside the ballroom, still dancing, toward the cool night air that drifted through the windows overlooking the bay. Their steps were slower, and he held her closer until her heart was beating against the velvet of his jacket and his face was bending low over hers. She looked up at him, and remembered with a sudden flash that other night so long ago, when he had carried her away from her wedding dance. Then his lips found hers and she trembled and clung to him.

In that one long, searching kiss all that had gone between her wedding night and this moment was lost in the sweet rebirth of joyous longing. She could feel the warmth of his hands on her body, the taste of his tongue in her mouth, and the vibrant sensations transmitted from his body to hers.

"Quint, oh, Quint, my darling," she whispered as his lips traveled from her mouth to the hollow of her throat. She stroked the soft mass of red hair and felt the hot progress of his lips over the soft curve of her breast.

He raised his head and smiled at her. "We could slip away for a while. Merciful Smith is outside. I could send him to discreetly take care of Des, who will soon pass out, if I'm not mistaken. Ah, Kyla, I've tried to resist temptation, but I can't. Come with me, be with me for a little while."

She could not fight the madness of her heart, or the longing of her flesh. She had been only half-alive for so long. Dumbly she nodded and pulled his face closer so that she might kiss his mouth again. Then they were in the carriage and Merciful Smith was whipping the horses forward and Quint's arms were around her as they traveled through the magic of a spring night. A small group of black-clad Chinese men moved aside as Kyla and Quint alighted in front of a bleak-looking hotel, but Kyla's eyes were full of stars and her body ached with desire. She did not see anything, or feel anything, but Quint's electrifying presence.

Later she did not remember undressing, or even all of the ways he made love to her. They explored each other's bodies with hands and lips and tongues and he turned her this way and that way and touched her and penetrated her and there were moments when she was not sure where his body ended and hers began. She thought wonderingly, fleetingly, that this was what was meant by being one with a man and it seemed that as their bodies joined, their minds also went soaring away together and there was no need for words, only for gentle sighs and soft cries of pleasure.

A long time later she lay still, studying his sleeping face, just above hers on the pillow. The handsomely chiseled features were less fierce in repose, almost vulnerable when the lion's eyes were closed. His red hair was tousled and the mouth was peaceful, despite the knotted muscles of his arm holding her in a hard grip. She was so happy she felt as though all of her joy must be flowing into him in a stream of happy solutions. When he awakened he would be able to tell her how they could be together always.

Somewhere in the back of her mind a door opened and several shapeless horrors appeared. *He has withstood the guile of women more worldly, persuasive and beautiful than you*, one of them whispered to her. *What about Des-*

*mond?* another accused. She blinked her eyes, trying to make the troublesome thoughts go away, caring for nothing but the warmth and vibrant proximity of the creature she loved most on earth. Desmond was not her husband. The marriage had never been consummated.

Her eyes drifted to the window as a faint light flickered in the darkness and then disappeared. A second later the breeze fluttered the curtain again and there was another flash of light and slowly, as she watched, the night sky began to take on an ominous red glow.

Quint stirred and mumbled something in his sleep as she tried to slip from his arms. She pressed her lips to the upturned palm of his hand, then gently disentangled their arms and legs and slid her feet to the floor.

At the window her breath caught in her throat. Fire was racing across the city under a cloud of billowing smoke. Flames leapt from one building to the next, borne on a strong wind. Below their window the street was rapidly filling with shouting people hauling their belongings from the doomed buildings. They were in the direct path of the wind-carried holocaust.

There had been many fires since the disastrous December blaze of 1849, but Kyla knew that none had been as bad as this. She turned to call Quint's name, but he was awake and moving to her side, taking in the ghastly picture framed in their window.

"Get dressed," he said. "Hurry. Go downstairs and look for Merciful. He'll be waiting for you with the carriage." Quint was dragging his trousers and reaching for his shirt.

"But you're not going to send me home alone?"

"I have to go and get Shansi," he said curtly. "She'll be lost in her magic cloud and roast to death."

"Shansi!" Kyla gasped. "But—"

"Kyla, I own this hotel. My living quarters are on the top floor, and so is Shansi. We are in the Chinese section of town. I must go to the waterfront. I've got gunpowder stored in a warehouse there, and I've got to reach it before the fire does. Merciful will take you home. Now hurry."

The next moment he was gone.

Disbelieving, she picked up her beautiful ballgown. He

had lain in her arms all night and left her to save his Oriental mistress. Shansi! She had put the lovely sloe-eyed girl out of her mind, but he had been living with her all this time and when it came to a choice of who he would save, it was Shansi he thought of first.

Feeling more ridiculous than frightened, dressed as she was in the previous evening's finery, Kyla stepped out into the hall and joined the guests, who were vacating their rooms in the silent and orderly fashion of the Chinese.

Out in the street it was a different situation. A swarm of hoodlums had poured out of the area south of Telegraph Hill known as Sydney Town and were advancing on the helpless citizens who carried their most valuable possessions. Kyla's horrified gaze took in several of the notorious Sydney Ducks sweeping down the street swinging clubs and pistols. An elderly Chinese fell under their blows, and the small box he was carrying was shot open and the contents fell out.

Kyla was swept along in a frenzied throng of people running as much from the thugs as from the flames. The air tasted hot, and smoke was in her eyes and mouth and lungs. She could hear the roar of the conflagration now, above the anguished cries of the fleeing populace and the shattering of doors as the Sydney Ducks looted in the path of the advancing flames.

Suddenly brawny arms seized her and she was plucked from the running crowd. The red glow of the flames illuminated the evil face of the man who held her helpless in tattooed arms. She screamed as his hand went to the necklace she wore.

"Hold still, you bloody whore," the man shouted in her ear in that peculiar whine that typified the corrupted Cockney speech of the Sydney Ducks. "Gimme the jewels. Tyke off the ring, blast yer." He was shaking her, as though to tumble fruit from a tree. Her dress was torn and her hair whipping wildly about her face. Oh, God, she thought, let me be dreaming, let it be a nightmare. The flickering flames illuminated the faces of the jostling crowd, casting an orange glow upon the alien features of the Chinese and the pockmarked countenances of thugs, who descended like scavenging vermin on the vacated buildings.

Struggling to free herself from the clutching hands, she slipped to the wooden sidewalk and cried out in terror as feet brushed her face. Her assailant was tugging at the rings on her fingers when he suddenly opened his mouth in surprise and a convulsive spasm passed through his body; then he pitched forward across her legs, soaking her in blood. She looked up and saw Merciful Smith slip a knife back into a scabbard concealed beneath his frock-coat. He rolled the culprit's body from her with an expert flick of his boot and pulled her quickly to her feet.

"Horses bolted, so no carriage," he said. "Come on, let's get out of here."

Seizing her hand, he propelled her through the crowd, using shoulders, elbows and feet to clear the way. She stumbled along in his wake, dress torn and covered with blood, her hair hanging over her face. She had lost one of her slippers.

The flames leaped and soared, devouring the night, sucking up the air into the chimney of the glowing sky. She felt dizzy from the heat and smoke and as the crowd surged away from the doomed building. Kyla felt as though she were drowning, being pulled below the steaming surface of some hellish cauldron. The sound of the fire rushed overhead like surf pounding a jagged shore. As warehouse after warehouse was engulfed, there came the staccato reports of exploding kegs of powder.

On the opposite side of the street a small shop burst into flames and a voice was heard to cry, " 'Ere, no need to set any more. The whole bleedin' town's ablaze now."

There had been rumors that more than one of the fires which had erupted in the city had been the work of arsonists and, as they turned the corner and came upon a group of volunteer firefighters racing toward the blaze, they heard the shout go up: "Shoot the incendiaries and looters!"

Over the roar of fire and wind and the human cries came the clanging of the great city bell, calling out the volunteers. For smaller fires the coded strokes of the bell pinpointed the blaze. Tonight there was no need. The entire city seemed to be burning.

I'm being punished, Kyla thought, for betraying Desmond. For being happy with Quint. Now I'm going to die. Her breath escaped in tortured gulps and shuddering sobs, but Merciful did not slow their pace until they were nearly to the top of the hill.

"All right. Catch your breath for a minute," he said. Oddly, his own rasping hoarseness seemed no worse for either the smoke or the mad dash through the crowded streets. Kyla leaned back weakly against a wall and tried not to think about the expression on the face of the Sydney Duck when Merciful's knife had slid between his shoulder blades.

"Listen, missus. I didn't get a chance to tell Mr. Delleroc," he went on. "But your 'usband went looking for you last night. Tried to get him to go home, but he wouldn't. He'd been to the other hotels they own, see, and would have come to the one in Chinatown if the fire hadn't broke out. 'E just didn't think Mr. Delleroc would take you there with *'er* being there."

Kyla closed her eyes, wishing she could cry. How could she ever face the hurt in those gentle blue eyes, oh, how could she have done this to him? He had been right. Quint Delleroc was the devil incarnate and she would hate him until the day she died.

"Did Mr. Delleroc find Shansi in time?" she asked, as her breathing became more even.

"When I saw 'im he was fetching Felice and the boy. Come, we'd best be moving on."

"Felice—has a child?" Kyla asked weakly.

"Just a little tyke," Merciful mumbled. He began to walk ahead of her, past a building that suddenly ignited as a shower of wind-driven sparks touched the roof.

The child. It must be Quint Delleroc's child! That was why Felice no longer worked in the gambling parlor, why Merciful had been embarrassed to tell her what Felice was doing. Oh, how stupid she had been! She had betrayed her husband with a man who boldly kept two mistresses and an illegitimate child.

"Come on, Lady Talmage," Merciful called to her gruffly. "You'll be able to think up some story by the time we get you 'ome. Just be glad you're alive, I always say."

He bent to pick up a burning stick that had fallen from the roof above, pulling a cigar from his pocket as he did so. He was about to touch the flaming brand to the cigar tip when the horsemen came galloping down the center of the street. Kyla was still several paces behind him and the scream died in her throat as the nearest horseman yelled, "There's one of them. Shoot that Sydney Duck!"

At least three bullets must have struck Merciful Smith simultaneously. He spun around grotesquely, dropped the cigar and the damning torch, then crumpled to the ground. The riders plunged down the street as Kyla flung herself down beside Merciful and cradled his head in her lap.

His eyes were open and staring and his lips twitched as he tried to speak. "Always—afraid—they'd hang me again—" He grinned briefly, as though greatly relieved, then slipped away from her.

She looked up at the building, which was now emitting gusts of smoke; the heat scorched her flesh. Gently she laid Merciful's head down and pressed his eyes closed. She removed the gun from his inside pocket, then she stood up and began to walk up the hill. Her eyes were wide and staring and her lips slightly parted. She was oblivious to everything but the flame-filled night.

At the top of the hill she turned and looked down on the burning city and silently vowed that like the legendary phoenix, she would rise again from the ashes of her life.

# 24

*Four hundred buildings had been destroyed. Gun barrels* were twisted into molten serpents and nails melted to form the shape of the kegs that had held them. Heaps of knives, forks and spoons formed sculptures that still emitted heat. An iron "fire-proof" safe had burst. Four men who had taken refuge in an iron-shuttered "fireproof" brick building had roasted to death as though in an oven. But before the embers cooled, merchants were planning to rebuild. Within forty-eight hours the city resounded to the din of hammers and saws.

A weary, soot-blacked Quint Delleroc climbed Nob Hill and pounded on the door of the Talmage household. "Ahoy the house!" he roared. "Let me in and feed me. Alone and unaided I saved our warehouse." The words were accompanied by enthusiastic thumps on the door.

He was unprepared for the blow when the door burst open and Desmond loomed over him. Desmond swung so wildly that he himself was thrown off-balance when his fist connected with Quint's cheekbone, and both of them tumbled down the steps to the street.

Quint shook his head and got up unsteadily. He offered his hand to Desmond, who lay in the dirt, eyes blazing. Desmond knocked the offered hand aside viciously and the effort laid him flat on his back.

Rubbing his cheek, Quint looked down at Desmond.

"If you will let me help you to your feet, you could try again." There was bewilderment as well as jocularity in his tone.

"Damn you! You ruined my name in India. You involved me in Santa Anna's plotting with the European governments. But you've manipulated my life for the last time," Desmond said hoarsely. He grasped the iron railing flanking the steps and pulled himself to his feet. He had completely forgotten the presence of Garett Ramsey in the house. Nor was he aware of how much of their quarrel Ramsey was overhearing.

"Vinegar," Quint was saying foolishly. He had been without sleep for forty-eight hours and it was possible he was at this moment caught in the absurdity of a dream. "I used vinegar. There were gallons of it in the warehouse next to ours. No water. Just the vinegar. So I poured it all over the roof and the sparks didn't ignite."

Desmond stared at him with a hatred that was palpable.

"Hell to pay, everywhere," Quint said after a moment's silence. "My place in Chinatown's gone, of course. The women are together in a house in the *barrio*. Just temporarily. Felice won't stand for Shansi and Old Woman's shenanigans for long. Not now. She—well, I heard Ramsey is in for it. He was with the Chinese prostitute when the fire started and had to jump from her window without his clothes. Maria will carve him up."

"Shut up," Desmond said, his lips white. "Shut up and get out of my life. I never want to see you again as long as you live. If you had returned yesterday instead of today, I would have called you out. But killing you isn't the answer. I won't face eternal damnation because of you, Delleroc."

"You really mean it, don't you?" Quint said in amazement. "I must admit I never thought we would split up because of a woman."

"If you speak her name, I will kill you," Desmond said through clenched teeth that emphasized the upward slant of his scarred lip.

"All right. Calm down. Tell me what you want me to do. Shall I just get out of town? Would that be dramatic enough? Or do you want me to do some other form of penance? Pity there aren't any stocks or flogging posts—though I understand the Vigilance Committee is considering hanging men from the upper stories of buildings and the yardarms of abandoned ships."

"Sooner or later, Quint Delleroc, you will pay," Desmond said in a voice filled with grief and pain. "I want you out of my life. Permanently. I am packing my books and personal belongings and leaving today for a mission in the south. As long as you never stray in that direction, it is immaterial to me where you go or what you do."

Quint's eyes narrowed, the pupils contracting to black lines. "And your wife? You'll bury her alive, too? Des, she's a warm-blooded woman, not a fossil, and there are worse sins than a little harmless romp—"

The words were cut off as Desmond flung himself at Quint's throat, squeezing with all the power in his one hand. Quint jerked his head free and his hands grasped Desmond's arm, flinging him backward to sprawl across the steps.

"Or is it because I had Merciful bring her home instead of bringing her myself?" Quint asked, his mind examining possibilities. "Des, come on, be fair. I knew Merciful wouldn't let anything happen to her. I'd trust him with my life. And I had to get to Felice and the—and Shansi and Old Woman. They were all on the top floor of the hotel." He paused, a dreadful thought infiltrating his mind as he looked into the impotent fury expressed in Desmond's eyes. "Des, she's all right, isn't she? She wasn't hurt? Merciful was on his way to her before I—"

"We found Merciful's body yesterday afternoon," Desmond said. "He had been shot, along with sundry other looters, incendiaries and innocent bystanders."

Quint drew in his breath, his face pale. "And Kyla?"

"Missing. She never came home. I've searched the entire city and there is no sign of her. Some of the burned bodies are unrecognizable, however. I know. I've looked at every one of them."

The miners and the storekeepers along the single street

of the boomtown paused as the exotically strange group
approached. Leading the riders was a handsome young
Mexican astride a magnificent white stallion, the silver
trappings of his carved leather saddle glinting in the afternoon sunlight. Next to him rode a woman, her slim body
encased in a dark skirt and simple silk shirt, a scarf
knotted at her throat. Her light golden hair hung down
her back in a single braid beneath a *vaquero's* hat.

Just behind them rode an Indian, his buckskins setting
off his bronzed skin, a shimmering feather tucked into
his rawhide headband. Half a dozen other Mexicans rode,
in single file, behind the three. All were dressed in color-
fully embroidered boleros and gold-buttoned *calzoneras*
unfastened over their boots to accommodate silver spurs.

They rode into town boldly, heads high, their horses
prancing as though in a parade. Dark eyes nonchalantly
returned the stares of the men on the street but the woman
stared straight ahead.

At the ramshackle building that served as a combination
general store, bar and roominghouse, the riders reined
their horses and dismounted, the handsome young leader
lifting the woman from her horse. His hands lingered about
her waist and he smiled down at her, white teeth flashing.
For a second they were alone in the world. Then they
went into the store.

"Good day to you," Miguel said politely to the man
behind the bar. "I am in need of rooms for my party and
supplies for a long journey. I will pay in gold dust, if
that is acceptable."

The man ran a filthy rag across the top of the bar and
his eyes over the blond woman. He snorted derisively.
"Ain't no rooms for greasers. You can leave the woman,
though."

Miguel continued to smile. He placed two bags of gold
dust on the counter. "Then you will permit me to purchase
flour and coffee and we shall be on our way."

Several of the other customers, some in an advanced
state of drunkenness despite the early hour, had risen to
their feet to study the Mexicans and their blond companion.

"They kidnap you, girlie?" one grizzled old miner asked her suspiciously. Her eyes regarded him coldly and only the upraised eyebrow acknowledged she had even heard the question. Then she turned her head in the opposite direction.

"Christ, you've got to admire their gall," one man muttered. "Walking in large as life and demanding service. Must be new in these parts. Hey, you, we string up greasers who don't know their place." The latter remark was addressed in the direction of Miguel's back and he turned slowly and regarded the man. For a few seconds they stared at each other and then the man turned to the other patrons of the bar. "See the way he's looking at me?" he asked indignantly.

Miguel's hands moved briefly in the sign language that caused Golden Feather to immediately place himself between the miner and Kyla, then swiftly usher her through the door into the street.

Miguel's teeth flashed again in a smile. "Señors, it is a pity you refuse to take my money, because now I must take what I need and teach you a lesson in how to treat your customers."

His arm snaked out, caught the proprietor about the throat and pushed him backward into the row of bottles that lined the wall. At the same instant guns appeared in the hands of two of the bar's patrons but before they could squeeze the trigger two of Miguel's men threw their knives with deadly accuracy.

The melee was soon over. Two other men dropped to the floor as chairs were broken over their heads. The sound of groans and splintering wood drifted out into the sunbaked street. While one Mexican held his gun on the remaining men in the store, Miguel and the others filled their buckskin bags with provisions.

Outside, Kyla and Golden Feather had mounted their horses and were riding slowly back the way they came. Only when they heard the thunder of hooves behind them did Golden Feather give Kyla's horse a jab on the rump to send it galloping forward.

Now the men on the street and the miners at the river

saw a display of riding that few had ever seen equalled.
Miguel and his men streaked out of town, riders and horses
a symphony of swift and graceful movement. There had
never been horsemen like the *californios*.

Long before the townsmen had stumbled to their own
horses, the party of Mexicans had vanished in the rolling,
wooded countryside.

"It would have been nice to sleep in a bed tonight,"
Kyla said somewhat wistfully when they were again
riding at a leisurely pace.

"Be patient, *chiquita*," Miguel said. "At the end of our
journey you will sleep in the *casa grande* at the Marques
*hacienda*."

"It seems too good to be true," Kyla said. "Tell me
again."

"It is simple. Only Alta California has been ceded to the
United States. Baja California is still ours. The border lies
just south of San Diego. Therefore, the Marques *hacienda*
is still in Mexico. Now that Santa Anna is no longer in
power, Apolo Ramírez has arranged for the *hacienda* to
be granted to me for my service in the army. We've lost
most of the land, but we will have the house and some of
the peons' huts and outbuildings. It is a beginning. We will
not be rich, Kyla, not in the way my father was rich, but
our home will be restored to us and we will not have to live
with the *norteamericanos* and their contempt."

"And does Apolo Ramírez know what you've been
doing north of the border?" Kyla asked, raising her eyebrows quizzically.

Miguel smiled. "He believes I have been living with
Maria and her rich *yanqui* husband. Ah, Kyla, *chiquita*,
life is good again! I am going home and my beloved rides
at my side."

Kyla forced her lips into a smile. The ice that had
encased her heart since the night of the fire was a welcome
barrier between her emotions and the outside world. She
was only vaguely concerned that Miguel was indisputably
a *bandido*. He was reckless and daring and flirted constantly with death. That she might lose him at any moment
was just another fact of life that she pushed into the back

of her mind, along with the knowledge that she herself now occupied a position in life that was a far cry from the honored role of Doña Talmage, mistress of the de Rivero *rancho*.

It was becoming easier for her to play a part, and even Miguel accepted the changes in her as being the result of her ordeal in the farmhouse. How could he know that the new Kyla who had calmly stolen a horse to ride to their rendezvous at the *Los Amigos rancho* had been born the night of the burning of San Francisco?

The Marques *hacienda* was the same, yet different. The surrounding land remained untouched by war, cattle still roamed the cliffs above the surf-edged Pacific Ocean, and horses ran free in the coastal valleys. East of the collapsed-elephant-train hills, the searing desert lay unchanged, serene, in its starkly unadorned beauty.

The *casa grande* had been occupied from time to time by friends of El Presidente and others who sought to take the place of the Padrone, but there had been too few peons to work it because of the war, and no one had the strength to rule the vast estate. All of the large *haciendas* had been broken up into smaller farms, some occupied by squatters and others by soldier-peons.

Through the good offices of Apolo Ramírez, the last family to occupy the Marques *casa grande* had been sent elsewhere at the end of the war. But Miguel had not come to take possession, and squatters and vandals had passed through leaving the house in a sad state of disrepair. Most of the original furniture was missing.

Miguel strode about his home angrily, dark eyes smoldering. Kyla stood watching him and for a moment saw the stern features of the Padrone superimposed in a ghostly manner over Miguel's face. She shivered in the warm sunshine.

"We will rebuild and restore," Miguel announced at last. "I swear I will make it better than before. We shall do it with *yanqui* gold." He looked across the litter-strewn floor to where Kyla stood silhouetted in the open doorway and then moved toward her, arms outstretched.

She went into his arms willingly, needing the comfort of

the closeness of a man who loved her, but when she felt him stirring against her she drew away.

His black brows came together in a frown. "We are home now, *chiquita*. You promised me. How long will you make me wait when my blood cries out for you?"

She turned away from him, pulling her hat from her head and shaking her hair free. "The men are outside and it is still broad daylight, Miguel. Besides, we have much work to do. We can't prepare a meal or even sleep here until we clear some of the debris left by the previous tenants."

"Pigs!" Miguel said, looking around again angrily. "I should have come home before. I had thought I would bring my *guerrilleros* to hide in the desert or to the cave of the *Bufadora* if ever the Yanqui soldiers chased us south of the border. But the *yanquis* never followed. They are afraid of our desert and our ocean. They are obsessed with being near fresh water at all times. Ah, Kyla, this land does not belong to them, not our beautiful California."

"The gold it yields, Miguel. That's what they want. But at least we still have Baja California."

"Broken in two like the wishbone of a chicken, that's what they did to our California," Miguel said. He stepped outside to look at the patio. The bougainvillea vines that once had brightened the adobe walls with their colorful red and orange blossom were now dead from lack of water. The handsomely carved door showed signs of entry by means of an axe. All except the hardiest and most drought-resistant trees and shrubs were withered. Tiles were missing from the roof, windows were broken, the intricate decorations adorning the front of the house were crumbling from the walls and the alcoves that had once contained miniature statues of the saints were empty.

Kyla peeled a hanging strip of tapestry from the interior wall and followed him, wanting to reach out and touch him comfortingly, yet afraid he would misunderstand the gesture.

"When my father acquired this land, he had three hundred years of Spanish rule behind him, the order and continuity of a vast empire. Yet within his lifetime, Mexico gained independence from Spain and in turn was conquered by the *Yanquis*. The rules my father lived by no longer apply to us." As he spoke, Miguel turned and looked down at her and there was lost pride and furious resolve in the words. For a moment she felt an old familiar bond as their thoughts met and blended, and she knew that love of the land was a more enduring passion than all others. He was her Miguel, companion of her childhood and she loved him dearly.

She put up her hand and touched his arm, slid her fingers downward to find his hand and looked at him, promising him with her eyes that she would no longer withhold that which he wanted most from her.

He smiled, the tight lines vanishing from his handsome features, and he pulled her to him and kissed her hungrily while his men, tending their horses, grinned and murmured *"Olé!"*

That night when they found the tattered remains of a sheet to cover the bed the Padrone had once shared with his bride, Miguel took her by the hand and drew her down, bending to kiss her eyelids, her lips, her throat. He slipped the nightgown from her shoulders, revealing her breasts and tiny waist and his eyes worshipped her as he pressed his mouth to the delicate pink areola, his lips parting and his tongue gently exploring.

She looked down at the dark head against the whiteness of her body and could not stop the shiver that rippled along her spine, or her teeth from biting down over her lower lip. *He mustn't know!* She placed her fingers on his head, drew his face upward toward her and, closing her eyes, kissed him with all the remembered fervor she had felt for Quint Delleroc. She felt the warm hardness of his body and wriggled out of her nightgown, guiding him as he tried to enter her, but her body knew it was all a lie.

She made soft little sounds and undulated her body and recreated in her mind the night her fevered blood had churned in unison with her lover. She learned, because she cared deeply for Miguel, to do what caring women have done since the dawn of time—to act the act of love.

# 25

*Shansi raised her head, her lips still parted as though*
in surprise. She ran her tiny exquisite hands over Quint
Delleroc's abdomen, exploring the taut muscles, sliding
downward to caress his strangely reluctant manhood. Her
long dark hair trailed across his thighs as she bent over
him again, her small breasts pressing, cradling. When her
lips sought him again he stopped her, his hand caught in
her hair to raise her face to look at him.

Her remote eyes met his and he shook his head wearily.
"It's no use, Shansi."

She shrugged her slim shoulders and rose from the
bed, slipping the curtain of her hair over her shoulder.
The dawn was breaking, damp and chill, but her naked-
ness was of no concern to her, despite the unheated
room.

Quint watched her for a moment. Then, with a quick
movement, he swung his feet over the edge of the bed.
He moved to the window and looked out at the awakening
city. "I'm going back to Monterey," he said, more to himself than to Shansi. "There has to be some way to reunite
all of the disintegrating elements of my life." Quietly he
continued to speak, to perhaps make sense of his thoughts.

"I was happy there, for a little while. It seemed then
that life was full of promise, after all. A strange and
exotic new land, the adventure yet to come in Mexico,

standing in for Desmond at his arranged marriage. I thought then there would be another war between England and the United States over the Oregon dispute, and perhaps I'd clash with the British officers who threatened us with court-martial in India. But for all the *yanqui* bleating about 'Fifty-Four-Forty or Fight' the whole thing fizzled out. They settled it peaceably and went to war with Mexico instead. And Des—I tried to make amends for ruining his name in India, and what did I accomplish? He simply traded his monastery for a mission." He turned from the window abruptly and looked down at Shansi. She lay still now, her eyes closed, her body glistening slightly. He pulled the sheet over her.

"And you, Shansi," he added softly. "What shall I do with you? You leave your magic cloud only long enough to satisfy the cravings it induces. Odd, that once I found you sensuously exciting and now only pitiable. You'll never be able to overcome your addiction, will you? There's no longer any point in my locking you up. There are too many Chinese sailors arriving with what you need. I would like to move back to Monterey and live respectably. I'm not sure why. I'll probably find it's merely another passing whim. Still, I can't leave you here, can I?"

But Shansi was not listening. She was sound asleep. Quint dressed and went along the hotel corridor to knock on Felice's door.

She opened it quickly, a finger to her lips as she gestured for him to enter. "He's asleep," she said. Even in a whisper her voice was full-bodied.

Felice had gained weight in the year that had passed since she willingly took up the role of surrogate mother to Delleroc's foundling. The child they called Victor was a foundling—that was all Delleroc had ever told her, just as she had told him only briefly of the husband and baby she had lost to cholera soon after her arrival in California. She pulled her wrapper more modestly over her expansive bosom and sat down at the table, where the coffeepot spread its inviting aroma into the room.

Next to the table was the wooden high chair Quint had made for Victor, smeared with the evidence of a recent bout with breakfast porridge.

She poured two cups of coffee and scratched herself absently. "You thought any more about a house, Mr. Delleroc? He's a handful to keep in a hotel room."

"I'm going to take you back to Monterey. I don't think the doctors here can do any more, it will be up to us now, Felice. Have you exercised his feet this morning? Shall I wait and do the manipulation when he wakes?"

"No, I haven't done it yet. He took the brace off in the night again."

"I'll have a word with him. He's bright, isn't he, Felice? Did you ever see a brighter child for his age?"

She smiled indulgently. "Maybe any child would be clever if it were talked to and read to and played with as much as he is. You've surprised me, Mr. Delleroc. I thought you would have lost interest in him months ago after the doctor told us we must manipulate his feet twice a day. And there still may have to be an operation, even after the casts and braces and all. Then, I thought you spent so much time with him because he was a little cripple, like Lord Talmage, and you seem to have a great compassion for them."

A frown descended over hawklike features, and his voice was sharp. "You are never to use that word in his presence. He has a shortening of the Achilles tendons, and by the time he is a man it will be forgotten."

Felice looked hurt. "You don't have to tell me. I love him as much as you do. And not just because he took me away from smoky gambling dens and the great paws of miners and sailors, either."

Her booming laugh rang out and she clapped a hand hastily over her mouth, her body shaking with suppressed giggles. It was not possible for Felice's exuberant personality to remain offended for more than a split-second. She ran her plump fingers through her hair, where an inch of gray showed at the roots. Her skin was still good and her features attractive, but Felice was enjoying moving into the calmer waters of middle age. Life had been hectic and there were enough memories to tide her over any dull afternoons.

She chided herself silently for speaking without thinking and comparing the child's clubfeet to Lord Talmage's frightful injuries. She should have realized there was a good reason Delleroc had sworn her to secrecy about his bringing the child to her. He had been particularly insistent that Lord and Lady Talmage must not find out. It must be, Felice reasoned, that Delleroc was afraid Lord Talmage would believe he adopted the foundling *because* of the clubfeet, rather than in spite of them. This thought was too deep, and she shrugged it away. Felice was not the first to be baffled by the mystical relationship between the two men.

"Fel—lice!" A strident young voice called from the adjoining bedroom. "Fel—lice. I'm awake."

They both went in to the room and Victor's busy little fingers stopped working on the braces when he saw Quint. "Morning, Quint. How are we?" the child asked, black eyes lighting up mischievously. His mop of golden curls had grown almost to his shoulders, but Felice refused to cut them, despite Quint's admonishment that Victor would shortly be mistaken for a girl.

"We are excellent," Quint responded gravely. "And does the young gentleman include himself in the royal 'we'? If so, let me help you with the braces, and we'll find out."

Felice hid a smile. Quint always spoke to the child as though he were a miniature adult. Surprisingly, Victor usually understood and often responded with grown-up phrases he surely did not fully understand.

He had Kyla's delicate cheekbones and full, sensitive lips, but his nose was bolder, and the chin jutting and stubborn. Even with the curls, he did not look like a girl.

"You going to pull my feet? I want Felice to do it."

"I've no doubt you do. Felice is too tender-hearted, and doesn't use all her strength when you look at her like a martyred cherub. How would you like to go and live in a house with a garden and patio? Other children to play with. Perhaps a school."

"No! I want to go with you!" Victor said. Then he added wheedlingly, "Take me to see the ships today— please?"

Felice did not stay to watch the manipulation and exercises that had to be done twice daily to keep the tendons flexible. When it became too painful, Quint would pretend to box with the boy so that the small flailing fists would help ease the tension.

"There are ships in Monterey too," Quint told him. "That's where our house is."

"I suppose you haven't forgotten that the Ramseys moved back to Monterey?" Felice called to him from the adjoining room. "They left San Francisco after the last fire." She was too polite to add that she knew there was no love lost between them.

On the anniversary of the May fire of 1850, a second blaze had swept through the city after the Sydney Ducks openly boasted there would be another conflagration. This time eighteen blocks with over two thousand buildings were destroyed—many supposedly fireproof brick structures with iron doors and shutters. Despite the fact that San Francisco now boasted of numerous enthusiastic, if somewhat gaudy, fire companies, the shortage of water had defeated them.

The criminals of the city had again rampaged through the night, looting and murdering and even the most moderate of the city's newspapers, the *Alta California,* had editorialized, "How many murders have been committed in this city within a year? And who has been hanged or punished for the crime? Nobody!" The paper went on to state flatly that lynch law was the only remedy.

Shortly after this, Ramsey, who was known to be actively recruiting a group of vigilantes, was set upon by a band of Sydney Ducks. He had been in Chinatown visiting Ah Toy. Ramsey was badly beaten, but managed to ward off his attackers. As soon as he was able to sell their house, the Ramseys unobtrusively departed for Monterey. After all, with the passage of time, the old guard in that fair city had surely forgotten Maria's earlier status.

"Yes, I know the Ramseys are in Monterey," Quint said, picking up Victor to give him a playful hug. Quint did not give voice to the thought that it amused him to watch Ramsey run around and collide with his own fear—that Delleroc was waiting to pay him back for what had happened in the Mexican desert. If Ramsey had not left him with the dying Sergeant Morgan, then Morgan would not have asked him to visit his brother at Sutter's Fort. And Quint would not have been one of the first to obtain gold when it was discovered there. He had taken enough to finance his journey to the East Coast to purchase a cargo of goods.

"I've had no contact with the Ramseys since Lord Talmage left town," Quint added.

"They never found her body, did they?" Felice asked.

"That's because she isn't dead," Quint answered.

"How do you know?"

"Because if she were I'd be able to put her out of my thoughts. But she lives on in my mind, Felice. And that's another little secret I'll ask you to keep."

Desmond had reopened a small mission far to the south. He found the climate in Southern California less cruel to his leg, and he had grown to love the desert. He was fascinated by the terrain, as different from his own misty green dells as might be the moon.

The mission was situated east of San Diego. There was a quadrangle of adobe buildings, a grove of cottonwoods and a cluster of palms around an underground spring. It was the only mission not built within easy access to the sea and connected by El Camino Real, the royal road of the Spanish civilization. Instead, an Irish priest who arrived in California under mysterious circumstances had founded the mission about the time of Mexican independence, using the Spanish missions as a model. Though it had been abandoned on the death of the priest, and for years unused, Desmond had learned about the place from wayfarers who had stopped at the mission south of Monterey while he and Kyla lived there.

The desert yielded little in the way of food, and the

few Indians who joined him sustained themselves by taking their handicrafts to the nearest settlement to barter for food. Desmond was also able to solicit donations from local *rancheros*.

He had taken to wearing the robes of a monk, and he was beginning to forget that there had ever been a world of commerce and bustle known as San Francisco. On the day his peaceful existence was shattered, he had spent a quiet hour in meditation before his simple evening meal. He had congratulated himself that at last he could remember Kyla without the accompanying pain and rage he felt. He was even able, occasionally, to think of Shansi and the earthly passions she had resurrected in him. Poor doomed Shansi, how lovely she had been.

In quiet moments he considered the years he had known Delleroc and how each had used the other and pretended what they shared was friendship. He felt as though he had ridden a ship through the wild waves of a tempest and had come at last into a calm harbor.

*"Padre! Padre!"* The voice that broke into his thoughts came from the shadows beyond the open door of his room and it did not belong to any of the men who lodged in the small mission.

"Who is it? Who is there?" he called back, feeling for his cane so he could stand up.

"Sanctuary, *padre*? Will you give us sanctuary? We have a wounded man and are being pursued by soldiers."

Desmond had not heard riders approaching, but a fugitive would have approached with stealth. There had been rumors that the notorious Joaquin Murrieta was riding this way from Los Angeles.

"Of course. Bring him in."

*"Gracias, padre."*

Desmond bent to light another taper in the branched candlesticks on the rough wooden table as two men carried a third into the room. "Over there. On the bed," Desmond said, searching for the bag which contained the precious bandages, the scalpel he had begged from a doctor in town, and a small bottle of brandy.

They placed the wounded man face down. The man

who was peeling off the blood-saturated poncho looked up at Desmond, and the candlelight caught the proud and handsome features.

"I was afraid I was dealing with Joaquin Murrieta," Desmond said. "Welcome to my house, Miguel Marques. I will do what I can for your friend."

Dawn was breaking, and all except Miguel and the wounded man had departed when Desmond went into the chapel to pray for divine guidance. The wounded man was dying, and Desmond was not a priest. He looked down at the monk's robes he wore. He was a fraud, an impostor not unlike Delleroc playing the part of Desmond Talmage. Perhaps, he thought wearily, he could send one of the Indians to San Diego to find a real priest—one who could be trusted not to report the presence of *bandidos*.

But it was too late. The soldiers who had been tracking the *bandidos* had surrounded the mission before anyone realized their presence. One of them appeared at the door to the sacristy and his hand was placed over Desmond's mouth to insure silence.

Minutes later Desmond saw them drag Miguel outside, his hands tied behind his back, and throw him over a horse.

The young lieutenant in charge came to the chapel door and removed his hat respectfully while the trooper released his hold on Desmond. "The other one is dead," the lieutenant said. "Hope my man didn't rough you up too much, Father. We knew there wasn't anything you could do except give them sanctuary."

Kyla was not concerned that Miguel had not returned to the hacienda with the dawn. Often he and his men slipped into a friendly *pueblo* to spend the night after one of their raids. Her Indian maid was placing a freshly sliced mango on the marble-topped table as Kyla came into the house after her early-morning ride.

As she sat down to breakfast, Kyla noticed a small lizard on the wall above the window. The tiny curved body was beautifully marked with vivid orange stripes,

unlike the common gray lizards that usually crept into
the house in search of insects. The bright coloring made
her think of Quint Delleroc. There were so few creatures
of gaudy brightness in the world.

She sighed as she sipped her chocolate and turned her
thoughts to Miguel. He had changed so much in the last
year, she hardly knew him. He was like a bowstring that
had been drawn too taut. They quarreled constantly, and
she had learned that an argument would not end until she
had grown as angry as he. It was as though he must bait
her until she became a screaming virago and then he
would watch her expectantly, as though waiting for her to
reveal something to him that would only be said in the
heat of anger.

Although it was apparent that at times, in her unguarded moments, Miguel could still read her thoughts,
she found herself unable to guess at his. It was, she decided, because his thoughts were in such a turmoil. There
were so many conflicting desires. Part of him wanted to live
a leisurely, gracious life like his father. He also wanted to
arouse the downtrodden peons and force them to demand
the kind of government the country needed. And yet
another part of him, perhaps the most dominant now,
*enjoyed* the role of *bandido* leader.

Miguel had learned to kill in the war, but he had not
learned how to stop. She was forced to admit that he
shared the booty they brought from the *yanqui* north with
the poor peons, but she lay awake at night and wondered
about the men he had killed and about how long she and
Miguel would have to live on stolen money. Once she had
tried to persuade him to give up the life of *bandido,* buy
some cattle, round up some of the wild mustangs. He had
turned on her angrily and said, "Tell me what you really
mean, Kyla. Tell me that you tire of living here with me.
That you miss the excitement of your San Francisco balls
and parties and theaters. Here you have only Miguel and
he is not enough for you."

"No! That's unfair, Miguel." Her own anger had flared.
"I fear for your life. You grow more reckless every time
you ride north. But perhaps you are right. Perhaps it is this

place. It is full of ghosts of a life that will never be again. And us? What about us? We are like children playing a game. You are the Padrone, and I am Doña Kyla, and we are rich and very, very respectable."

He clasped her shoulders and spun her around to face him, his dark eyes blazing. "It is not I who plays a game, Kyla. I am well aware that I am a desperado with a price on his head, and that you are a woman who has been used by other men. And it is not I who lies in the arms of my lover and pretends he is someone else."

She tried to wrench herself free of his hands, but as she struggled, he pulled her closer and kissed her on the mouth, a fierce hungry kiss that was full of despair. They had made up, as always, and he had made love to her, but his hands and his lips still conveyed the anger he felt. She suffered his caresses and the coupling of their bodies, but there was no joy in her heart and no release for her own flesh.

Afterward, when he slept, she rose and went to the window to look at the play of light and shadow across the flagged patio. Why, she thought, why can't I love him the way he loves me? She knew now that she must never again indulge in the fancy that it was Quint Delleroc making love to her, for Miguel had surely read her thoughts and known. We do the same things, she thought, Miguel touches me and caresses me and kisses me. But there is not that spark of wild joy, a joy that makes us whole when we are together.

She tried to recall what she had read in one of Desmond's books. Was it the poetry of Lord Byron? Something about a woman loves her lover only in her first passion, that in all others all she loves is love. Why did her first and only love have to be Quint Delleroc, who was incapable of loving only one woman? Miguel had never loved anyone else. He was young and handsome and brave, and she was twisting a knife in his heart because he saw through her pretense. Yet she could not love him with the passion and abandon she had given to Quint. She turned and looked at Miguel's dark hair against the pillow, his arm outstretched about the place where she had lain beside him. She must learn to be an actress. She must practice concealing all of her emotions, from Miguel and from everyone else. She would never see Quint Delleroc again, but if the fates were cruel and their paths did cross, she would never again let him use and discard her.

No matter how hard she tried to create the illusion of happiness with Miguel, he became more unhappy, more reckless in his raids and more boastful as the days passed. He was the small boy again, strutting and showing off and trying to surpass each daredevil feat with another even more dangerous, just to impress her.

The fact that he and his men had not returned from their latest raid meant that once again they had been unable to cross the border because their pursuers were hard on their heels. They would be hiding somewhere in a settlement of *californios* or Mexicans. And what if they clashed with Joaquin Murrieta and his pack of cutthroats? Kyla knew that Miguel had agreed not to raid in his territory. Yet he struck in Southern California so that he might return to her at the *hacienda*.

It was high noon before Golden Feather rode through the hacienda gates on a lame horse, followed by a weary group of riders. Kyla saw at once that Miguel was not with them.

She came through the door and waited, a feeling of dread sweeping through her. She thought, He can't be dead . . . no, please don't let him be dead . . . we quarreled again before he left. . . .

Miguel and two others were missing. One was Carlos Ramírez, younger brother of Apolo. Golden Feather slipped from his horse and moved his hands rapidly in the sign language that she only partly understood. There was, however, no mistaking who the *padre* was who was sheltering Miguel and Carlos. Desmond Talmage. Golden Feather's fingers clearly indicated Desmond's missing arm and stiff leg.

Late the following afternoon the messenger arrived from Desmond, bringing the news that Carlos was dead and

Miguel had been captured by *yanqui* soldiers. Desmond was going to do all he could to prevent Miguel's execution.

Kyla immediately went to her room and began to pack a bag, while Golden Feather saddled their horses.

# 26

*Maria stamped her foot and screamed, "I tell you he has* moved back into his house here. And brought Felice and a child—about four years old, undoubtedly his own bastard, or why would he put them in his house? Just when we were making a new start here with all the new settlers. Now someone will remember that Felice used to run a gambling parlor behind Merciful's undertakers and that I dealt cards for her."

"Among other things," Garett muttered under his breath. He frowned and blew a cloud of cigar smoke across the bed quilt. Why the hell did Delleroc have to return to Monterey? Garett Ramsey spent a good deal of time in San Francisco "attending to business" and when he came home to the pleasant town on the breathtaking peninsula, he was able to cloak himself in respectability and gracious living. As a businessman interested in community affairs, and an avowed and generous patron of the arts, it was only a matter of time until he was elected to the state legislature.

The Vigilance Committee had already acted on one of his suggestions, and had imposed a twenty-dollar-a-month tax on all foreign miners. But in the mining camps and among the merchants, the assessment had caused havoc. Foreigners were unable to pay both the tax *and* the sky-high prices for food and lodging. They left the country in

266

droves. The tax also fanned feelings between Americans and Mexicans to white heat. The Mexicans did not think of themselves as foreigners. They felt they had as much right to the gold as the *yanqui* newcomers.

Having stirred up the citizens of San Francisco, Ramsey created a reputation as a fearless proponent of law and order. It was also no secret that he enjoyed the charms of the Chinese prostitutes. In Monterey, however, Ramsey's alter ego dwelled as chastely as any deacon. Because the two cities were far enough apart he was able to maintain his dual lives with ease.

Maria was right. They did not need Quint Delleroc in Monterey. He belonged in San Francisco with the Sydney Ducks and the other scum.

"Oh, I wish you wouldn't smoke that thing in here," Maria said, furiously fanning the cigar smoke from the air. "You remind me of that terrible man Merciful Smith with his perpetual cigar. Thank goodness *he* won't be able to move back here." She went to the window and flung it open.

Garett stared moodily into space, the ash growing in length on the cigar stuck between his lips. Maria's rages were one of the reasons his visits to Monterey were as brief as possible. He harbored a secret fear that, if sufficiently goaded, she might slip a stiletto under his ribs while he slept. Strangely, it was this very quality in her that he most admired. She was a spirited and fearless woman, and he was proud of her looks and breeding, despite the fact that they lived in a society suspicious of Mexicans. No one meeting his wife for the first time thought of her as anything but Spanish royalty. It was a pity she had not conceived a child before he became impotent with her. That was another reason to keep Maria contented in all other respects; she kept her mouth shut about their domestic relations.

"Well?" she demanded. "What are you going to do about Delleroc?"

"Keep an eye on him. If he tries to open up any seedy gambling dens or any other kind of business here, we can do something about it. But I don't see what we can do about him moving back into a house he owns."

Maria paced angrily in front of the latticed windows overlooking the azure sweep of the ocean. Their house stood at the crest of a hill and enjoyed a panoramic view of the bay. But Maria's dark eyes saw only the hateful image of Delleroc's hawklike features and flaming mane of hair moving back into her life to plague her. She had carried a seething resentment of the man since he humiliated her by accepting an assignation and then appearing at her door in the company of Kyla and her husband.

"And what about Felice? And the child?"

"I don't suppose she'll come calling. But I'll stop by and tell her we have to be careful who we associate with now. And maybe I'll send a couple of letters of inquiry to England and to Mexico City, see if I can find out anything we can use against Delleroc. He and Desmond had a fight after Kyla was burned to death. Desmond said something about Delleroc ruining his name in India. He was in the British Indian Army, so perhaps I can learn something from them. He also mentioned a plot with Santa Anna."

Maria began to calm down. "Don't lose any time," she said sharply. "And be sure to go and see Felice before you return to San Francisco. You *are* going back tomorrow?"

"Yes. Is everything ready for the dinner party here tonight? I'd like it to be a prelude to the party we throw next time I'm home. The Vigilance Committee is going to make some dramatic moves shortly, and next time I'm in Monterey I expect to be preceded by some interesting news stories. Did I tell you I was speaking with Sam Branigan—"

Maria looked out of the window and shut out the sound of his voice droning on about his political cohorts. Their house was well situated, with a pleasant view, but Maria could not understand why Garett postponed the sorely needed bolstering of their hurriedly built frame house. When she complained that the entire wall shook if she slammed the front door, he would make vague promises and hint that perhaps there would be a house in Washington in their future—or even a governor's mansion.

Standing at their bedroom window, she looked over the flimsy verandah roof and decided the main advantage to their Monterey house was that Garett spent little time in it. She gave a shiver of anticipation. Tomorrow she would be alone again, free of Garett's clumsy and cumbersome presence. Thank goodness he stayed only long enough to keep up appearances, for Maria had a lover whose hot Spanish blood matched her own and whose profession was an added fillip to their affair.

She had been the only female passenger on the stagecoach journeying from San Francisco to Monterey the day the *bandidos* came riding alongside, firing their guns and causing the horses to bolt. She had stared, fascinated, at the flashing-eyed leader, with his red serape flying in the wind as his sleek black horse shot past the window. He caught up with their lead horses and within minutes they came sliding to a halt, the driver dispatched by a bullet between the eyes and the other male passengers relieved of their valuables, stripped and running for their lives.

Maria had waited, her heart hammering, but her chin tilted defiantly, while the *bandido* leader walked in a slow circle around her. She studied him as intently as he studied her. She noted the straight black hair and level eyebrows that gave his head a sculptured look, the thread of moustache and small goatee accentuating his mouth, the lean features and piercing eyes that said this was a very dangerous man. He had thrown the red serape back over his shoulders and beneath it wore a low-cut vest of black velvet under a dark jacket.

"Your jewelry, *por favor*, señora," he said politely.

Maria started to slip the heavy gold wedding band from her finger, with some pleasure.

"No. You may keep your wedding ring. Just the necklace and your other rings."

Regretfully Maria pushed the ring back and began to fumble with the clasp of her necklace, but her hair hung in lustrous waves over the nape of her neck and she gave a little exclamation of annoyance.

"Allow me, señora," the *bandido* leader said. His fingers were warm against her neck and she looked up at him from under curling dark eyelashes as he freed the necklace but allowed his fingertip to linger against the soft skin of her throat.

"What do you propose to do with me?" Maria asked, slightly breathless. She felt no fear, some instinct telling her he would display Spanish chivalry toward a woman, despite his occupation. The rest of the *bandidos* maintained a respectful distance, sitting motionless on their horses. Besides, she thought carelessly, if he wanted to possess her body—well, he was very handsome. There had been few men in her life as attractive. "Will you shoot me, or perhaps you would like to strip me naked also and send me running into the woods?"

The man smiled, his white teeth flashing in the deepening twilight. "Joaquin Murrieta does not shoot beautiful women, señora, but I must admit, the picture you conjure up of your lovely body naked in the moonlight—ah, that is enough to tempt a saint."

She smiled, too, a slow seductive smile. "Surely, the famous Joaquin Murrieta will not leave a helpless woman alone? You will at least escort me to a lodging for the night?"

Joaquin paused for a moment while their eyes met and held in a long eloquent glance and then he called over his shoulder, "Claudio, unhitch a horse from the stagecoach for the señora. We shall take her with us."

*Murrieta!* Her blood raced with excitement as she rode along the pine-shrouded trail. They took her to a small house hidden in a thicket of tall trees. The house was built of wood, in the American style, rather than of adobe brick, and Maria wondered casually what had become of the American settlers who owned it. There were also several tents nearby, and women were cooking an evening meal.

Joaquin slid gracefully from his horse and his hands went about her waist to lift her from the saddle. But there was a long moment before her feet touched the ground as he held her and feasted his eyes on the full lips and long column of her neck. Just before he put her down, his lips brushed against the hollow of her throat.

"In the morning," he said huskily, "I will see you are delivered safely to your husband. Meantime, you are my guest."

They dined surprisingly well, although Joaquin apologized profusely for the food and accommodations, telling her this was only a temporary hideaway since he was newly arrived in Northern California. There had been too many close brushes with the law in the south.

As she sipped a fine red wine, she found herself chattering as though they were old friends. It was such a pleasure to speak Spanish again; her thoughts flowed with the wine. They commiserated with each other about the treatment meted out to their people by the *yanquis* and Maria let a single tear slip down her cheek as she explained she had been forced into marriage with a great oaf of a *gringo*. Joaquin's lean brown fingers closed comfortingly over her pale ones, the piercing eyes softening sympathetically.

"There are probably at least half a dozen Joaquin Murrietas who ride and plunder from one end of the state to the other," he told her as one of the women brought a large pot of *sopa de carne seca y arroz,* and ladled the jerky and rice soup into earthenware bowls. "I could not possibly have committed all of the crimes the *yanquis* attribute to me." He smiled again and she felt his knee press against hers beneath the rough wooden table.

There was one bedroom in the house, and when he led her into it, his men were eating outside, seated in a circle about their campfire. One of the women was playing a guitar softly, a hauntingly sad melody that spoke of times gone by and lost loves. In the darkness of the room, lit only by the firelight flickering through the window, Maria gave a little sob as Joaquin's arms went around her.

The touch of his lips brought a flame leaping inside her that scorched its way to the tips of her fingers, her toes, her inner thighs, the nipples that thrust hard against the silk of her bodice. Then his hands were freeing her breasts from the restraining silk, caressing, encircling, fingers tracing the nipple points.

Impatiently she shrugged her shoulders free of the dress, letting it fall about her ankles. Her chemise followed, and Joaquin sighed as his dark eyes caressed her body. He laughed softly as she tugged at the sash wound tightly about his middle, and he helped her unfasten the buttons beneath. "Eh, señora, it is good that first I removed the knife I carried there, *sí*?"

She pressed her lips to the taut skin of his chest, letting her hands explore his body. "Maria," she murmured. "My name is Maria." Then she slipped to her knees and her lips found his pulsating manhood and he exclaimed sharply that she must wait and let him first make love to her in all the ways he desired, that he would worship at the altar of her beauty.

He lifted her to the bed and began to kiss her. She felt the soft hair of his moustache and goatee making a tantalizing trail over the tightening flesh of her stomach and she seized his head, feeling the thick black hair beneath her fingers. Her hips were writhing wildly in some pagan pirouette of their own, and when his tongue flicked lightly downward over the yielding flesh of her inner thighs she moaned and her head rolled from side to side. "Joaquin!" she gasped, "I want you inside me— ah!" Her words ended in a cry of pleasure as he swung his body up over hers, poised for a moment with his member throbbing against the center of all of her desire, then thrust inside her so swiftly and surely that dizzying lights exploded in the darkness.

They moved together, their bodies plunging and soaring in a dance of abandon that increased in tempo until the driving force that united them exploded into an apex of delight that rippled through their bodies and numbed their minds in its afterglow.

"*Caramba!*" Joaquin mumbled weakly against her hair. "I never expected to find such a woman. Maria— Maria!"

There was no sleep for them that night as they found different ways to excite and please each other—many exotic positions in which their lithe young bodies could be joined. The music of their lovemaking throbbed deep in the realm of their flesh, blotting out everything that existed beyond the small circle of their arms and sighs.

When he escorted her to Monterey the following day, disguised in the traveling robes of a priest so that he might accompany her all the way to her door, she was wearing the necklace and rings he had removed the evening before, as well as a new gold bracelet. And a place had been chosen where she could send him a message when her husband was away.

In San Diego, it was at first believed the army had captured the notorious Joaquin Murrieta. But then the word of the Englishman was accepted. The defiant young Mexican who refused to answer questions was actually Miguel Marques, who had served in the Mexican Cavalry and then become a *guerillero*. Still, only the fact that Miguel was captured by the army saved him from a prompt hanging.

In San Francisco, the Vigilance Committee had personally placed the nooses around the necks of several Sydney Ducks and hauled them, kicking, into the air. Other vigilantes throughout the state quickly followed their example.

In response to Desmond Talmage's pleas, the army held Miguel while a civil judge was sought to conduct a trial. Desmond looked for a defense lawyer.

As the lieutenant who captured Miguel was told—somewhat cynically by his commanding officer—"The end result will be the same, no matter what. The Mex will dance on the end of a rope. But the whole country is up in arms about the lawlessness here and about California's vigilante justice. A trail will help show the rest of the country that we can be just as civilized with our hangings as they are. I want you personally to get as many newspapermen as possible to cover the story of the capture and the upcoming trial."

"Yes, sir," the lieutenant said. "I reckon you know the Mex had another visitor today? A woman."

"Pretty?"

"Very. A blonde, with blue eyes."

The commanding officer's eyebrow went up. "I don't suppose she's his wife?"

The lieutenant grinned. "Hardly. You want her mentioned in the story?"

The sergeant, who had been waiting patiently for his turn to speak now coughed and said, "Begging the major's pardon, sir. But the blond lady is the wife of the Englishman."

Both the commanding officer and the lieutenant looked disappointed at this news.

When the story was carried in the local newspaper, a young reporter waxed eloquent about the good-looking young Spanish blue-blood who had been driven to a life of crime, and who had the championship of an English nobleman and his lovely, golden-haired wife. The reporter was able to weave a thread of pathos, hinting at doomed destinies in the tragic aftermath of war that was in sharp contrast to the usual inflammatory coverage of the activities of Mexican bandidos.

Later, the reporter asked himself, in amazement, what had prompted him to write in such a manner. His only conclusion was that it had been impossible to resist the combined appeal and persuasiveness of the pathetically scarred Englishman, and the huge, sad eyes of the woman. In those misty blue eyes the most hardened cynic had to see the anguish of lost love. The reporter decided against mentioning the fact that the woman had not been living with her husband for over a year, but did go into great detail about Kyla being brought up on the Marques *hacienda* as Miguel's sister. The Indian attack on her stepfather's *rancho,* the loss of the *rancho* at war's end, and a few hints about *californios* being swindled out of their land by shrewd Yankees also appeared in his original story. However, his editor saw no need to stir up the many California Spaniards who had also lost their land, and this portion of the story was deleted.

The story attracted a great deal of attention. There were those who demanded the hanging of a *bandido* without the frills and unnecessary expense of a trial, and there were those who were intrigued by the connection among a crippled but nevertheless titled Englishman, a beautiful woman and a *bandido*. There did seem to be all the elements necessary for dark romance.

When the story was picked up by several newspapers in northern California, Quint Delleroc read it and went immediately to his bank to arrange transfer of funds to Desmond. A lawyer to defend Miguel would be expensive, and Lord Talmage never had money for necessities, let alone emergencies.

# 27

*Until they were alone, Desmond was able to conceal his* shock at Kyla's resurrection from the dead. When he had caught his first glimpse of her, leaving the army stockade after visiting Miguel, he at first thought she was just someone who looked like Kyla. That had happened to him before. Sunlight catching blond hair, a certain incline to a slender neck, a gesture with long-fingered hands—all of these reminded him, painfully, of Kyla. He had learned long ago to disregard the sudden wave of joy that always preceded disappointment as he realized he was merely seeing a woman who looked a little like her.

This time, however, he stopped in the middle of the compound, leaning on his cane, a pulse beating unsteadily in his temple. No, he thought, I'm mistaken. She walks, strides, almost, with too much authority. This woman tosses her head too imperiously. There is more impatience in the movements of her hands. She cannot be sweet, gentle Kyla.

But she was. He could not prevent the tears from springing to his eyes, and he brushed quickly at his face with the fist clasped about his cane.

The troopers accompanying her to the gates saw only a restrained greeting pass between the two before they climbed into a waiting carriage.

"I thought you were dead, Kyla. It was cruel of you to let me think so," Desmond said.

"I couldn't face you, Desmond. Shall we wait until we can be truly alone before we discuss it?" she said, with a glance in the direction of their driver. "I've taken a room at a hotel. We can go there."

She was not the woman he had known and lived with. During the days that followed, he realized how many changes time had wrought. There were moments when a hard and reckless gleam came into her eyes that reminded him, disturbingly, of the defiant gaze of Miguel Marques —and, although Desmond was not sure why he recalled it, the speculative sparks that flashed in Delleroc's eyes, just before he contemplated instigating some kind of mayhem.

When Desmond asked her if she would like him to arrange an annulment of their marriage she had stared at him in surprise. "Annulment? After all this time?"

He looked awkwardly at the floor. "There was no— consummation."

"Oh, I see. No. No, I see no reason why either of us should have to suffer the embarrassment of telling a judge that. I won't live with you again, Desmond, but I have no desire to marry anyone else."

Delleroc's name was never brought up by either of them.

"Kyla, I don't wish to be pessimistic, but you must consider what you will do if we are unable to get Miguel acquitted."

"I have already decided what I shall do," she replied in a tone that precluded further questioning. And that recklessly determined look flashed into her eyes again.

The trial lasted only a few hours. Witnesses for the prosecution told of robbery, murder and rape perpetrated by *bandidos*. And when they added to their testimony the demand for swift justice, they were loudly cheered by the spectators. The crowd was unruly and threatening as the nervous young defense attorney tried in vain to cross-examine the witnesses. But it was not the crowd that swiftly demolished him. The combination of a suave prosecutor and the damning identification of Miguel by witness after witness—most of whom could not possibly have seen the prisoner's face in the raids they described —finally acted to convict Miguel.

Desmond and Kyla were called as character witnesses only, but the case was already lost. An hour after the jury found Miguel guilty, Desmond arrived at Kyla's hotel, puzzled to find her enjoying a leisurely meal in her room.

"Come in, Desmond. I'm glad you're here, you can speak to the newspaper reporter who is waiting to interview us downstairs. I had my dinner sent up here so I wouldn't have to see him."

"Yes, of course," Desmond murmured, taken aback by her aplomb.

"Tell him I am so upset I am lying down."

"Yes. Kyla, are you all right? You seem—unnaturally calm, in view of the verdict."

"I'm perfectly all right. Sit down, Desmond, and have some dinner. You are so dreadfully thin. Do you ever eat? What will you do now, go back to your mission in the desert?"

He lowered himself slowly into a chair. "No, I'm afraid I can't go back. Some of the men from town rode out there a few days ago and drove off the Indians and burned everything that would burn."

"I'm sorry. I suppose your support of Miguel enraged the townspeople?"

"I can understand their feelings. Many isolated farms were robbed, the men killed. Some of the women were raped. Feelings naturally ran high against the bandits, although I am still convinced that the more brutal robberies were executed by Joaquin Murrieta's men, not Miguel's. Then too, there were those who felt I had been masquerading as a priest."

"I never understood why you wore those monk's robes. They must be uncomfortably hot. Where will you go now? Do you ever get homesick for England?" She asked the questions between bites of food that were consumed more methodically than with gusto.

Watching her, Desmond was uneasy. Again he was reminded of Quint Delleroc. The atmosphere between them was like that peculiar tension in the air just before thunderheads appear on the horizon.

"I'll find a place somewhere. I've grown to love this country, Kyla. There is something about the peace and stillness of the desert that is more soul-satisfying than any other terrain on earth. Then, too, the dry air seems to have a therapeutic effect on my—aches and pains. Kyla —you won't—please don't stay in town for the execution."

She raised her head and looked at him, and there was that reckless flash of steel in her eyes again. Her full lower lip curled slightly, and he saw her breasts rise and fall beneath the simple white blouse she wore. She hesitated for a moment, as though about to tell him something, then she lowered her eyes and began savagely to hack another piece of meat from the beefsteak on her plate. "Tell me more about your desert," she said, chewing furiously.

"I believe that no matter what the hordes of immigrants do to the rest of your beautiful California, the desert will prevail, untouched. I pray it will. The delicate balance of life, each creature, each clump of cactus and plant has its own space. Nothing is crowded in the desert. Sunrise is a holy moment. The light sweeps down over timeless hills so simple and unadorned they might be the bare bones of the earth itself. Perhaps I feel that in the desert there is space for even a creature like me. There I will not offend anyone. No one is forced to look upon me."

Kyla looked up again, and this time her eyes were bright with unshed tears. She dropped her fork on her plate and rose and crossed the small space between them. Her arms went about his shoulders, her fingers touched the hair that curled over the nape of his neck and drew his face to her breast. Then, slowly, deliberately, she placed her hand under his chin and forced him to look up at her.

"Desmond, you are the most beautiful human being I have ever known," she said softly, and her hands were on his cheeks, the pressure no less on the cruel scars than the unblemished side of his face. Her fingers gently caressed him as she spoke. "Your every thought has always been for others. You are even more concerned with how other people view your scars than with your own pain. Desmond, how can I tell you—when one gets to know you, the scars disappear. Please believe me, I didn't run away from you, but from myself."

He reached up and took her fingers in his, bending to kiss the palm of her hand. When he looked up at her, his eyes glowed with an emotion she had not seen there before. "Kyla—I know. I've always known. What you ran away from was your love for Quint Delleroc. No, please don't pull away from me. You see, I love him too. Oh, not in the way you love him, but in the way a father loves an errant son, or a brother loves his truant brother. And I, too, ran away from him."

"Not—" she said, her fingers closing around his hand, "not because of me?"

"At the time I told myself that was the reason. But I believe that ever since that day in India, when he saved my life, there have been times when I have tried to escape him. He is an individual so vibrant that he eclipses everyone around him. No one is ever indifferent to Delleroc. They love him or they hate him, and I believe loving him is a harder burden, because he cannot accept the love we offer. I've tried to analyze why this is and all I can come up with is that his birth and early childhood must have taught him that it will hurt to love or be loved. You know how he is. Every time he tells the story of his beginnings, it comes out differently. I don't believe anyone really knows where Delleroc was born, or of what parentage."

"You say you ran away from him," Kyla said. "Where is he? Was he well when last you saw him?"

"I left him in San Francisco. He was well. But knowing Quint, I imagine by now he is somewhere else. He has never stayed this long in one place." It would be better, Desmond decided silently, not to tell her about the anonymous donation of money he had received to pay for Miguel's lawyer.

"I won't deny that I loved him, Desmond. But I love Miguel too, in a different way. And I love our land, fiercely, rather than the quiet way you love your desert. I hate to see turmoil where once there was order and gracious living. Surely there is enough here for everyone? And Desmond, I love you. No matter what happens in the future, I want you to remember that. I love you for the beauty of your soul and for your fine, quick mind. You gave me, in a way, more than either Quint or Miguel gave me. You opened the doors of my mind." She paused and looked over his head toward the window where the sunset was painting the sky in vivid hues. "Desmond, will you go now and speak with the newspaperman downstairs? Explain to him that I'm resting."

He stood up reluctantly and looked deep into her eyes. "Kyla—you aren't—you wouldn't—"

She cut off his words with a finger to his lips, then stood on tiptoe and kissed him lightly on the mouth. "Good night, Desmond."

He dragged himself to the door, turned and looked at her with his sad eyes and half-smile. "Good night, my dear. I'll see you in the morning."

Kyla slipped the bolt across the door and moved swiftly. The long skirt and petticoats were quickly discarded and she pulled on a pair of *vaquero*'s *calzoneras*. A dark jacket went over her blouse and a rough wool poncho over all. The long braid of pale hair was fastened to the top of her head and covered with a battered sombrero several sizes too large, held under her chin by a rawhide thong. The derringer she had taken from Merciful Smith's body was slipped into an inside pocket. From the chest of drawers beside her bed she withdrew a Colt revolver and pushed it into her belt beneath the poncho.

At the window she looked down on the street below. There were few people about as it was the dinner hour. Quickly she slipped out onto the ledge, feeling for the drain spout that ran from the roof. Oh, please, she prayed silently, let me be able to do this. She looked up and saw him then, silhouetted against the night sky, the single feather standing proudly above his head. Golden Feather leaned over the roof to offer her his strong hand.

They went silently across the rooftop and she stopped when they reached the edge, looking at the gap between the hotel roof and the next building. In the daylight it had appeared to be only a few feet in width, but now in the darkness it was a yawning chasm. Golden Feather looked down at her, then his hand closed on hers again and he led her back, away from the edge.

A low cry escaped from his throat as he suddenly dragged her forward. It was the first sound she had ever heard him make. In her surprise, she ran with him, and their momentum carried them across the space between the buildings. She felt the jolt of their landing but quickly recovered. They scrambled over a roof with a steeper incline, downward toward the alley behind the buildings. Then they were on the ground, running toward the waiting horses.

They rode furiously, regretting the time that slipped away, the seconds measured by heartbeats. At the ill-lit *cantiña* in the Mexican part of town, Kyla leaped from her horse. A hand closed around her arm, and she looked up into a pair of fierce black eyes. The man's other hand found the pale gold braid of hair that had slipped from her sombrero during the wild ride. "She is waiting for you. Come," he said.

Above the *cantiña* were two private rooms, and in one of them a woman reclined on a disordered bed, clutching a sodden handkerchief, her eyes red and her cheeks still wet with tears. She wore a bright red dress and her dark hair fell loosely about her shoulders. She rose immediately and flung herself into Kyla's arms, sobbing.

"Maria, it's all right," Kyla said. "We are not going to let them hang him. Please, Maria, calm down. We must leave immediately."

Maria's clutching hands fell away and she looked at the man who stood watching them. "Joaquin has promised to help us," she said.

Kyla tried to keep her hand from shaking, as the man

bent to kiss her wrist. She did not have time to wonder how Maria came to know the infamous Murrieta.

"Garett didn't come with you?" she asked Maria.

"He would not let me even speak of Miguel," Maria said angrily. "When we read the story in the newspaper, he told me we must not let anyone in Monterey know that my name was once Marques. I simply left and did not tell him where I was going."

"Maria. Listen to me. We must free Miguel tonight." Kyla interrupted, sensing Maria wanted to go on talking. "We are grateful to you, señor," she said to Joaquin, "but we do not need your help."

"Oh? And how shall two women break into an army stockade to free Miguel?" Joaquin asked with keen interest. "You knew the army still holds him? They were afraid there would be a lynching if he were transferred to the local jail."

"Maria and her manservant will go to say goodbye to Miguel, who is to die in the morning," Kyla said. "Then they will leave. The plan is as simple as that."

Joaquin's eyes went over the man's clothing Kyla wore: nondescript clothing except for the distinctively patterned poncho with its riot of reds and blues, and the battered sombrero that was too large for her small head. "I see. It is good. You are a brave señorita. But we can help. My men will create a diversion in the plaza after you are inside, to be sure the guards do not notice that the small man under the sombrero and poncho has suddenly grown much taller and broader."

Kyla said, "I had thought that perhaps Miguel could simply walk with his knees bent, crouching under the poncho. But a diversion will help."

"I don't understand—" Maria began.

"One woman and her servant will go into the stockade and the same servant, with his bright poncho and disgraceful hat, will come out," Kyla explained. "Maria, you must hide this in your clothing somewhere." She thrust the derringer into Maria's hand. "When they demand our weapons, we will give them this." She pointed to the Colt tucked into her belt.

Maria stared, in some awe, at her adopted sister. "You would do this for him? You will take his place in prison? What will they do to you when they find out?"

"It doesn't matter," Kyla said. "I don't suppose they will hang me. Whatever else they do—well, it doesn't matter. Maria, you must be sure the men guarding Miguel keep looking at you. I have some dye which Golden Feather prepared to darken my skin, but we must be sure the soldiers see only my poncho and hat."

Maria smiled tearfully. Attracting male glances would be easy.

The soldiers fell over their feet staring at Maria, dressed as she was in her most alluring gown, surrounded by fragrance, her eyes dark and tragic, but Golden Feather proved to be an unexpected problem. Instead of remaining with the horses, which he and Kyla had used to rendezvous with Maria, he followed the two women into the fort. No amount of gesturing on Kyla's part would turn him back. He walked behind their buggy and moved to hold the horses when the sentry admitted the two women to the commanding officer's quarters.

Maria was crying again. They had passed through the square in front of the jailhouse where a scaffold had been erected, a grim reminder of what would happen to Miguel if they failed in their mission. The town was proud of the scaffold. It proved that not only could they give a bandit a fair trial, but they could also hang him from a real gallows. The usual method of dispatching criminals throughout the state was to dangle them from an upper-story window or the limb of a tree.

"I am Maria Consuela Augustine Marques," Maria announced, dabbing her eyes. "I have traveled all the way from Monterey to see my brother Miguel before you murder him."

"Not us, ma'am. We were just about to turn him over to the civilian authorities. Come inside, please," the commanding officer said. "Another hour and he would have been gone."

The sentries stood aside to let Maria pass, but barred the path of the shuffling Mexican youth.

"Please, allow him to come in," Maria said. "The *indio* can remain outside, but—Juan—must stay with me."

The commanding officer nodded to the sentries and Kyla followed Maria into the lighted room, keeping her head bent low.

"Sorry, ma'am," the officer said, "but only you can go to see your brother. Your man will have to wait here."

"No!" Maria cried. "Juan must go with me. I would be afraid if he were not at my side. A señorita is always chaperoned. Señor Commandant, please, look at your men, how they stare at me." She moved closer to him, her hands lifting imploringly. Her fingers lightly touched the buttons of his jacket and her dark eyes looked up at him beseechingly. She was so close, the warm scent of her assailed his nostrils, and he saw his grinning men crowding around the doorway.

The commanding officer glanced at the small-statured Mexican huddled beneath his hat. A boy only, and the Indian outside was a man well past his prime. "Your men will have to be searched for weapons."

"Oh no!" Maria gasped. "I mean—wait. Golden Feather will not understand. And Juan—he has a revolver. He will give it to you willingly." She added a rapid order in Spanish in Kyla's direction.

"Somebody take that Colt. The Indian can wait there with the buggy and your other servant can go with you, ma'am. Sergeant?"

Maria played her part to perfection, alternately flirting with the sergeant and then sobbing softly at her brother's fate. The sergeant paid no attention at all to the Mexican in the bright poncho who shuffled along behind them.

"Your brother is locked in a storeroom, ma'am," the sergeant said. "We put him in here to keep him safe. Figured if he was in the stockade there might be a necktie party. Oh, begging your pardon."

Maria stopped him with an upraised hand as he was about to follow them into the storeroom. "Señor, please, just one minute alone with my brother? I implore you." Her hand touched his chest and he looked at her then stepped back, closing the door after him.

Miguel wrapped his arms around Maria, looking over her shoulder in puzzlement at the brightly clad youth behind her. Then he saw the smoky blue eyes and the streaks on sculptured cheekbones where tears washed away rivulets of brown dye.

"No!" Kyla whispered as he reached for her. "They can see. Through the window." She spoke quietly in Spanish, jerking her head toward the narrow, barred window. "Move to the corner of the room where you will be out of sight. Maria stand in front of the window so that the guards outside will be looking at your back. Miguel, you will wear this." She was removing the poncho as Maria moved to block the window.

"Ah, Kyla, *chiquita,*" Miguel said brokenly. "You would do that for me? But I am a man. I will not let you take my place."

"Miguel, you must. They won't hang me."

"Look, Miguel, we brought you a gun," Maria whispered, slipping the derringer from under her skirts.

Miguel took the tiny gun from her hand. "I will save myself after you are gone."

At that moment there was a shout outside, followed by the sharp report of a rifle. The storeroom door burst open. "I'm going to have to get you out of here," the guard shouted.

Through the open door behind him they could see troopers running across the compound as the sound of more gunfire shattered the night.

Kyla looked wildly at Miguel, then sprang at the sergeant. "Run!" she screamed.

The second guard plunged into the storeroom to find himself reeling under tearing fingernails as Maria flung herself upon him. By the time he had pushed her aside, Miguel had brought the barrel of the derringer down on the sergeant's head, and he slumped at her feet. The gun spat flame as a second guard pulled his revolver from his belt. As the man fell, Kyla was already pulling the uniform jacket from the unconscious sergeant. "Miguel, quick —put it on. Take his cap."

Joaquin Murrieta and his men were riding in a wild

circle around the walls of the fort, firing into the air and yelling obcenities at the soldiers who shot at them from the walls but could see little in the blackness of the moonless night. A lieutenant was organizing a group of troopers to ride out to deal with the troublesome Mexicans.

"Get those civilians inside," an officer yelled at the uniform-clad Miguel from amid the confusion.

"Miguel, you must ride out when they open the gates," Kyla said. "Please. Go now. We will be all right, Golden Feather is here."

"Look!" Maria clutched at Miguel's arm and pointed. Hurtling toward them through the mélée of confused soldiers was the buggy, Golden Feather standing erect, whipping the horses.

"Sergeant! Get those civilians the hell out of the way!" someone shouted as Miguel pushed Kyla and Maria into the buggy and jumped in behind them. They lurched forward, racing along behind the troopers who galloped out to pursue the bandits rapidly fading from view along dark and deserted streets.

The buggy was halfway across the plaza when a trooper wheeled back after a fruitless dash into a dead-end street. Shots thundered through the night and the bodies of two blue-clad soldiers were sprawled on the ground, their horses running in circles and whinnying in fright. The returning trooper saw the bodies of his comrades, and then looked up at the Indian whipping the buggy away from the scene.

As the bullet smashed into Golden Feather, the horses felt the convulsive jerk on the reins and at the same moment collided with the riderless mount of one of the dead troopers. The buggy balanced for a second on one wheel, then as Golden Feather plunged forward across the horses' backs, the buggy went over on its side, sending its occupants rolling in the dust.

Scrambling to his feet, Miguel looked around in time to see Kyla on her feet and seizing the dangling reins of the riderless horse. The trooper who had shot Golden Feather was charging toward him, and Miguel sprang aside, pulling the man from his mount as he went by. They both hit the ground in a flurry of dust, Miguel's hands finding the man's throat as he struggled to reach the gun that slipped from his hand.

Maria was still lying dazedly on her side in the center of the plaza when the great black horse came leaping from the shadows. The figure on its back was a man with fierce eyes, and a red turban wound about his head. He leaned to the side of his mount, almost touching the ground as he scooped Maria into his arms and placed her in front of him. Only a *vaquero* could have accomplished the feat with such grace. The troopers returning to the plaza were momentarily distracted by the bandit's horsemanship. Golden Feather crawled unnoticed into the shadows, his hand staunching the flow of blood from his thigh. One of Murieta's men dragged him into a darkened adobe hut.

Miguel leaped to the back of the second riderless horse and he and Kyla rode in the opposite direction from that taken by the flamboyant Joaquin.

By the time the troopers realized that the uniformed sergeant riding at the side of the slim Mexican youth, was the condemned bandit Miguel Marques, the *Californios* had disappeared into the blackness of the night.

# 28

*Desmond wore a frock coat and linen shirt, a trifle loose*
on his spare frame. The clothes were borrowed from the
sympathetic young lawyer who had defended Miguel and
who had hastily left town. The trousers were a little short,
but since Desmond leaned heavily on his cane as he
walked, this was not noticeable.

"Who was the woman?" the reporter persisted. "Do
you know who she was? Was she really his sister? Where
is your wife, Lord Talmage? They said the woman who
helped him escape was a beautiful Spanish girl. That
doesn't sound like your wife, but no one has seen your
wife since the trial ended."

"I've told you and everyone else, I do not know."
Desmond limped doggedly toward the stagecoach station.
"My wife is indisposed. She is in seclusion with friends."

"How would you feel about your wife running away
with a Mexican bandit, Lord Talmage?" a second reporter
asked, falling into step on Desmond's other side. "If it
was your wife, perhaps wearing a dark wig?"

"Her brother," Desmond said. "He is her brother."

"Well, not exactly. His father adopted her, but she was
not actually related to the family. What did the law say
about your part in the affair? They sure interrogated you
for a long time."

"I could be of little help. As you can see, I am

physically incapable of involvement in either the escape or pursuit. I understand a civilian posse has been formed, as well as the army patrol that has gone after them. I will pray for their safety."

"You think they'll try to cross the desert, head south into Mexico?"

"Please, gentlemen, you are impeding my progress."

"You leaving on the stage, Lord Talmage? How are folks going to feel about that?"

"I'm not leaving. I'm meeting an old friend."

An hour later when the stagecoach from the north rattled into view and stopped to disgorge its passengers, the two reporters discovered the friend of Lord Talmage was not a man to harass. He was the first off the coach, standing in the doorway for a moment while his eyes sought and found the crippled Englishman. The man was hatless, and the sun blazed on a fiery mane of hair, giving it a vibrant life of its own. He jumped down from the coach and strode toward the Englishman, eyes lighting up despite the casual greeting he offered.

"What, no sackcloth and ashes, old sport? For shame!" His hand went out to touch Desmond's shoulder.

"May I ask your name, sir, and why you are here?" the younger reporter asked.

The man's eyes turned to meet his and a slight frown appeared on the swarthy features. "No, you may not." He had Spanish blood, despite his hair and eyes, the reporter noted. His path was suddenly barred by an extended arm and when he angrily tried to push forward he found himself flung back into the arms of the second reporter. They both looked into a challenging glare for a moment, before deciding they had better things to do than pursue the story of the escape of the convicted bandit.

At Desmond's hotel a meal was sent to his room.

"Thank you for coming, Quint. And thank you also for the money. I realized when it came that you must have read the newspaper stories. I had no right to expect you to come, but I knew you would not fail me."

Quint shrugged. "I was all ready to come anyway. Your invitation didn't make any difference. I would have been here before the trial ended, but I had—other matters to take care of in Monterey. Was the mystery woman the papers are talking about Maria? Ramsey put out the story in Monterey that she is ill and not seeing visitors, but I noticed she disappeared shortly after the first news story about Miguel's capture appeared."

"I had absolutely nothing to do with the escape, Quint, although I see now I should have expected it. I don't know who the woman was, but it seems likely it was Maria. I believe the slightly-built Mexican youth she called Juan was actually Kyla disguised as a boy. She disappeared from her hotel room just before the escape. Quint, if they attempt to cross the desert at this time of year without sufficient water—" He paused and closed his eyes for a second, then added, "I must confess I was surprised when the money arrived for me. I knew at once you had sent it, of course, and that you'd get my message through your bankers. I mean, I was surprised you were still in the country."

"You're still here too," Quint said. "It seems we may both have fallen under a spell more powerful than female seduction this time, old sport. Damn funny, isn't it? We came here for a lark and to see that your betrothed was not done out of her inheritance. And here we are, nearly five years later. But no time to be looking back. What have you done with the Indian?"

"He is waiting for you at a *cantiña* in the Mexican part of town. He was shot in the thigh, as you know, but I believe he will be able to ride. He will be invaluable as a tracker as he knows the Californian and Mexican deserts, but he may slow you down because of his wound."

"I'll leave at dawn," Quint said. "And you, Des, will travel north on the first available stage."

"But I thought I would wait here."

"If I am to go after Kyla, then you will oblige me by traveling to Monterey to take care of Shansi."

Desmond's sudden pallor was not noticed by Quint, who was privately debating how much he should tell Desmond about Felice and the child. "Felice is with her. Felice has a child, a boy she adopted, and she's not too happy about living with Shansi. Felice has a severe case of respectability since she acquired the child and doesn't want him to be exposed to Shansi's more unusual pastimes. Shansi needs someone to take care of her."

"She is ill?" Desmond asked, his eyes downcast for fear Quint would read his thoughts.

"She's an opium addict. I tried to wean her away from it, Des, but it was useless. Old Woman is still with her, but Shansi no longer seems to be aware of the real world and I'm afraid for her. The new Californians have a mortal fear of Orientals, and the persecution of the Chinese has reached epic proportions in the north. On top of that there's Murrieta and his sidekick, the one they call Three-Fingered Jack, who collects Chinese people's ears. My dread is that Shansi will wander away from the house."

"I'll go north," Desmond said in a low voice. "We'll wait for you in Monterey."

Kyla and Miguel could not stop to rest until they were sure they were far enough ahead of their pursuers. Serenaded by the eerie howl of a distant pack of coyotes, they rode all night. As the sunrise blazed over the hills and swept mauve shadows down the rocky canyons, their weary horses plodded along dry washes. Kyla and Miguel sat in their saddles, heads slumped on their chests, drifting rather than riding.

The gravelly sand crunched beneath the hooves of the horses; jackrabbits and kangaroo rats scurried under cactus. Kyla reined her horse to allow a slow-moving desert tortoise to amble by and high on a rocky ledge a bighorn sheep watched their progress.

By mid-morning the sun was a saber, crashing earthward in a blinding ray of heat. Kyla's eyes burned, her lips parched and cracked; her hair seemed to sizzle beneath the sombrero. She could feel the heat generated by her body blending with the heat reflected by giant boulders. Beneath the saddle the horse lost its precious body moisture in a lather of sweat.

"We'll stop—over there—and rest now," Miguel's voice was a hoarse croak.

Ahead of them the boulders marked the beginning of a slow sweep of foothills. Kyla urged her mount toward a formation of the giant rocks, her heat-hazed senses seeing them as pagan idols reaching for their sun-god. Despite the size of the boulders, there was little shade as the summer sun climbed high in the vivid sky.

When she took only a sip of water from her canteen, Miguel said, "No, don't save it. Drink all you want now."

"But we have only one canteen each."

"It will do you more good inside you than carried on your back."

"What about the horses?"

"They will die. Perhaps they will carry us for a while longer if we wait until evening. Tomorrow we will reach water. You are sure that Maria knew the man who carried her off?"

"Yes. I met him at the *cantiña*. He is a friend of hers." Kyla thought of the disarray of the bed upon which Maria had been lying and the familiar way Joaquin Murrieta looked at her, but kept these thoughts to herself.

"Do you know who that man is?"

Kyla looked at his dust-covered face and tried to read his expression or his thoughts, but they were closed to her. She sipped water and he did not wait for her answer.

"He is Joaquin Murrieta."

"How do you know?"

"I met him once. Rest now. We must not waste our strength in idle conversation."

Occasionally, during the long slow baking they endured, Kyla drifted into a misty world of forgotten dreams and half-remembered images. Not quite asleep, nor awake, she seemed to be a child again, scrambling down the cliff trail to watch the giant plume of spray billow forth from the Bufadora at high tide. Down on the beach Miguel was leaping from one slippery rock to another as the sea rose inexorably. Strutting, posturing. "Look at me, Kyla! Look at me!" The ghost of the long-dead Cervantes moved silently into the foreground, glowering, resentful.

Then Maria's shrill taunts and her pinching fingers would jolt Kyla's eyes open and she stared at the searing rocks and white heat of the cauldron that was the desert, their escape and their prison. Miguel was motionless, leaning against a lichen-covered rock, his eyes closed. Both horses were down.

The day Golden Feather had carried Miguel home slowly materialized in her mind. Golden Feather—the childish name they had given him was the only name by which they knew him. The *indio* had come riding slowly through the *hacienda* gates, Miguel's motionless body clasped to his bronzed bare chest. The dead cougar that had clawed Miguel's arms and legs was being slowly dragged through the dust behind Golden Feather's pony. Miguel's wounds had already been treated with a mixture of herbs and clay. The *indio* placed Miguel gently into the arms of the nearest *vaquero* and faded back into the hills.

Miguel: always the daring one, so brave and so reckless. At least he won't die at the end of a rope. Why could I not find joy in his arms when I love him so much?

The air being sucked painfully into her lungs tasted like molten lead. Her hands and feet were swollen and throbbed persistently. She peeled off her boots and gasped as her bare feet touched the scorching sand. Poor blistered feet, dancing feet. She was dancing the fandango, castanets clicking, hot dark eyes following her movements. A strong hand closed around her waist and now it was the waltz she danced, whirling faster and faster and the eyes that burned into hers were green, lit with flashes of golden fire. She slipped deeper below the surface of consciousness and thought she heard a slight moan escape her lips. Was she dancing, or was she running? Running from those green eyes. The cougar. The green eyes of the cougar. No, the cougar was dead, bumping over the ground at the end of a lariat.

The green eyes smiled. A fiery mane of hair declared a warning she should heed. There was something she could not remember, something important in her life, but it was veiled from her memory. The green eyes looked into hers and made her forget. Why?

She groaned and stirred. "Quint?"

Miguel was shaking her. "Riders coming."

She blinked open her eyes. Miguel was desperately trying to get the horses to their feet, but it was useless. He turned and pointed to the hills and she began to scramble up the ridge, her breath rasping in her throat, wanting to cling to the rocks with her hands but afraid to put her fingers in places her eyes could not see for fear of disturbing a rattlesnake. The hill rose sharply after the first gentle incline. Horses would not be able to follow. Miguel was at her side, taking her hand to drag her at a faster pace.

They reached the top of the ridge and lay prostrate. The line of riders moved across the plain below. The riders and their mounts blurred together, the image shimmering and growing larger. They had extra horses to carry water.

"Kyla, it's hopeless," Miguel panted. "They'll find the horses and I have only one bullet in the derringer. You must give yourself up to them. They won't harm a woman."

"And you—oh, no, Miguel."

"I will try to reach the border on foot."

"And I will go with you. You are forgetting Josefa—" She had read of the dance-hall girl hanged by the San Francisco Vigilance Committee during Miguel's trial, a news item Kyla had forgotten till now, which she had not repeated to either Miguel or Maria. Miguel's hand closed tightly over her wrist and she saw he was staring, pointing to the west. "Look!"

Two riders had appeared, galloping furiously toward the hills on the far side of the plain. The posse wheeled about to follow, and a great cloud of dust rose in the hot still air.

"They must believe those other two—are—" the words would not come, her mouth and lips were too dry. She lay back limply, closing her eyes. The unknown riders had led their pursuers in the opposite direction, but had perhaps condemned Miguel and herself to a more lingering death.

Shansi tried to shake free from the clutching hands of Old Woman. "Let me go. I want to go out. I am tired of the company of women. I don't want to look upon your ugliness for another minute, Old Woman."

The talons would not release her, and Felice came hurrying to see what all the commotion was about. "Can't you two be quiet? Victor is taking his nap," she said, trying to keep her own voice at a low pitch, despite her annoyance.

"She won't let me go out," Shansi said sullenly.

"Quite right too. Mr. Delleroc said none of us is to leave the house until he gets back, or Lord Talmage arrives. What is it you want that we can't get the Indian couple to bring? You've got enough damned opium for an army. And that's another thing. Mr. Delleroc said you were to keep your blasted magic cloud at the far end of the house with all the windows open, yet the whole house reeks of it. Do you want the child to smell it?"

Shansi looked venomously at Old Woman. "Make her let me go."

Felice jerked her head at Old Woman, whose clawlike brown fingers slowly relaxed their grip on Shansi's wrist.

Shansi pulled away, turning her back. "I hate her. I wish I didn't have to look at her. If I can't get away from here for a little while, I shall go mad."

"Now come on, honey. What's this all about? You don't mean that. Mr. Delleroc told me she's been with you all your life."

Shansi turned to face her and she was trembling. "Look at her. Look how ugly she is! That terrible toothless smile. Her skin is like dried-up leaves. I cannot bear to look at her and know I am looking at myself in a few years." She covered her face with her hands and her long fingernails made little crescents in the smooth forehead. "I want to be admired and loved while there is still time," she said from behind the screen of her fingers. "I want a man to make love to me and tell me how beautiful I am. Mr. Delleroc—does not want me any longer."

Felice looked from one woman to the other and began to understand. "Tell her to leave us alone for a minute."

"She understands you. Go, Old Woman," Shansi said, dropping her hands. Silently Old Woman backed away from them, her tiny beadlike eyes fixed on Shansi until the moment the door closed on her toothless grin.

"Listen, Shansi. It's too dangerous for you to go wandering off by yourself. Thousands of your people have been pouring into California, because of the gold. Things aren't the same as when you first came here, when there probably weren't more than half a dozen of you in the entire territory. They frighten people, see. They will wear their outlandish clothes and speak their heathen tongue and they brought their secret societies with them. What are they called? Tongs. It seems there's a tong in every mining town and the Lord knows how many in San Francisco. People say there will be wars between them, and if we don't stop the Chinese immigrants now, pretty soon there'll be more of them than us."

"You are speaking of peasants," Shansi said coldly. "I am not one of them. I speak your language better than you."

"Be that as it may," Felice said, "Mr. Delleroc wants a respectable home here for little Victor. We've got to act like ladies. He won't want you going down to the waterfront to pick up some sailor to sleep with."

"Mr. Delleroc will not sleep with me. I need someone. He is not the man who used to make love in every way it was possible, and ways you cannot dream of. He began to change, when he went to Mexico to arrange the wedding of Lord Talmage. When he returned, he was not the same. Little things. He would look at me as though he were seeing someone else. And he was more—gentle. I did not like him to be so. I wanted my lord and master to be the man he had always been with me. But someone had tamed my tiger. Oh, there had always been other

women since I have known him. But he always came
back to me. I have lost him to the woman he cannot
have."

"Kyla Talmage," Felice said, with a sigh. "He never
did believe she died in the fire. Now he's gone after her.
But you're right, he can't have her. He and Lord Talmage,
no matter what they say, they won't hurt each other. No
woman will come between them, so you've no need to
fear Mr. Delleroc will bring her back here if he finds her.
He'll take her back to Lord Talmage."

Shansi's eyes had drifted away in the remote and
dreamy manner that Felice was beginning to recognize.
"Shansi, don't leave the house. Garett Ramsey came
around making threats, and he's got people all stirred up
telling them Mr. Delleroc has some kind of den of evil
here. There was an editorial in the newspaper yesterday
about the undesirable elements in town—"

But Shansi was no longer listening. She walked to the
door, moving sinuously as a silken serpent, her fingers
brushing her narrow hips like fluttering birds.

Felice sighed again and went after her. There was no
need to stop her from leaving, however, as a carriage
was coming to a stop in front of the house and Lord
Talmage was being helped out by the driver.


Garett Ramsey slammed the newspaper down on the
desk and pounded it with his huge fist. All he had worked
for—and most especially his triumphant return to his
family in the East—would be lost if he was connected to
the Marques family. Worse, if they found out that the
mysterious señorita who aided the bandit to escape was
actually Mrs. Garett Ramsey. Damn them, he should have
known better than to marry a Mexican.

He had locked Maria in her room when she demanded
that he travel south for Miguel's trial, but she had somehow got out and disappeared, even while he was in the
house. At least she had not arrived in time to identify
herself at the trial. But if she were fleeing through the
desert with Miguel now and they were caught—damn

them. A political career would be impossible with such scandalous family connections.

There was a sudden sound outside the window and he tensed, the hair standing up on the back of his neck. The hour was late and the house silent. His hand slid across his desk to the top drawer, found the revolver and pulled it slowly into his lap.

He spun around in his chair, the gun pointing toward the window. Another sound, a faint tapping on the glass. He stood up, his bulk casting a shadow over the curtained window. At times like this he regretted building a wood frame house with windows exposed to the street. The Spanish idea of windows opening to an inner courtyard offered more protection from prowlers.

The gun barrel lifted the curtain from the edge of the window and he almost pulled the trigger in fright as the disembodied head appeared, glowing whitely in the light from the house. Then he recognized Maria, wrapped in a hooded cloak that blended with the darkness.

"Let me in! I did not want to come to the door in case a servant answered, and I have lost my key," she whispered as he opened the window. She was alone.

He let the curtain fall and went quickly to the front door, opening it only wide enough to allow her to pass through. She walked, unconcerned, into the living room, removing her black cloak and dropping it into the nearest chair. "*Dios!* I am tired."

"Where the hell have you been?"

She looked at him contemptuously. "Sit down. You make my neck stiff when you loom over me like that. I have been helping Miguel escape."

"Do they know—does anyone in the South know who you are? Where is Miguel now? What about the Talmages?"

"Stop! I cannot answer all your questions at once. Miguel and Kyla are riding to Mexico."

"Kyla? Thank God, I thought it was you who helped him."

"It *was* I who helped him escape," Maria said impatiently, "but Kyla was there too, dressed as a peon.

Desmond sent for Delleroc; I saw him arrive on the stagecoach. I was waiting to take a coach north, watching from the hotel across the street."

"But the newspaper said the woman who helped Miguel escape was one of Murrieta's women, that he was seen pulling her up on his horse." He reached out and caught her wrist, pulling her to her feet. "You'd better talk fast, Maria, or I'm going to beat you within an inch of your life."

Her eyes flashed. "Take your hands off me! If you touch me you are a dead man. I *am* Joaquin Murrieta's woman. I only came back because he thought it would be safer for me to be Madame Ramsey until Miguel is safely on Mexican soil. How dare you look at me like that? You—I know all about your Chinese prostitutes. Did you believe I would meekly stay home and run your household unless I had a lover? Pah! It is not I who will tell your conniving political friends about this matter. It is Delleroc you had better worry about. Why would Desmond send for Delleroc unless he wants him to go after Kyla? Kyla has been living with Miguel. I think you had better make sure that Delleroc doesn't return to Monterey if you want to keep this whole affair quiet."

Garett released her, his face contorted with rage. "You little slut. I never should have married you. But you are Mrs. Garett Ramsey and we're going to see that no one ever connects us with Miguel, or the Talmages, or Delleroc, ever again. And you'll never see Murrieta again either, I promise you. His days are numbered. We've got rangers scouring the state for him and wanted posters plastered in every settlement from Sonoma to San Diego. I'll put out the word that he's going to try to ride into Monterey, and I'll watch you every minute."

Maria glared at him for a moment and then tossed her head contemptuously. "You will not catch him. Why don't you occupy yourself with a task more suited to your capabilities? Perhaps you ought to knock some nails into this flimsy house you are so proud of, which is falling down about our ears." She swept out of the room.

Ramsey kicked a chair over. She never lost an opportunity to point out the inferior workmanship of their hastily constructed wooden house, comparing it to the stout durability of the adobe houses. Maria . . . Murrieta . . . *Delleroc*. Delleroc had been biding his time, waiting for the opportunity to revenge himself, Ramsey was convinced, and now the Marques family had given him his chance to get even for what Ramsey had done to him. A man like Delleroc could not forget being dragged behind a horse, being abandoned with a dying man in the desert. Delleroc had just been waiting. Ramsey kicked the chair again, splintering it with his boot as though it were made of matchsticks.

# 29

*At Miguel's side, Kyla concentrated only on placing one* foot in front of another. All that could be heard in the endless, silent desert were their grainy footfalls and labored breathing.

"The next ridge, Kyla. We'll rest there."

The horizon danced dizzily, slashed with pink and yellow light, as though painted on the sky. The hot white sand swam up to meet her and then the sky was all she could see in the second before she fell into a merciful void.

Unaware that Miguel had picked her up and was carrying her, she hovered on the brink of consciousness, borne on a dream that she was again being swept through the burning streets of San Francisco. Through the dense smoke she could discern the sinister faces of the marauding Sydney Ducks, Merciful Smith hacking his way calmly through the seething sea of humanity.

Somewhere ahead in the swirling smoke she could see Quint Delleroc. He had come back for her. He had not left her after all. She could see his hair, brighter than the leaping flames, his eyes reflecting the golden sparks.

"Quint?" Had she said his name aloud?

He was beckoning to her. Guiding her through the flames. She wanted to call out to him that she was coming to him, beg him to wait for her. But her skirts were held fast by the rushing crowd and he disappeared in a great column of black smoke.

She could feel something deliciously cool and moist. It touched her lips and then descended over her burning brow. She opened her eyes as the last crimson streaks of the sunset gave way to the deep blue of the desert night. She could feel the hard ground under her body, but there was something soft under her head. Someone was bending over her, dabbing the wet cloth to her cracked lips.

His face was in darkness and she blinked and started to raise her head but he whispered, "It's all right, Kyla, just lie still. You're safe now." The voice was gentle, speaking in English with a lilt that softened the meticulously pronounced words.

"Miguel?" she croaked hoarsely.

"He's all right. Asleep."

"Quint? Is it you? What are you doing here?"

"Leading the posse a merry chase, I hope. Golden Feather is here too, taking care of Miguel. You were both in poor condition when we found you. Unfortunately, we couldn't let you rest until we were sure we had lost the posse. You've been sharing a horse with me for the past few miles."

She wanted to know more. There were many questions to be answered, but she was too weary. She felt his fingertips press lightly on her eyelids, and his voice came to her from far away. "Sleep now, Kyla."

The three men were still sleeping soundly when Kyla awoke, just before dawn, and she had time to lie on the cool ground and study them, collect her thoughts and make her decisions.

To the east, the first silver rays of the coming day blazed on the hills as the stars faded. Miguel lay with his face buried in his arm, and Golden Feather, as ramrod-straight in repose as he carried himself while awake, lay nearby.

Quint Delleroc was closest to her, lying on his side facing her, his arm extended toward her across the cold sand. She studied his features as he slept, the chiseled cheekbones and slightly pointed chin, the bold nose. When his eyes were open they dominated the face, as the setting of an emerald enhances the stone, but with the eyes hidden beneath heavy lids, red lashes bristling along high cheekbones, Kyla realized it was possible for Quint Delleroc to look like one of the tormented saints in the chapel. He opened his eyes suddenly and instantly his face became that of a satyr, handsome and deadly.

"Good morning," he said. "How do you feel?"

"Thirsty." Her voice was still a painful croak.

Before Quint could stand up, Golden Feather was unhooking the canteen from one of the horses and Miguel blinked open his eyes.

"Your Indian friend rode back to retrieve the extra horses and the mule while you slept," Quint said. "We had to leave them hidden in an arroyo while we led the posse away from you."

"Then we will all have horses?" Kyla saw now that there were four horses and a mule.

"Yes, and we must be on our way quickly." Quint handed her the canteen and then went over to Miguel. "I'm not sure I understand all of Golden Feather's sign language, but I believe you should reach the border before nightfall. I will take Kyla back with me."

Miguel's jaw hardened and he climbed stiffly to his feet. "Kyla goes with me. But I will allow Golden Feather to accompany you, if you prefer not to come to Mexico with us."

"You are still a hunted man. A condemned murderer with a rope waiting for you if you are caught," Quint said. "You'll travel faster if you travel alone, or at least not slowed down by a woman. Besides, I cannot allow you to endanger her life any further. She must leave this territory before anyone realizes it was she who helped you escape."

"I will protect her," Miguel said angrily, taking an unsteady step closer to Quint, his fists clenched. Behind them Golden Feather tensed, his eyes fixed on Quint.

"Stop it!" Kyla scrambled to her feet and swayed dizzily for a moment, then stumbled between the two men. "I will decide where I will go and what I will do.

I don't belong to either of you," she said stormily. She took several deep breaths and then added in a calmer tone, "Quint, you might as well know right away that I'm not going back to live with Desmond. I know it must have been he who asked you to come after us. I'm already a fallen woman in the eyes of civilized society, so I might as well go a step further and start making my own decisions about my life. Wasn't it you who once told me I should? You'll be glad to know I'm all finished letting men make my decisions."

Golden Feather held up his hand for silence and dropped to his knees, pressing his ear to the ground. When he looked up, his hands pointed to the north, made a sweeping motion and then came together.

"Riders coming," Miguel said.

"We'll all head for the border. Kyla, you can decide what you want to do when we get there," Quint said.

When they were mounted, Golden Feather consulted briefly with Miguel, then the Indian took the mule and started riding to the southwest, while the other three beat a path due south.

"Golden Feather will make slower time with the burro, and if they catch up with him they will see only a lone Indian whose features are the same to their eyes as are every other Indian's," Miguel explained.

The sun blazed over the horizon, and a bee hummed by Kyla's ear as she bent over the neck of her horse, urging him forward.

"The water I told you about, it is not far from here."

Yes, she thought, bees meant an oasis somewhere near.

"We can't stop there. The posse will go directly to any water," Quint said, his horse catching up with them and edging between their mounts.

Already the heat was rising from the white sand in shimmering waves. Quint handed her a strip of beef jerky. "Chew on this as you ride." He offered a second piece of the dried meat to Miguel, who took it silently.

"Have you considered," Quint said to Kyla, as they allowed the horses to slow to a walk, "that if you cross the border with him you will never be able to return to

Alta California? He is too well known now to have a career left as a bandit."

"Kyla, I have had enough of banditry," Miguel said. "The time has come to fight the corruption in our own country. We cannot regain what we have lost, the territories to the north. There are too many *gringos* to fight. I shall not go back, you need have no fear. The governor of Oaxaca, a man named Benito Juarez, may be the leader we are looking for to reunite Mexico and overthrow the tyrants. Kyla, you were right. We were playing at life in the *hacienda,* I pretending to be the Padrone and you—" he broke off, embarrassed that he must speak in front of Delleroc, yet feeling as though time were running out.

"You are not going to the *hacienda?*" Kyla asked quickly.

"No. I shall ride to Oaxaca, and join the men who are supporting Juarez. You will come with me."

"No, Miguel. I'm sorry."

"Because of him? Because of the man who betrayed you? Used you like a *puta?*"

"And what exactly has *your* relationship been with her for the past months?" Quint asked in a voice like the hiss of a snake.

Miguel turned his horse deliberately into Quint's mount, and the two animals stamped their feet and snorted in fear.

"I love her," Miguel said defiantly.

They had conversed in English, but now Quint looked into Miguel's eyes and said softly, *"Ama a quien no te ama, responde a quien no te llama, y andaras carreras vanas."*

Miguel's dark eyes blazed in his dust-streaked face, then his mouth clamped shut and he jerked the reins. His horse cantered, putting distance between him and the words for which he had no answer.

Kyla watched Miguel's back straighten, his shoulders square as he held his head high. That proudly held head came closer to breaking her heart than anything he could have said. She turned angrily to Quint. "Who are you to taunt him with the fact I don't love him?"

"Then you admit it *is* a fact?" Quint said. "Kyla, don't go with him out of a sense of pity. I see it in your eyes, but it would be more cruel to let him hope than to end it now."

"Cruel! I can't believe I am being censured about cruelty by the master in the art," Kyla said bitterly.

"*A quien mala fama tiene, ni acompanes ni quieras bien,*" Quint quoted. "Do I have it right? He who has a bad reputation do not accompany nor love dearly."

"Advice I shall certainly take. As soon as Miguel is safely across the border, I never want to see you again, Quint Delleroc."

"I should be happy to hear you say that, Kyla, but for some reason I'm not. There was a time when I thought that if the hidden fires in you could be lit, you would be one of the most exciting women I had ever known. You were like an uncut gem when I first met you, full of unfulfilled promise. Now you are a polished woman and you have, I suspect, moved out of my reach."

"If you believe I shall ever again melt into your arms, you are a fool. I learned my lesson in San Francisco. Since then I have learned what you men knew all along. All men are the same in the dark." She jabbed her heels into the flanks of her horse and galloped forward to ride with Miguel.

Quint Delleroc watched her ruefully. Echoing in his mind were Desmond's words, flung at him in that rare and enlightening moment of anger: *Sooner or later, Quint Delleroc, you will pay.*

The two figures riding ahead of him looked right together. She so fair, he so dark. They rode with the effortless skill of their forebears. They had shared their childhood, grown up together, descended from proud and aristocratic families. Watching them ride side by side, Quint Delleroc felt regret for the first time in his life; coupled with a deep longing that transcended any emotion he had ever known.

He had thought about her constantly during their time apart, and seeing her again, lying limply within the protection of Miguel's arms, Quint had been overwhelmed with jealousy and rage. It was, he decided as reason returned, a good thing they were both prostrate from the heat and lack of water, or he might have killed Miguel and ridden off with Kyla like some primitive swain.

Was it, he wondered, because he had come to love her child? He had never felt love before, but the fierce protective pride he felt in the boy was easy to recognize as being love. It was a simple and uncomplicated emotion that had grown gradually and naturally and which he knew was reciprocated. Ah, but love between a man and a woman, that was something else. Quint had seen that kind of love fade and swiftly die. Perhaps it was merely an illusion, he thought, conjured up in the heat of passion to explain why one woman pleases more than another.

Since Victor had come into his life, Quint had observed families together. There was an invisible bond, he had noticed, an aura that surrounded them; shutting out everyone else. He had been denied that bond as a child, but perhaps he could experience it now, with Victor.

He was deluding himself. That thought rose unbidden. He wanted Kyla. For herself alone, not just for Victor or the warm comfort of creating a family. He wanted her for her sweet purity of mind, her generously shared affection, her loyalty. With Kyla he was better than he had been before. He was whole.

Without mercy the sun seared the air. The horses moved listlessly, dragging their hooves over the hot ground in flurries of yellow dust. It is the heat, Quint told himself. Worse than India. Perhaps not as bad as the Sahara. It plays tricks with a man's mind. *Sooner or later, Quint Delleroc, you will pay!*

Desmond Talmage regarded Shansi gravely, his piercingly blue eyes unflinching in their steady gaze. "You will not smoke opium. There is no more opium in the house. I have destroyed it."

The empty eyes stared back at him uncomprehendingly for a moment. "I must have my magic cloud," she said in a small voice. "You do not understand. Without it I see— I see—"

"What do you see, Shansi?"

"The nightmare comes. I see—her body. We are in China again, in the burned ruins . . . and there, in the ashes . . . I am pushing the ashes away from her hand . . . her arm. If I don't have my magic cloud, I will see the rest! Oh, please, Lord Talmage, I beg of you—" she dropped to her knees, her tiny hands clutching at his boot, her mouth trying to kiss his foot.

Desmond's hand caught her chin before she could press her lips to his boot. "Felice!" he called. "Help me."

Felice had been standing in the doorway, and now she moved forward to pull Shansi to her feet. Groveling in a corner of the room was Old Woman, her wrinkled face shrunken without her usual grin. Her frail old body twitched and jerked spasmodically and her hands plucked at her legs as though trying to remove crawling insects.

Shansi's face glistened with perspiration, but her eyes were alive now, burning with hatred as she looked at Desmond from within the circle of Felice's restraining arms.

"We must have it! I tell you we must. Look, see what you are doing to Old Woman. Soon I will be like that—ahhh—" She began to wail.

"Felice, stay with her until I fetch the servant to help me. Then you and Victor must leave. The next few days will be the most difficult. I don't want you and the child here then. Could you return to Quint's hotel in San Francisco for a little while?"

"Are you sure you can manage the two of them?" Felice asked doubtfully.

"Yes. I will speak with you privately before you leave."

Shansi screamed, struggling, "I will see my mother's body!"

Desmond limped about the house, seeking the Indian and his squaw who were the only servants. They were cowering in the cookhouse, built away from the main house, as was the custom. They had seen the madness overcome the Oriental girl and were afraid of the lurking evil spirits. It took all of Desmond's gentle tact to persuade them to even enter the same room as Shansi and Old

Woman. "As soon as Miss Felice and Victor are on their way," Desmond told them, "I will return to take care of Miss Shansi. After that you will lock the door and not allow anyone to enter or leave. You will bring food and leave it outside. Do you understand?" The two nodded fearfully, glancing at each other for reassurance.

Within the hour Felice had packed two bags and was buttoning Victor's velvet coat. The child's eyes were fixed on Desmond. "Will Quint be at the hotel?"

"No, dear. But we'll see him again soon," Felice said.

"Why did *he* come here? Everything was all right until he came. Now he's made Shansi cry and we have to go away. I want Quint."

Desmond stretched out his hand to the child. "Come here, Victor," he said gently. In order to keep his balance, it was necessary for Desmond to lean against a table.

The child stared at him suspiciously for a moment, then, compelled by the brilliant eyes, moved toward the outstretched hand. Victor walked on his toes. The shortened Achilles' tendons would not allow his heels to touch the ground, but his tottering steps were the proud accomplishment of the man he loved most in the world.

"Shansi is ill," Desmond said as his hand clasped the small fist. "And for a little while she will not be herself. It will be better for her if you and Felice don't see her. You understand, Victor, I know you do. You and I both know how much it hurts if other people look at us with pity. Shansi will be more a subject of pity in the next few days than either of us. Do you understand? I'm afraid I've never known how to speak to a child."

"Pity," Victor repeated. "What does that mean?"

"People feel sorry for you because of your feet. Because of my missing arm and my scars."

"You have more to pity then," the boy said with satisfaction.

"Yes. Much more. Some day your feet will be like everyone else's. Felice tells me your problem will be solved by the time you are a man. You are fortunate. Now we must help Shansi overcome her problem."

"But why did Quint go away?"

"He went to help someone. He'll tell you all about it when he returns. Now I want you to go out to the kitchen and see if you can find some apples to eat on your journey on the stagecoach."

When the child had gone Desmond looked at Felice and said, "Quint never told you who the child was? Did you not guess?"

Felice looked at him blankly. "Just that Victor was a foundling. I did wonder if the boy was his son, perhaps by a Mexican woman, because of those dark eyes. I thought surely no man could be so patient with a child not his own flesh and blood."

"Quint Delleroc's son would have bright red hair," Desmond observed. "Victor has blond curls and delicate cheekbones. If he were Quint's son he would have those fierce features and bold nose."

"You know who the child's parents are then?"

"No. I don't know who the child's parents are. He is returning. Are you ready to go?"

As he dragged his aching body back to Shansi's side, Desmond wondered for the hundredth time since his arrival in Monterey what Quint Delleroc would tell Kyla about the child. Desmond thought about what Quint had done and was awed by the compassion of the man. He must have sought and found the child during that supposed journey to the gold towns. All that time in San Francisco, he cared for the child and yet told neither Desmond nor Kyla about him. Would he ever have told them? What he had done, he had done for the child's sake, or had he done it because he loved the mother?

Desmond prided himself on his own compassion for the unfortunates of the world. Yet what had he ever done to compare with this? he asked himself. But there was no time to ponder the enigma that was Quint Delleroc. There were Shansi and Old Woman, and caring for them would take all of his strength.

As he pushed open the door, Shansi sprang away from the Indian servant, flinging herself on the bed and tearing her clothes. "I must have my magic cloud," she shrieked, ripping frantically at the silk of her dress until her breasts were exposed. The two servants quickly departed.

As the bolt slid along the outside of the door, Shansi tore away the last of her clothing and began to writhe on the bed. "Come to me. I will make you happy, I will give you anything you ask. Please, please," she implored. She looked wildly toward Old Woman, who was still plucking at her legs. "Look at her! Don't you see? Don't you understand? That is how I shall look, old and ugly and used up. No one will want me. There will be no man to make love to me and I will not be able to bear it. Mr. Delleroc, he does not want me any more. It is beginning—I am afraid—ah, Lord Talmage, I am so afraid—I don't want to look like Old Woman."

He limped to the bed and sat beside her, taking her hands in his warm grip as she scrambled closer, pressing her face to the thin shoulder.

"We are going to talk, Shansi. You are going to tell me all about those nightmares. And I am going to make you understand that Old Woman is not the mirror image of what you will become. You are the most beautiful and desirable woman in the world and you will always be so, if you will overcome this terrible addiction. Shansi! No! If you do that I shall strike you with my cane."

The tiny hands that had been fumbling with his trousers drew away, startled by the violence in his voice. "You like Shansi, Shansi made you happy once," she whimpered, her body trembling.

"Shansi, Shansi," he sighed. "Perhaps I love you. We shall find out. But first we are going to exorcise all of the demons. You are going to tell me about your nightmare."

Two harrowing nights and three days passed, however, before Desmond and Shansi together experienced the end of her nightmare.

The tiny child who had uncovered her mother's mutilated body in the ashes of her home was buried deeply inside the lovely and wanton woman. When at last the torment of her mind was laid bare, Shansi's eyes were no longer empty and remote. They glowed with hope, despite the misery of her aching limbs and sweat-drenched body.

# 30

*The rocks were still warm from the heat of the day, but* the desert air cooled rapidly as darkness fell. Above them, the stars pierced the blackness of the sky with beckoning points of light.

Miguel jumped from his horse, pulled the sergeant's hat from his head and tossed it into the air. He let it lie in the cactus where it fell. The jacket had been discarded long ago. "We're across the border! We're safe now." He was elated, the weariness of the long hot ride slipping away from him as he reached up to help Kyla from her horse.

"As soon as Golden Feather catches up, we can go on to Oaxaca. And you, Delleroc, you can come with us or go on your way."

Quint slid from his horse and flexed his aching shoulders. "Perhaps you'd better listen to what Kyla wants first, before you make too many plans."

Miguel held Kyla about her waist, looking down at the starlight reflected in her eyes. "You would not have risked your life to help me escape, ridden across the desert with me, if you did not love me, *chiquita*," he said softly.

"I do love you, Miguel. I've loved you all my life. But I can't be your woman any longer." Kyla's voice was as gentle as his.

"Then you will get a divorce and marry me. Kyla, I'm sorry, I should have realized that we could not live together in sin. That is why it has not been good with us, little one. The act of love is merely a barbarous ritual without meaning when a man and woman are not joined by the sacrament of holy matrimony. I thought that it was denied to us because of all that had happened to you."

"Happened to me?" Kyla repeated, a sudden edge to her voice.

Miguel's hands slid up her arms and came to rest on her shoulders. "It doesn't matter any more. I can forget that other men had you before me. That you bore a bastard child."

Kyla froze. It seemed that all sensation had left her body except for a dull throbbing in her temples. "And you, Miguel, you would have come to your marriage bed a virgin?"

His hands dropped to his sides and he stared at the pale blur that was her face. "Virgin is not a word that applies to a man, Kyla. I've told you, it doesn't matter to me now. There was a time I would have cut out the heart of every man who possessed you, when the torment of not being your first and only lover drove me to the brink of madness. These past months, when we were together, I knew you were remembering other men. Can you imagine what that does to a man? But I swear to you, it will not be so in the future. We will be married."

"No, Miguel," Kyla's voice cut him off and she continued to speak even when he tried to interrupt. Her voice was brittle, almost shrill. "I wouldn't think of trapping you or any other man into marriage. After all, I am soiled merchandise. But apart from that, I want my own life. My very own private life. I've always been dominated by a man, first your father, then Quint Delleroc and Desmond and then you. I have never been mistress of my own destiny. Well, all that has changed. I've decided what I want out of life. I am going back to Los Angeles and I am going to fight for my inheritance. My mother died on the de Rivero *rancho,* and my stepfather went to a great deal of trouble to leave it to me—and I allowed the invaders to take it away from me. Well, I want it back and I'm going to fight for it. And I don't need a man to help me, you or any other man. Go and find your Juarez in Oaxaca. Fight your revolutions. Kill or be killed. I will pray for you, but I will not go with you."

They had both forgotten the presence of Quint Delleroc, who quietly sat in the shadows and listened.

"I do not know you any more, Kyla," Miguel said, bewildered. "You speak like—like a man."

Kyla turned away from him in a single swift movement of her lithe body. Watching her, Quint Delleroc was reminded of the proud and imperious way Miguel moved. This woman, Quint thought, could be told of the existence of Victor. This woman had learned to bend like a willow in the wind. The girl she had replaced would have been broken by the revelation that her child lived. He felt a surge of pride in her and his strong teeth came down over his lower lip to prevent the words of praise that sprang to his tongue. He would have to be patient. First she must have time to accept herself.

Golden Feather reached their camp as dawn was breaking and he rested only briefly before Miguel told him they should ride.

Miguel looked at Kyla. "You won't come with us?"

"No. When we meet again, I pray we will both have attained what we want most in the world. *Vaya con Dios,* Miguel."

Miguel bowed his head. "I cannot force you, Kyla. Perhaps in time I shall learn to live without you." A moment later his horse was streaking toward the silver sunrise.

Quint said respectfully, "I'll ride with you as far as Los Angeles, if you don't mind."

Kyla shrugged. "Suit yourself. I can't promise I'll be good company." She pressed her fingers to her forehead. The throbbing headache was back early today. She had put it down to heat prostration and lack of water, and tried to ignore the other miseries of her stiff and sore limbs.

"Let's head due west," Quint said. "It will take longer, but be more pleasant riding the coastal route. My royal

Spanish ancestors chose a splendid path for the king's highway."

Kyla climbed wearily into her saddle. "Every time you mention your ancestors, Quint Delleroc, you tell a different story. Please spare me your fantasies."

"I'm sorry. I was just trying to take your mind off your parting from Miguel. It must be quite a wrench for you. Kyla, don't feel too sorry for him. You know, it's never as exciting to be loved as it is to love."

She turned her eyes toward him, and in their depths he saw a flicker of pain before the veil of indifference was carefully lowered and he cursed his clumsiness.

"Kyla, once I told you a story about myself. I'd like to tell you more, if you'll listen."

They began to ride, Quint leading the mule. Kyla's breakfast of a strip of jerky and sip of water lay heavily in her stomach and her headache grew worse with every movement of her horse.

Quint glanced at her, his expression concerned, then said, "I spent my life searching for something to believe in. I told myself I was looking for my father, my country, a cause, a religion. Something to make some sense out of my being, a reason for my existence. Kyla, the malaise I endured was as real as hunger or thirst. I searched, not for my soul, but for myself."

The sun came up, hot against her back; her fingers were cold and numb on the reins.

"And all the time I was angry," Quint continued. "Because I could make no sense out of it all. So I defied all the conventions, broke all the rules, deliberately invited the wrath of my fellow man. I found it impossible to either hate or love, but I was fascinated by these emotions in other people. Forgive me, Kyla. I wanted you to love me. Just as I wanted Des to love me, and Ramsey to hate me, and Shansi to need me. You see, if I were loved and hated and needed, then I must exist. Kyla, do you understand?" *Lead up to it—carefully, but oh, God, let me say it the right way!*

"You don't have to bare your soul to me, Quint. Oh, it's true I loved you once. I think I would have died for you. But you see, love can die, or fade away, or be killed. So there is no need for you to be concerned about me. My love for you no longer exists." She was shaking violently. Her hands had slipped from the horse's reins.

"Kyla, do you feel well?"

"Oh come now, Quint! Surely even you are not so conceited as to believe I must be ill if I no longer love you!"

"You look very pale, and your eyes are unnaturally bright. When I handed you the canteen of water I noticed your hand was hot. Do you have a fever?" *It's too late. She no longer cares.*

"Tell me about you and Desmond. I know you saved his life. Why did you stay with him, involve yourself so deeply in his life?"

"At first I suppose I enjoyed playing the part, being addressed as 'your lordship.' What bastard wouldn't? I used Desmond's name and position, even his commission in the army. I believe I forgot at times that I was not actually him."

"And he—apart from being grateful to you, why did he allow this?" It seemed important to continue talking, to keep at bay the faintness she was experiencing.

Quint bit down on his lower lip. The past would have to be swept away, somehow.

"Each man has two sides, his good side and his evil one. Somewhere along the way my life and Desmond's became fused into one. When we were together he was all good and I was all evil. It seemed every scrape I got into was a victory of sorts for him, just as I was redeemed by his good deeds. I know it sounds mad. We were bad for each other, but I was especially bad for Des because he was vicariously *living* my sins, while I merely basked in the reflected glory of his saintliness. But inevitably one of us had to tire of being only half a soul in two bodies. Ah, Kyla, if only Desmond's goodness and capacity for love could have been part of my makeup. He loves you, you know. I think perhaps he has from the moment he met you. But he'd die before he'd tell you."

Kyla was silent, remembering Desmond and how considerate he had always been. But her future belonged to herself alone. Her plans did not include sharing her life with a man. Not even the man who still had the power to make her knees buckle merely by standing near.

When she did not respond, Quint said, "I believe coming to the New World was the salvation of two half-mad men. Des has been more useful here than he ever was in the army or moldering in that monastery, and I—Kyla, what is it?" He leaped from his horse and caught her as she slipped into unconsciousness.

For a time Monterey had been a ghost town, deserted by its citizens who were lured away to the gold fields, but as the first flush of gold fever faded, the people returned to the fine old homes that had been their town houses in *rancho* days. New arrivals, mostly American, came to join the Spanish *Californios* and seamen, merchants and disillusioned argonauts began to build wooden American-style houses among the whitewashed adobe buildings. Some of the new houses were hastily constructed and would not survive a fraction of the time the adobe buildings stood, but it was fashionable to bring "American" architecture to the Spanish town.

In the fertile valley of El Rio Carmelo, many American ranchers settled, plowing the land to the very walls of the mission San Carlos. California acquired its first theater when an Englishman named Jack Swan built a lodging house complete with barroom on Calle Estrada and allowed some New York volunteers, stationed in the old *presidio,* to put on plays.

In the Pacific House the county of Monterey had a courtroom, jury room and the county clerk's office. There were a newspaper, law office, ballroom and temperance society.

As Monterey grew and prospered, so did Ramsey's hope for his own future and the concomitant fear that his plans would be thwarted. Sooner or later, Delleroc would return to kill Ramsey, or ruin him by the revelation that Miguel Marques was his brother-in-law. Or perhaps Murrieta would return and his relationship with Maria become public knowledge. As time passed, Ramsey's obsession with Delleroc's destruction, and his fear that Maria would cuckold him, grew until he could think of little else. He became a quivering bundle of nerves, unable to sleep or attend to his own business.

Ramsey smiled uneasily when a conversation inevitably came around to the misdeeds of Murrieta and the other Mexican bandits. Maria, on the other hand, sadly lit a candle in the chapel, convinced that her lover was dead. She was sure if he lived he would not have stayed away from her for so long.

"You must never mention Miguel's name to anyone," Ramsey cautioned her. "We were lucky to be living in San Francisco when he visited you. No one here must know he is your brother. Fortunately the name Marques is common among your people, but avoid telling them it is also your maiden name. When California is admitted to the Union, and it will be soon, I am going to be one of its first senators."

Maria's dark eyes slid over him speculatively. It was possible he would achieve his ambitions. He was so very *norteamericano* with his blond good looks, his education and, she thought spitefully, his love of money and power. One could not, after all, have everything. A handsome and hotblooded Latin lover made the calculating husband's presence bearable. She would simply have to replace Joaquin if he did not return soon.

"And what will you do if Delleroc returns to town? Or if Kyla's husband ever comes out of seclusion? You know he is still living in Delleroc's house with the Chinese girl. People are whispering about them, of all the strange occupants of that house who come and go. Felice and the child left. They say servants won't stay there. If they knew about Shansi—"

"Knew what about Shansi?" Ramsey asked, careful not to look at his wife. The lovely Oriental mistress of Delleroc still lingered in his thoughts and it had been some time since he visited Ah Toy in San Francisco. There was something about the Chinese, an exotic sensuality that drove away the fears he had harbored about his manhood since his voyages on the *Constantia*.

"She smokes opium," Maria said. "She and Old Woman. I did not know what it was at first. It has a most peculiar smell. Felice told me about it when I worked for her. Felice said Shansi went to meet the ships coming in to see if there were Chinese seamen aboard who had opium to sell. I wonder what she is doing for her supplies now? No one has left the house for weeks."

Ramsey made a great show of stirring the embers of the dying fire. He kept his back turned to Maria.

"I forgot to mention—" he said casually, "I'll probably have to make a trip to San Francisco to look in on all my business interests there. While I'm gone, I want your word you won't see Murrieta. He's a dead man, Maria. It's only a matter of time until the Rangers catch up with him, so if you want to keep your own pretty skin whole, it will be in your own interest to forget him."

Maria tossed her head and stormed from the room.

"My lord, you gave me life," Shansi said, taking Desmond's hand in hers and pressing it to her lips. She had come to him silently, dropping to the ground beside his chair in the garden.

He closed the book he was reading and looked at the sleek black hair shining in the sunlight. "Desmond. Call me Desmond, Shansi."

She raised her head and looked up at him, her eyes dark polished jewels. "I feel the sunlight—warm upon my skin. I taste the air. I rest in untroubled sleep. Food lingers on my tongue and delights me. The singing of the birds gladdens my ears. Ah, Desmond, you cannot know what you have done. I have just entered the world, I am born. Delleroc tried to make me stop, but always I was able to deceive him. I did not stop. But you stayed with me, night and day, until you drove away the demons. I love you, Desmond. I want to be your woman."

"You are just lonely for Quint, Shansi, and feeling a little grateful to me. You shouldn't be, the struggle and the victory are yours alone." He looked at her fondly, secure in the knowledge that she would not shrink from his scarred face. There had never been a woman, not since India, who had been able to look upon his face without flinching.

"Delleroc does not love me. He does not even want me any longer. He began to change when——" Shansi stopped herself before she mentioned the name of Desmond's wife. She had known Delleroc was captivated by the pale-haired woman when he returned after the proxy wedding. Shansi had known it before Delleroc himself had known.

"When I lived at your *rancho*," Shansi said, "while he was away, I came to your bed and we were happy together."

Desmond drew in his breath, his eyes sweeping about the fragrant garden as though seeking escape. "Shansi, you do not have to offer yourself to me in gratitude. I told you the battle was yours." His voice was strangled with emotion.

"Why do you turn away from me, Desmond? Why do you pretend you do not want me? You are not a priest that you must live without a woman's love."

Slowly he turned to look at her again, at her porcelain skin and tenderly curved lips. It's true, he thought, I even wore a monk's robes. I set myself up as an unordained priest, smug in the good works I believed I performed. Was this the reason? To pretend to myself that if I embraced the priest's vow of chastity, I would not need a woman's body?

His fingers gripped her hair tightly and the brilliantly blue eyes lit up with hope as he pulled her close to him. Shansi. She was real, a flesh and blood woman. Kyla had been a beautiful goddess he had worshipped from afar, but Shansi had lain with him in the starry southern nights, and his body had been whole again. Damn Delleroc. Even if Quint still wanted Shansi, he could not have her.

# 31

*Kyla did not know how long she had been sitting on the* battered chair beneath the cottonwood tree. The shifting patterns of light and shade seemed to drift toward her from nowhere. She saw the small stone house across the narrow creek; a thin plume of smoke rose from the chimney. She could not remember coming to the cottonwood grove.

Her hair was a dead weight and she wanted to adjust it. But her arms refused her brain's command to raise her hands. She looked down at them, lying limply on the lap of a faded calico dress. Surely those thin fingers and shrunken wrists could not be hers? She studied them for a moment, as though they belonged to a stranger. Kyla at last summoned the strength to lift her hair away from her neck, then she gripped the arms of the chair and tried to rise. The effort brought beads of perspiration to her brow and a quickening of her shallow breathing. She was so weak she began to tremble.

For a moment the restless branches of the cottonwood, the creek and the stone house faded from view. She blinked and the scene came back. This time she saw the flash of the axe, swung high over a mane of flaming hair. The crack of splitting wood came a second later. Quint Delleroc. She must never let him know she still loved him. Why, was that her first thought, she wondered, as she

began to remember—riding through the desert toward
the Mexican border. Miguel was safe. She and Quint had
been riding—where? El Camino Real. . . .

He was coming toward her, his long legs devouring the
distance so swiftly she did not have time to prepare her
thoughts.

"Kyla, you're awake. Would you like a drink?" He
stepped over the trickle of water moving sluggishly over
the rocky streambed.

"How did we get here?" Her voice sounded strange,
she had not used it for a long time.

His hand went to her forehead and then closed over her
wrist, and she was too weak to pull away. "I carried you
in front of me on my horse. Found this place abandoned
by prospectors, I expect. That dress you're wearing must
have belonged to a very lonely woman. There was water
and game to sustain us. You've been very ill, Kyla. A
fever, I'm not sure what, but not yellow fever or cholera,
I'm sure of that. Anyway, you're better today. I knew you
would come back to me if I brought you out here."

"How long—how long have we been here?"

"A couple of weeks, maybe longer. I lost count of the
days."

"I'm sorry I kept you here."

"Don't be. I had nothing pressing to return to."

"Not even your son?"

His eyes opened wider. "My son?"

"There's no need to feign surprise, Quint. Merciful
Smith told me about Felice's child that night of the fire
in San Francisco. I'm sure you must be anxious to return
to them."

He was staring at her in amazement. "You think
Victor is my son? Mine and Felice's? Is that why you—
oh, my God, no. This is too priceless. Kyla, Victor is an
orphan I adopted, neither Felice's child nor mine."

"In any case, I'm sure they must be wondering where
you are. It's really none of my business who the child is.
I just feel guilty about keeping you here, caring for me."

"You can't travel yet. You're too weak. When you can
travel I am going to take you to Monterey with me,

because you're going to need a long convalescence before you do battle with the *yanquis* for your land. No, don't argue. You are also going to see Desmond and decide what you want to do about your marriage. It is unfair to leave him hanging. You never know, he might want to marry again, even if you do not."

His eyes searched her face for a moment, then he continued, "I would like to help you regain your *rancho*. I've already decided to sell my house in Monterey. That is, if I can find someone who appreciates the durability of adobe. Finding a Mexican with enough money might be difficult. But whether or not you agree to let me help you, I intend to try living in your dusty pueblo of Los Angeles, so I'll be nearby if you need me." The words he wanted to say were choking him, but he could not get them out. *Kyla, I love you.*

Kyla stared at him, her eyes enormous pools of tropical blue in her pale and pinched face. "I shan't need any help. As soon as I get my strength back, I want to fight my own battles. But thank you for the offer."

Her casual dismissal was not feigned, he knew with chilling certainty, and he felt a moment's panic that he had lost her forever.

"Kyla," he said, a small vein throbbing in his temple. The pause lengthened and there was no expectant waiting in her expression. "Would you like me to wash your hair for you?" he finished lamely.

She smiled. "I can't think of any greater bliss at this moment than having my hair washed."

Ramsey went to Delleroc's house in the early hours of the morning, casting furtive glances up and down the deserted street to be sure no one saw him as Desmond admitted him.

"Maria told me everything," Ramsey said after a perfunctory greeting. "About herself and Kyla helping Miguel escape. No doubt Kyla has crossed the border with him by now, but frankly, Desmond, I'd like to know what you are doing here in Delleroc's house, and when Delleroc is coming back. You understand that because of the connection between your wife and my wife's family, I have to make this my business."

"I haven't heard from either of them," Desmond gestured for Ramsey to sit down and he limped across the room, to the *trastero* containing wine and glasses. "You need have no fear about my divulging your wife's part in the escape. As soon as Quint returns, I shall be leaving Monterey."

"And Felice and the child? Are they coming back?" He accepted the offered glass of wine.

Desmond lowered himself into a chair. Each day he had promised himself that he would send a letter to San Francisco and tell Felice she should return. But the hours slipped away, and with only Old Woman moving inobtrusively in the background, he and Shansi had created an intimately shared world. Felice's booming laugh and the demands of a child would be intrusions. His happiness with Shansi was still such a fragile bubble that it might burst at any moment.

"Yes. Yes, I expect they will be back shortly also."

The scent of jasmine drifted into the room and they turned to see Shansi standing in the doorway. "Desmond?" she said sleepily. She wore only a petticoat and chemise of fine lawn and the laces were unfastened to the waist, revealing the curve of her breasts. Her hair was a black cloud about delicate shoulders. "Oh! I did not know *he* was here." There was venom in 'er voice as she looked at Ramsey with dislike.

"Shansi, perhaps you should go and put on a wrapper?" Desmond suggested.

"I do not want this man to come here," Shansi said. "I do not understand why Mr. Delleroc did not kill him."

Ramsey laughed, his eyes darting over her body hungrily. "Bloodthirsty little heathen, isn't she?"

"*You* tried to kill *him*," Shansi said.

"Someone shot at him from ambush," Ramsey said. "Probably one of Felice's customers who lost too much at his gambling tables."

Ramsey stood up, his eyes still fixed on Shansi. "I'll be on my way. Sorry to have got you out of bed. By the way, Desmond, there is one thing. My wife feels hurt that you haven't been to see her, and she asks that you stop by the house tomorrow night. She's going to be alone with the servants because I have to go out of town. No offense, but it would be better if Miss Shansi didn't go with you, and if you went after dark."

"Yes, of course, I'll go. She can perhaps tell me more about Kyla and Miguel. You won't mind, will you, Shansi?"

Lost in the unspoken message their eyes communicated to one another, neither Desmond nor Shansi noted the smirk of satisfaction on Ramsey's face.

Desmond had been gone only a few minutes the following evening when the front door of the house reverberated to the sound of pounding fists.

Shansi nodded to Old Woman to go and answer the impatient summons, and she turned her attention back to the silk shirt she was making for Desmond from one of her dresses. The Indian servant and his wife had departed during the turmoil of her withdrawal frenzy, and Desmond had never bothered to find other servants.

The footsteps coming down the tiled hallway were too heavy to be Old Woman's soft tread. Nor was the sound the shuffling step and tapping of Desmond's cane. Shansi looked up in belated realization and fear as Ramsey burst through her bedroom door.

He stood still, watching her as she sprang across her bed, pressing herself back against the wall to get as far away from him as possible. That other time, she thought desperately, I did not care—I had the magic cloud to make everything all right. But now, now I cannot bear to have him touch me.

"Now, what kind of greeting is that?" Ramsey asked. "When I brought you a nice present?" He slowly withdrew a small package from his pocket and tossed it on the bed.

Shansi stared at it, hypnotized, knowing what it contained. A sick fear gripped her stomach, her knees trembled. "No. No," she whispered. "I don't want it. I don't need it any more. Please."

He smiled. "Oh, I think you do. And Old Woman—where are you, Old Woman? You want some happy powder, too?" He glanced over his shoulder to where Old Woman cowered in the dim hallway.

"See, it's like this. Delleroc is coming back here. I'm going to smoke him out. Smoke him out, that's pretty funny," Ramsey chuckled, pleased at his own wit. "He'll have to come back when he finds out his mistress is being deported for smoking opium and his good friend Lord Talmage is dead."

"Desmond? What are you going to do to Desmond?" Shansi cried, the horror of their predicament causing her to collapse to the bed, her fingers inches away from the sinister package.

"Pity about my house," Ramsey said. "But then, Maria always said it was ready to fall down." He blinked, realizing he was thinking aloud. No need to tell the girl everything. Just enough to scare her. There was no need for her to know that burning down his house would solve all his problems. He would be rid of a wife who was becoming a real embarrassment, and Delleroc would come rushing back because of the death of his friend. With the information obtained from the British Army in India, having Delleroc deported should be a simple matter. Aloud, Ramsey said, "Your people aren't too popular in California, Shansi. It's the heathen practices you follow." His eyes flitted from her body to the package lying beside her and he ran his tongue slowly over his lower lip.

"Desmond—what are you going to do to Desmond? Or have you already—you said Lord Talmage is dead—"

"Not yet, China girl. Maybe you can save him. Depends on how nice you are to me and how long he makes his visit to my wife tonight." His eyes slid down the length of her body and he hooked his thumbs into his belt.

"Please don't hurt Desmond. Please. I will do anything you ask if only you won't hurt him." She crawled across the bed toward him, stretching out her hand in mute appeal.

Ramsey grinned. "Sure you will. Come on, get out the opium paraphernalia. Oh, I know you've kept it. I saw enough Chinese at sea to know they never entirely give up the habit once they've started it. You, my pretty China girl, are going to be thoroughly saturated with opium when they come to tell you about the unfortunate accident—the fire at my house tonight—and I am going to be in San Francisco."

"But why—why do you want to hurt Desmond? He never harmed you."

Ramsey was irritated by her concern for the cripple, angry that the remote eyes now were filled with anguished pleading, not for her own skin, but for half a man. "I'm doing him a favor. He probably wishes he were dead anyway, looking the way he does. What the hell is he to you? I don't care about the cripple. I want Maria out of the way and Delleroc back here. Lord Talmage's name will get into the newspapers. See, he's well known since Miguel's trial."

Ramsey paused, glancing over his shoulder to be sure Old Woman was still there, cowering in the hallway. Delleroc, Delleroc, he thought with rising rage, there's no way to kill the swine. I'll have to settle for deportation. "There's no more time, China girl. I've got a hard ride ahead of me." He laughed again, recognizing an amusing double entendre.

Slowly he unfastened his belt, his eyes fixed on her and his lower lip slightly moist.

Maria could not believe her eyes when she opened her door to Desmond Talmage. Silently she cursed the fates that brought him calling on this of all nights, when at any moment she expected Joaquin Murrieta. She forced a smile to her lips as she admitted Desmond. "Why, Desmond, I didn't expect you. Garett left for San Francisco this afternoon and I was going to retire early."

"He didn't tell you I was coming?" Desmond asked, bewildered. "But he—do forgive me. I must have misunderstood. May I sit down for a moment to rest? If I could have a glass of water, I shall be on my way. I'm afraid walking the short distance from Quint's house to yours has done me in."

Maria glanced at the grandfather clock standing in the hall beside her. "Of course. Come into the *sala*, I'll get you one. How are you, Desmond? I heard you were here, but I've been so busy——" She wore an extremely low-cut red satin gown and her dark wavy hair hung loosely, free from combs, decorated by a scarlet hibiscus. "I sent the servants away tonight, so I'm all alone. That's why I was surprised to see you. But I'm sure a few minutes alone——" Her eyes and the gesture of her hands completed the admonishment.

"Do you think Miguel and Kyla reached the border?" Desmond asked, sipping the glass of water she handed him.

"Of course. They had horses. No one can outride us *californios*," Maria said scornfully. "Even Kyla is a *californio* when it comes to riding. We were all born to the saddle. The *gringos* sit their horses with all the grace of a grizzly bear. Even the *indios* are better horsemen." She looked pointedly at the grandfather clock and covered a wide yawn with her hand.

"Thank you. If you hear from Miguel, you will let me know?" Desmond placed his weight on his cane and struggled to his feet.

"Yes, yes. Now if you will excuse me?" she said impatiently, good manners forgotten as the last of the twilight faded.

Less than an hour had elapsed since he left Shansi, but he was glad to be limping down the moonlit streets to return to her. Another half hour and he would be at her side. Desmond dragged his stiff leg determinedly, despite the pain, but had to pause at the corner of the street and lean against the adobe wall to rest.

A bougainvillea vine trailed down the wall, blowing in the sea breeze, and the scent of roses was heavy in the air. The smell of flowers reminded him of Shansi. She was always so fragrant.

Desmond heard the sound of a horse, coming toward him at full gallop. He drew back against the wall for fear of pebbles flying up from the churning hooves.

Desmond had almost reached Delleroc's house, the last

one on the street, when he again had to stumble to the side of the road to allow another horseman to pass. There was not time for him to cry out, even though he instantly recognized the large horse and the bulk of the man in the saddle. Garett Ramsey. Who was supposed to be in San Francisco, who had sent Desmond to Maria even though she clearly did not expect him. Shansi! Her name came to his scarred lips as he tried to run toward the house, losing his cane and falling in the dust in his agitation.

His chest was heaving and his hand clammy as he reached the open front door. The house was ominously silent.

"Shansi!" He called her name again.

He almost fell over the shriveled body of Old Woman. She lay half into the bedroom, her spindly legs in the hallway. The lamp was burning low, and in the faint light Old Woman looked up at him with a toothless grin. The air was heavy with a sickening smell; the opium pipes lay on the floor.

Shansi was sprawled on the bed, her hair hanging over the edge in a dusky cloud. She was naked and her legs were still parted. Her thighs glistened slightly.

An anguished sob that began deep inside him seemed to echo around the disordered room. His hand went under Shansi's neck, raising her head.

She looked at him through half-closed eyes that were as remote as a distant dark star, and she murmured, "Des-mond, are we dead?" then her head rolled to the side and she snored softly.

His stiff leg was forgotten, his single hand did the work of two hands. While she slept, he bathed her body, washing away the traces of Ramsey. There were no bruises, he noted. He was surprisingly calm as he prodded Old Woman with his foot until she rose to help him pack their belongings.

"We are leaving on the first stagecoach in the morning," he told her. "We are going far from ships and sailors who bring this noxious substance that destroys your mind. There is a small mission, far to the south, in the desert.

We shall go there. I will take care of you both until you are well again."

Old Woman grinned toothlessly.

Ramsey had made careful preparations. The kerosene had been hidden beneath the hedge along the rear wall of the house, the newspapers that would be pushed around the windows and doors were neatly stacked in the cookhouse. The log that would jam the rear door to prevent escape was lying near the outhouse. Everything was in order.

Place the log across the rear door first, he thought, as he tied his horse to the post in front and went quickly along the verandah that ran completely around the house. There was no glimmer of light from within the house and he wondered where Maria and Desmond were. Must have gone into the *sala* in the rear.

Ramsey stopped short when he reached the back of the house. A large black horse was tied to the verandah rail. The only light came from the upper story, Maria's bedroom.

He was sure Talmage had not brought a horse to town. There had been no sign of one at Delleroc's house. But it must be his. Talmage, in Maria's bedroom? She must be desperate, he thought with some amusement. The mental picture of Talmage making love to Maria flashed into his mind, and with it curiosity.

Ramsey grinned in the darkness. Easy enough to climb up the posts of the verandah roof and have a look. The window was open, and he heard the faint murmur of voices, then Maria gave a low and throaty laugh.

Trying to keep from laughing out loud, Ramsey placed one foot on the verandah rail, his hands closing around the post, then hoisted himself up to the roof.

The wood groaned under the impact of his weight and his boots slid as he clutched at the nearest window ledge, momentarily losing his balance. The sounds he made caused the murmuring within the bedroom to stop abruptly.

Holding his breath, ignoring the splintering wood, he

began to slide toward Maria's window. Hell, what could Talmage do, even if he had heard the creaking wood? He'd have to hurry though before they stopped whatever they were doing. Ramsey's hands went up over the window ledge and he slowly raised his head and looked into the fierce black eyes of Joaquin Murrieta.

# 32

The new, larger-capacity stagecoach was making its first run from Monterey to San Francisco. The last couple who entered the coach stopped the buzz of conversation for a moment and interested eyes followed the striking pair. The woman had a mass of pale gold hair and arresting dark blue eyes. She was lovely, if a trifle pale.

At her side was a tall man with bright copper-colored hair, hypnotic green eyes and fierce, hawklike features that were handsome in the aristocratic Spanish manner. Several of the female passengers allowed their eyes to drift in the direction of the flame-haired man, but he was oblivious to their inviting glances and seemed totally engrossed in his companion, with whom he conversed in quiet and rapid Spanish during most of the journey.

"I hope you won't regret selling your house in Monterey," Kyla said.

Quint shrugged. "I'd already kept it longer than any previous possession. Besides, how could I resist the temptation of selling a house, in the best part of town, to the notorious Joaquin Murrieta?"

Kyla smiled. "Señor Sanchez, you mean, goldminer from the Sierras, expected and accepted by the bankers and merchants of Monterey, thanks to you. Is he really Murrieta, did you think?"

"Probably not. I don't believe there is such a person.

It's a name conjured up by half a dozen bandits to confuse the *gringo* and imbue the *bandido* with mythical powers. But our particular Murrieta, well, you said yourself he was the same one who helped you and Maria— you know where." Quint glanced about the coach at the other passengers. Their expressions were blank, but one never knew how much Spanish they understood.

"In time, of course, either he will move in with Maria or she with him. After a respectable period of mourning. I'm still surprised at the way Ramsey died. Talk about a freak accident." The news of Ramsey's death had been given them by Maria upon their arrival in Monterey. She had also begged them to help her find a way for Joaquin to give up his banditry and live respectably in town.

"What was Ramsey doing on the roof, do you suppose?" Kyla asked with a shiver.

"Perhaps sneaking in after a night on the town? From what Maria said, he wouldn't have broken his neck if there hadn't been a log propped against the door, which apparently administered the *coup de grace* as he dislodged it during the fall. Seems it was a mystery how the log came to be there, but apart from that it was clearly an accident. The verandah roof had a great splintered hole in it, and Maria certainly isn't strong enough to have shoved him out of a window. In fact, few *men* would have been able to, what with Ramsey's size and weight."

"She wasn't very grief-stricken, was she?" Kyla asked wryly. "Quint, what about Desmond? I promised myself I wouldn't ask you what he wrote to you in the letter he left for you, but, well, he *is* still my husband."

His eyes were opaque and Quint watched the misty green countryside float past the window for a moment, not speaking.

"You persuaded me to go to San Francisco with you, Quint, and led me to believe Desmond would be there," Kyla persisted. "But I've had the uneasy feeling that you are concealing something. There was a moment after you read his letter that your face expressed—relief. You usually have an expression that is difficult to read, but in that one moment it seemed an enormous weight had been removed from your shoulders."

His white teeth flashed in a smile. "If you're able to read my expressions, it's probably time for me to run. Kyla, I wanted you to come to San Francisco and meet Victor, the orphan I adopted. Desmond is not there. I'm sorry. I should have been honest with you. Old habits die hard, I expect. I've always found it more interesting to make up a story than to tell the plain truth."

He fumbled in his inside pocket and produced the folded sheet of paper that Kyla recognized immediately as the one left by Desmond. Silently Quint handed it to her and she read:

> *Goodbye, Quint,*
> I never believed there was anything to your theory about our mutual karma. But you may believe it has ended if you wish. I'm taking Shansi with me because I love her; where we are going I doubt you will ever find us.
> This will shock you in view of your opinion of me, but the formality of marriage seems unimportant to Shansi and me; however, I shall arrange in due course for Kyla to receive word of my "death." She was brought up strictly in the Roman Catholic faith, Quint, and I don't believe even an annulment of our marriage would allow her to consider the ties broken.
> I believe the only way you and she will be able to come together without guilt is for you to know that I love and will care for Shansi, and for Kyla to believe that I am dead. I want you to tell her this letter informs you that I am sailing for England. My ship will conveniently be lost at sea.
> I never dreamed when I asked you to sail to the New World to be my proxy that I was sending you to the one woman on earth who would reform you, Quint. Sometimes it seems a great pity. You were such a doughty rogue.

Kyla read the words twice and then looked up at Quint.

"Why did you change your mind about letting me know the truth?"

"It's as old Des says. I've reformed. Besides, Desmond was wrong about you. You told me in no uncertain terms that you have no desire to marry again. And I believe you were fond enough of old Des to be glad he's alive and happy, rather than dead."

Kyla smiled. "Yes. I am. I wonder what gave him the idea that you—that you and I—"

Quint turned innocent eyes toward her. "Perhaps he knows something you and I don't know?"

"I don't love you any more, Quint."

"I know. You told me that. Several times. However, the offer of my services in the matter of regaining your *rancho* still stands. I must say there's enough of the old Quint left to relish the prospect of a fight, legal or otherwise. After we've seen Felice and the boy and you've regained your strength, will you at least consider the offer? I promise I'll be a perfect gentleman."

Kyla looked down at her hands, folded on her lap. "We'll see," she said. He *had* been a perfect gentleman, and more, these past weeks. She had been sorry when they left the little stone house in the cottonwood grove. A quiet companionship had grown between them; it was, in a way, as satisfying as the passion they had shared earlier. Even when her strength began to return, they had lingered, neither wanting to end the simple life they shared.

But the meager supplies left behind by the prospectors could not last forever and the outside world waited. Kyla had suggested she was well enough to travel.

Quint *was* different, she thought as the stage journeyed toward San Francisco. Could it be that the man who had nursed her back from the brink of death, and contentedly shared long quiet hours with her, no longer felt the need to go tearing off in pursuit of excitement in some remote part of the world? How ironic if he should want to settle down just when she was ready for adventure.

He had spoken to her often of the boy, Victor, he had

adopted. She was looking forward to meeting the child, and felt she already knew the boy, from Quint's descriptions and fond anecdotes. Kyla realized now that one of the reasons she had been so unhappy with Miguel at the *hacienda* had been the absence of children. She had been happy caring for the Indian children at the mission before Quint came riding back into her life.

She remembered once when she and Desmond had been discussing Quint that Desmond had said his friend sought—what was the word he used? Catharsis. Yes, that was it. That Quint had roamed the earth in search of the experience that would purge him of the unknown devils that tormented him. Perhaps Quint's catharsis had been the child, Victor.

During their time together Quint had told her often that he hoped she would spend some time with the boy before she went to reclaim her *rancho*. Felice, he said, was kind and loving, but the boy needed exposure to a younger woman. Felice was the ideal grandmother figure, but Victor's family would not be complete until there was a mother figure for him too.

Kyla's reaction to this was mixed. Had Quint been trying to tell her that he wanted a wife and family? *Family*, she thought. There was something comforting about just the word.

Quint added, "I hope Felice received my letter telling her we would be traveling on today's stage."

Glancing out of the corner of her eye, Kyla saw Quint was watching her intently. He had watched her in that strangely hopeful way ever since the moment she had opened her eyes and found herself sitting in the cottonwood grove.

At her side, Quint wondered what she was thinking that caused her breathing to quicken and then her shoulders to droop suddenly as a deep inward sigh passed through her body. She was so lovely. Tragedy and hardship and illness had, if anything, made her more beautiful. Every man on the coach was surreptitiously watching her. But they could not see beneath the skin to the beauty Quint had discovered which even the most hardened cynic in the world had eventually recognized.

Quint's senses quickened as his thoughts drifted again to his plans for the future. It would not be easy, but then, little in his life had been easy. And he wanted Kyla more than anything he had ever wanted before. He must move slowly and with infinite caution, to earn her respect before he dared seek her love again.

She must not know, for instance, that no matter what the situation was in regard to her *rancho* in the South, that he was wealthy enough to buy it back for her. Quint believed that fortuitous arrival at Sutter's Fort had been the only time in his life he had stumbled into something without seeking it. It was not in his nature to consider that he went there to keep a promise to a dying man—whom he had helped at considerable risk to his own life. He had always felt that a man made his own destiny, that nothing was because of chance, and it had seemed that his timely arrival at Sutter's Fort was the one random incident in his life that had been the exception to prove the rule.

The stagecoach had been rolling along so smoothly that no one aboard was prepared for the sudden lurch. Quint's eyes had drifted to the green hills to the east and, as he watched, the grass rippled slowly and trees shook as though a great wave had passed across the earth.

Instantly the lead horses reared in fright, the animal sounds of terror blending with the grinding of wheels as the coach slid off the trail and into the rocks. Almost at the same instant, a large tree swayed for a second, then toppled into their path, its roots wrenched from the ground.

They could hear a low rumbling sound now that vibrated upward from the ground, through the carriage floor. One of the women screamed.

Quint wrapped one arm around Kyla. "Out of the coach, everybody," he called calmly. "Get out and into the nearest clearing. Stay away from trees."

Kyla looked up at him and whispered in Spanish,

"Wouldn't it be better for them to stay in the coach, in case there are fissures?"

He shook his head and answered, "That fallen tree is the only thing stopped the horses from bolting. If the horses turn around—" It was unnecessary for him to finish. They had just decended a steep trail cut into the side of a hill.

"Speak English, damn you!" one man shouted. "What's happening?"

"Please, everyone keep calm. It's just an earth tremor." Quint didn't have time to finish as the frightened passengers leaped for the doors.

The second tremor began after only a few people had alighted and the rest were flung back as the coach shook violently on the heaving ground. The driver lost his balance and fell. He was blinded by the dust churned by the plunging horses as they tried frantically to free themselves from the restraining harness.

In the split-second before the horses turned and bolted, Quint shoved aside the passenger who had landed on him and swung his legs through the coach window to fling himself up into the driver's seat. The coach lurched forward, tossing the remaining passengers about like rag dolls.

Wedged between a large woman who was sobbing hysterically and an apologetic man who kept closing his eyes as though to make everything go away, Kyla whispered a silent prayer. The horses were bolting along the narrow trail beaten around the side of a steep hill. Another tremor, or the first sharp curve, would surely send them plunging into the boulder-strewn gorge below.

Quint . . . Quint was out there, desperately trying to stop the horses. Kyla struggled to free herself from the smothering flesh, her fingers reaching for the window. *He might die,* she thought in panic. *What does foolish pride matter now?*

For a dizzying second she looked at the canyon below, then, leaning as far out the window as she could, she caught a glimpse of red hair and heard Quint's voice calling to the horses. "Steady. Steady there. Whoaa. Steady."

Kyla realized what he was about to do as he jumped to the back of the nearest horse. No! He would be killed. There were six horses bolting madly. He could not reach the lead horse without falling and being trampled—

"Quint Delleroc, if you get killed I'll die—" she screamed at him.

His head jerked backward for a second, startled, as the cry reached him. Ahead the trail disappeared ominously where the sky touched the hilltop. A sharp curve—

His feet were up on the horse's back now as he prepared to crawl along the harness to attempt to reach the lead horses. Just before he jumped, he shouted over his shoulder, "I love you, Kyla."

Blinded by tears, she closed her eyes and prayed as she had never prayed in her life before.

The horses slid to a panting, trembling halt with the coach perched precariously on the edge of the cliff. Obeying the quiet command of the red-haired man, the shaken passengers climbed out cautiously as he warned them another panic-stricken rush would dislodge the coach. When everyone was safely away, he unharnessed the horses a moment before the coach toppled over the edge and went crashing out of sight.

Before the dust had settled, Quint turned to Kyla and in one swift movement wrapped his arms about her, holding her close. He held her tightly for a long minute then she raised her face and they kissed, a slow and deliberate kiss, oblivious to the wide-eyed watchers. It was the kiss of two people meeting after a long absence.

When the earth stopped trembling, the stagecoach driver took one of the horses and rode to the nearest station to pick up another coach, and it was almost dawn before they resumed their journey.

When the stage came to a halt amid the bustle and noise that was San Francisco, they were met by a plump amazon, with a small boy whose unruly mop of golden curls brightened the gloom of a foggy morning. The two had been on hand for the arrival of every stage since the previous day.

The child's carefully cut trousers and specially constructed shoes did not quite disguise his clubfeet, but he came close to jumping up and down for joy when he caught sight of the copper hair of the man above the crowd. ·

"Quint! Quint!" he yelled excitedly, tugging at the hand of the large woman to draw her forward as the stage passengers disembarked.

Quint swung Victor up in the air, hugged him closely and then placed him astride his shoulders. "How are you, Felice?" Quint asked, his arm going around her ample shoulders as she giggled and chattered and assured Kyla she was going to feed her until she was as plump as herself.

Kyla moved along beside them to where Felice's carriage waited, her eyes straying repeatedly to the boy on Quint's shoulders. He was an appealing little boy. Quint had told her Victor was the most courageous child as well as being very intelligent. Kyla was surprised that meeting the child had given her an almost physical jolt. She rationalized that she was still weak from her illness, the ordeal of their brush with death——

She pushed aside the thought that if her own child had lived, he would have been about the age of this little boy. How strange it was that there were still moments when she thought of the lost child with such profound sorrow and regret. She had carried the child within her, feeling his movements under her heart; she supposed it was natural that she should have such feelings. All at once she remembered praying in the mission chapel so long ago, and seeing the imprint of the child's bare feet in the adobe tile. Her own child had left the imprint of tiny feet upon her heart. She blinked away a tear.

"You won't go away again, will you, Quint?" the boy was saying. "We missed you so much, didn't we, Felice?" He had the same accent as Quint Delleroc. Kyla supposed it was that which made the child seem so familiar to her. She longed to hold him in her arms, but she must get to know him first.

"I promise you will come with me next time," Quint said, glancing sideways at Kyla.

"Are you thinking of leaving again?" Felice asked, as they came to the carriage and Quint lifted the child into a seat and then turned to help Kyla.

"If the lady agrees to allow me to be of service, yes. She has this extraordinary desire to own a large area of semiarid land near a dusty pueblo. What is it called again, Kyla? Ah, yes. Los Angeles. And, of course, when we achieve our goal—and never fear that we shall—she will undoubtedly need a *mayordomo* to run the place for her. And what good are horses unless there is a small boy or two to ride them? Victor, you will learn to ride like a true *Californio*. I shall buy you one of their carved leather saddles with all of the silver trappings."

"Quint!" Kyla protested. "How you do run on. Don't you know you should never make a promise to a child that you aren't absolutely sure you can keep?"

Quint smiled enigmatically. "But I *am* absolutely sure I can keep the promise," he said.

He leaned back, his eyes moving with satisfaction from the child to Kyla. There is plenty of time, he reflected silently. After he had wooed and won her and they were safely married, perhaps even after there were several red-haired playmates for Victor—or perhaps never. It didn't matter, really, they were together at last and the terrible searching emptiness that had driven Quint Delleroc on one useless quest after another was ended. He knew who he was now. He was Victor's father and soon, Kyla's husband.

"*Amor con amor se paga,*" Quint said.

Kyla did not meet his eyes as she translated for Felice. "Love with love should be repaid."

But he knew by the tone of her voice that she took his declaration seriously.

Their carriage rolled down the steep hill toward the

deep blue bay. Golden fingers of sunlight stirred the fog and gilded the tall ships in the harbor, and the boisterous young city stretched and yawned and prepared for a new day.

# EPILOGUE

Kyla watched the three riders coming over the crest of the hill. The sunlight cast a fiery glow on two bronzed heads and gilded the blond locks of the third rider with yellow flame.

She stood on the verandah, watching her husband and sons approach, feeling the familiar surge of love and pride. Her small daughter was at her side, laying bright curls against her mother's skirts. As far as they could see in any direction the land belonged to them.

The years had been turbulent and life with Quint Delleroc never dull. Kyla smiled, remembering the peaks and valleys. There had been more peaks, she reflected. They had regained the rancho. Desmond had quietly had their unconsummated marriage annulled so that he might be free to marry Shansi, and she Quint. But, of course, there had not been an easy courtship between Kyla and Quint. He had realized long before that he couldn't live without her. To convince Kyla, with her new-found independence, was no easy task for the volatile Quint.

Victor had been the link that kept them together. Kyla had loved the child from the very beginning. There had been a bond between them that seemed to transcend time and space. A bond that surprised everyone but Quint.

Kyla remembered the exact moment she realized Victor was her son. Quint had insisted they name their own first-born Desmond, while Kyla insisted upon naming him Quintero. Desmond Quintero was nicknamed "Tero" by Victor. Victor was a patient and ever-watchful older brother. Since Tero was a carefree and reckless child, full of his father's bravado, Kyla was grateful for Victor's vigilance.

The *vaqueros* were breaking wild horses that afternoon when Kyla heard shouts of horror. At almost the same instant Tero's nursemaid burst into the room, weeping. She had taken her eyes off the baby for only a second and he had climbed out of his crib and wandered outside.

Kyla rushed from the house, but the small drama had already ended. Tero had climbed into the corral just as the first bronco was released. Victor had seen the child and leaped into the dust, placing himself between the thrashing hooves and the wide-eyed toddler. The skill of the rider had averted tragedy. By the time Kyla arrived on the scene Tero was enclosed in Victor's arms. Two dust-streaked faces looked up at her.

Kyla stopped, her heart in her throat, her eyes locked with Victor's dark and compassionate gaze. She felt his fear for her baby's life and his love for both of them. Victor's emotions were as tangible to her as her own. The bond of the blood-tie between them was there, as plain to see as the tears that flowed and blended in wordless gratitude as they flung themselves into each other's arms.

Afterward, Kyla reflected that she had felt Victor was her son for some time before that day. She had simply been unable to ask Quint to confirm what she hoped and prayed to be true. She wanted it so much that she had not dared ask, in case she was wrong.

Gently, Quint told her the whole story.

Victor held her hands tightly and shyly confessed that he, too, had felt she was his mother—long before Quint told him.

Kyla had laughed and wept and embraced both of them. Her heart had been so full of joy she thought it surely must be the supreme moment of her life. But there were still other moments of wildest happiness to come.

The day their daughter was born. The day Victor strode toward his horse, both heels digging firmly into the golden earth.

She walked down the verandah steps, holding her daughter's hand. The riders slid from their horses and Quint gathered his daughter and wife into his arms as their two sons grinned and watched.

# Victoria Holt

*Here are the stories you love best. Tales about love, intrigue, wealth, power and of course romance. Books that will keep you turning the pages deep into the night.*

| | | |
|---|---|---|
| ☐ BRIDE OF PENDORRIC | 23280-8 | $1.95 |
| ☐ THE CURSE OF THE KINGS | 23284-0 | $1.95 |
| ☐ THE HOUSE OF A THOUSAND LANTERNS | 23685-4 | $1.95 |
| ☐ THE KING OF THE CASTLE | 23587-4 | $1.95 |
| ☐ KIRKLAND REVELS | X2917 | $1.75 |
| ☐ LEGEND OF THE SEVENTH VIRGIN | 23281-6 | $1.95 |
| ☐ LORD OF THE FAR ISLAND | 22874-6 | $1.95 |
| ☐ MENFREYA IN THE MORNING | 23757-5 | $1.95 |
| ☐ MISTRESS OF MELLYN | 23124-0 | $1.75 |
| ☐ ON THE NIGHT OF THE SEVENTH MOON | 23568-0 | $1.95 |
| ☐ THE PRIDE OF THE PEACOCK | 23198-4 | $1.95 |
| ☐ THE QUEEN'S CONFESSION | 23213-1 | $1.95 |
| ☐ THE SECRET WOMAN | 23283-2 | $1.95 |
| ☐ SHADOW OF THE LYNX | 23278-6 | $1.95 |
| ☐ THE SHIVERING SANDS | 23282-4 | $1.95 |

Buy them at your local bookstores or use this handy coupon for ordering:

**FAWCETT BOOKS GROUP**
P.O. Box C730, 524 Myrtle Ave., Pratt Station, Brooklyn, N.Y. 11205

Please send me the books I have checked above. Orders for less than 5 books must include 75¢ for the first book and 25¢ for each additional book to cover mailing and handling. I enclose $_____ in check or money order.

Name_____
Address_____
City_____State/Zip_____

Please allow 4 to 5 weeks for delivery.

B13

W0101-W

# Mary Stewart

*"Mary Stewart is magic"* is the way Anthony Boucher puts it. Each and every one of her novels is a kind of enchantment, a spellbinding experience that has won acclaim from the critics, millions of fans, and a permanent place at the top.

| | | | |
|---|---|---|---|
| ☐ | AIRS ABOVE THE GROUND | 23868-7 | $1.95 |
| ☐ | THE CRYSTAL CAVE | 23315-4 | $1.95 |
| ☐ | THE GABRIEL HOUNDS | 22971-8 | $1.75 |
| ☐ | THE HOLLOW HILLS | 23316-2 | $1.95 |
| ☐ | THE IVY TREE | 23251-4 | $1.75 |
| ☐ | MADAM, WILL YOU TALK | 23250-6 | $1.75 |
| ☐ | THE MOON-SPINNERS | 23073-2 | $1.75 |
| ☐ | MY BROTHER MICHAEL | 22974-2 | $1.75 |
| ☐ | NINE COACHES WAITING | 23121-6 | $1.75 |
| ☐ | THIS ROUGH MAGIC | 22846-0 | $1.75 |
| ☐ | THUNDER ON THE RIGHT | 23100-3 | $1.75 |
| ☐ | TOUCH NOT THE CAT | 23201-8 | $1.95 |

B-1